THE MARRIAGE WAGER

SHE HAD BEEN SURE SHE COULD BEAT him, Colin thought. And she had not planned beyond that point. He waited, curious to see what she would do now.

She pounded the table again, thwarted determination obvious in her face. "Will you try another match?" she said finally.

A fighter, Colin thought approvingly. He breathed in the scent of her perfume, let his eyes linger on the creamy skin of her shoulders. He had never encountered such a woman before. He didn't want her to go. On the contrary, he found himself wanting something quite different. "One hand," he offered. "If you win, the notes are yours."

"And if I do not?" she asked

"You may still have them, but I get . . ." He hesitated. He was not the sort of man who seduced young ladies for sport. But she had come here to his house and challenged him, Colin thought. She was no schoolgirl. She had intrigued and irritated and roused him.

"What?" she said loudly.

He had been staring at her far too intensely, Colin realized. But the brandy and the strangeness of the night had made him reckless. "You," he replied.

BANTAM BOOKS BY JANE ASHFORD

THE MARRIAGE WAGER

The Marriage Wager

Jane Ashford

Bantam Books
New York   Toronto   London   Sydney   Auckland

THE MARRIAGE WAGER
A Bantam Fanfare Book / November 1996

ISBN 0-553-57577-5

Published simultaneously in the United States and Canada

Bantam Books are published by Bantam Books, a division of Bantam
Doubleday Dell Publishing Group, Inc. Its trademark, consisting of
the words "Bantam Books" and the portrayal of a rooster, is
Registered in U.S. Patent and Trademark Office and in other
countries. Marca Registrada. Bantam Books, 1540 Broadway, New
York, New York 10036.

The Marriage Wager

Chapter One

Colin Wareham, fifth baron St. Mawr, stood at the ship's rail watching the foam and heave of the English Channel. Even though it was late June, the day was damp and cool, with a sky of streaming black clouds and a sharp wind from the north. Yet Wareham made no effort to restrain the flapping of his long cloak or to avoid the slap of spray as the ship beat through the waves. He was bone-tired. He could no longer remember, in fact, when he hadn't been tired.

"Nearly home, my lord," said his valet, Reddings, who stood solicitously beside him. He pointed to the smudge of gray at the horizon that was England.

"Home." Colin examined the word as if he couldn't quite remember its meaning. For eight years, his home had been a military encampment. In the duke of Wellington's army, he had fought his way up the Iberian Peninsula—Coruña, Talavera, Salamanca—he had fought his way through France, and then done it again after Napoleon escaped Saint Helena and rallied the country behind him once more. He had lived with blood and death and filth until all the joy had gone out of him. And now he was going home, back to a family that lived for the amusements of fashionable London, to the responsibilities of an eldest son. His many relatives, at least, were pleased. According to them, as baron, he should never have risked himself as a soldier in the first place. Their satisfaction at his return matched the intensity of the outcry when he had joined up at twenty.

Reddings watched his master with surreptitious anxiety. The baron was a big man, broad-shouldered and rangy. But just now, he was thin from the privations of war and silent with its memories. Reddings didn't like the brooding quiet that had come to dominate St. Mawr, which the recent victory at Waterloo had done nothing to lift. He would even have preferred flares of temper, complaints, bitter railing against the fate that had decreed that his lordship's youth be spent at war. Most of all, he would have rejoiced to see some sign of the laughing, gallant young lad who had first taken him into his service.

That had been a day, Reddings thought, glad to retreat into memories of happier times. His lordship had returned from his last year at Eton six inches taller than when he left in the fall, with a wardrobe that had by no means kept up with his growth. The old baron, his father, had taken one look at Master Colin and let off one of his great barks of laughter, declaring that the boy must have a valet before he went up to Cambridge or the family reputation would fall into tatters along with his coat. Colin had grinned and replied that he would never live up to his father's sartorial splendor. They had a bond, those two, Reddings thought.

He'd been a footman, then, and had actually been on duty in the front hall of the house when this exchange took place in the study. He had heard it all, including the heart-stopping words that concluded the conversation. The old baron had said, "Fetch young Sam Reddings. He follows my man about like a starving hound and is always full of questions. I daresay he'll make you a tolerable valet." And so Reddings had been granted his dearest wish and never had a moment's regret, despite going off to war and all the rest of it. It was a terrible pity the old baron had died so soon after that day, he thought. He'd be the man to make a difference in his lordship now.

The ship's prow crashed into a mountainous gray wave, throwing cold spray in great gleaming arcs to either side. The wind sang in the rigging and cut through layers of clothing like the slash of a cavalryman's saber. It had been a rough crossing. Most of the passengers were ill below, fervently wishing for an end to the journey or, if that were not possible, to their miserable lives.

The pitch and heave of the deck left Colin Wareham unscathed. What an adventure he had imagined war would be, he was thinking. What a young idiot he had been, dreaming of exotic places and wild escapades, fancying himself a hero. Colin's lip curled with contempt for his youthful self. That naïveté had been wrung out of him by years of hard campaigning. The realities of war made all his medals and commendations seem a dark joke. And what was left to him now? The numbing boredom of the London Season; hunting parties and the changeless tasks of a noble landholder; his widowed mother's nagging to marry and produce an heir; the tiresome attentions of insipid debutantes and their rapacious parents. In short, nothing but duty. Wareham's mouth tightened. He knew about duty, and he would do it.

The pale cliffs of Dover were definitely visible now as the ship beat against the wind to reach shore. The mate was shouting orders, and the sailors were swarming over the ropes. A few hardy gulls added their plaintive cries to the uproar as the ship tacked toward the harbor entrance.

A movement on the opposite side of the deck caught Colin's eye. Two other passengers had left the refuge of their cabins and dared the elements to watch the landing. The first was most unusual—a giant of a man with swarthy skin, dark flashing eyes, and huge hands. Though he wore European dress, he was obviously from some eastern country, an Arab or a Turk, Colin thought, and wondered what he could be doing so far from home. He didn't look very happy with his first view of the English coastline.

The fellow moved, and Colin got a clear look at the woman who stood next to him. A gust of wind molded her clothing against her slender form and caught the hood of her gray cloak and threw it back, revealing hair of the very palest gold; even on this dim day, it glowed like burnished metal. She had a delicately etched profile like an antique cameo, a small straight nose, and high unyielding cheekbones, but Colin also noticed the promise of passion in her full lips and soft curve of jaw. She was exquisite—a woman like a blade of moonlight—tall and square-shouldered, perhaps five and twenty, her pale skin flushed from the bitter wind. His interest caught, Colin noticed that her gaze at the shore was steady and serious. She looked as if she were facing a potential enemy instead of a friendly harbor.

As he watched, she turned, letting her eyes run along the coast to the south, her gaze glancing across his. Her expression was so full of longing and loss that he felt a spark of curiosity. Who was she? What had taken her across the Channel, and what brought her back? She turned to speak to the dark giant—undoubtedly her servant, he thought—and he wondered if she had been in the East, a most unlikely destination for a lady. She smiled slightly, sadly, and he felt a sudden tug of attraction. For a moment, he was tempted to cross the deck and speak to her, taking advantage of the freedom among ship passengers to scrape an introduction. Surely that pensive face held fascinating secrets. He took one step before rationality intervened, reminding him that most of the truly tedious women he had known in his life had been quite pretty. It would be unbearable to discover that only silly chatter and wearisome affectation lay behind that beautiful facade. Colin turned and saw that they were approaching the docks. "We'd best gather our things," he said to Reddings, and led the way below.

The other pair remained at the rail as the ship passed into the shelter of the headland and the wind lessened. The dark giant huddled his cloak closer, while the woman faced the waves head-on. She seemed to relish the cut of the spray and the salty damp of the air. "There it is, Ferik," she said after a while. "Home." Her tone was quietly sarcastic.

The huge man viewed the buildings of Dover without enthusiasm. A gull floated by at the level of his head, and he looked at it as if measuring it for the roasting spit.

"When I left here seven years ago," said the woman, "I had a husband, a fortune, six servants, and trunks of fashionable gowns. I return with little but my wits."

"And me, mistress," answered the giant in a deep sonorous voice with a heavy accent to his English.

"And you," she replied warmly. "I still don't think you will like England, Ferik." He looked so odd in narrow trousers and a tailcoat, she thought, utterly out of place.

"It must be better than where I came from, mistress," was the reply.

Remembering the horrors she had rescued him from, Emma Tarrant had to agree.

"Except for maybe the rain," he added, a bit plaintively.

Emma laughed. "I warned you about that, and the cold, too."

"Yes, mistress," agreed her huge servitor, sounding aggrieved nonetheless.

Emma surveyed the shore, drinking in the peaked roofs of English houses, the greenery, the very English carriage and pair with a crest on the door, waiting for some passenger. Seven years, she thought, seven years she'd been gone, and it felt like a lifetime. Probably it was a mistake to come back. She would find no welcome, no feast spread for the prodigal daughter. Indeed, she had no intention of seeing anyone from that old, lost life. She only wanted to live among familiar surroundings again, to speak her own language, to feel other than an alien on foreign soil. She was asking so little. Surely, it would not be denied her.

The sailors were throwing lines to be secured and readying the gangplank. Men bustled on the docks. "Come, Ferik," said Emma. "We'd best see to our boxes."

On the steep, ladderlike stair leading below deck, they had to squeeze past a tall gentleman and his valet who were coming up. Even their few pieces of worn, battered luggage jammed the opening, so that for a moment, Emma was caught and held against the ship's timbers on one side and the departing passenger on the other. Looking up to protest, she encountered eyes of a startling, unusual blue, almost violet, and undeniable magnetism. From a distance of less than five inches they examined her, seeming to look beneath the surface and search for something important. Emma couldn't look away. She felt a deep internal pulse answer that search, as if it was a quest she had been pursuing for a long time. Her lips parted in surprise; her heartbeat accelerated.

Colin Wareham found himself seized by an overwhelming desire to kiss this stranger to whom he had never spoken a word. Her nearness roused him; the startled intelligence of her expression intrigued him. It would be so very easy to bend his head and take her lips for his own. The mere thought of their yielding softness made him rigid with longing.

Then the giant moved, backing out of the passage and hauling one of the offending pieces of luggage with him. The woman was freed. "Are you all right, mistress?" the huge servant asked when she did not move at once.

She started, and slipped quickly down the stair to the lower deck. "Yes," she said. "Thank you, Ferik."

"Beg pardon," murmured Reddings, and hurried up.

Colin hesitated, about to speak. One part of him declared that he would always regret it if he let this woman slip away, while another insisted that this was madness. Reddings leaned over the open hatch above him. "Can I help, my lord?" he asked. The outsized man started down the stair again, effectively filling the opening. It *was* madness, Colin concluded, and pushed past the giant into the open air.

A week later, Emma sat at a card table in Barbara Rampling's drawing room and pondered which suit to discard. It was a matter of some importance, because for the past year her only means of support had been her skill with games of chance. She considered a minor club, then a diamond. Her opponent was a wretched player, but overconfidence was always a mistake. It had been the downfall of her late husband, Edward, who never stopped believing that the next hand of cards, or the next turn of the wheel, would favor him. He had run through all of Emma's substantial fortune on the basis of that belief, and had managed to maintain it up to the very moment he was killed in a tavern brawl over a wager.

Emma laid down her card. While her opponent considered it, she glanced up and caught Barbara Rampling's eye. Though she had only just met the woman, she felt she knew her. Barbara, too, had had a husband whose grand passion was gaming rather than his wife. When his insurmountable pile of debts had caused him to put a bullet through his head, Barbara had opened this genteel gaming hell in her own house in order to keep from starving. Emma was quite familiar with such places; she had spent the last year in them. She was even grateful. She could not enter the clubs where gentlemen played deep. It was only thanks to people like Barbara that she could survive at all.

Edward's only legacy, besides debts and disappointments, had been the lessons he gave Emma in gambling.

Under his tutelage, she had learned to play all sorts of
card games and, surprisingly, had proved to have real
talent. It had driven Edward nearly mad—that she could
be so skillful and yet have no desire whatsoever to play.
In the last days she had kept them afloat for a while by
winning. But no one could have kept pace with his continual losses. His death had ended an accelerating spiral
of ruin that had very nearly pulled Emma under with it.

Her opponent frowned. She was a careless player
who did not seem to grasp the principles of the game.
She was also, Emma had been reliably informed, easily
able to afford substantial losses. Emma need not feel
guilty if she came out of this evening set up for a month.

Hiding her impatience while her partner decided on
her play, Emma gazed around the room once again, au-
tomatically cataloguing the crowd at the tables. Most of
them were tiresomely familiar types; she had encountered them in grand salons and mean inns all across the
Continent and as far away as Constantinople. They
made up a floating international population of sharps
and gulls, the cunning and the lost, who shared just one
overriding characteristic—they cared for nothing but
the game. The usual mixture of contempt, pity, and dislike that assailed her in such places gathered in Emma's
throat. Sir Edward and Lady Emma Tarrant, she
thought with bitter humor. She had certainly never
imagined it would end like this.

Her gaze paused and then froze on a young man at a
corner table, playing faro with a single opponent. He
could not be more than seventeen, she thought, and he
exhibited all the terrible signs she knew so well—the
obsessed glitter in his eyes, the trembling hands, the
intent angle of his body bent over the cards. He was
losing money he did not have. The sight made Emma
sick. She would have stopped him if she could, but the
last seven years had made her only too familiar with the
gamester's mania. He would not hear anything she said.

She started to turn her back on that corner of the
room, refusing to watch the debacle, but just then, the

young man made a quick gesture and turned his head so that she could see his full face. Emma frowned. The gesture, his hair, the set of his shoulders—his features were at once hauntingly familiar and completely new to her. There was only one person he could be.

Emma's heart began to pound, and she grew hot. She had not expected to find any of them in a place like this. As the fat woman on the other side of the table at last laid down her card, Emma said, "Do you know that young man in the corner?" Though she fought to keep her voice steady, it wavered a little.

The woman was too engrossed in the game to notice. She glanced idly at the boy and said, "Name's Bellingham, I believe. Your play."

The name rang in her ears, confirming her suspicions. It could not be, but it was. The past, which she had thought to evade, had surfaced despite all her plans.

Somehow, Emma got through the rest of the rubber. She even won, for the other woman was hopeless. Refusing another round, she gathered her winnings and took a glass of wine to a window seat. From its obscurity, she watched the young man lose hand after hand, hundreds of pounds, as the candles burned down and the night waned and Emma's nightmares came to vivid life to torment her once again.

How many evenings had she spent this way, she wondered, watching gambling wreck her life—the insatiable lust for the luck of the draw, the toss of the dice. How often, in the beginning, had she tried to reason with her husband and discovered his crazed anger, his cruel disregard for anything but his need to play.

Hatred began to rise in Emma for the boy's opponent, also a familiar figure. Much older than his partner, perhaps thirty, he had the saturnine expression Emma had seen on the faces of countless hardened gamesters. He wouldn't care about the boy's age or his means, Emma thought bitterly. In fact, he had probably lured him here, pretending to be his friend, just in order to enrich himself. Rage built in her as the minutes passed.

How she loathed him and all his kind. They were parasites, scavengers on human misery. Once, she had had to go to such a man and plead with him to forgive a debt. The man had shown no more feeling than a stone when he refused.

It was past midnight when the game broke up. The young man looked sick and terrified as he murmured some final words to his partner and then hurried from the room. Emma rose as the older man strolled out, his careless ease infuriating her further. Something had to be done, she decided. She could not allow this. This time, she *would* be able to stop it.

Rising, Emma followed the man from the room, keeping just out of sight as he descended the stairs, received his cloak from a servant, and went out into the night. When Ferik rose from his place in the hall to accompany her home, Emma gave him a silent signal. Obediently, he fell in two paces behind as she trailed the man to a cluster of hackney coaches awaiting passengers. Only when Emma told one of the drivers, "I wish to go where that gentleman goes," pointing to the hack pulling away ahead of them, did Ferik say, "Mistress?"

"Get in," replied Emma, her anger evident in her tone.

Silently, he did so, and they clattered through the dark streets of London toward a more fashionable part of town. Emma took out the loo mask she always carried in her reticule, in case she wished to go somewhere unrecognized, and put it on. It covered all her face except the lips and chin.

"What has happened, mistress?" asked Ferik. He frowned. "Did that man insult you? Shall I kill him?"

Emma waved him to silence as both hackneys pulled up in front of a large stone mansion. She leapt out, thrust a coin at the driver, and hurried toward the door, which the man was just unlocking. Ferik ran to keep up.

She made it, as she had meant to, just as he walked inside. And thus she and Ferik entered his house on his heels as the wide door swung shut.

"What in blazes?" The man lifted his ebony walking stick like someone who knew what to do with it. "Who are you? What do you want?"

"I've come for Robin Bellingham's notes of hand," said Emma. She had seen the young man scribbling one after another promise to pay as he lost more and more to this villain. Rage at the man burned in her. How many young men had he ruined already? she wondered.

He lowered his cane slightly and stared. There was something familiar about these two, he thought.

"I'll offer you what you can't refuse," the woman added, her tone heavy with scorn. "I'll play you for them."

Colin Wareham let his stick fall. He eyed the bronze giant and the cloaked and masked woman beside him. "I saw you on the ship from France," he said. The entire incident came back to him, particularly the feeling this woman had roused.

She ignored this as irrelevant. "Did you hear me? I challenge you to a game, the stakes to be those notes."

Colin examined her. The mask didn't matter; he clearly remembered that beautiful face, and the unfathomable complex of emotions he had thought he saw in it. No woman had ever spoken to him in this way, or offered such a proposition. "Why?" he asked. "What's young Bellingham to you?" He absorbed the pale gilt hair, the sensuous mouth, the gentle curve of breast and hip, more exciting somehow than voluptuousness. "Your lover?" The idea was ridiculous. He didn't believe the boy had it in him.

"That is no concern of yours!" she responded with icy ferocity. "I shall not let you ruin him."

Colin was oddly disappointed that she did not deny the connection. There must be more to young Bellingham than was readily apparent. Then he noticed that the woman's giant servant was gaping at her with obvious astonishment. This was a puzzle indeed.

Colin felt as if something lost was stirring and wakening inside him. It had been months since he had felt curiosity, or the least hint of amusement. He could not resist prolonging the situation. "Very well," he said. "I'll play you. You leave the choice of game to me?"

She gave a curt nod.

"You are very confident of your skills."

She made no reply, but Colin could see contempt in the set of her head, the quick involuntary gesture of one hand. His competitive instincts began to stir. "Why not?" he said, half to himself.

A thin smile curved her lips. She looked, Colin thought, as if he had done precisely what she expected, and as if she was anticipating a thorough rout. Growing even more intrigued, he took up the candlestick that had been waiting for him and opened a door off the hall. Walking into the library, he rang the bell, then lit more candles with the one he held, illuminating the beautiful room. "Does your fearsome friend stand over me as we play?" he inquired.

"Ferik will wait in the hall," she replied. "Where he can *easily* hear me if I call out." At her words, the giant folded his legs under him and sank to the hall floor, leaning his back comfortably against the wall.

"He can have a chair," said Colin.

Silent, enigmatic, Ferik slowly shook his head. He looked like a dark statue guarding some ancient monument, Colin thought. The image surprised and delighted him. Giving in to the impulse, he laughed, and the sound in the quiet of the house startled him. How long had it been since he had felt moved to laughter?

A surprised, and very sleepy, footman appeared at the back of the hall. He gaped at Ferik, then at the masked woman standing next to him. "My lord?" he said.

"John. Good. We require brandy and several piquet decks." Taking in his guest's set expression, he added, "Unopened packs, mind you, John." A smile continued to tug at his lips.

"Yes, my lord," said the young footman, closing his

mouth with a snap and turning to do his master's bidding.

Emma walked into the library and took a seat at the card table to wait. She was somewhat surprised to find that it was just the sort of room she liked. The shelves of leather-bound books beckoned against the dark green walls. The thick patterned carpet and heavy draperies shut out all external noise. In a corner was a comfortable armchair with a footrest, a book open on the small table beside it. Probably his wife had been reading there alone while he gambled away their funds until the early hours, Emma thought. She had never met a gamester who cared a snap of his fingers for books.

The footman returned with a tray containing the cards, a decanter of brandy and two glasses. He took his time as he set it down, arranged the table, and poured, casting curious sidelong glances at the masked woman sitting rigid in the gilt chair. The baron had had no guests at all since his return from France. His disappointed staff, expecting lively parties of gentlemen at least—along with the opportunity for lavish tips—had murmured among themselves. Cook had gone so far as to approach Mr. Reddings with a question, and had been roundly snubbed by the valet for her pains. But now it seemed as if their master was beginning an intrigue. This opened up new possibilities. John could scarcely wait to tell the others in the morning. "Will there be anything else, my lord?" he said, his face showing none of these thoughts.

"No, thank you, John. Nothing more. You may go to bed."

His avid gaze taking in every detail, the footman went. Wait until Nancy heard about the foreign giant sitting on the hall floor, he thought. He would be the center of attention below stairs for days and days.

Emma faced her host across the inlaid card table and prepared to deal. She had no doubt that she would win, and she could scarcely wait to see his face when she did. One of the few pleasures left in her life was defeating these despicable creatures who preyed on the young and unwary. They thought themselves invulnerable, and when they were bested, and by a woman too, it rocked them to their very foundations.

They began to play. The room was warm. The footman had made up the fire, though the evening was mild. The ranks of candles threw a wavering golden light over the cards as Emma surveyed her hand and began to calculate choices. The scent of leather and beeswax furniture polish permeated the room.

Her host offered her one of the glasses. "Brandy, miss . . . ? What is your name? I never heard it on the ship."

She ignored him, deciding on a discard.

"Mine's Wareham, Colin Wareham." He sipped from his glass, his eyes roving over her, then examined the card she had put down. His brows rose slightly. "Clever," he said. "You play well. But it's odd; you don't have quite the manner of the ladies who haunt the gaming tables."

"I'm not like them," replied Emma in a voice full of loathing. "Like *you*. I don't lure unwitting youngsters into losing their fortunes to me."

"Neither do—"

"I don't care to talk while I play," said Emma. She had no intention of chatting with a man like him.

In the next half hour, she discovered that he was a formidable player. He calculated the odds to a nicety, and played his cards well. He seemed also to have an uncanny ability to predict what cards she held. It was clear that a fine mind lay behind those slender, finely boned hands. As time passed, Emma noticed with some surprise that they were not the soft, white hands she usually saw at gambling tables. His skin was browned by the sun, and there were nicks and calluses to show that he did other things besides fleece youngsters of their money. His manner, too, was not quite that of the hardened gamester. But she had the evidence of her own eyes, and she steadfastly ignored any distractions.

Emma lost the first game of the rubber, but not by much. And the fall of the cards had obviously been in his favor. She was not at all worried as he dealt the second hand and she sorted through it, planning her strategy.

"You don't even like cards, do you?" said Wareham, curiosity clear in his tone.

Startled, Emma looked up. She had not expected him to notice anything but the game. Men like him had no other interests. She met his eyes, and abruptly remembered all the details of their encounter on the ship as she lost herself in their violet depths. They really did have depths. And they hinted at intelligence and compassion and humor and numberless other traits that were utterly alien to the kind of man she knew him to be. As on the boat, she was transfixed by the power of his gaze.

Thoroughly unsettled, she examined him. She'd gotten only a general impression before—of a tall, dark man, slender though broad-shouldered, dressed in well-cut, fashionable clothes. Now she noticed his face—narrow, with high cheekbones that slanted upward, leaving a slight hollow beneath them; an aquiline nose; a determined chin with an unobtrusive cleft. His black hair was cropped short, but it had a slight curl that was not wholly disguised by brushing it severely back from his forehead and temples. His lips were firm and chiseled, his eyes deep set and that unusual shade of blue. He was quite handsome, she admitted to herself, and there was something definitely attractive about him. Of course, there would have to be, she reminded herself severely, if he was to lure unsuspecting youngsters to their ruin. All these Captain Sharps had a certain superficial charm.

"It's almost as if you hate playing," he added.

"I do," she replied crisply. For Emma, there was no thrill at the risk. Gambling, for her, was more like the tedious mathematical problems her governess Miss Crane used to set her in the schoolroom, or translation of a tricky bit of French. She won not through love or luck but through intelligence and cool calculation and sheer necessity.

"You find no joy in it at all?" he said.

"Joy?" repeated Emma in accents of loathing. "The moment I begin to enjoy gaming, I shall abandon it forever." She had to suppress a shudder.

"Why, then, do you play?" he inquired.

"Because I must!" she snapped. "Will you discard, sir?"

He looked as if he wished to say more, but in the end, he simply laid down a card. Focusing on her hand, Emma tried to concentrate all her attention upon it. But she was aware now of his gaze upon her, of his compelling presence on the other side of the table.

She looked up again. He *was* gazing at her, steadily, curiously. But she could find no threat in his eyes. On the contrary, they were disarmingly friendly. He could not possibly look like that and wish her any harm, Emma thought dreamily.

He smiled.

Emma caught her breath. His smile was amazing— warm, confiding, utterly trustworthy. She must have misjudged him, Emma thought.

"Are you sure you won't have some of this excellent brandy?" he asked, sipping from his glass. "I really can recommend it."

Seven years of hard lessons came crashing back upon Emma as their locked gaze broke. He was doing this on purpose, of course. Trying to divert her attention, beguile her into making mistakes and losing. Gathering all her bitterness and resolution, Emma shifted her mind to the cards. She would not be caught so again.

Emma won the second hand, putting them even. But as she exulted in the win, she noticed a small smile playing around Colin Wareham's lips and wondered at it. He poured himself another glass of brandy and sipped it. He looked as if he was thoroughly enjoying himself, she thought. And he didn't seem at all worried that she would beat him. His arrogance was infuriating.

All now rested on the third hand. As she opened a new pack of cards and prepared to deal, Emma took a deep breath.

"You are making a mistake, refusing this brandy," Wareham said, sipping again.

"I have no intention of fuzzing my wits with drink," answered Emma crisply. She did not look at him as she snapped out the cards.

"Who are you?" he said abruptly. "Where do you come from? You have the voice and manner of a nobleman's daughter, but you are nothing like the women I meet in society."

Emma flushed a little. There was something in his tone—it might be admiration or derision—that made her self-conscious. Let some of those women spend the last seven years as she had, she thought bitterly, and then see what they were like. "I came here to play cards," she said coldly. "I have said I do not wish to converse with you."

Raising one dark eyebrow, he picked up his hand. The fire hissed in the grate. One of the candles guttered, filling the room with the smell of wax and smoke. At this late hour, the streets outside were silent; the only sound was Ferik's surprisingly delicate snores from the hall.

In silence, they frowned over discards and calculated odds. Finally, after a long struggle, Wareham said, "I believe this point is good." He put down a card.

Emma stared at it.

"And also my quint," he added, laying down another.

Emma's eyes flickered to his face, then down again. "Yes?" he urged.

Swallowing, she nodded.

"Ah. Good. Then—a quint, a tierce, fourteen aces, three kings, and eleven cards played, ma'am."

Emma gazed at the galaxy of court cards spread before her, then fixed on the one card he still held. The game depended on it, and there was no hint to tell her what she should keep to win the day. She hesitated a moment longer, then made her decision. "A diamond," she said, throwing down the rest of her hand.

"Too bad," he replied, exhibiting a small club.

Emma stared at the square of pasteboard, stunned. She couldn't believe that he had beaten her. "Piqued, repiqued, and capotted," she murmured. It was a humiliating defeat for one of her skill.

"Bad luck."

"I cannot believe you kept that club."

"Rather than throw it away on the slender chance of picking up an ace or a king?"

Numbly, Emma nodded. "You had been taking such risks."

"I sometimes bet on the slim chances," he conceded. "But you must vary your play if you expect to keep your opponent off balance." He smiled.

That charming smile, Emma thought. Not gloating or contemptuous, but warm all the way to those extraordinary eyes. It almost softened the blow of losing. Almost.

"We said nothing of your stake for this game," he pointed out.

"You asked me for none," Emma retorted. She could not nearly match the amount of Robin Bellingham's notes.

"True." Colin watched as she bit her lower lip in frustration, and savored the rapid rise and fall of her breasts under the thin bodice of her satin gown. "It appears we are even."

She pounded her fist softly on the table. She had been sure she could beat him, Colin thought. And she had not planned beyond that point. He waited, curious to see what she would do now.

She pounded the table again, thwarted determination obvious in her face. "Will you try another match?" she said finally.

A fighter, Colin thought approvingly. He breathed in the scent of her perfume, let his eyes linger on the

creamy skin of her shoulders. He had never encountered such a woman before. He didn't want her to go.
On the contrary, he found himself wanting something
quite different. "One hand," he offered. "If you win,
the notes are yours."

"And if I do not?" she asked.

"You may still have them, but I get . . ." He hesitated. He was not the sort of man who seduced young
ladies for sport. But she had come here to his house and
challenged him, Colin thought. She was no schoolgirl.
She had intrigued and irritated and roused him.

"What?" she said, rather loudly.

He had been staring at her far too intensely, Colin
realized. But the brandy and the strangeness of the night
had made him reckless. "You," he replied.

There was a moment of shocked silence, as if that one
simple word had frozen them into a static tableau. Then
his beautiful visitor stiffened in her chair. On the table-
top, her hands curled into fists. "How dare you?" she
replied.

"You might be surprised at what I would dare."

"You are despicable. If you think that I came here
to—"

"You are the one who suggested another game," he
interrupted. "I have merely set the stakes."

"Outrageous stakes," she answered. "Out of the
question."

"You'll never be offered better odds," he said, his
senses filled with images of her in his arms. "However
the cards fall, you get what you want." Unable to resist
the impulse any longer, he reached across the table to
touch her.

She jerked out of reach and sprang to her feet,
knocking over the delicate chair she had been sitting in.
It clattered against the table leg and fell with a loud
thump onto the carpet.

A spark of keen disappointment made him say, "I
suppose I shall have to collect from young Bellingham,
after all."

"You *are* nothing but a rapacious swindler," was the furious response.

She said it as though she had begun to form some other opinion, Colin thought, and felt a pang of regret for his unconsidered remark. "On the contrary," he began, "but you must admit—"

"Mistress?" said a deep, resonant voice from the hallway. "Did you call?"

Emma took a step back from the table. Colin started around it. "Ferik has made himself very much my protector," she warned. "He is not fettered by English notions of law and fairness, and his methods are direct and extremely effective."

"If he interferes with me, he will find himself in serious trouble," replied Colin between clenched teeth.

The library door opened and Ferik filled the doorway, his dark eyes suspicious. He eyed the overturned chair, then turned his belligerent gaze on Colin Wareham. "What has he done to you?" he demanded.

"Nothing," she said. "We must go." She retrieved her things from the card table and donned her cloak.

The giant hesitated. He was contemplating Wareham with his fists clenched.

"Now," she commanded, already in the hall, turning the lock on the great front door.

Reluctantly, Ferik moved to follow.

"Tell me your name," demanded Colin. "Where can I find you again?"

Ignoring him, she hurried out, and as Colin moved to intercept her, Ferik's massive bulk blocked him.

"I'll find you," called Colin, standing in the open doorway. The shaft of light from the library made him a black outline against a glowing golden rectangle. The shapes of light shifted as he raised an arm. "Have no doubt. I will," he added fiercely.

She disappeared into the darkness without answering.

B aron St. Mawr sat at his breakfast table and contemplated with disgust the array of food the cook had
sent up. As all of his servants who had come into contact with him this morning already knew, he was in the
foulest of foul moods. He had scarcely slept in the few
hours since the mysterious woman left his house, and
the effects of the brandy he had drunk were oppressive.
But most of all, he was furious that he had let his lovely
visitor escape without finding out anything about her.
For a brief time, she had lifted the cloud that now shadowed his existence. She had brought curiosity and
amusement and challenge, the urgent sweetness of desire. And like an utter fool, he had let her slip away
without even learning her name. Silently, savagely, he
cursed his stupidity, his fingers white with tension on
his coffee cup. Then he cursed her blasted servant—
what was his name?—Ferik. Damned silly name. Beginning to enjoy himself, he cursed his morning engagements, which prevented him from beginning to search
for her at once. He was about to move on to other

"Yes, my lo...

"Wait. Who is it?"

"A Mr. Robin Bellingham, my lord."

Bellingham. Colin sat up straighter, his jaw tightening. He had forgotten all about Bellingham. Here was a
link to his visitor, though he still did not understand
what sort exactly. But he very much wished to speak to
young Bellingham. Draining his coffee cup, he rose.
"Where have you put him?" he asked John.

"In the library, my lord."

"Fitting," jibed Colin.

As he opened the chamber door for his master, John
observed the steely glint in his lordship's eyes and felt
rather sorry for young Bellingham, who looked unhappy enough already.

Striding into the library, Colin found Robin Bellingham standing before the fireplace looking very young
and quite miserable. There were dark circles under his
eyes and his hands showed a slight tremor. He stood
straight, however, when Colin entered and said, "I've
come to speak to you about my notes of hand, sir."

"Ah, heard they're still outstanding, have you?" he
snarled. What connection could that magnificent creature possibly have with this reedy youth? Colin wondered.

"I beg your pardon?"

"I want the whole story," he demanded.

Bellingham looked bewildered.

"Didn't come off quite as you'd planned, eh?" All of
Colin's frustration and anger came to a point and focused on the young man standing before him. All the
reasons he could think of for his mysterious guest of
last night to go to such lengths for this poor specimen

filled him with rage. "She didn't quite manage the thing."

"My lord St. Mawr, I don't understand you," said Robin Bellingham stiffly. "I have come to discuss the money I lost to you last night at Barbara Rampling's house."

"Who is she?" demanded Colin, goaded by his bland deception. "You will tell me or I will choke it out of you!"

Bellingham backed away. "Mrs. Rampling?" he stammered. "I scarcely know her, my lord. I believe she is the widow of—"

"Blast Barbara Rampling! You know very well I was not speaking of her. Who is the woman who came to reclaim your notes?"

"Woman?" Bellingham goggled at him as if he'd gone mad. "I have no notion what you're talking about, my lord."

Wareham examined the boy's face. His confusion looked genuine. Then he noticed something else. He took a step closer, surveying his features.

Bellingham took a step back. "I . . . I hoped . . . that is, I came to request a little time to redeem the notes," he said with difficulty. "I find myself a bit strapped just now. I know that you—"

"I don't win money from striplings," interrupted Wareham, brushing his apologies aside as if the whole matter didn't interest him in the least. "I would have told you last night, if you hadn't hurried off. Indeed, I would have refused the game altogether if I could have done so without insulting you." He stared at the boy's silver-gilt hair, at the shape of his jaw. He suddenly noticed the trick he had of cocking his head to listen.

"Sir," said Robin Bellingham, drawing himself up in outrage. "I am not a schoolboy. I have been on the town for—"

"Oh, all of six months," interjected Wareham. There was something haunting about the shape of the lad's face. And that hair—he should have realized—it was a most uncommon color. "I've no intention of taking your blunt," he said.

Bellingham flushed and clenched his fists at his sides. "You may do as you like," he replied in mortified accents. "But you should know that I shall consider myself obligated to pay nonetheless."

"Then you may consider yourself an ass," replied Wareham indifferently.

"My lord!" Bellingham clenched his jaw. He was white and trembling. "I shall . . . I shall . . ."

"Don't call me out," said Wareham wearily. "I shan't meet you." He sighed, realizing he must placate this young sprig if he was to get anything out of him. "This is not aimed at you personally, you know. I do not take large sums of money from men ten years younger than I. It's against my principles."

"But I . . ." Bellingham was clearly humiliated, but a hint of relief was beginning to creep into his tone. "I cannot fail in a debt of honor," he objected tentatively.

"You can clear it by doing me a service," answered Wareham.

The young man stood straighter. "Anything in my power, my lord."

Colin leaned a little forward. "Tell me, do you have a sister?"

"A . . ." Bellingham gaped at him.

"A sister," repeated his host meditatively. "An older sister. A good bit older, I would imagine."

The young man's mouth hung open. He looked as if he had been stuffed.

"Come, come," said Colin impatiently. "Is this a difficult question? You must know whether you have a sister?"

"Yes. That is, no. That is, I did, but . . ."

"But?" encouraged Wareham.

"I'm not supposed to speak of her," blurted Bellingham. "Father has forbidden it."

"Ah." His theory confirmed, Colin relaxed. The resemblance of this youngster to his nighttime visitor really was striking once you began to observe details. And her reasons for trying to rescue the lad were explained quite satisfactorily by such a relationship. Best of all, now he would find out everything he wanted to know. Clearly, there was a mystery involved. "I will not mention it to your father. But in exchange for your notes, I should like to hear all about your sister," he declared.

Bellingham stared at him.

"Would you care for coffee?" he asked, all cordiality now. Indeed, his headache had greatly diminished. "Breakfast?"

In a very few minutes, they were seated across from each other in the deep library chairs while the footman served coffee. When he had gone, Colin leaned forward, putting the tips of his fingers together. "Now," he said with anticipation. "Your sister."

Bellingham cleared his throat. "I didn't know her very well," he said. "She is eight years older than I, and we never saw much of each other. By the time I was out of short coats, she was getting ready to leave the schoolroom and be presented to society."

Wareham waved this aside. "Tell me what you do know," he urged.

"Very well." Bellingham cleared his throat nervously again. "My sister's name is Emma," he confided.

"Emma," echoed the baron, savoring the sound. It was a fine name. He liked it very much.

"Yes. I remember she was very beautiful, and always laughing. She used to dance around the drawing room, teasing Father." Robin grimaced. "He was a different man in those days. He—"

"You speak as if she was dead," said Wareham, with a sudden chill. Had he been wrong after all?

"No. Not dead." Bellingham moved uneasily in his chair. "Well, that is, my father has declared her dead to our family."

Here was the crux of it, Colin thought. Now he would discover her secret. "Why?" he prompted.

"He didn't approve of her marriage."

"Marriage!" The word crashed down on Wareham like a falling tree.

"Yes. She, er, chose someone he didn't like, and then she defied him when he objected." Robin sounded rather wistful, as if he would very much like to do the same.

"Tell me the whole tale," Colin said harshly. "From the beginning."

Bellingham nodded. "As much as I know, sir. In her first season, Emma fell in love with Edward Tarrant. The eldest son of Sir Philip Tarrant."

"The one who ruined himself at Newmarket?" growled Colin, the phrase "fell in love" echoing unpleasantly in his ears.

"Yes. I think that happened the same year Emma met his son. At any rate, the Tarrants were left without a penny, and my father forbade the match. Emma had a large fortune, you see, left her by our grandmother, and my father thought Tarrant was after her money. I gather he hadn't liked Tarrant much in the first place, because he had a bad reputation as a gamester."

"Ah," said Wareham. Some of the things Emma had said about cards came clearer for him.

"But Emma wouldn't listen to anyone. They say Edward Tarrant is very handsome and dashing." Robin hesitated. "Did you speak, my lord?"

Colin, who had let out an involuntary growl, shook his head. "Go on."

"They married as soon as Emma turned eighteen and went to live abroad. I believe my father tried to keep Emma's fortune from Tarrant. I know he spent a great deal of time talking with solicitors. But in the end, he couldn't. He was like a madman. I remember *that* quite well, the way he raved about the house cursing Tarrant and calling Emma names. He said Tarrant would run through her money at the tables in five years and leave her destitute."

"And did he?"

Bellingham shrugged. "No one has heard from Emma for years."

"Or her husband?" Colin inquired. It was curious, he thought. He had never before realized how much one could dislike a word.

"No. That is . . . not that I've ever heard. I suppose he must have had friends, but . . ."

That could be looked into, Colin thought. "She . . . they are not back in England?" he asked.

Bellingham shook his head, then hesitated. "Well, I don't know where they are," he admitted. "I wouldn't recognize Tarrant if I passed him in the street." He frowned. "Why do you want to know all this?"

"I believe I saw your sister last night," replied Wareham absently.

"Saw Emma? Where?"

Colin started to say, "here," then stopped. "At the card party, after you left," he substituted.

Bellingham leaned forward, excited. "Did you know her? I have so often wanted to speak about her, but my father . . ."

"No," interrupted Wareham. "I did not know her." If she had come out seven years ago, he thought, he would have been in a filthy military camp in Portugal at the time.

"Oh." Robin looked disappointed. "Well, did you speak to her? Where is she staying? I will call on her, no matter what Father says."

Any hopes Wareham had had that Bellingham was actually hiding his sister vanished. It scarcely mattered now in any case, he thought. She was a married woman, nothing to do with him. "I have no idea," he said. "I was merely curious."

"Oh." The young man's face fell. He was too self-absorbed to wonder at his host's unusual curiosity. "I wish I had stayed. I would like to see her."

Weariness had descended on Colin again. Rising, he went to his desk and got out Bellingham's notes of hand. "Here," he said, handing over the small bundle. "We are quits."

Slowly, the young man reached for them. "You are certain?"

"I have told you," was the impatient reply. "And now I must bid you good day. I have an appointment."

"Of course." Bellingham rose. "I . . . thank you."

The baron waved this aside. "Be more careful at the tables," he suggested.

At this, the young man's face reddened and his pale brows came together in anger. With a set jaw, he turned his back and strode from the room. Colin stared after him thoughtfully for a moment. Clearly, he had hit a nerve. But then he shrugged. Bellingham was no concern of his. Nor was his *married* sister. The gloom that had possessed him for so long descended upon Colin again. It was like a black fog, muffling everything and taking all the joy out of his life. Morosely, he went to pour himself another cup of coffee.

In a much less fashionable neighborhood on the other side of London, Emma also had risen early after a restless few hours tossing in her bed. She sat in a small, shabby breakfast room drinking tea and supporting her aching head with one hand. She had created a dreadful tangle and accomplished absolutely nothing, she thought irritably. She had exposed herself to scandal by visiting a man's house alone late at night, and this after years of struggle to keep her good name, as she lost everything else. On top of that, the wretched man had recognized her from the boat, and now he would know her if she appeared at any of the card parties where she had planned to win enough money to survive. And to crown her folly, she had not erased the debt still hanging over her young brother.

The door of the breakfast room opened and a small, bustling woman of nearly sixty came in. Gray ringlets clustered about her head, and her amber gown, lavishly trimmed with yellow braid, suited neither her age nor her surroundings. Her face was pale, her features small and undistinguished. The smile she gave Emma didn't seem to penetrate below the surface of her gray eyes. "Good morning, my dear," she said, taking a seat opposite Emma and ringing for fresh tea. "Did you sleep well?"

"Not very." Emma watched Edward's aunt, the only person she had been willing to contact on her return to England, hesitate over the choice of a muffin. She had remembered Arabella Tarrant as an established, if minor, member of the *ton.* She had returned to find her reduced to genteel poverty by the flight of her husband to the West Indies, accompanied by a pretty young housemaid. Best not even to *think* of that subject, Emma told herself hastily. When Arabella got started on the sins of her husband, she could go on for hours.

"It didn't go badly at the tables last night, I hope?" said the older woman, spreading butter with a liberal hand. Her hot tea arrived, and she poured a cup.

"Very badly," replied Emma, thinking of Robin.

"You lost?" Arabella clutched at her thin bosom.

"No, no. I won. It's all right." They had made an agreement that Emma would contribute part of her winnings to Arabella's household expenses, and she saw now how important that promise was to her hostess. Another person she would be disappointing, Emma thought with a sinking heart, now that she had spoiled her chances of appearing at card parties. "Aunt?" she asked, "do you know a man named Colin Wareham?"

Arabella's eyes grew round. "St. Mawr?" she replied. Emma shrugged to show her ignorance.

"Colin Wareham is the baron St. Mawr," explained the older woman. "A very old family. Vastly wealthy and well connected. Caroline Wareham, his sister, is married to the earl of Wrotham. I believe St. Mawr is just back from the French war. There was a great to-do when he joined the army. You would not remember. You were still in the schoolroom, I imagine."

Emma sipped her tea. Arabella enjoyed recalling times when she had been privy to the gossip of the *ton.*

The older woman clasped her hands before her. "Emma, you haven't met St. Mawr? He's one of the most eligible bachelors in London. What a splendid thing it would be if—"

"There's no question of anything like that," interrupted Emma.

"But, my dear, you are still quite lovely. And you have an air about you—I don't know how to describe it exactly—but I swear that a man might find it extremely—"

"I am not on the lookout for a husband," stated Emma.

"But why not? It is most comfortable for a woman to be married. And I am certain St. Mawr would never be so vulgar and *disgusting* as to take up with a servant and leave the country with her. When I think what I put up with from that man, the sacrifices I made to his whims, the—"

"I am hardly a desirable partner," put in Emma, hoping to stem the flow before Arabella hit her stride. "Penniless, a widow, disowned by my family."

"What? Oh. No, I suppose not." She looked like a child deprived of a promised treat, but whether it was the dream of a splendid match or the opportunity to rehearse her grievances yet again, Emma couldn't tell.

"Even if it were possible, I do not care to marry again," Emma admonished. "I have not formed a high opinion of the married state."

Arabella sighed dramatically. "I cannot say I blame you there," she answered. "When I think of the *years* I devoted to—"

"What do you know of Colin Wareham?" Emma interrupted. "He is a gamester, is he not?"

Arabella looked thwarted briefly, then made a vague gesture with one hand. "He has been abroad for years with the army. I don't think anyone knows much about him."

Which meant only that Arabella knew nothing, Emma thought.

A look of concern crossed the older woman's pale face. "Did you win a great deal of money from him?"

"And if I did?" wondered Emma.

"Well . . . it is just . . . some gentlemen don't care to be beaten by a woman, and that is a very powerful family. You wouldn't want them to be angry with you. They could destroy all your chances."

This was even worse than she had thought, Emma saw. Robin would be helpless before such a man. If he could not pay—and from his expression last night she was sure he couldn't—he would be ruined in society's eyes, which would only push him to even greater excesses at the tables.

Emma's jaw tightened. She had to free her brother from this threat. It didn't matter that after the long years of fighting for respectability, she would have to put it all at risk—to go against everything she had been taught, every code of proper behavior. She had no choice. She would have to do as Wareham asked, to go back to him and accept his scandalous wager.

The prospect was not completely repugnant to her, Emma found. There was something about Colin Wareham, something rather compelling. But all she wanted was to beat him soundly at cards, Emma thought quickly, and to wipe that look of smug assurance from his handsome features.

She had a good chance of winning, she told herself. She had the skill. But so did Wareham, a skeptical inner voice argued. He had a great deal of skill. In the end, it would all come down to luck. Emma grimaced. There were ways, of course, to be more certain of the outcome. She knew how to cheat at cards. She had a notion, however, that Colin Wareham was very well able to recognize such underhanded methods, and the idea of being caught at them by him made her cheeks grow hot. She would have to rely on her wits, Emma concluded. But she had been doing that for quite some time now.

"My dear, what is it?" exclaimed Arabella.

"What?"

"Why, for a moment, you had the oddest expression."

"It's nothing to worry about," replied Emma. "Just something I must do."

"Something involving St. Mawr?"

"Don't be concerned," repeated Emma.

Arabella watched her doubtfully. Emma's arrival had been like an answer to her prayers, for she was badly in need of the extra money she promised. If Emma got embroiled in some dispute with a man like St. Mawr, that promise would be empty. Arabella determined to do whatever she could to make certain that did not happen.

Colin sat in his library, the brandy decanter once more at his elbow, and brooded over the flames leaping in the fireplace. At the insistence of his mother, he had spent another dull, empty evening at Almack's. He had thought that by now she had introduced him to all the insipid young ladies of high birth on the marriage mart, but tonight she had produced a few more. And he had been required to talk to them and dance with them and take one of them in to supper. Though he was never other than polite, his patience had been stretched to the limit. He was sick to death of wide innocent eyes, white muslin frills, and meaningless conversation. He had tried to explain to his mother that the girls she presented as potential wives were utterly uninteresting, their minds filled with trivialities, their hearts vacant with youth. But she brushed his objections aside as stubbornness, or an incomprehensible desire to thwart her and evade his responsibilities to his name. "Damn," he muttered, and emptied his glass.

As he refilled it, he allowed the image of Emma Tarrant to float once more into his mind. Here was a woman very different from the witless debs. He had seen character in her face, an understanding of tragedy in her eyes. She had daring and courage. And a husband, an inner voice interjected savagely, causing his fingers to tighten on his glass. Letting his fist fall on the chair arm, he tore his mind from the memories of her hair, her scent. She was not worth his regrets.

The library door opened. "A lady to see you, my lord," said the footman.

Emma was right behind him, once again wearing her mask. She stepped into the room quickly, before she could change her mind, and faced Colin, still sprawled in his armchair. "I've come to do as you asked," she blurted out.

Colin stood. He had drunk a good deal, he realized, when his legs revealed a tendency to wobble. "Thank you, John," he said. "That will be all." He waited while the footman, agog with curiosity, slowly pulled the door closed again.

"Did you hear me?" said Emma, pulling the mask from her face. "I've come to play you for Robin's notes."

"Have you indeed?" replied Colin sardonically.

"Yes." Emma stood very straight, defiant. This was worse than she had expected. The kindness she had thought she glimpsed in him at times last night seemed to have disappeared. The man who stood before her now, raking her with his eyes, was rather frightening. He was exactly what she'd thought him, she saw with a sinking heart—a cold, hardened gamester who cared for nothing and no one. She drew a shaky breath. That was all the more reason to save Robin from him, she told herself, and took a step forward.

What a poor creature her wretched husband must be, Colin thought. Should he ever possess such a vibrant, desirable woman, she would have no opportunity to visit other men's houses late at night and offer herself in exchange for a few paltry notes of hand. She was not his, however. And never would be. Colin felt a wave of savage regret. Why should he hesitate? She was no innocent maiden; she knew quite well what she was doing. "Very well," he said, turning away from her and walking over to the card table.

They took their places facing each other. If luck went her way, she could beat him, Colin thought. Their skill was nearly equal. But somehow, he felt that the cards would fall for him tonight. "You may deal," he offered, and found himself savoring the defiant look she gave him in return.

Emma picked up the cards and began to shuffle them with a decided snap.

He watched her as she finished, stacked them in one pile, and started to deal. She'd been goaded into this, he saw, and now she was going through with it with fierce determination. Anticipation coursed through him as he picked up his hand and began the contest between them.

It was a rout. Luck was indeed on Colin Wareham's side tonight. Every card seemed to go his way, every strategy Emma tried only aided him. He could hardly believe it himself, and he did not blame her when she paused after the second hand and examined the deck as if it might be marked. But even with a fresh packet of cards, he won the final hand as well, and by a large margin.

When the last trick was played and the points tallied, Emma pulled the brandy bottle across the table, poured a large glass, and swallowed it in two throat-searing gulps.

He ought to let her go, Colin thought. He ought to tell her that he had returned her brother's notes of hand, and that they were quits. But he couldn't resist rising to stand beside her chair and brush a hand lightly along her bare shoulder. The feel of her skin was like warm silk. Everything about her roused him.

Emma shivered at his touch. "You will not hold me to this ridiculous wager," she said, her voice higher than usual.

One kiss, Colin thought. He deserved that. He pulled her to her feet and around to face him. This whole venture was insane, and he had gone a little mad himself. She was lovely. Her eyes were a fathomless dark blue.

Emma gazed up at him. He was so very large. Despite her height, he loomed over her, his astonishing violet eyes burning into her own, his handsome face stark with some strong emotion that she could not identify. She was at once fascinated and a little afraid. She opened her mouth to protest, only to have it captured by his, her arms imprisoned in an iron grasp. She started to struggle, then stopped, astonished by what was happening to her.

Colin Wareham did not grind her lips against her teeth, as Edward had done. He did not grapple with her as if she were a large parcel he was trying to shift. He did not push her impatiently, as if angry that she did not know exactly what he wanted every moment and eager to get things over with.

Colin Wareham's kiss was gentle and pliable. It was warm and soft and went on and on, coaxing her to respond, growing more urgent as she yielded to him, step by step. It was incredible. She had never felt anything like it before, and she could not tear herself away from the thrill of it.

When his arms slipped around and drew her close, leaving her own free, Emma swayed. She felt the hard muscles of his chest against her breasts and the pressure of his powerful thigh along her own. And still he did not maul her. His lips drifted down her neck as his hands gently caressed her back. He dropped quick kisses along her shoulder and the swell of her breasts above the low neckline of her gown. They felt hot on her skin. When he took her lips again, she let him. He gently teased her to greater arousal with the tip of his tongue.

Her tentative, unpracticed, but clearly passionate, response roused Colin to a fever pitch. Though he meant to draw back, he couldn't. It was as if life was returning to him, pouring back in, intensified, after long months of arid emptiness. He let his hand slide up to cup her breast, teasing the nipple through the thin silk of her gown.

"Oh," breathed Emma, clinging to him, overwhelmed by the things he was making her feel.

Colin eased his thigh between her legs, holding her close.

"Oh," said Emma again. A thread of alarm penetrated her daze of sensation. "No. Wait."

"I can't," he breathed, letting his lips slide down her neck again. His hands a little rough, he pushed the small puffed sleeves of her gown off her shoulders and pulled down her narrow bodice, exposing her breasts, their tips rosy and inviting in the candlelight.

Emma gasped. An old fear flooded her. As her husband had so terrifyingly shown, men had another, darker side hidden behind their dash and gallantry.

"What is the matter?" Colin asked.

"Nothing, my lord," replied Emma mechanically. She had to endure this for Robin, she told herself.

Watching the shifts of her expression, Colin grew puzzled. Her behavior didn't match the things he knew about her. Commanding men under extreme conditions for long years, he had become a keen judge of character, and he could see no guile in Emma, no slyness. She seemed a warm and beautiful creature scarcely awakened to the intimacies between a man and a woman. She also looked genuinely afraid.

That, he couldn't bear. Bending his head, he kissed her again, very gently, slowly tantalizing her lips until, after a long while, they relaxed under his and yielded up the honey of her mouth. His desire sharpened with her response, but he kept it in check. Leading her to the long sofa before the fireplace, he eased her onto the cushions and knelt at her side. She started to sit up, but he kissed her again, drugging her with the exquisite gentleness of his touch. Colin bent to one bare breast and took the tip in his mouth, fluttering his tongue.

Emma gasped again. She hadn't realized a man could,

or ever would, make her feel this way. Her mind reeled in confusion. What was this man? Cold and contemptuous one moment and now making her feel as if she was drowning in sweet sensations.

Colin's hand crept under the hem of her gown and slid up the soft skin of her leg, his fingers like whispers.

Emma stiffened again. "No. Wait," she said, struggling to sit up.

Colin wanted her more than he had ever wanted any woman. Something about the combination of sadness and passion he discovered in her answered a deep need that he hadn't even known he had. "Darling Emma, I don't think I can," he replied.

A thrill of shock and apprehension crackled through Emma at these words, and she sat up straight despite his confining embrace. "How do you know my name?" she demanded.

Cursing his own clumsiness, Colin gathered his scattered wits, trying to ignore the urgent demands of his body. What story could he give her? How could he divert her enough to return to the business at hand? But seeing the fear rise again in her dark blue eyes, he could not carry on with the deception. "I guessed your identity," he admitted. "From the resemblance to your brother."

"Brother?" she wavered, trying to hang on to the ruins of her anonymity. "I don't know what you mean, my lord."

"He called on me this morning," Colin said gently. "It took a bit of time, but then I began to notice. Your hair is quite distinctive, you know. And though he is not much like you in feature, there are mannerisms which are unmistakable. I got the story from him at last."

Story! Emma groaned silently. The story of her disgrace. She was truly unmasked now. Her hopes of leading a quiet existence in her own country were shattered. And even worse, somehow, this man knew the full extent of her folly and humiliation. She had wagered everything for a brother who didn't even know her, and lost.

"I will not speak of it to anyone," Colin assured her in response to the look on her face.

She didn't believe him. In her experience, men could never resist boasting of their triumphs. He would tell just one crony over a bottle about Robin Bellingham's wanton sister and the way she had put herself in his power for the sake of a wager, and then the tale would begin to fly. Robin himself would hear it. Emma flushed crimson. Slipping one sleeve of her gown back onto her shoulder, she said, "Will you give me the notes?"

"Ah. I must explain about those."

Emma's hand clenched on her sleeve. "Will you still hold me to this dreadful wager?" she cried.

"No, but you see, I can't give them to you. I have already—"

"What a fool I am," Emma burst out. She clenched her hands together in front of her. "A man like you has no honor. I *knew* that. But somehow, I allowed myself to believe. I was lulled by your manner, just like the victims you fleece." She struck her fists together, not noticing the pain. "I have created a scandal for nothing. Ruined my—"

"If you will allow me to tell you," put in Colin, raising his voice above hers. "There is no need for this ranting. I—"

"Oh yes, I see," said Emma bitterly. "Now you will say I have not fulfilled my part in the agreement, despite the fact that you have destroyed all my chances. And if I should meet your demands, there will be yet more after that. You are the lowest form of humanity. You care for nothing but the wager. You have no heart."

"Like your husband?" he snapped, goaded by her tone and her refusal to listen to him.

Emma's jaw hardened. "We will not speak of this," she replied. "It was men like you who ruined him."

"Oh, indeed? A truly fine specimen he must be. Does he know where you were last night?" Colin taunted. "Did he send you to see what you could get out of me?"

Emma gasped at the insult. "Edward is dead," she cried. "He was killed a year ago by someone just like you!"

Colin had barely a moment to assimilate this news, before the footman opened the door a crack and said, "A gentleman has called, my lord. I told him it was late and you were occupied—"

"I can hear him shouting through the door, you idiot," broke in a second voice. "Let me through, damn you!"

Colin saw Emma go still as a statue, her eyes widening into pools of darkness. Instinctively, he jumped to his feet, striding around the sofa and standing behind it so that he shielded her from the doorway. In the next instant, a tall, upright old man pushed into the library and faced him, pounding his ebony cane on the floor for emphasis. "Sir, I expect you know why I am here."

Colin examined his visitor's shock of white hair and hard, lined features. Only the fact that Emma was staring at him like a bird at a snake kept him from having the man thrown out. "I haven't the faintest idea," he answered.

"I've come about my son," roared the other. "I've just heard what he's been up to. I have ways of keeping tabs on that young jackanapes. He had no business playing with you. I forbade him the tables after his last losses, and I told him I'd cover no more gambling debts." He pounded the cane on the floor again. "Do you hear me, sir? No more. He'll have to pay this out of his allowance. I shan't rescue him another time. Let this be a warning to you not to play with striplings. Though I should think any gentleman would know as much already."

"Your son and I have already settled the debt," said Colin icily. "There is no need for you to concern yourself. Indeed, I do not understand why you have done so." In the background, he heard Emma gasp, and he mentally consigned his infuriating visitor to perdition.

Bellingham glowered. "He hadn't the money to pay it."

"He has cleared the debt," Colin repeated. "I have returned his notes of hand to him."

A small cry escaped Emma just as her father opened his mouth to reply. Bellingham, goaded, took another step into the room so that he could see and face down this intruder. "This is none of your—" he began, then stopped. His bushy white eyebrows drew together in a terrific scowl. His pale blue eyes bulged. Blood darkened the harsh lines of his face. "You," he said.

Colin looked from one to the other, and deeply regretted the part he had played in this affair.

"What are you doing here?" shouted Bellingham. "What in blazes have you done with your dress? I suppose you are looking for some new way to disgrace me?"

Emma took a shuddering breath and restored the other sleeve of her gown to its proper place. Though she was very white, she sat straight and faced her father full-on.

"Where's that scapegrace husband of yours? Deserted you, has he? I expect your money's gone, then. I hope you don't imagine that I will support you."

"No," said Emma tonelessly.

"You haven't come back to live in London?" Bellingham looked outraged. "I won't have it, you know. I told that blackguard Tarrant if I ever saw his face in England again I'd put a bullet through him. And I'm not so old that I can't do it, either!"

"Edward is dead," said Emma in the same lifeless voice. She gathered her courage, reminding herself that she was no longer a child, to be intimidated by her father's bluster. "And I had no intention of seeing you at all. I would rather die than ask you for anything."

Bellingham glowered at her. Then he looked from

her to Wareham. "What are you doing in this house?" he asked.

"I came to speak to Baron St. Mawr about Robin's notes," said Emma, and Colin's betrayal raked her again.

"At this hour? Alone? And with your gown pulled down around your shoulders like a common lightskirt? Don't try to cozen me, girl!"

Emma swallowed. She wanted to stand and face him, but she was afraid her legs wouldn't support her.

"What have you sunk to under Tarrant's influence?" her father jeered. "Are you this man's mistress? Will you drag our family name still deeper into the mud?"

"I . . ." Words stuck in Emma's throat.

"We are old friends," said Colin smoothly. He couldn't bear the hunted look on her face. "We met in Europe some time ago."

"Friends?" Bellingham made the word sound scandalous. "And do you customarily require of your female friends such a state of undress, my lord St. Mawr?"

Emma looked near tears. Colin felt an irresistible urge to protect her.

"I believe, sir, that you have dishonored my daughter," roared Bellingham. He banged his cane on the floor once again. "What else am I to think, eh? I find her here, half naked. What is your explanation for that?"

"I have nothing to do with you," cried Emma. "You cast me off. You have no right to—"

"I've a family name to think of," said her father. "The Bellinghams never were touched by scandal until you ran off with that damned Tarrant. I won't have any more such goings-on." He turned back to Colin. "What amends do you intend to make, sir?"

Colin had caught the sudden gleam in the old man's eye and was well aware of the scheme he was hatching. "Do you expect me to marry her?" he asked, curious to see his reaction.

"What?" cried Emma.

"You've put her in a compromising position," said the old man with visible satisfaction. "It would be the honorable thing to do."

"Don't be ridiculous," said Emma.

"It would, wouldn't it?" Colin answered meditatively. It was an insane notion, he thought. Out of the question, really.

Emma whirled to stare at him. "Have you gone mad?" she said.

"Well, now." Bellingham began to smile. His free hand rubbed the back of the one clutching his cane. "Baroness St. Mawr," he added. "Who would have thought it?"

"Wait a moment," cried Emma. "Both of you. I have no intention of—"

"This is wonderful news," said her father, growing more jovial by the moment. "Far more than I ever looked for. My dear Emma."

"I haven't said that I would—" began Colin.

"I am not your dear Emma," she snapped. "And I shall certainly not marry St. Mawr. Or anyone else, for that matter."

Her father chuckled, driving Emma to rigid fury. "Women," he said to Colin. "Emotional creatures, eh? Part of their charm."

Colin was not foolish enough to reply.

"So, we'll consider it settled then," he went on. "You will be married from Bellingham House, of course."

"Nothing is settled," said Emma through clenched teeth. "Didn't you hear me? I refuse."

"This is a matter that requires more discussion," agreed Colin. It was impossible, of course. The antithesis of what was expected of him. Although, as the idea worked in his mind, he started to see certain advantages.

"Of course, of course. I'm sure you'll make it all up between you," replied Bellingham, turning toward the door. "Baroness St. Mawr," he repeated, looking extremely pleased with himself. As if afraid someone might contradict him, he hurried out.

"What the devil do you think you're doing?" Emma demanded before the door had even shut behind him.

The more he thought of Emma as his wife the more attractive the notion grew, Colin realized. "Offering for you?" he ventured, as if trying out the concept.

Her mouth opened, but no words came out.

He thought about the time before he had met her, when he had looked forward only to an endless round of meaningless duty until the day he died. Emma had brought first curiosity, then laughter, and finally desire back into his life. "Might we not deal very well together?" he wondered, half to himself.

"You cannot be serious." She seemed stunned.

"From the time we met—"

"Yesterday!" exclaimed Emma.

"Yesterday," he agreed. "From that time, I have felt a striking interest in you."

"Interest?" she echoed in a strangled voice.

He nodded, pleased to see that she was getting his drift. "And we have the problem of your presence here."

"My . . . ?"

He raised his eyebrows, his gaze full of implications about the caresses they had shared.

"How dare you!" exploded Emma.

His brows snapped together. "How dare I offer for you?" He was not accustomed to this sort of reception.

"I am not some mindless object, to be tossed back and forth between you and my father," she declared.

"That is the way these things are customarily settled," he pointed out.

"These . . . !" Briefly, Emma was speechless. "Am I a blushing debutante?" she cried. "Are you a young man in need of a parent's advice?"

"My point exactly," agreed Colin. "We are well matched in that."

"We are most ill matched," contradicted Emma. "I will not be shackled to another gamester."

"I gave your brother's notes back to him," Colin pointed out. "I never intended to demand payment. I wouldn't have played with him at all, but he made it such a point of honor that—"

"And you allowed me to believe," said Emma, nearly choking on her rage, "that you *would* demand it. You deceived me in an effort to lure me into your bed!"

"You deceived me as well," he argued. "You never mentioned a husband."

"What had that to do with Robin's debt?" she cried. "There was no reason for me to tell you anything."

"I think—"

"Think whatever you like," she cried, her brain whirling. "I shall certainly not marry you. The idea is completely ridiculous." For some reason, she was about to burst into tears. She could not bear for him to see that. In a flurry of ruffled skirts, she fled the room, wrenching open the great front door and careening down the steps into the street. She had to get away, to be alone and sort out her hopelessly jumbled feelings. And when the Baron St. Mawr had an opportunity to do the same, Emma thought, he would most certainly regret his rash proposal.

Colin was not far behind her, but Emma managed to catch a hansom cab just down the street and escape into the London traffic. Realizing that he still had no idea how to find her again, Colin stood in the middle of the pavement and cursed, loudly and creatively. "That's it, guv," said a workman passing by. "Give 'em 'ell."

Chapter Three

When Colin Wareham descended to breakfast two days later, he was once again in a foul humor. Oblivious to the worried looks being exchanged by his staff, he rejected the offer of sausages with revulsion. He crumbled bread on his plate as if he quite enjoyed destroying it and reduced his napkin to a crushed ball of linen on the floor, which the footman stepped around as carefully as if it contained explosives. Colin had found no clue as to where Emma might be staying in London. Barbara Rampling did not know, and discreet inquiries among habitués of her house had turned up nothing. He felt a compelling need to speak to Emma, a sense that a stroke of fortune was slipping away, and yet he had no way to find her. It was a damnable situation.

When he did not find the *Morning Post* folded beside his plate as usual, Colin rang the bell with uncharacteristic force. Very promptly, his valet Reddings appeared, laid the newspaper near his hand, and lingered to pour his master a fresh cup of coffee. This was an odd enough occurrence for Wareham to raise his eyebrows at the man.

"Very interesting news in the paper this morning, my lord," said the valet stiffly.

"Is there?" Colin examined the front page. "Something from the congress?" In the aftermath of Napoleon's defeat, the nations of Europe were meeting at a great congress in Vienna, and he had been following events with interest. After all his years of fighting the little Corsican, he felt he had some stake in what became of his empire.

"No, my lord," replied Reddings in a very strange tone.

Colin examined him irritably. Their years of hard campaigning together had formed a relationship far closer than the common master-servant bond. Colin had no trouble interpreting the small man's compressed lips and half lowered eyelids. It was plain that he had somehow offended Reddings, or at least that Reddings thought he had. And yet the valet had seemed just as usual while helping Colin dress not half an hour before. "What is the matter?" he asked.

"Nothing, I'm sure, my lord," said Reddings. But he remained standing beside the table, far from his regular orbit at this time of day.

"Something about this news in the paper?" asked Colin, not fooled. "What the deuce is it?"

"I'm sure you have no obligation to inform me—that is, the household staff—of any of your plans, my lord," Reddings burst out. "But when you are contemplating such a change in all our situations, I should think you might communicate it yourself." He stood very upright, gazing at the far wall with an intensity that the bland painting hanging there clearly did not deserve.

"Change?" said Colin, mystified. He looked down at the newspaper, wondering what in blazes the man could be talking about.

Reddings stiffened further. "Indeed, my lord. Perhaps you do not realize what a large change it will be."

"What will be? You're making no sense, man."

The valet looked reproachful. Without speaking, he opened the newspaper to the announcements page and pointed to one particular item. Irritated, Colin read it. "Oh, lord," he said.

"A new mistress always makes changes," said Reddings. "Cook has become convinced she will be replaced by a Frenchman, and the housemaids—" Seeing Wareham's scowl, he broke off.

"Bellingham," exploded Colin. "This is his doing." He reread the announcement of his engagement to Lady Emma Tarrant, daughter of the honorable George Bellingham. The old devil had had the inconceivable gall to add a wedding date only two weeks away. "Lord," he said again. Emma would be furious. Any hopes of a calm discussion of their situation were lost.

"Is the item incorrect, my lord?" wondered Reddings, scanning his face. He had been with his lordship through the rigors of battle, through the stretches of boredom and highjinks that came between the bouts of fighting, through the unsettling melancholy of recent days, and he had never seen him as exercised as this. "Is something wrong?"

But Colin had been galvanized by a sudden thought. "My God, my mother!" he exclaimed, rising from the table so abruptly that he nearly overset his chair. "Order my horse saddled at once. I'm going out."

"Certainly, my lord." Rampant curiosity had replaced Reddings' stiffness. "May I inquire where?"

"Where no one will find me until I set this straight," was the harassed reply. "Hurry, man."

On the other side of London, Emma had no opportunity to go down to breakfast. Arabella Tarrant burst into her bedchamber with only the most cursory of knocks before she was even finished dressing. "Oh, my dear!" the older woman cried. "So secretive. And the way you pretended to reject any thought of marriage.

You deceived me completely. But I think you might have said something when he actually made an offer. This is beyond anything!"

Emma turned from the dressing table, her hands frozen in the act of putting up her pale hair. "What do you mean?" she asked.

"So very rich!" exclaimed Arabella, clasping her hands on her meager bosom. Her dress this morning was an alarming shade of puce. "You will never want for *anything*." She looked quite wistful. "And I understand he is quite handsome as well."

"What are you talking about?" demanded Emma, but she had a sinking feeling that she knew.

"Why, the announcement of your engagement. In the *Morning Post*. Didn't they tell you it would be in today?"

"Where is it?" said Emma through clenched teeth.

Arabella happily fetched the newspaper. As Emma read the brief lines, the older woman kept up a stream of chatter about bride clothes and furnishings and the latest fashion in barouches, as gleeful as if it were her own marriage she was anticipating. Emma let the paper drop. She could not believe Wareham would have inserted this notice after the things she had said to him. It was insufferable, an unforgivable trampling on all her rights and wishes. The action said, quite plainly, that her opinions meant nothing. "Father," she concluded. "Damn him!"

"Emma!"

"He cares *nothing* about me," she said vehemently. "I don't believe he ever did. It is all appearances and what people will say and his position as the second son of an earl. I'm sick to death of it!" She threw the newspaper onto the floor and then kicked at it. When the result was unsatisfying, she kicked a stray shoe across the room. It bounced off the opposite wall with a loud thump. "Men think they can do as they please with us," she added. "But I'll give them all a surprise. I'll leave today." She turned back to the mirror to finish dressing her hair.

"Leave?" The other woman gaped at her.

"We will catch the boat to France tonight," Emma declared.

She had been up most of the night worrying over how to remedy the wretched tangle she had made of things here. Her means of support was gone. Gaming was bad enough, but to do it in a cloud of whispers about her past and present indiscretions was an unbearable prospect. And the renewed contact with her family, which she had never wanted, could only bring discord and pain. She had made up her mind that she must leave England again. She and Ferik would return to the Continent, to living in small, shabby hotels, subsisting on the money she won in grubby gaming houses. She felt a wave of reluctance—how she had hated it!—and ruthlessly suppressed it. It was the only choice. She did not understand what Colin Wareham was playing at, what quixotic mixture of obligation and perversity was driving him. But this newspaper notice was the last straw—she would not be forced on any man. "I was going anyway. I will simply leave a bit sooner."

Arabella had regained the use of her voice. "But . . . but what about St. Mawr?" she said incredulously. "You're *deserting* him? One of the greatest catches in England?"

Against her will, Emma remembered his hands on her skin, the look in his eyes when he touched her. Tightening her jaw, she pushed the memories away. "Baron St. Mawr may pity me," she said. "Or he may be a victim of unsteady humors. I do not know. But I *am* certain that he was as surprised to see that notice as I was." And extremely sorry for his impetuous words, Emma added to herself. That would teach him to give in to passing impulses.

"But, my dear." Arabella tugged at her sleeve to emphasize her point. "The announcement has appeared. Everyone will have seen it. He can't cry off if you hold him to it."

"I would never do such a thing," said Emma, revolted.

"You would not have to *do* anything. You could simply go ahead with the arrangements as if—"

"No." She lifted her chin. Her life in recent years had deprived her of many things, but not of her self-respect. "I do not wish to be married, in any case, Aunt. As I have said, I have no great opinion of the state."

"But this would be totally different," cried Arabella. "You would be a baroness, and rich. You would be a figure of influence in the *haut ton.* You would be invited everywhere and . . ."

Emma imagined the storm of gossip that must even now be sweeping the *ton.* "Impossible," she murmured. She turned to go. "I must tell Ferik to begin packing up our things," she said. "My mind is made up."

Arabella stood staring at the door long after Emma had disappeared through it. She simply could not comprehend Emma's position. Given any chance to reenter society, Arabella would have snatched it without a thought of consequences. To throw away the opportunity to marry into a fortune and a title seemed to her an act of madness. And not only for Emma. For if her young relative did marry St. Mawr, Arabella would have a connection to him as well, and who knew what chances for an escape from her current dreary existence?

A mulish expression settled over Arabella's pale features. She was not going to sit by and see her chances ruined once again. She had been helpless when her wretched husband had run off—taken by surprise and thrown into confusion. But matters were quite different now. She would not let this man—and all he might do for her—slip through her fingers. Going to her own chamber, Arabella sat at the writing desk and spent twenty minutes chewing on a quill pen and composing a note to Baron St. Mawr. When she was finished, she folded and sealed it, then sent it off with strict orders that it be delivered at once, no matter where the baron might be. Finally, she gave her maid certain instructions, and then retired to await events.

An unearthly shriek rang out in the opulent bed-chamber of Catherine, present Baroness St. Mawr. The shattering sound brought her dresser, her butler, two housemaids, and a footman at a dead run and left them jostling one another in her bedroom doorway in a most undignified manner. The dresser, a superior female with extraordinarily sharp elbows, won through first. "My lady?" she said, straightening her cap and trying not to pant from exertion.

"My salts!" cried the baroness, clutching her throat. "Brandy. Send for the doctor. Send for my daughter."

As the large group of servants dispersed to fulfill these requests, their mistress continued to recline on her bed in a welter of pink silk pillows. A discarded break-fast tray, a hand mirror, and a scattering of morning mail lay around her. The *Morning Post* was a crumpled mass on the carpet, as if she had wadded it up and thrown it there.

Though past fifty, Colin Wareham's mother was still very attractive. Her son had inherited his dark hair and violet eyes from her. His size, and the stern lines of his features, had come from his father, however. Her face was much softer. Indeed, her entire figure was gently rounded without being in the least fat. She had small, plump hands and cheeks like a squirrel. The delightful cupid's bow of her mouth had excited many young gen-tlemen to raptures thirty years ago. Everything about her appearance encouraged observers to conclude that she was a placid, pleasant little person whose deepest thoughts would be devoted to gossip, shopping, and dress. In short, she was a total and utter deception. For the baroness was a sharp, determined, and decisive woman who managed her own investments, took a keen interest in politics, and terrorized much of her family with her acerbic opinions and interference in their lives.

Her servants were well aware of her true nature, and did her bidding speedily and efficiently. In a very few minutes, the respected physician entrusted with the baroness's health was knocking at the front door, and her daughter, Caroline, countess Wrotham, was stepping into her fashionable barouche to go and call upon her mother.

"Have you seen it?" the baroness cried as soon as her daughter appeared.

"What, Mother? Are you ill? The footman said you had taken a fit."

"The *Morning Post*," was the reply, emphasized by a dramatic gesture toward the crumpled newspaper on the carpet.

"I haven't yet had time to read it. The nursery was in an uproar this morning, and I have had to—"

"Well, do so," snapped her mother, abandoning her languishing pose and brushing the doctor aside.

Sighing, Caroline went to retrieve the paper. "Was there something in particular that you . . . ?" she began as she smoothed it out.

"Indeed! Look at the engagements."

Obediently, Caroline leafed through the pages until she came to the announcements. Her expression impatient, she started to read. "The Merton chit caught Harriman," she commented. "I didn't think she would. Oh, Amelia Franklin is engaged. I am so glad. She . . ." Caroline's jaw dropped.

"Now you see," said her mother triumphantly.

"Colin?"

Having gotten the effect she wanted, the baroness waved her servants and the doctor away. "Go, go. I am perfectly all right."

With a sigh, but no surprise, the doctor packed up his bag and departed. The housemaids scattered. Only my lady's dresser, experienced in the ways of her mistress, waited behind. Her prescience was rewarded when the baroness said, "Bring the blue merino. I'm going out in a little while." With a small, tight smile, the dresser went to prepare her ensemble.

"What can this mean?" asked Caroline when they were alone.

Her mother looked at her. Even more than Colin, her daughter resembled the late baron. She had the same high slanting cheekbones and cleft chin, along with her father's auburn hair and pale blue eyes. Even the spray of freckles, which she was continually trying to eradicate with exotic lotions, was exactly like his. She ought to have been a formidable woman. But for some reason, she had not inherited any of her parents' keen intellect or incisive manner. She looked impressive, but she was simply a nice young woman wrapped up in her growing family, with an annoying tendency to dither under pressure.

"It means that some wholly unsuitable female has trapped Colin into offering for her," snapped her mother.

"Trapped Colin?" Caroline looked astonished. She was rather in awe of her older brother.

"She must be exceedingly clever," acknowledged the baroness.

"But who is she?" Caroline consulted the *Morning Post* again. "Tarrant? Do you know the family?"

"Oh, yes. They are a pack of wastrels who have gambled away more than one fortune at the tables and the track. I don't know precisely which one this is, but I shall soon find out. *And* I shall let her know that Colin is not a pigeon for her plucking."

"Colin?" repeated Caroline. She frowned as if working out a difficult mathematical problem. "But no one can fool Colin." Her brother's coolheaded omniscience had been a dominant feature of her youth.

The baroness felt a moment's doubt. She herself had tried more than once to . . . not trick, of course, but *guide* Colin into marrying a suitable girl. And none of her very clever schemes had had any success. Her irritating son saw through them immediately. And what was most exasperating, he would go along with them for a while, allowing her to hope that this time she had succeeded. And then a moment would come when he would meet her eyes with a sweet, gently mocking smile and slip effortlessly out of her toils. A woman who could succeed where she had failed must be clever indeed. "She may have resources which others do not," she concluded grimly.

"What do you mean, Mama?"

"Colin is, after all, a man," was the reply.

Caroline looked puzzled. "Of course he is, Mama."

"And men are susceptible in . . . certain ways. No doubt this creature took advantage of that weakness."

"Weakness?" It was the last word she would apply to her brother.

"Caroline, do stop repeating everything I say like Sara Clarington's parrot," complained her mother. "You know perfectly well what I mean."

Her daughter continued to frown as the baroness started to dress. She had donned her gown and was sitting at the dressing table having her hair arranged when light finally dawned. "Mama! You don't think . . . ?"

"I shall find out," answered her mother. "But the first thing we shall do is see Colin and ask him about this nonsense."

"I . . . I ought to go home," attempted Caroline. "Nicky has a cold, and—"

"I'm sure Nurse can look after him. I need you with me."

Drooping a little, Caroline conceded. She disliked rows, and it was obvious that a very large one was looming ahead. If only she had taken Nicky into the country as she had considered doing, she might have avoided what was rapidly developing into a major family wrangle.

Robin Bellingham turned his gleaming chestnut mare through the gates of the park just at the fashionable hour for the promenade. He was feeling extremely pleased with himself. His new dark blue coat was from Weston, and it fitted his slender form to a nicety. His buff pantaloons showed nary a wrinkle, and his tall Hessian boots gleamed. His neckcloth, while not aspiring to the complexities of the Mathematical or Oriental tie, was quite credible. His beaver hat sat jauntily on his silver-gilt locks. All in all, he thought, he looked the picture of what he longed to be—a true pink of the *ton*.

"Robin!"

Turning, he found himself hailed by a group of his cronies, young men he had known since his first years at Eton, who were now making their bow to society together. His best friend, Jack Ripton, was among them, and Robin urged his mount in their direction, going slow enough to give them ample time to admire his new rig.

"You're in prime twig," was Jack's comment.

Robin took this, as it was meant, for a compliment. "Weston," he couldn't resist saying.

"The devil you say? Top of the trees, ain't we?" Jack responded, his grin lighting a rather homely face and transforming it into warmly attractive lines.

The small group began riding along the path, one eye out for pretty girls strolling the lawns or in carriages, the other evaluating the men they passed, judging their own style and manner against those of the leaders of society.

"Say," said Jack after a while. "I nearly forgot. Appears felicitations are in order."

There were murmurs among the others, and Robin found they were all looking at him. "What?" he said.

"Odd part of it is, I didn't know you *had* a sister," complained Jack. "I mean, I think a fellow would mention a thing like that. You know very well that I've got two."

"What are you talking about?" asked Robin.

"You've met them," Jack continued accusingly.

"That time you stayed with us for the hunting? Played silver loo with Amelia."

"Jack," said Robin.

"All these years, and not a word about a sister," his friend marveled. "I can't understand it."

"Jack, what are you talking about?" demanded Robin through clenched teeth.

"Sister's engagement," replied Jack, as if it must be obvious. "Saw it in the paper this morning."

"My sister? You must be mistaken."

"It was in there, plain as day. Wasn't it, fellows?"

The others agreed.

"But . . . but . . ." Robin stammered over his father's long-standing orders that he was never to mention Emma. "My sister's abroad," he settled on finally.

Jack looked at him kindly. "Can't be, if she's going to marry St. Mawr, can she?"

"St. Mawr?" The baron's questions came back to Robin, and his forgiveness of a large debt in exchange for answers. A frown settled over his handsome features. Something very queer was going on here, he thought.

"Good match," said another of the group laconically.

"Good?" said Jack Ripton. "It's beyond good. My mother would have crawled down Bond Street on her knees to get St. Mawr for Amelia. Fellow's got fortune, family, position. Girls have been setting their caps for him in droves." He contemplated this interesting position, wondering what it would feel like to have all the prettiest debs giving him the eye. Then he remembered his grievance. "But Robin," he continued, "why've you kept mum about your sister? She must be a diamond of the first water to have caught St. Mawr. Might have given the rest of us a chance, you know."

"She's a good deal older," offered Bellingham, knowing the excuse was lame. His father might have said something, he thought bitterly, prepared him a bit. It was no wonder the old man had been so pleased with himself this morning, if this was really true.

"Older. Abroad. We're making scant headway with this mystery." Jack Ripton shook his head. "Come now, Robin. We're all friends here."

What had happened to Edward Tarrant? Robin wondered silently. How had Emma ended up at Barbara Rampling's house, where few respectable ladies went? And why had St. Mawr engaged himself to her? It was beyond unexpected; it was an incredible match.

"One good thing, you might get a hand with your debts," Jack went on. "I hear St. Mawr's a pleasant fellow. All the go, too. I daresay he might advance you a few hundred, and your father can stick his head in a bucket."

There was general laughter. All of the young men were familiar with Robin's troubles with his father. Universally, they characterized him as a tightfisted old killjoy.

For a moment, Robin was distracted by his own problems. His father seemed to have no conception of what it cost to be on the town these days. One needed the proper rig-out and some blood cattle to drive, which was dashed expensive. Most of all, a man had to show himself ready to play the tables or wager something on a race. He couldn't be always drawing back because of a few losses. He certainly could not tell anyone he was *forbidden* to gamble by his father. Might as well say he was still in short coats and couldn't go out alone. But even so, Robin didn't care for Jack's suggestion about St. Mawr. The scene with him yesterday had left a bad taste in Robin's mouth, as if he had committed some social solecism. He'd go to the moneylenders before he asked St. Mawr for funds.

"So when can we meet this sister?" asked Jack. "I warn you I won't stand for any more mystery. I want to see her, and I want to see her soon." The others added laughing agreements.

"I, er . . ." He would have to speak to his father, Robin thought, wheedling information out of him when he should have been told in the first place. He wished he had the nerve to blow up at him about this. Sometimes, it seemed as if his father thought he'd never left the nursery. The thought filled him with a familiar sullen resentment.

"There's the Boyntons' carriage," said Jack.

The others' heads turned like a pack of hounds catching a scent. Sally Boynton was one of the acknowledged beauties this Season.

"Come on," urged Jack, leading the group over to pay its respects. Robin, lagging behind, wondered what other surprises might be in store for him before he found out what the devil was going on.

At seven o'clock that evening, Colin Wareham, still in morning dress, entered the small shabby drawing room of Arabella Tarrant's home. Outwardly, he appeared calm, perhaps even a little bored, but his appearance belied considerable inner turmoil. He had spent the day at Cribb's Parlor, his club, and several other all-male establishments where he could not be accosted by any female relative. But that had not prevented his mother from pelting him with outraged written summonses, or his great-aunt Celia from inquiring in an acid note whether he had lost his mind. He had also been the target of felicitations of varying sorts from men he knew. Some had been appalled, others amused, and a few even sympathetic, as if he had contracted some embarrassing, fatal disease that it was best not to mention. All of them appeared to believe that he had been lured into lifelong captivity. He had not foreseen this emotional storm that was breaking over him, along with the fever of curiosity roused throughout the *ton,* when he had considered marrying Emma Tarrant. And only considered, he reminded himself bitterly; it was her blasted father who had roused this furor of shock and speculation with his notice to the paper. That man had much to answer for.

He looked around the room. When he had finally

received the note informing him that Emma was staying here and asking him to call, he had at first been relieved, for he wanted nothing more than to talk to her. But now, examining the threadbare carpet and draperies, the worn chairs, he felt wariness descend. He had found out a great deal more about the Tarrant family in various conversations today, and he wondered if this Arabella would fit the descriptions he had received of heedless, grasping individuals who cared for nothing but games of chance.

A loud voice from another room interrupted his thoughts. "*Where* are my trunks?" it demanded. "You cannot have misplaced anything so large. Everything I possess is in those trunks. You had better find them. Now!"

Colin smiled slightly. He recognized Emma's accents and the outraged tone. She certainly was a spirited woman. There was a clatter from the rear regions of the house, and then a deep male voice let loose a spate of incomprehensible words. They sounded like curses to Colin, and it was obvious they came from Emma's odd foreign servant. Some domestic upheaval, he thought, but for some reason this knowledge did not fill him with the desire to flee. He recalled the flash in Emma's eyes when she was angry, the color in her cheeks and the animation of voice and gesture. The picture was as far removed as it was possible to be from the meek debutantes who had been paraded before him for the last few weeks. He had to marry, Colin thought. It was his duty to his family and title, and he always did his duty. But what if he could have a woman who challenged and interested him rather than a frightened little mouse? Despite the gossip and annoyance, it was still an interesting concept. It was, he supposed, the main reason he was here. He was about to follow the sounds and find Emma when a small, thin woman burst into the room, her hands pressed to her pale cheeks. "Oh, dear. Oh, dear," she said.

Colin examined her. Her garishly colored gown had

a streak of dust along the hem. Her graying brown hair was coming out of its pins on one side. With her eyes darting nervously about the room and her rather prominent front teeth, she looked like a cornered rabbit.

"My lord!" she gasped. "So sorry. Things are a bit . . . I have been trying to keep her here, you see, until you . . . but Emma is so . . . forceful. I am afraid I have made her angry."

"You are Arabella Tarrant?" he asked, thinking that this Tarrant, at least, did not seem to fit the profile he had been given.

"Oh! Yes. I beg your pardon. I am so . . . Edward's aunt, you know. I believe I had the honor of meeting your mother at a ball years ago. Not that she would remember me, of course, but I thought at the time how—"

"What is going on?" Colin asked, recognizing that she would veer off onto irrelevancies unless he intervened.

Arabella clasped her hands together on her chest and assumed an excessively pained expression. "You will have to excuse me, my lord," she said. "I am all at sixes and sevens. There has been such scolding, and running hither and thither, and that creature Ferik keeps bellowing at my maids. I really do not think he is a suitable servant for—"

"Yes, yes," interrupted Colin, losing patience. "May I speak to Lady Tarrant?" One of his discoveries today had been Edward Tarrant's knighthood, which he had found both incongruous and annoying.

"Yes, that is why I wrote to you. Emma is leaving, you see, and I . . . I thought she . . . that is, you . . . er, that the two of you should talk before she goes."

"Leaving this house?" asked Colin. He was very much in favor of that. It was not only shabby, but as far as he could see it was totally disorganized as well. And he wished Emma's association with the Tarrant family cut as soon as possible.

"No, no, the country. England. She planned to take the boat to France tonight, but . . ." Arabella's timid glance grew sly. "I, er, managed to hinder her preparations a bit." Her thin features took on a sanctimonious expression. "I don't know what may have passed between you, but I thought you should at least say farewell," she added.

Colin looked at her. She was not the sort of person he encountered in the normal course of things. But his life seemed to have toppled right out of the normal course, he thought wryly. "Thank you," he said.

Arabella beamed at him. "*Very* happy to be of service, my lord."

He sighed. It was clear he would pay for this favor in some as yet unstated manner.

"Ferik," cried Emma's voice from the back of the house. "Have you found them, Ferik? If not, hang Jim by his toes over the cookstove until he tells you what he has done with those trunks."

"Yes, mistress," replied the deep voice, in a tone that said the giant interpreted her orders quite literally.

An inarticulate squawk of protest followed this threat. "Oh, dear," said Arabella. She wrung her hands. "I had better go and see . . ."

"Why not tell her that I am here?" Colin suggested.

"Yes. Yes, I will. One moment." She scurried out.

There was a short silence, then Emma's voice came again, saying, "What? What have you done?"

The silence that followed was thick and ominous. Colin felt his lips twitch as he imagined the confrontation. By the time Emma swept into the room a few minutes later, he was having to work hard to suppress a smile.

Her appearance sobered him, however. In a traveling dress of dark green, with long sleeves and a high neck, Emma looked coolly elegant. Her jaw was set, and her eyes frosty. She was breathtakingly beautiful, and formidably angry. "Have the trunks turned up?" he could not help asking.

She gave him a glare. "They have, now that Arabella has accomplished her purpose."

"You intended to leave England without even telling me?"

"I didn't see that it was any of your concern," Emma snapped. The last few hours had frayed her temper beyond mending. Having to face Colin and the jumble of feelings he roused was the crowning touch to an infuriating day.

"So I was to be left to face the gossip and conjectures while you fled abroad?" asked Colin.

"Yes!" she cried. "This whole muddle is your fault. If you had not said we were to be married—"

"I didn't say so."

"Well, implied it then," said Emma through gritted teeth. "If you had not spoken in such an impulsive and irresponsible way—"

"Then your father would not have put the notice in the *Morning Post*, neatly closing the trap," he finished.

Emma flushed crimson. "Exactly so," she replied. His use of the word "trap" was the final straw. She wanted to scream with frustration.

With a swift gesture, he conceded the point. "So, you are running away?" he asked.

Emma turned from him, walking across the threadbare carpet to the empty hearth and gripping the mantelpiece so hard her knuckles whitened. "I am not running away," she said when she could master her temper again. "I am simply returning to the Continent after a visit home." Her voice wavered slightly on the last word.

"Returning to what?" he asked her.

Emma shrugged and said nothing.

"Did Tarrant leave you provided for?"

A great wave of weary bitterness washed over Emma. Things had been so easy for this man. He had no idea of the kind of life she had been forced to lead. "Edward left me a skill with cards," she responded icily. "And a most thorough knowledge of the gaming houses where money is to be won. I shall manage quite well, thank you."

A picture of her in those sorts of places rose in his mind with appalling vividness. As an officer, he had often had to haul one or the other of the men in his regiment from such dens. "No," he said.

Emma ignored it. "If there is nothing further, my lord St. Mawr, I am eager to get on the road."

"No," he said again, all his protective instincts alerted.

"I beg your pardon?"

He could not allow it, he thought. He could not let all her vibrant life be leached away in the smoky gray rooms of gaming hells. He could not think of her enduring insults and privation, forced to depend on an activity she hated for her very bread. It was intolerable.

"There must be some other choice," he said.

He had always had choices, Emma thought. He couldn't even imagine what it was like to be beaten and squeezed down to one perilous path with nothing but dull misery ahead. Resentment made her speak more freely than she might have wished. "I am penniless, disgraced and disowned by my family, and alone," she said with great clarity. "I have no choices."

The mixture of courage and despair he saw in the set of her shoulders and the firmness of her jaw moved Colin beyond common sense. "You will marry me," he declared. "You will not return to that kind of life."

"Don't speak to me as if I were a servant," retorted Emma, her eyes flashing. "I shall do nothing of the kind. I wish you would stop this ridiculous talk of marriage."

Colin Wareham, Baron St. Mawr, was not accustomed to this sort of reaction. The men under his command had jumped to obey when he spoke in that tone. In London, he was used to fawning eagerness and delighted hope from any young lady he deigned to approach, let alone offer for. And though he despised such behavior with his whole heart, Emma's attitude nonetheless provoked him. "Do you call it ridiculous?" he replied in a dangerously quiet voice.

"Everyone in London must do so. Or worse. They would think you mad to form an alliance with me."

"If you care so much what people think, I'm surprised you don't feel obliged to marry after the way your father found you in my house," he said cuttingly.

Emma gasped as if he had slapped her and flushed crimson again. "How dare you? When you deceived me in order to get me into that position!"

"I did try—"

"Letting me think you still had Robin's notes when you had already returned them to him," she accused.

"I was about to tell—"

"Playing the hardened gamester, so that I would think there was no other way to get them back," she railed. "And all just to lure me—"

"Will you be quiet!" shouted Colin.

Startled, Emma closed her mouth and stared up at him. Colin, surprised by his own vehemence, gathered his scattered control. "This is exactly what happened that night," he complained. And when she started to speak, he held up a hand to silence her. "I was trying to explain then, too, and you would not allow me to finish a sentence."

Emma struggled with herself, and managed to remain silent.

Wareham's lips twitched once again at the look on her face. "It was very wrong of me not to tell you," he said. "I offer you my sincere apologies. But the thing was . . ."

Emma raised her eyebrows.

Just like her, Colin thought. Now, when he would have welcomed an interruption, she had nothing to say. "The thing was, I could not resist you," he added. He couldn't keep a caressing heat out of his voice.

She met his violet gaze without wavering. "I was doing what had to be done to aid my brother," she said coldly. "I excuse my actions on those grounds, and do not believe they were immoral."

"Are you denying that you enjoyed our embraces?" he asked incredulously. He remembered, all too vividly, the way her mouth had softened under his, and her soft, surprised gasp of pleasure.

Now her eyes dropped. "I . . . I was taken by surprise . . ." she stammered.

"And . . . ?"

"And nothing!" declared Emma.

"I see." He took a step toward her. "My memory of the incident is quite different. It seemed to me very far from nothing. Perhaps we should put the matter to the test here and now."

She backed quickly away. "That won't be necessary." She moved away from the fireplace and nearer to the door. "And in any case, it is really quite . . . quite irrelevant to this discussion."

"Irrelevant?" he exclaimed.

Emma stood straighter and faced him directly. "Physical attraction is not a sound basis for a marriage, my lord. I have learned that lesson in my life, at least."

It took Colin a moment to realize that she was equating him with the miserable, and completely unlamented, Edward Tarrant. Rage, always slow to wake in Wareham, and all the more powerful for that very reason, engulfed him. "Enough," he shouted. "We will not continue this pointless discussion. We will marry, and that is the end of it." And then he would show her the difference, he thought, between himself and the contemptible Edward. "We may as well stand by the date your father gave the *Morning Post*. I see no reason for delay."

"My lord," said Emma.

"We will go down to Trevallan afterward, and then return for—"

"Will you stop!" she cried.

He scowled at her.

"I won't be forced into marriage by blind convention," insisted Emma. "Nor will you be. I will not be any man's obligation."

"You have completely missed the point—"

Her dark eyes were afire. "Nor do I want your pity. I will *not* be pitied. In any case, this is all useless. I don't wish to be married. It is . . . I am not suited to the state."

"Have you listened to one word I—?"

"Why do you wish to marry me?" Emma broke in, as if it was a vitally important question to which he had not yet given her a satisfactory answer.

"I should think that was obvious."

"Well, it isn't," she retorted, and waited.

Colin tried to marshal a rational argument, but he found he was still too angry.

"Perhaps you are mad," she said after a moment. "But I am not. I will not marry on an insane whim, or out of some misguided sense of obligation. Please leave now. If you do not, I will have to ask Ferik to escort you out." Emma hurried from the room. And as she did, without warning, a heavy pain like muffling cloth settled around the regions of her heart.

Colin strode after her, then heard her speaking to someone else in the corridor, and stopped. His jaw and fists clenched, he stared into the mottled mirror above the mantel. He had handled this badly, he thought. It was so damned difficult to think when she began throwing accusations about.

He drew in a deep, calming breath. She really was an extraordinary woman, he thought. After admitting that she was penniless and alone, still she refused a match that would bring her wealth and security and an assured position in society. She put her principles ahead of material gain with a fierce courage and integrity such as he had rarely seen in anyone—let alone a female. Colin saw again the flash of her eyes, the regal set of her head. He had no doubts now; this was the sort of woman he wanted for his wife.

He took another breath. She had roused his fighting

spirit. The iron courage and lightning power of decision that had supported Colin through innumerable military skirmishes rose in him. She would marry him. He would find a way to convince her that she must.

Looking up at a sound, Colin found Arabella Tarrant in the drawing room doorway, looking pale and very disappointed. No doubt she had listened to the whole, he thought. "You must not let her leave tonight," he said. "I will be back tomorrow morning, and I must find her here."

Arabella brightened visibly. "Yes, my lord."

"You think you can do this?" he asked.

"Oh, yes." Once again, Arabella looked sly. She didn't tell him that Emma had already missed the last coach to the coast, and there was no question of her leaving until noon tomorrow. It was far better if he thought she had delayed her and was correspondingly grateful. "You may count on me, my lord," she added.

"I do," he replied curtly, and with a nod, he left.

Arabella, whose hopes had been nearly dashed by the acrimonious exchange between the baron and Emma, rubbed her hands together in anticipation. Perhaps, after all, the cause was not lost. She might yet achieve her connection with Baron St. Mawr. She would use the rest of the evening to try to bring Emma to her senses. And if that failed—well, no doubt she would think of something else.

At precisely the same moment, Colin Wareham's mother was pounding one plump fist on the arm of her comfortable chair. "He is still avoiding me," she raged. "I know he has received my notes, and he is ignoring them. This woman has bewitched him."

Her daughter Caroline, sitting on the edge of the sofa and wishing fervently that she could go home, did not bother to remind her that Colin often failed to appear the moment he was summoned. She certainly did not mention her opinion that their mother's abrupt commands always seemed to annoy him a good deal.

"He is ashamed," the baroness concluded. "He is afraid to face me and admit that he has been entrapped by a scheming female. But I shan't regard it. I shall save him anyway. Men are always completely helpless in these matters."

"Save him?" wondered Caroline. Guiltily, she prayed that Colin would not arrive while she was in her mother's house.

The baroness's small, plump face looked triumphant. "I intend to discover all I can about this woman. I'm sure that there are things about her he does not know, which will break the spell she has put on him."

"What things, Mama?"

"That is what I mean to find out," answered the baroness impatiently. "Really, Caroline, you can be irritatingly dense."

"But how do you know . . . ?"

"I'm certain her life will not stand up to close scrutiny," said her mother. "Colin has resisted every respectable girl I presented to him. Possibly he picked up low tastes in the army. But we will soon cure that!"

Caroline received a vivid picture of how Colin would react to such interference. She shuddered quietly. "Mama, I must go home. Nicky *is* ill, you know. And Frederick is returning from the country today."

Her mother waved this aside. "I'm sure Wrotham can look after himself."

"But I *wish* to look after him," replied Caroline, greatly daring.

Seeing the stubborn set to her jaw, the baroness took another tack. "Oh, very well, if you insist upon leaving me alone at this difficult time." She let her head loll back in the armchair as if half fainting. "I suppose I can struggle along on my own. I know I must not spare myself. The honor of the family is at stake."

Caroline sprang to her feet, determined to take advantage of this small opening without feeling guilty.

"Thank you, Mama. Good-bye," she said, and fled before her mother could react to this defiance.

The baroness sat up straight again and stared after her daughter with a mixture of outrage and disbelief that was almost comical. Then, seeing that she was really gone, she leaned back and began to tap her fingers impatiently on the chair arm. She didn't like being left without an audience.

Fortunately, it was only a few minutes before her dresser appeared in the doorway. "My lady?" she inquired.

"Crane. Are you back already?"

"Yes, my lady."

"What have you found out?"

The servant looked smug. "A good deal, my lady."

"Come in and tell me at once." The baroness leaned forward. She had sent her spy out into the underground of the *haut ton,* the interlaced network of servants who cared for its members. Crane maintained an extensive web of contacts in other households and always knew every disreputable piece of gossip before her mistress. The baroness did not doubt she had found out whatever this Emma Tarrant would most like to hide.

Crane stood before her, head lowered, arms crossed at the wrist. She was the picture of demure submission, but the baroness knew what she demanded. "Sit down," she said, giving it. "You must be worn out with walking."

Not deigning to smirk, Crane took a chair opposite her mistress. She enjoyed exacting such petty payments for her spying services. It confirmed her conviction that in asking, the baroness put herself on the same level as her dresser. "She was married to a very disreputable young gentleman," she said.

"Ah!" The baroness looked like a cat before a bowl of cream.

"Sir Edward Tarrant," continued Crane. "His father lost everything at Newmarket, and the son was known as a gamester almost before he was out of short coats.

The whole family's tainted with it. No one knows what has become of him, though it seems likely he's dead."

"How?" wondered the baroness.

Crane looked regretful at having to admit her ignorance on this point. "He is thought to have gambled her fortune away, however."

"She had a fortune?" asked the baroness, displeased.

Crane nodded. "From her grandmother, the old Countess Lindley."

"Countess," sniffed Colin's mother, not at all glad to hear this piece of information.

Crane nodded. "As the notice in the paper said, she's the daughter of George Bellingham. He was married to Rose Gresham, of the Lincolnshire Greshams."

The baroness pursed her lips. Much to her chagrin, she could not fault the family.

Crane, seeing her disappointment, smiled thinly. "There was something odd about her marriage," she added. Her smile broadened slightly when her mistress looked up like a hound on the scent.

"What?"

"They were married very privately," she said. "With no family present as far as I can discover. And no announcement until afterward."

"An elopement?" breathed the baroness, delighted.

Crane shrugged. "It's not known for certain. But suspected? Yes, indeed."

Baroness St. Mawr clasped her hands together. "Wait until I tell Colin," she exulted.

"There's something else."

"Yes?"

Crane paused, making her mistress wait. It was one of the small hoard of pleasures in her life.

"What?" said the baroness.

"It's possible this woman has visited your son's house alone, and late at night," Crane offered triumphantly.

The baroness smiled. "I knew she must be that sort of person. There was no other explanation."

"The thing is," added Crane. "It isn't certain. One can't get anything from St. Mawr's staff." Her tone implied that this was an affront directed specifically at her.

"Oh, I'm sure it's true. The wicked creature has seduced him and lured him into a proposal."

Crane, who shared Caroline's opinion of the baron, merely looked doubtful.

"I'll show him she is not worthy of marriage," continued the baroness happily. "If he wishes to take her for his mistress—well, such things are none of my affair. But I will not yield my place to a vile hussy such as that. Crane, you are a jewel."

"Thank you, my lady."

"You have given me just what I need to defeat this dreadful woman."

"Happy to be of service, my lady." Crane rose and made as if to move toward the door. "Oh, my lady?" she said casually.

"Yes, Crane?"

"I meant to tell you. That dark blue merino—it doesn't really become your ladyship."

"My new walking dress?" cried the baroness. "But of course it . . ." She stopped suddenly and bit her lip. Another part of the price was being exacted. Crane would be paid for her efforts, though only in ways she herself chose. "The blue?" The baroness's mouth turned down at the corners. "You know, I believe you are right. There is something about it. Why don't you take it, Crane? The color might suit you better."

"Very well, my lady. If you insist?" replied the dresser, squeezing the final bit of satisfaction from the transaction.

"Yes . . . well, I do. Take it," said Colin's mother, with a gesture as if she were throwing something away.

"Thank you, my lady," answered Crane, and left the room with a self-satisfied smile.

Really, she was insufferable, the baroness thought. If she weren't so very useful, she would be impossible to tolerate.

• • •

"But what is going on?" said Robin Bellingham to his father. They sat together in the fine old library of the Bellingham townhouse, the elder man holding a glass of brandy.

"Nothing that need concern you," he said.

"Nothing?" Briefly, Robin was speechless with exasperation. "For nearly half my life, I am not permitted to so much as mention my sister's name. Now, without a word of warning, she reappears in London engaged to St. Mawr. What has become of her husband?"

"He is dead," replied his father, with obvious relish.

"What happened to him?"

With an airy gesture, his father dismissed this as unimportant. "What matters is that he has been removed from the picture, and now Emma will take her rightful place in society." His tone was highly self-satisfied.

"When did she return? How did she meet St. Mawr? What is she like?" wondered Robin.

"Don't worry yourself over the details. It is enough that she is to be creditably established at last." He sighed contentedly. "I had given up any hope for her, you know. This is beyond anything I expected."

"But, Father, my friends are asking about her. They want to meet her. And let me tell you, they think it's deuced odd that I never mentioned having a sister."

"They will meet her soon enough. I daresay Emma will become one of the chief ornaments of society. She has kept her looks charmingly," he finished, as if reassuring Robin on a point of concern.

"I am in society, too!" he protested, jealous of his father's prediction of success for Emma in an area where he so wanted to excel. "And this has made me look a perfect fool."

"Nonsense. No one expects you to be involved in such things. Don't make a fuss over nothing, boy."

"They expect me to know I have a sister," Robin

muttered under his breath, furious at being called "boy."

"An unlooked-for ending indeed," said George Bellingham, sipping his brandy meditatively. "Let it be a lesson to you, Robin. Never imagine that even the most disastrous situation cannot be mended."

He was extremely tired of his father's lessons, Robin thought rebelliously.

"Take your gaming, for example," the older man continued.

Robin's handsome face fell into mulish lines. Here it came, he thought, another lecture on his numerous failings.

"You have been heedless and fallen into debt," his father went on pompously. "You have refused to listen to wiser heads and, inevitably, have gotten yourself into difficulties. No doubt bad company was a large part of the problem. That Jack Ripton, now——"

"Jack is my best friend!" cried Robin. "He's a splendid fellow."

His father shook his head. "Rather wild, I think. A care-for-nobody. And what is his family? They do not seem to be known in London."

"His father has a small estate up north," snapped Robin. "And I won't hear anything against Jack, so you may as well save your breath."

"Well, well," responded his father genially, "loyalty is a fine thing in young men. But what I am trying to tell you is that it is by no means too late to salvage the situation. You are——"

"Can I at least go and visit her?" Robin burst out, unable to stand it any longer.

"Who?"

"Emma. My sister. I hardly remember her. I would like to make her acquaintance."

"Oh, well, as to that . . ." The older man shifted in his chair. "You will meet her at the wedding, which is quite soon."

"Where is she staying?" Robin demanded. "Why is she not with us if we are now reconciled?"

"She is, er . . . she preferred to find her own lodgings," his father replied.

Robin did not blame her in the least. He had waged a fierce battle for rooms of his own at the start of the season, and lost, of course, he thought bitterly, since his father persisted in thinking of him as a child. "Where are they?" he asked again. "Surely I am allowed to call on her now?"

"I daresay she is very busy with wedding preparations," ventured his father. "That sort of thing wholly preoccupies females, you know. Best wait until after, when she will have more time."

"You think she cannot spare twenty minutes for her brother?" he asked, affronted.

"These matters overset the calmest of women," his father insisted. "I remember when your mother was—"

"I will let her inform me if she is too busy," Robin interrupted. "Where is she staying, Father?"

"Ah . . . er . . ."

A great light dawned on Robin. "You don't know, do you?"

"Of course I do!"

"Where, then?"

"I . . . I am certain she does not wish to be disturbed," answered his father gruffly.

"She didn't tell you her direction," marveled Robin. He was filled with awe and admiration for his newfound sister. Effortlessly, she had escaped their father's overbearing presence. Or, could it be even more than that? "Did you even know she was in London before you saw the announcement?"

"Of course," the older man exploded. "I was deeply involved in, er, settling the engagement."

That had the ring of truth, Robin thought. But it was clear his father knew little more. He exulted in his long-lost sister's defiant spirit. She had done precisely what he had longed to do for months and months. His wish to meet her grew keen. She would be his example, he thought. He would follow her lead in dealing with the old man's rules and lectures. Together, they would rout him! Robin grinned in anticipation. He would show him that his son was not a child, but a grown man, who must be treated accordingly.

"You find something amusing in that?" demanded his father, not at all pleased by the exposure of his ignorance.

"No, Father," replied Robin dutifully. There was no need to wrangle now. He would save his energy until Emma was on the scene. And then they would see something! Suppressing another grin, Robin rose and bid his father good night.

Chapter Four

At nine o'clock the next morning, Colin Wareham once again knocked on the door of Arabella Tarrant's small house in an unfashionable corner of London. The baron was immaculately turned out in sleek buff pantaloons and a long-tailed coat of olive green superfine. His tall Hessian boots gleamed like mirrors, and his black hair was brushed into a perfect Brutus. When a maidservant opened the door and ushered him in, he walked calmly to the drawing room and positioned himself beside the fireplace, his handsome face utterly composed.

Colin had spent a good part of the night thinking over the events that had swept through his life in the last few days. Alone, in the calm serenity of his own library, he had examined his motives and behavior in light of the very sensible question Emma had asked him. And he was now satisfied that he understood why he was contemplating a match that almost every person of his acquaintance saw as insane.

He could understand that it might appear, from the

outside, to be an ill-considered, impulsive mistake. But that was not the case at all. It had become clear to him in the early hours of the morning that instinct—that sudden comprehensive knowledge all good military commanders learned to trust—had led him to this decision. He hadn't seen it himself at first. He had been diverted by . . . irrelevancies. But fulfilling his duty by wedding a woman like Emma was exactly the ticket.

She had asked him for the reasons he wished to marry her, and he would give them to her. He had prepared very carefully for this meeting, and he was determined that it would go exactly as he had planned. He would not succumb to emotion; he would not let Emma's vibrant beauty divert him. He would make such a compelling case that she had to agree.

It was all very simple, he told himself as he waited for her to appear. At a very young age, Emma had been overcome by a false infatuation and drawn into a disastrous match. She feared marriage as a trap, even though the situation was completely different now. He must appeal to her formidable intellect and her scrupulous principles before she would allow herself to give in.

Arabella Tarrant entered the room. "She does not wish to come down," she told him. "She says you have nothing further to discuss."

A spark of annoyance ignited in Colin. Ruthlessly, he suppressed it. "Please inform Lady Tarrant that that is not the case," he said civilly.

"I don't think—"

"Please," he repeated in a tone that brooked no argument.

Looking doubtful, Arabella went out.

He was in complete control here, Colin told himself. There would be no outbursts, no unfortunate slips that would cause her to bolt. With studied casualness, he laid his arm along the mantelpiece, forcing his fingers to relax. He took a deep breath.

A few moments later, Arabella reappeared. "She

won't come down," she informed him uneasily. "She said . . ."

"Yes?" prompted Colin when she fell silent.

"Er . . ."

"What the dev—that is, please tell me what she said."

"She said if you did not go, she would send Ferik to throw you out," blurted Arabella on one long breath.

"Did she indeed?" Dispassionately, Colin noted that his hand had balled into a fist. He consciously relaxed it again. "Tell her," he said, his voice clipped, "that I rather think I could hold my own with Ferik. But in any case, should he injure me, he would be put in prison or hanged." He prolonged the last word, savoring its long stretch of vowel.

"My lord," began Arabella.

"Do me the courtesy of conveying my message," he answered.

Looking hunted, once again, his hostess scuttled away.

His teeth were not clenched, Colin thought. Nor were his brows drawn together in a dark scowl, as the mirror seemed to imply. He was simply primed and ready to make his case as soon as he was given the opportunity to do so. All would be measured and reasonable; there would be no raised voices, no grasping her by the shoulders and shaking her until some sense made its way into that lovely, stubborn head and . . . Shocked at the gratification this picture held for him, Colin banished it.

Arabella peered around the door frame. "She refuses, my lord. She is quite unshakable. Indeed, I fear she is—"

Without another word, Colin strode from the room and up the narrow stairs, Arabella fluttering agitatedly behind him. In the upper corridor, he looked to her for direction, and she indicated a door on the left with shaking hands. Colin unhesitatingly threw it open and stalked into a small bedchamber hung with faded pink chintz. "You are the most infuriating woman I have ever met," he said to Emma, who sat in the far corner at a rickety writing desk, "and possibly the most interesting I ever shall meet."

"My lord!" she cried, springing to her feet. "How dare you burst into my room in this way?"

"I dare because you would not come down," he said. "You left me no other choice."

"On the contrary, I asked you to leave."

"Well, I did not wish to do that," Colin pointed out, as he tried to regain his careful calm. She looked particularly beautiful this morning, in a crisp gown of white muslin sprigged with blue flowers. The very air around her seemed to crackle with vitality—and anger. He must seize his chance. "You asked me the reasons I wish to marry you," he said. "Well, that is one of the foremost among them."

"What is?" snapped Emma.

"That you are the most interesting woman I have yet encountered," he repeated. "I don't believe you will ever bore me, or plague me with foolishness."

"The same might be said for many women in London," replied Emma.

"I have not met them," he countered.

"It is a large city," she replied coldly. "It must be filled with interesting women. I know it is teeming with much better matches."

"That depends upon your requirements," Colin said. "I have had rather too much experience of the marriage mart recently, and I can assure you that the qualities I mentioned are exceedingly rare. Indeed, I have found them nowhere else."

"Then you have not tried, my lord."

"Have I not?" He grimaced, remembering countless hours of insipid conversation and longing for escape. "These great matches you talk of so freely—do you know what they come down to? I am expected to marry some chit of seventeen who has just left the schoolroom."

"Well, she needn't be . . ."

"That is what my mother plots. She has been parading these girls before me since the day after I returned home, trussed up like Christmas parcels in ribbons and lace and well-schooled admiration."

Emma suppressed a smile at the picture.

"They are polite and obedient and terribly eager to please," he added.

"What more could a man want?" asked Emma tartly.

"And they are all dead bores," he finished.

"Because you do not know them well," suggested Emma, though she found she did not really wish to argue this case.

"I know them," he replied. "I do not say it is their fault. They have had no time to develop thoughts of their own, and no encouragement to do so. But I will not be saddled with one of them."

"Then don't be," exclaimed Emma, throwing up her hands. "But your preferences have nothing to do with me."

"Yes, they do," he said, in a tone that made her turn to look at him.

"There is another side to this, you know—the woman's. I am not such a great catch."

Emma started to disagree, but he silenced her with a curt gesture.

"I have spent the last eight years at war," he continued—slowly, because this part was more difficult. "My mind is still filled with images from the battlefield. My temperament has . . . darkened. I am . . ." He groped for words. "I believe I am forever changed."

She was watching his face as if she could see something disturbing there.

He had meant to tell her everything, but the look in her eyes made him veer off. "I have lost whatever patience I ever had with stupidity or ignorance," he added. "I can no longer tolerate fools. I believe that you can understand this. I believe, even, that you may feel some of the same things."

Emma met his eyes. Depths, she thought; she had been right about that.

"We have both endured much," Colin went on. "We can offer each other the compassion that comes out of such experiences, and perhaps lighten the burden somewhat."

He had truly caught Emma's attention now.

"I do not wish to spend my life with someone who is constantly asking me what I mean or cajoling me for smiles that I do not feel."

A chord of fellow feeling rang through Emma. She knew precisely what he meant. "Alone amid laughter," she murmured.

Colin's face lit. "You see? You do understand me."

"Yes." Emma looked at him with new eyes.

Encouraged, he stepped forward and took her hand. "When I was twenty, I assumed that I would one day fall head over heels in love and be swept into marriage by strong emotion. I am nearly thirty now, and I fear emotion has been burned out of me by long years of battle." He gazed down at her. "Perhaps you understand this, too, somewhat."

Their eyes held steadily. Emma was finding it difficult to breathe.

"I have found a great deal to admire in you," he continued. "You are extremely intelligent. You have a great deal of integrity. I believe we could offer one another comradeship. And perhaps that is the most we can expect at this point in our lives."

Shaken, she scanned his face. "Comradeship?"

He nodded.

"You are offering me a bargain?" she concluded.

"Yes. You can't wish to return to the life you left. I require a wife who will not drive me to murder within a week. Our needs seem . . . suited."

Emma gazed up at him. She was thinking not of the barren and precarious life she would face abroad, or even of the luxurious existence she could expect as Baroness St. Mawr. What transfixed her was his voice as he spoke of the dark days he had endured in the war and their common understanding of hardship. Something deep inside her had come awake at those words, had responded profoundly to the tone of them, to the reminiscent shadow in his eyes. She had never before met with such kinship. She had never expected it. Emma trembled with the strength of her emotion, though she wasn't sure what it was. "I . . ." she began, and could not finish.

"You cannot condemn me to be surrounded by people who know nothing but sunlight," he said. "I will not abandon you to that fate either," he added.

A bargain, thought Emma. A clear agreement between two people who understood each other, which offered advantages to each. Not, most emphatically not, a heedless, headstrong leap into disaster. Not the risks and stupidities of a naive young girl's illusion of true love. This was safe. It was sensible. And it did offer her many things. Comradeship, Emma thought. It was a pleasing concept. "No," she said.

"No?" he repeated.

"No, I could not condemn you to that," she added, conscious that it was the truth, even if she was making a serious mistake.

Arabella Tarrant, peering through a crack in the door, put her hands to her mouth to stifle a gratified squeal. This was really a splendid development. Though she hadn't understood half of what they said, this pair had clearly come to an agreement at last. And the Baron St. Mawr and his new wife would both have reason to be grateful to her for bringing them together. Surely, she thought, as she watched Colin offer his hand, and Emma take it as if sealing a business transaction, surely they would be very grateful indeed.

A pang of envy shot through her, like a sour surge of bile. Emma would have everything now. It wasn't fair, she thought vaguely. Nothing in her life had been fair. But perhaps she was going to make up for that at last, she thought as she crept away.

"There is one—rather delicate—thing I must ask you," Colin said then.

Emma raised her head at his tone. "What?"

"I owe my name and title an heir," he said evenly.

It took Emma an instant, then she understood. "I . . . I was with child in the first year of my marriage," she said. "I lost the baby during a rough journey to Vienna." She swallowed at the pain of the memory. "The doctor told me there was no reason for concern in the future. But then, after that first year, Edward spent most of his nights at the gaming houses, and drinking. He hardly ever . . . that is . . . it became obvious that his true passion was gaming."

Colin felt a mixture of compassion for her and jealous contempt for the man who had treated her so.

A moment passed before either of them spoke again. Then Colin took a breath and contemplated the opposite wall. "First thing tomorrow, I will visit my greataunt Celia," he told her. "I believe I can make her our ally in this, and she has great influence in society." He smiled slightly. "Even better, my mother is terrified of her."

"Your mother will not be pleased," concluded Emma.

"She will make a great fuss, but you must pay no attention. My mother has not been pleased with anything I did since I left the nursery. You should have heard her screech when I accepted a commission in the army."

"You do not get along?" she wondered.

"I get along perfectly well," Colin replied. "But my mother is overfond of her own way. And she will not be convinced that I have no desire for her . . . guidance."

Emma sighed.

"I should go and begin to put things in motion," he said. "Do you . . . need anything to help you prepare for the wedding?"

Emma stood straighter. "I shan't take money from you. I'll do quite well with what I have."

"Of course." He hesitated. "It's just that my mother is very . . . susceptible to appearances."

"Is she?" Emma's chin came up. "I shall do my best to, er, satisfy her."

Colin smiled slightly. "I'll call again this afternoon," he said. "All will be well," he assured her.

Emma wished she could believe him.

Colin rang the bell at his mother's townhouse and was admitted by her butler, Riggs, with a somber greeting. Moving with austere dignity, Riggs escorted his lordship to the drawing room and sent a footman to inform their mistress of her son's arrival. Then, finding himself unobserved, the butler raced down two flights of stairs to inform the senior staff that a blow-up of major proportions was about to take place. Those with the least excuse to loiter near the drawing room promptly took their places. Thus, the baroness had a gratifyingly large audience when she swept down the staircase and along the corridor, like a frigate under full sail, to confront her erring offspring.

"So," she said accusingly when she entered the drawing room.

Colin turned from the window, where he had been observing the coaches passing in the street. "Good afternoon, Mother," he replied. He was still immaculate in pale pantaloons and a dark green coat, his neckcloth a perfect Oriental. "You look well."

"I do not," replied the baroness, irritated by his refusal to acknowledge her dramatic manner.

Colin raised his dark eyebrows.

"I am prostrate with anxiety," added his mother pettishly.

"Indeed. Do you wish to lie down?"

"No!"

"But if you are prostrate . . . ?"

"Colin! Stop trying to goad me by pretending that all

is as usual. I insist upon discussing this impossible engagement of yours."

"I am here to discuss my engagement," he acknowledged.

"Well, there is only one thing to be said about it. It must be broken off immediately. It is the most scandalously unsuitable, ridiculously—"

"Before you say more, Mother, I should warn you that I fully intend to go ahead with this marriage."

It was like running into a wall, thought the baroness, trying to control her temper. One had just about the same chance of having an effect. "And that is that?" she asked. "Without hearing my opinion, without consulting your family, or indeed, anyone?"

"I'm afraid so," he said, with a slight smile.

His mother's jaw set. "You have not heard what I have to tell you about this woman," she continued.

"I don't think there is anything you can tell me that I do not know," was his calm reply.

Though this idea rattled her a bit, the baroness refused to give up. "Really? Did you know that it is almost certain her first marriage was an elopement? And that her husband was fleeing England because he could not pay his debts of honor? He left unpaid bills all across London. They spent their life in gaming hells, and I have just today learned that her husband was killed in a filthy tavern brawl, over a game of dice he had fallen into with a common carter." She crossed her arms on her chest and gazed at him as if daring him to contradict her.

Colin looked calmly back. "You have made a strong case against Edward Tarrant," he said. "And I agree that the man must have been a thorough blackguard. But I don't see what that has to do with Emma."

"Don't . . . ?" The baroness struggled for words. "A woman who has lived in that way? A creature of gaming hells and low alehouses? A ruined, grasping—"

"Mother!"

His voice was like a whiplash; she clamped her lips shut on further epithets.

"Your excuse must be that you have never met her," said Colin more gently. "Emma is very little touched by the life she was forced to lead. It's remarkable, really."

"She *has* bewitched you," exclaimed the baroness. "She has used her wiles to addle your wits."

"On the contrary . . ."

"She did not scruple to visit your house," snapped his mother. "And *before* there was any talk of engagement, I would note."

Colin went very still. Foolishly, he had not expected this. "You are mistaken," he said coolly.

His mother felt a surge of triumph. Finally, she had penetrated past his infuriating, imperturbable surface. "I don't think so," she said. "I have it on the best authority."

"You have been *mis*informed," he said.

"I have not. Crane had it directly from . . ." She stopped and flushed slightly.

"Servants' gossip, Mother? I hadn't thought it of you."

"Yes, well . . ."

"Did Crane's 'informants' give you my visitor's name? Was she known to them?"

"No, but the description was quite detailed and—"

"Misleading," he declared.

"Are you trying to tell me that you had some other female in your house only days before you offered for this . . . this . . ."

"I am telling you to cease this interference," he replied. "The matter has come up between us before." He was terrifically angry, Colin realized dispassionately. The threat had roused every defensive instinct.

"Will you abandon your family for a woman with no background, a creature of the gaming hells and—"

"Emma is as well-born as you," he said crisply.

The baroness's head jerked back. It was a sore point with her that she was the child of a mere country squire, with no pretensions to nobility. The subject was not customarily mentioned, and she could not believe he had brought it up.

"She is intelligent, well-mannered, with a strong natural dignity," he went on. "You will accustom yourself to the idea that we will be married. And you will not"—he fixed her with an icy gaze—"not repeat any gossip about her. Is that clear?"

His mother blinked. Colin did not sound like a man enmeshed in the toils of passion. Could she have misjudged the situation after all? "I do not understand you," she complained.

"Very true," he agreed blandly.

"I have presented every eligible girl in the *ton* to you," she wailed. "A number of them were *quite* ravishing, and all of them were above reproach. Any one would have been overjoyed to receive an offer. Why must you—"

"As you pointed out, you do not understand me," he answered. "Now, let me tell you about the plans I have made."

The baroness sank onto the sofa, her plump face creased into petulant lines. "You are the most annoying person, Colin."

"Doubtless," he said, brushing this perennial complaint aside. "Great-aunt Celia is giving a dinner to celebrate the engagement Wednesday week."

"Aunt Celia is taking your side in this?" His mother looked uneasy.

"She has . . . come to appreciate my point of view." He did not tell her that their formidable relative had made her help completely probationary. Or that she had said, "Mind you, young jackanapes, if I don't care for the girl, I'll put an end to the match. And if you think I can't, you don't know who you're dealing with."

"How could she?" complained the baroness.

"All the family will be invited," Colin continued. "And I shall expect them to attend."

"We couldn't refuse an invitation from Celia," she said faintly.

Which was exactly why he had gone to her, thought Colin. "Afterward, we will attend the Cardingtons' ball together," he told her. "Will you ask Lady Cardington to include Emma among her guests?"

"Ask her?" exclaimed the baroness. "She will fall over herself to invite her. Do you have any idea of the gossip you have stirred up, Colin? Felicity Cardington will be the envy of every other hostess in London if she has you and your . . . intended at her ball."

Colin nodded, his mouth tight.

"I suppose you realize that we will be the targets of rude stares and every fool who fancies himself a wit?" she added pettishly.

"It can't be helped," he said. "We must just see that the talk dies down as soon as possible."

"But—"

"I expect your help in this, Mother," he warned.

"I don't—"

"And Caroline's as well."

"You want us to help you ruin yourself?" she complained.

"On the contrary, Mother. On the contrary."

She watched him, puzzled by the look on his face. "Do you care for this woman, Colin? Is there something that you're not telling me?"

"She will do very well," he replied.

"That does not answer my question."

"It is all the answer you will get."

"I declare I hardly know you anymore, Colin," said his mother peevishly. "It is the war, I suppose. It has changed you."

"I believe it has," he acknowledged. "But if your memory suggests that before the war I allowed you to order me about, it is seriously flawed, Mother."

"You have been impossible since you were eight years old," she complained. "I remember distinctly the day you turned to me, with precisely that superior look on your face, and informed me that you did not wish to see boiled carrots on your plate ever again." She sniffed. "Independent, your father called it. Headstrong and ungovernable is nearer the truth."

He smiled very slightly. "Good day, Mother. Until Wednesday."

"Colin!" But he left the room without acknowledging her protest. "Arrogant, too," said the baroness. "Not to mention incredibly irritating." She vented her frustration on a small embroidered footstool, kicking it aside as she stalked from the room.

Emma carefully restacked the pile of coins and banknotes she had set out on the small table in her bedchamber. The last time she had contemplated marriage, she thought, she had had her own secure income of six hundred a year and very little understanding of money. This time, her entire fortune consisted of four hundred seventy-nine pounds and some odd shillings, most of it won from the fat woman at Barbara Rampling's card party, and she had become a frugal and efficient manager of her funds. She fingered the two pieces of jewelry she had been able to keep through the downward progress of her life—a modest string of pearls she had inherited from her mother and an exquisite cameo brooch in tints of peach and ivory that had belonged to her wealthy grandmother. She had sold her wedding ring in Constantinople to pay Edward's final debts, which had seemed to her a suitably symbolic gesture.

Emma swept the money into her reticule and put the jewelry away. It was not much on which to rig herself out like a baroness, but she had great faith in her own powers of contrivance. As she moved toward the door, she caught a glimpse of her reflection in the mirror and gave it a wry smile. Two things she had learned in recent years—gambling, and how to clothe herself stylishly on nearly nothing.

Finding Arabella in the drawing room, she inquired

about shops. When the older woman began to name some of the fashionable Bond Street establishments, Emma shook her head. "Not where the *ton* goes. I cannot pay for an address. There must be other places."

"Well, I have heard that one can get things very cheap at the Pantheon Bazaar," replied Arabella doubtfully. "But I have never been there."

"We shall take a look," said Emma cheerfully. "That is, if you care to come with me?"

"Do you think it's safe?" wondered Arabella.

"Ferik will be with us. No one has ever dared accost me with him present."

"I suppose not," she replied doubtfully. Arabella had not developed a fondness for Ferik. "But will you really find anything suitable in such a place?"

Emma smiled. "I will tell you a secret, aunt. Cities are full of interesting places where the fashionable people never go. There are thousands of respectable women in London who cannot afford to shop in Bond Street— wives of barristers and shopkeepers. I wager they have no trouble buying a length of fine muslin or some trimming for a gown."

Arabella looked shocked. "You cannot think to dress like a shopkeeper's wife?"

"No. But I may use the same materials. Come, I'll show you."

Arabella went to fetch her hat. Knowing that it would take her some time to prepare to go out, Emma used the opportunity to summon Ferik to the drawing room.

"Yes, mistress?" he said in his deep voice a few minutes later. Entering the room, and immediately making it seem much smaller, he stood like a great bronze statue beside the open door.

"Ferik, I am going to be married," said Emma.

He took this in without reaction.

"To the gentleman who was here this morning," she added.

"The English milord with the wonderful eyes?" he inquired.

"Er . . . well, yes." Emma gazed up at him in amazement. "What do you know of his eyes, Ferik?"

"Ellen says it," he informed her.

"Ah." Ellen was one of the housemaids.

"He is rich?" asked the giant.

Emma allowed that he was.

"And an important bey?"

"Well, he is a nobleman," agreed Emma, not certain about Turkish equivalents.

Ferik nodded, looking satisfied. "That is good. You should be married to a great man, who can give you many jewels and a fine house. He has no other wife?"

"Other . . . ?" Emma recalled that in Ferik's home country, men were allowed more than one. She had found the idea quite shocking when she first heard of it. "No," she said firmly. "No other wife."

"Then you will be chief wife," he replied complacently. "That is very good. I will head your household."

"Men have only one wife in England," Emma felt obliged to tell him. "And the household is all the same. You will remain my servant, of course, but Baron St. Mawr has a staff already, and you will have to get along with them." This last came out somewhat sternly. There had been incidents with Arabella's servants.

"One wife!" exclaimed Ferik. "But you said he was rich."

"He is."

"So, then, he could provide for more than one wife, mistress?"

"I . . . I suppose he could," said Emma. "If he wished to."

"All men wish to," Ferik assured her. "But of course not all can afford more than one." He scowled. "Perhaps this man is not as rich as he tells you," he added suspiciously.

"He is quite wealthy, Ferik, but—"

"Then he will wish for another wife." Ferik nodded.

"Not now. And none will ever be as noble and lovely as you, mistress, but someday he will."

"Men can have only one wife in England, Ferik," Emma repeated loudly.

He frowned at her.

"One," she insisted.

"No matter how rich they are?" inquired Ferik.

"No matter."

"Even if they could buy a dozen houses and a thousand slaves?"

She was not going to get into the issue of slaves, Emma thought. "That's right," she responded firmly.

Ferik looked bewildered. His huge hands were open and raised to the ceiling in helpless amazement. "But, mistress, that isn't fair."

"It is the way things are," declared Emma. "Now, we are going—"

"It isn't right to cheat a man of the rewards of his wealth." The giant spoke with sweet reasonableness, as if he had only to point out this truth to have her see the light.

Emma had no wish to argue moral principles. "It is against the law," she said with finality.

"The law?" He looked astonished. "What law?"

"The law of England. Ferik, I have told you many times that England is very different from your country," she pointed out in her own defense.

"Yes, but if a man can afford to keep more than one . . ."

"It is not allowed, Ferik." Emma moved toward the door, hoping to signal a definite end to this subject. "Now, we are going out. You will accompany us."

This diverted him. "But it is raining again, mistress," he protested. "You will get wet."

Emma hid a smile, knowing that he meant he would get wet. "We will take a covered hack, Ferik. Get your hat."

His massive shoulders sagging slightly, her giant servant turned away. As he left the room, Emma heard him

mutter. "Rain, soft white food, one wife. It is a barba-
rous country."

A short while later the three of them were prowling
the crowded aisles of the Pantheon Bazaar. Arabella was
exclaiming at the cheapness of the goods while the other
shoppers eyed Ferik with openmouthed uneasiness.
"Look at this velvet," said Arabella. "This is less than
half what I paid three years ago for the same stuff! And
the blue satin; it's dirt cheap. If I had known about this
place before, I might have twice as many gowns as I
do."

Eyeing the almost painful brightness of the satin,
Emma said nothing. She went back to looking through a
pile of sprigged muslins, picking out the finest.

"Gloves ninepence the pair," cried Arabella. "Ribbon, braid, bugling. Everything you could want is
here." She wandered off through the aisles, picking up
items at random and exclaiming aloud at their value.

Emma did not allow herself to be distracted by
branches of artificial flowers or a special price on ribbon
of a particularly virulent yellow. She knew precisely
what she wanted, and she went about the aisles filling a
mental list that she had spent some time compiling. As
the neatly wrapped parcels accumulated in Ferik's stout
arms, she began to feel a certain excitement. It had been
a long time since she had spent so much on things for
herself. The thought of appearing before Colin in the
gowns she had envisioned was pleasant, as was the idea
of going out in public without worrying about winning
enough money to pay the next month's expenses. A hint
of the enjoyment she had once found in society returned to her, like an animal struggling to life after a
long hibernation.

"Now I must find a dressmaker who is very good
and very reasonable about her fees," Emma said as they
rode home together in a hansom cab.

"I have just the person for you," replied Arabella.

"She is a friend of mine, and, like me, in, uh, difficult circumstances since the death of her husband last year."

Emma frowned. "I would like to help your friend, aunt," she said. "But I must have a truly fine seamstress who can create as well as sew. If it were not so important . . ."

"No, no. You don't understand. Sophie is a French-woman, an émigré. She has the most exquisite taste. She is starting up her own dressmaking business, and she already has a number of customers, but she is not well known as yet. I'm sure she would be happy to make your gowns for next to nothing if you would mention her name when you are a baroness." Arabella rubbed her hands together. This was just the sort of transaction she enjoyed. Sophie would owe her a few gowns for making this connection.

"Well . . ." This sounded promising, but Emma did not want to be put in the position of rejecting a friend of Arabella's.

"Why not meet her and talk with her?" suggested the older woman. "If you don't think she will do, that will be the end of it."

After all, thought Emma, she had no other candidates. "Very well."

"Splendid." Arabella clapped her hands. "Isn't this fun? It is all just like a fairy tale."

"We haven't yet met the dragon," answered Emma dryly.

The moment Sophie Fisher walked into Arabella's drawing room, Emma knew she was the right choice. She wore a gown of thin muslin in a rich amber shade that perfectly complimented her dark coloring. With its scooped neck, high waist, and wide ruffle along the hem, the dress looked as if it had come straight from Paris. It had tiny tucks in the bodice and puffed sleeves executed with exquisite skill, and was stylishly trimmed with knots of gold ribbon. The combination of taste and workmanship was exactly what she wanted. After a brief greeting, Emma simply got out her lists and the models she had found in various fashion periodicals and began to show them to Sophie. Within five minutes they were seated side by side on the sofa poring over these, and Sophie was offering such good advice that Emma resolved to put herself entirely in her hands. She foresaw only one problem. "I must have these very quickly," she pointed out.

Sophie, who had been thoroughly drilled by Arabella on the situation, waved an airy hand. "I have three ladies who sew for me, and I can add two more. We will have your trousseau for you like this." She snapped her fingers. "I will send someone for the cloth today, and we will begin to cut. Tomorrow afternoon, a fitting. It will go like a flash, you will see."

"Splendid," said Emma.

Sophie gave her a shrewd glance. There was no need to mention the fact that she was doing herself a service also, she decided. This was a very intelligent young woman. She would not forget her part of the bargain. For a moment, Sophie Fisher lost herself in an agreeable vision of the future—an exclusive shop on Bond Street, duchesses clamoring for her designs, a fat bank account, respect and independence. With only a very little help, she would make a great success. She was certain of it. Then her bone-deep practicality reasserted itself. There was much to do before that time. Best get to work at once. She stood. "I will go then," she told Emma. "My boy will come for the cloth very soon."

"It is ready."

Sophie bowed her head. She was turning to go when she hesitated. "Perhaps I will just take the satin now," she decided.

"Certainly. I'll fetch it for you."

In a few moments, the package was in Sophie's hands. "Good," she pronounced. "You will be *ravissante* in this," she promised as she departed. "And in everything I make for you. Be assured."

Emma was.

She closed the door behind Sophie in great good spirits, and when a knock sounded on the panels a few minutes later, she answered it smilingly herself. "Did you forget . . ." she began. But the words died on her lips. It was not Sophie who stood there, but someone quite different, someone she had never thought to see again in her life.

The worst man in the world walked nonchalantly over the threshold. As if he owned the house. As if he had no doubt at all of an enthusiastic reception. He smiled at her warmly, intimately, as if they knew each other very well indeed.

Emma swallowed a bad taste in her mouth. She had not encountered Count Julio Orsino in nearly a year, and she certainly had not thought of him. She never thought of men like him unless she had to. He represented everything she hated most in the world. And yet here he was, standing before her with his hand held out in greeting as if they were on the best of terms.

"My dear Lady Tarrant," he said. "I so hoped to find you here."

"Really?" replied Emma coldly. "Why?"

He looked hurt. "Why, for the pleasure of renewing our acquaintance," he declared.

Orsino hadn't changed at all, Emma noted. His black hair was still flat and smooth as leather on his round head; his dark eyes were liquidly expressive. His face remained blandly pleasant, effectively masking a host of evils. His exquisite mode of dress made the best of a short, stocky frame. All in all, his appearance gave no clue to his true nature. Emma felt her fingers curl into claws and made an effort to relax them.

Footsteps sounded in the hall behind them. "Was that the door?" wondered Arabella's high-pitched voice. "Oh," she added, seeing the caller.

Orsino was not the sort of person anyone should know, Emma thought. She wished she didn't know him herself. But she didn't see how she could avoid introductions. "Mrs. Arabella Tarrant," she said tersely.

Orsino stepped forward and executed a sweeping bow. "I am Count Julio Orsino," he said. "From Italy. Enchanted." He grasped Arabella's limp hand and kissed it.

"Oh my," she fluttered. She looked at Emma, silently requesting more information.

"We were acquainted with the count in Europe," Emma said tonelessly.

"Acquainted?" he protested. "Surely more than that? I was a close friend of poor Edward," he informed Arabella. "Your nephew, I believe?"

"Friend," repeated Emma with contempt. "You encouraged his excesses, applauded his worst behavior. You led him into ruin and profited from every step. If he had listened to me, he would have severed the connection with you years ago."

"You are very hard," he commented, without seeming offended.

"Indeed, Emma, you are being horribly rude to the count," put in Arabella, who had clearly been impressed by his manner. "Come in, sir. May we offer you a glass of Madeira?"

"Thank you." With urbane effrontery, he followed the older woman into the drawing room.

What did he want? Emma wondered. For it was certain he wanted something. Orsino did nothing except for his own advantage. Then she remembered the newspaper announcement. No doubt he had seen it. And now he expected to profit somehow from her connection to St. Mawr. Her expression hardened. He'd find he'd misjudged things this time, she thought.

"Yes, London is a fine city," Orsino was saying when she came into the room. "Although it cannot compare with, say, Vienna, can it, Lady Tarrant?" He gave her a meaningful look, as if he were referring to some deeply significant shared experience.

Emma fumed. She was certain he knew that she despised him. "I fear you have caught me at an awkward moment," she said crisply. "I have another engagement in a short time."

"What engagement?" asked Arabella tactlessly.

The count sat in an armchair and said nothing, merely keeping his gaze on Emma with a half smile.

"Some errands I must do," replied Emma through gritted teeth.

His smile grew even broader. "You do not make me feel entirely welcome."

"What do you want?" she answered.

"Emma!" exclaimed Arabella.

"Won't you sit?" Orsino asked, gesturing toward the sofa.

"No."

"Ah."

He seemed much amused by her annoyance, Emma thought. "What do you want?" she repeated.

He spread his hands and looked blandly innocent. "This is merely a courtesy call," he claimed. "I wished to offer my felicitations on your forthcoming marriage."

Arabella threw Emma a reproachful look. "Isn't it wonderful," she said. "Such a splendid match."

"If you have come here looking for money, you have made a mistake," said Emma.

"Emma!" exclaimed Arabella again.

"No, no, I want no money," he replied, surprising her. "I thought only to see an old friend. Friendship is so important, don't you think?"

Now it comes, thought Emma, bracing herself.

"One can get so lonely, in a foreign country, knowing no one. You have felt this yourself."

Emma simply waited.

"But you have done so well here in London. Perhaps you would take pity on a poor stranger and introduce me to some of your acquaintances."

"Ah," said Emma. "You want me to bring you into

society, so that you may cheat people out of their money at the gaming tables."

Arabella made a scandalized sound.

"Cheat?" echoed Orsino, as if shocked.

"Everyone knows you cheat," declared Emma.

"If you were a man, I might call you out for such an accusation," threatened the count silkily.

"If I were a man, I'd happily put a bullet through you," said Emma. "I will not present you to anyone. You may as well go back where you came from."

"That is not . . . possible," he said. "I plan a stay of some duration in England."

"Are the authorities after you? I'm not surprised. You may as well leave. I have said I won't—"

He held up a hand to silence her. His expression was so malicious that Emma hesitated. It was not wise to take Orsino lightly. Behind his bland exterior, he was ruthless. She could call to mind numerous examples of men and women he had destroyed.

The count seemed to consider. The mantel clock ticked into the silence for a long moment. Then, Orsino appeared to make a decision. He rose. "We will talk again, when you are in better spirits," he said.

He thought he had some lever to use against her, Emma saw, and he was saving it. But it didn't matter. She wouldn't give him what he wanted. "My spirits have nothing to do with it," she told him. "I will never change my mind."

The count smiled unpleasantly. "Never is a very long time," he replied as he went out.

As Arabella began to upbraid her for her impolite behavior, Emma gazed at the empty doorway. Unsavory characters from her past had been no part of the bargain Colin Wareham made, she thought uneasily. And she knew she had by no means seen the last of Count Julio Orsino.

Chapter Five

Emma put the finishing touches on her ensemble and stood back to look in Arabella's ancient full-length mirror. The ball gown was even better than she had imagined. The underdress, of midnight-blue satin, reflected back the blue of her eyes. The skirt that fell from the high waist was overlaid with silver net, which matched the gleam of her silver-gilt hair, caught up now at the back of her head and allowed to fall in a cascade of ringlets. The miraculous Sophie had found a thin silver braid to trim the neckline and the tiny puffed sleeves. The dress was exactly what Emma had wanted—elegant, sophisticated. It was also the most beautiful dress she had had for a long, long time.

Arabella peeked around the half-open door. "He's here," she said. She was as excited as if she, and not Emma, were the one being presented to the Wareham family and the *ton* tonight. In fact, Emma wished she could restrain her excitement a bit; she was making her nervous.

"Oh, you look perfect!" the older woman exclaimed. "I told you Sophie is a genius with cloth."

"So she is," answered Emma. Picking up a gauzy silver scarf, she settled it around her shoulders, then took one last look in the mirror. Colin's family would not be able to find fault with her appearance, she thought. Which was fortunate, because they were more than likely to find fault with everything else.

"St. Mawr looks terribly handsome," Arabella confided, following Emma from the room. "You will be the envy of every girl at the ball tonight, my dear. How I wish I could see it!"

Emma said nothing as she made her way downstairs. Arabella had been angling for an invitation to join tonight's party since the moment she had heard of it. But though she felt a twinge of guilt over the matter, Emma emphatically did not want her there. A member of Edward's family would be wholly out of place in any case, she reminded herself.

When she entered the drawing room, Colin had his back to her, looking out the front window. Emma watched him for a moment while he was still unaware of her presence. He stood very straight, like a former soldier. His broad shoulders and fine athletic figure were perfectly set off by his dark evening clothes. His black hair curled just slightly on his neck. And yet, despite the richness of his attire and the assurance of his bearing, there was something sad about him. She couldn't even see his face, but she could sense the melancholy hanging over him like an enveloping mist. Emma moved farther into the room. "I am ready," she said.

He turned, and smiled, with no hint of sadness visible. Then, as he took in her gown, her hair twisted in a glinting knot, the delicate set of her head, his smile altered a little. She was stunning, he thought. He had expected beauty, and a suitably fashionable dress, but she went far beyond what he had pictured. She had a presence, an impact, that filled the room. He couldn't take his eyes off her. "Beautiful," he said, inadequately.

Emma enjoyed the admiration in his eyes. She did a little pirouette and said, "The lamb is ready for the slaughter, my lord."

He laughed. "Nonsense. They will be bowled over." He offered his arm. "Unless we are late. Then Great-aunt Celia will drag us both over the coals."

Taking his arm, Emma looked up at him. This moment felt weighted with significance. After tonight, it would be impossible to go back, to change their minds about the marriage or admit they'd made a mistake. Had she? Emma wondered. For a woman who hated gaming, she was taking a huge gamble, wagering her entire life. She had made such a reckless choice seven years before, she thought, and regretted it bitterly ever since.

"What is it?" said Colin.

Emma swallowed. "Are you sure?" she asked, a wealth of meaning vibrating in the three words.

He did not ask what she was talking about. "As sure as it is possible to be," he replied.

She drew back a little. "What does that mean?"

His eyes, steady on hers, were full of shadowed depths. "I have spent the last eight years of my life never certain whether I would see another day," he said. "There were so many times when I might have been killed."

"But you weren't," she put in, unsettled by the thought of such an existence.

"No. But friends were, men under my command. Cut down before they were twenty, some of them."

Emma's eyes widened.

"I concluded that you cannot count on the future. There is no guarantee of tomorrow. We must simply do the best we can with the moments we have."

A dark philosophy, Emma thought; not one she shared, despite everything that had happened to her. But something in his face, his eyes, had answered her inner questioning. "And I must spend some of my precious moments being scrutinized by your family?" she asked in a much lighter tone.

"No one will slight you," he said. "You *may* count on that."

Slightly startled by his vehemence, Emma blinked.

"We must go," he added. "Aunt Celia is rabid on the subject of punctuality."

"Then by all means, let us go," she said, moving with him toward the door. "I don't wish to set her against me from the very first."

Arabella, lurking at the darkened front parlor window, watched them walk out together. They were the handsomest couple she had ever seen, she thought. Both tall with long, easy strides; both powerful personalities, although she was not sure they were fully aware of it; both charming when they wanted to be; and both somehow different, not like the rest of the fashionable set. She tried to put her finger on just what it was that set them apart. A certain solitude, even in the midst of people, she thought; an almost brooding quality? Arabella shook her head. She was being fanciful. What mattered was that it was an excellent match, and that she had had a hand in making it. Once again, she congratulated herself. Better times were definitely ahead.

"Tell me who will be at dinner," said Emma when they were settled in his carriage.

"My mother; my sister Caroline and her husband Wrotham; several cousins and their assorted spouses. Remarkably assorted, in one or two cases. All presided over by Great-aunt Celia, whom I've told you about."

"Too much, perhaps," responded Emma. "I'm all in a quake."

"Yes, you look it," he said ironically, scanning her serene expression.

"I am mastering my emotions," she informed him severely, "just as my dear old governess taught me to do."

"Admirable," he replied with a smile. He did not believe she was truly afraid. Slightly nervous, yes. But he thought she might actually be rather excited at the challenge the evening presented, and he liked her attitude. Because he didn't want to spoil it, he waited until they had stepped down from the carriage and were being admitted to his great-aunt's elegant townhouse to add, "Your father and brother will be present as well, of course."

Emma froze in the act of tucking up a curl. "What?"

"We could not do this without them," he said. "It would look odd."

Her jaw set. "I don't want to see him."

"Your father will be on his best behavior. Aunt Celia will see to that. I've told her to keep him at her side all evening."

Emma looked mulish.

"You must see that to exclude your family, when they live right here in London, would look strange. It would appear that we were ashamed of them."

"I am! Of him, anyway."

"They would think it was my doing," Colin pointed out, "that I did not care for the family I was marrying into. I wouldn't want to give that impression." He had thought this out carefully. Though Colin had never paid much heed to society's rules or to what others thought of him, now that he was about to present Emma as his future wife, all that was changed. He was determined that she would not be slighted by the *ton*, and he was ready to do whatever was necessary to make certain of it.

"Oh," said Emma. He did not want to appear churlish in the eyes of his friends, she thought. No doubt their opinion was important to him. "Oh, very well."

"You need never see him again once we're married," he promised, half teasing.

Emma's features relaxed in a smile. "Is this how you intend to treat me then, my lord? Springing unpleasant truths upon me too late for me to do anything about them?"

"Of course," he said. "Invariably."

As he had hoped, this made her laugh a little. Thus, when they entered the drawing room side by side, the people waiting there saw a slightly smiling, apparently confident, unworried Emma, absolutely dazzling in her beautiful gown. Though her expression grew serious at once, the critical first impression had already been made, and an advantage established.

Colin escorted her around the room with a fine sense of protocol. "My great-aunt Celia, Lady Burrington," he said first.

Emma dropped a small curtsy to the massive old woman who sat in a great carved chair clutching an ebony cane. The rigidly boned and constructed bodice and wide billowing skirts of her brocade gown echoed the fashions of fifty years ago. Her lace cap was perched on snowy white hair, and her hands were gnarled and twisted with age. There was nothing old about the look she gave Emma, however. It was shrewd and challenging, daring her to show her mettle. "Where'd you find that gown?" the old lady barked without preamble.

She looked like an extremely successful bird of prey, Emma thought, one whose claws were always kept razor sharp. "A very clever Frenchwoman made it for me," she responded evenly. "Sophie Fisher."

"Fisher? Never heard of her."

"She is not well known in London as yet," conceded Emma.

"I daresay you'll be the making of her, then," said Lady Burrington, giving the gown another critical but approving examination.

"That is her hope," said Emma.

Her hostess raised one white eyebrow. She did it just as Colin did, Emma thought. Or, she supposed, the other way around. If Emma had not seen the twinkle in the old woman's eye, she might have thought she had offended her.

"My mother," said Colin, moving Emma a little to the left. "Catherine, Baroness St. Mawr."

"For now, at least," was the sharp rejoinder.

Emma was surprised to face a small woman, inches shorter than she, and very plump and pleasant-looking.

She realized that she had been visualizing a large, frowning harpy, with a beak of a nose and thick eyebrows, in the role of Colin's mother. A slight flush stained her cheeks. "How do you do?" she said.

"Humph," was the only reply. The baroness was openly dismayed. This elegant, imperturbable young woman was not what she had expected. Beauty, yes; that was inevitable. But Emma Tarrant had far more than beauty. She did not look at all like an interloper, or a schemer after Colin's money and position. Where in the world had she found such self-possession, the baroness wondered, such an air?

"My sister Caroline," said Colin, not lingering in dangerous territory.

"How lovely to meet you," said Caroline, who had thrown her mother's apprehensions to the wind at the first sight of Emma. "This is my husband, Frederick."

"Lord Wrotham," supplied Colin in a murmur.

"How do?" said the large, phlegmatic earl. Tall, broad, and blond, he looked as if his whole mind was occupied with thoughts of dinner.

Warmed by the open friendliness in Caroline's expression, and the lack of any hostility in her husband's, Emma smiled. It was the first full smile she had given the group. There was a ripple of reaction. One of the young male cousins gasped audibly.

Radiant, thought the baroness. There was no other word for the wretched woman. This was disastrous.

They went through the line of cousins very quickly. At the end, Colin said, "And of course I do not need to introduce the rest of our party."

Emma had prepared herself by this time. "Of course not. Father." She inclined her head, but did not offer to kiss him.

"Good evening, my dear." George Bellingham was beaming. "You're looking very fine."

"Thank you."

Though several of the Warehams noticed the marked coolness in Emma's voice, her father was oblivious to it.

Nothing could penetrate the buoyancy of his mood tonight. This was the sort of marriage he had always imagined for his only daughter. And he was reveling in it.

"You might have to present me," said Robin. "I was still in short coats when Emma . . ." Realizing that he was about to make a serious social error, Robin Bellingham blushed to the roots of his pale hair. "Er . . . married," he choked out.

"But of course I know you," said Emma warmly. "You are the image of our mother, Robin. How good to see you again."

Her brother mumbled something and effaced himself, to Colin's profound relief. It was like riding patrol in dangerous country, he thought. The room was simmering with potential flare-ups, and he was the one designated to see that none of them erupted. He steered Emma back toward Caroline.

The butler appeared and announced dinner. Two footmen followed close behind him. Taking up positions on either side of Lady Burrington's great chair, they heaved her up and out of it. "Come along, Bellingham," she commanded when she had gained her feet. "In honor of our coming relationship, you may take me in."

Looking both gratified and a bit cowed, Emma's father hurried forward to offer his arm. One of the footmen remained for support on her ladyship's other side, and in this manner she led the way into the dining room.

Emma found herself seated between Lord Wrotham and the eldest of the male cousins, a plump, complacent man of fifty who looked like a cross between their hostess and a sheep. Colin was several chairs away, but so, she saw with gratitude, was his mother. She had no difficulty making conversation. Wrotham was happy to talk about the splendidly prepared food they were served, his two-year-old son, and hunting, which did not tax Emma's knowledge, as he required little in the way of reply.

When the table turned, things grew more difficult. At first it seemed that the cousin had nothing at all to say for himself, and, like a sheep indeed, he shied from the innocuous questions Emma asked. But then she happened to hit upon the subject of paintings exhibited at the Royal Academy. The timid man brightened at once, and it emerged that he was a passionate collector of all sorts of art. From then on she only had to listen while he catalogued every piece he possessed, how he had come to find it, the intricate negotiations involved in acquiring it, and how beautifully it graced his walls or cabinets or vaults. The man had an amazing memory. It appeared that he had never forgotten a single detail having to do with his collection in thirty years.

Emma realized that she had forgotten how little was required of a younger female in society. Nodding and smiling got one through nearly anything. Except the boredom. Looking down, she noticed that she was savagely twisting her napkin between her fingers. She stopped, and when she looked up again, she found that Colin was gazing at her with such obvious, and amused, understanding that she had to smile. The baroness, intercepting the look they exchanged, saw at once that her cause was lost. She would not be separating this couple. Frustrated, she bit down hard on a lemon wafer, shattering it to crumbs that showered over the tablecloth. "Wretched thing," she muttered, looking at the remains of the wafer with loathing. "Dry as dust."

Soon after this, their hostess was hoisted up again, and the ladies withdrew, leaving the men to their port. Emma entered the drawing room with caution, knowing that this was the truly hazardous part of the evening, when the guards would come off and tongues grow sharp as rapiers. She moved as far from Colin's mother as she could, seating herself next to the wife of her dinner partner. "Your husband was telling me about his wonderful art collection," she said.

The lady, who didn't look anything like a sheep,

sniffed. "I'm not surprised. He thinks of little else," she replied. "Certainly not his family."

"Ah," said Emma, immediately conscious that she had made a mistake.

"He will spend hundreds of pounds on some moldy painting," continued the other bitterly. "But when it comes to clothing his daughters in proper style or setting a reasonable table, then we must economize. Oh, yes. Suddenly, our income becomes modest. Suddenly, we are barely able to meet our expenses. Until he uncovers some other wretched old bit of canvas or stone. Then, miraculously, money appears." She made a broad gesture, attracting the attention of the whole room. "It is a disease," she continued, her voice rising. "I have told the family time and again that something should be done about him. But of course, no one listens to me. No one cares that I—"

There was a sharp thump, followed by silence. Lady Burrington had struck the floor with her ebony cane, Emma realized. And now, she was looking at each of the women in turn, like a hawk evaluating a flock of chickens. The cousin's wife shrank down in her chair exactly like an anxious hen, her eyes fixed on the floor. Emma hid a smile.

"Come here," commanded their hostess, pointing at Emma.

There was an almost imperceptible stir of relief among the others as she rose and moved to the chair beside Lady Burrington. From the frying pan into the fire, Emma thought.

"So," said Lady Burrington when they sat side by side. "You are to marry St. Mawr?" She did not make it sound like a settled thing.

"It appears so, ma'am," Emma answered.

"Appears?" barked the old woman. "Is there some question?"

"I have the feeling that your approval is an important point," Emma replied, conscious that a number of the other guests were listening closely to their conversation.

"Mine!" Lady Burrington snorted delicately. "You think St. Mawr cares for my opinion?"

Emma considered. "He should," she said finally, having thought it over.

Looking fierce, the old woman stared at her. "Are you trying to flatter me, young woman? I despise toadies, you know."

She hadn't realized it would look that way, Emma thought. She noticed Colin's mother, sitting not far away. She looked very pleased with the way things were going. Abruptly, Emma was tired of fencing. "I wasn't," she said. "But think what you like."

"I always do," declared her ladyship.

For a moment, they faced each other like adversaries. For some reason, Emma remembered an occasion three years ago when an unsavory acquaintance had burst into her and Edward's rooms at an inn and drunkenly threatened them with a pistol. Whatever happened, she thought, Lady Burrington could not shoot her. And then she realized that the strictures of society truly had no hold on her any longer. "Colin and I understand each other," she said quietly. "Can you say the same?"

Lady Burrington's gaze sharpened. She looked as if she intended to search Emma's very soul. "I don't know," she said finally, also in a low voice. "Possibly not."

Emma saw the baroness straining to overhear. She spoke even more softly. "You have heard gossip about me." It was not a question. She knew that Lady Burrington would have gathered any information she could.

"It does not do you justice," was the dry reply.

"Perhaps I am not what you wished for in Colin's wife."

"I have not said so."

"I am not what others wished for," said Emma with certainty. "But I think he needs . . ."

The old woman waited.

Emma still hesitated. She didn't know how to say

what she meant. "Something other than what they wished for," she concluded finally.

Lady Burrington's eyes were as unwavering as those of a diving eagle. "You are not an adventuress," she said.

Emma said nothing.

"You are not a fool," said the old woman with even more conviction.

"I don't think I am."

"But what are you, eh?"

Emma stared at her, caught by the question. She didn't know how to answer.

Colin's great-aunt gave a crack of laughter. "Not so sure of that one? Well, I'd be suspicious if you were, at, what—five and twenty? But I believe I'm rather sorry I shan't live to see you work out the answer."

The door opened, and the gentlemen entered the drawing room.

"You'd best get on if you're going to that ball of Felicity Cardington's," declared Great-aunt Celia to the party at large. "I don't intend to keep all the men here for ten minutes just for form's sake."

Seeming used to this sort of statement, the family members began to stand. Emma looked to Colin, who came over to join them as the room emptied. "Has Aunt Celia been grilling you?" he asked, his tone light but his expression probing.

"Of course I have," replied the old woman. "What else did you expect?"

Colin looked at Emma, who smiled.

Lady Burrington gave a great sigh. "I'm tired," she said. "How I loathe being old."

Colin put a hand on her shoulder.

"Pleased with yourself, aren't you?" she responded. He smiled down at her.

"You've set society abuzz, outraged your mother, and wound me around your little finger."

"You?" he protested. "Never."

"Well, you haven't," she barked. "So don't preen

yourself. Either of you." Turning, she looked at Emma again. "Well, girl, from what I can see, you'll make a decent match for him. Better than the children Catherine was pushing forward at any rate. You've my 'approval,' if you actually care for it."

"Thank you, ma'am. I do," said Emma, and meant it.

"Go along now. I'm for bed."

"Can we help . . . ?" began Colin.

"No, no." Irritated, she waved them away. As they left the room, they passed the two footmen coming to help her upstairs.

"Well," said Emma when they were in the carriage once again. "Thank God that is over."

"It appears that you did splendidly."

"She made me quake in my shoes," said Emma.

"She's known for it," Colin acknowledged. "But somehow, I think you held your own."

"Perhaps." Emma gave him a sidelong glance. "I think I shall make your Aunt Celia my model," she declared. "I intend to be just like her when I am older."

"Then I shall cast up my accounts like Uncle Harold and leave you to it," Colin answered at once.

"When did he die?" wondered Emma.

"Five years ago. She was a different creature before that. I understand they were very happy together."

"Ah." Emma contemplated this new information, trying to imagine the intimidating Lady Burrington as a happy wife.

"However, I cannot believe you could be as crusty as Aunt Celia, not after watching you charm Wrotham and Cousin Gerald at dinner."

"I sat and smiled and agreed with whatever was said to me," she retorted.

"The perfect woman," he teased.

"If you truly think so, my lord, you have made a disastrous mistake in offering for me."

"I know."

"You know what? That you have made a mistake, or that I am not—"

"I know that I have made a very wise bargain indeed," he said. "I expect that in a week or so, you will have my mother eating out of your hand as well."

"You expect too much, my lord. I don't think anything will reconcile her to this match."

"You will find a way."

Emma looked doubtful.

"You will be meeting many of the leaders of society tonight," Colin continued, his tone businesslike.

Emma nodded. This must mean a great deal to him, she thought. He was marrying her against the wishes of his mother and amid a storm of gossip. No doubt he wanted her to impress his friends. She listened carefully to his descriptions of the people they were about to encounter.

The baroness, Caroline and her husband, and the Bellinghams met them, as prearranged, in front of Cardington house, and they went in to the ball together. The room was already filled with dancing couples when they entered, but their striking group still attracted a good deal of attention. The baroness wore violet the color of her eyes. Caroline's gown of deep orange set off her russet hair to perfection. Emma was like the moon on water in her blue and silver. And the men were all handsome, in different ways, in their evening dress. However, the extended stares and murmur of talk had little to do with appearance. The unexpected announcement of baron St. Mawr's engagement to an unknown woman had raced through the *ton* and roused wild speculation.

"Courage," said Colin, his hand at Emma's elbow. "Let us greet our hostess." Gathering his party with a glance, he led them to the corner where Lady Cardington was standing.

She broke off her conversation at once and stepped forward, her eyes gleaming with curiosity. Colin fixed his mother with a stern gaze. Obediently, she moved to meet Lady Cardington. "Felicity, may I present Lady Emma Tarrant?" she said.

"How do you do?" She examined Emma closely, seeming a bit surprised by what she found.

Conscious of the gaze of many pairs of eyes, Emma greeted her in return.

"How odd that we have not met before," said Lady Cardington. "I thought I knew positively everyone." Her tone implied that those she did not know were of no consequence.

"I have been living abroad," Emma replied, keeping a rein on her temper.

"Really? Where did you find to live with that monster Napoleon on the loose?" Once more, her tone was incredibly patronizing. It implied that since Lady Cardington did not know of any place where she might have lived, Emma must have resided in a back slum.

"I was last in Constantinople," said Emma tartly, "well out of his reach."

"Ah."

Emma was certain that Lady Cardington had no idea where Constantinople might be.

"Such a lovely city," she added, gazing right at her hostess. "And in such a vital position for English interests."

"Er . . ." said Lady Cardington.

"There is nothing more beautiful than the flush of dawn on the straits of the Bosphorus with the golden dome of Sofia hovering over them. Don't you agree?"

Coldly, Lady Cardington met her eyes. She was not to be bested as easily as this, her expression insisted. "I really couldn't say," she responded, as if Emma had asked about something quite uninteresting, and vaguely inappropriate. "I find travel so fatiguing, and most of the places one is urged to visit are so dirty and common. How glad you must be to be home again, among *fashionable* people."

Her threat was entirely clear. If Emma truly joined battle with her, she would spoil her chances in society. Bristling, Emma started to speak. Then she hesitated, remembering Colin's wish for her success. Presumably, this insufferable woman was a friend of his family. Emma became conscious of the baroness at her side. She would enjoy it so much if Emma was rejected by her peers. Swallowing her stinging reply and smiling blandly, Emma answered, "Of course."

"Shall we dance?" said Colin, taking her arm and leading her away. They joined a set forming at the end of the room and waited for the musicians to strike up.

"I cannot remain mute and smiling under that kind of questioning," said Emma, her anger reemerging now that the chance of offending Lady Cardington was past.

Colin shook his head.

"If you want a sweet, compliant ninnyhammer, you can no doubt find one," she added.

"Scores of them," he answered.

"Do you not think you have made a mistake, my lord?" said Emma through gritted teeth. "I despise that sort of woman—saying the most cutting things she can imagine in that syrupy voice, implying the worst without having the courage to accuse one of anything."

"I can't bear her myself," agreed Colin.

This startled Emma out of her anger. "Then why are we here?"

He took her hand as the music began, and they executed the opening steps of the quadrille before he answered, "Because others do not share your very sensible attitude toward Lady Cardington. She is one of the leaders of fashion, and this invitation will establish you, get you vouchers for Almack's, show society that you are to be reckoned with."

"I am surprised she invited me, then," replied Emma. "She certainly did not seem pleased to have me here."

Colin looked suddenly haughty. "She had no choice."

This made Emma's eyebrows come up. "Really, my lord baron? Why not?"

"I have a certain amount of influence."

"Over that woman?" Emma looked skeptical.

"Over her youngest son, who is botching his military career."

"I see. Enough to get me invited, but not to make her polite to me."

Colin smiled. "I do not think anyone could manage that."

"Thank you very much, my lord."

"She isn't polite to anyone," he assured her. "She is one of the most disliked women in London."

"And still a leader of fashion," marveled Emma. "I begin to see what I have missed, being abroad all these years."

Colin laughed down at her, and realized he was enjoying himself. This was the first of these social gatherings he had enjoyed since he came home from France, he thought.

What he did not realize was how evident this was to others in the crowd. A dozen mothers saw their hopes of a grand match definitely die. Several very young ladies grew quite petulant with their partners. And a number of men were greatly intrigued. Emma's beauty had already struck them. Now, they wondered what sort of woman could draw a smile like that from the somber Baron St. Mawr.

When the music ended, Emma found herself besieged by partners seeking an introduction and a dance. When she glanced at Colin, he shrugged slightly, leaving the choice to her. She hesitated. She had almost forgotten how much she loved dancing. Going through the measures with Colin had been exhilarating. But of course she could not stand up for every set with him. She looked up at him again. He was smiling at her, as if he followed her thoughts. A spark of the excitement she had felt years ago at her first ball reawakened in Emma's breast. She acknowledged one of the hopeful gentlemen and was presented. In another moment they were taking their places on the floor.

"She is making a great hit," said the baroness sourly to her son some time later.

He merely nodded.

"I think *you* might dance with someone else," she accused.

"No."

The baroness glared at him. She was extremely annoyed at the way things had fallen out. She was not a good loser. "Aren't you afraid she will lose her heart to one of those gallants?" she asked, following Colin's gaze to where Emma twirled in the arms of a duke's heir.

"No," he said again. It was obvious to him that Emma was finding joy not in her partners but in the act of dancing and freedom from the worries that had plagued her for years.

"You are the most infuriating person in existence," fumed his mother.

"So you have often said, Mother," was his absent reply.

Which positively proved her point, the baroness thought, watching him gaze at the woman who was to be his wife with absolutely no concern for her own feelings about the matter.

When the last set was announced, Emma rejected all offers and went in search of her promised husband. She found him saying good-bye to his sister just outside the ballroom. When she approached, Caroline held out her hands and said, "I hope we will be friends. Will you come and see me?"

"I'd like that," replied Emma.

"Nicky will love your hair," Caroline added obscurely.

"He'll likely rub barley sugar in it," warned Lord Wrotham, his tone indulgent.

"Caroline's son," said Colin, in answer to Emma's look.

"He doesn't do that any longer," objected Caroline at the same time. She seemed ready to argue the point, but her husband urged her toward the stairs. "Come soon," she called over her shoulder.

"Mother is gone as well," said Colin. "Your father escorted her home."

Emma made a face.

"Are you ready to leave?"

"The last dance is a waltz," objected Emma.

"Ah. We could not possibly go, then."

Looking up at him, Emma felt a tremor in the region of her heart. She was in danger of developing feelings for this man, she realized with a jolt. That would never do. It was no part of the sane, sensible bargain she had made. "Perhaps we should go," she said.

"No, indeed," he responded, and offered his arm.

In the ballroom he encircled her waist and she put a hand on his shoulder. His fingers curled firmly around hers—solid, reliable. Whatever the future held, this man would not publicly humiliate her as Edward had done, Emma realized, and her eyes briefly threatened to fill with tears.

"What is it?" asked Colin.

"Nothing."

He guided her expertly onto the floor, and they began to whirl in a great circle of dancing couples. "Do you wish to make a wedding journey?" asked Colin after a while.

"Out of England? No. I have had more than enough of foreign travel."

He nodded. "I thought we might go down to Trevallan."

"What is that?"

"The seat of the St. Mawrs. In Cornwall."

"Your home? Certainly. I should like to see it."

"It is traditional," he answered, almost apologetic.

"Of course," said Emma.

He gazed down at her. "It remains only to set the wedding day."

"I am at your disposal, my lord."

She looked so cool and elegant, everything a nobleman could want in a wife, Colin thought. So why did he feel a twinge of disappointment? "It makes no difference to you?"

"I need some time to prepare," she conceded. "But there is not a great deal to do, since we will have a small private ceremony."

"The date your father gave is one week from today," he pointed out.

"A week!" She looked startled, and somewhat anxious.

"We are not bound by it," he added.

"No. I . . . I suppose I can be ready by then."

An awkward silence fell between them. Neither appeared to know exactly what to say. They turned through the dance for several long minutes, outwardly calm and graceful.

The music ended. Colin and Emma faced one another. "So, shall we stay with that day then?" he asked, a bit abruptly.

"I . . . all right," she answered with equal unease.

He gave a single nod as they made their way off the floor and went to wait for their cloaks.

Robin Bellingham was lying in wait at the foot of the stairs. "I wanted to speak to you," he said to Emma.

Very conscious of Colin at her back, she stopped and smiled at her brother.

"I . . . we've had no chance to get acquainted," he stammered. "I should like to."

"So should I," replied Emma warmly. "We will have many opportunities now. Come and see me."

"Yes. Thank you." Robin flushed a little, obviously wanting to say more. Emma waited. "I never liked what Father did to you," her brother blurted out. "I think it was wrong. If I could have done anything, I would. Truly. It was just that I was . . ." He faltered, clenching his fists.

"You were ten years old," said Emma. "There was nothing you could do."

"I might have said something," said Robin. "If I had understood what . . ."

"But you did not. And you must not feel yourself responsible in any way." She smiled. "Besides, that is all past. We shall make up for it by being very good friends to one another now."

His face cleared. "Yes. I should like that."

"Come and see me," repeated Emma.

He nodded and watched Colin lead her off to where the carriage waited. Only when they were driving away did Robin remember that he still did not know where she was staying. Colorfully, he cursed his own ineptitude.

Chapter Six

Emma and Colin were married at Saint George's in Hanover Square on a July morning that glowed with rich golden light. The climbing rose that twisted about the church door waved like a scarlet banner against the deep blue of the sky as they went in to take their vows. Only the families had been invited, and a few of Colin's friends from his military days who were in London. Yet it was still a marked contrast to her first hurried marriage ceremony, Emma thought, as the music rang through the church and the bishop, a connection of the Warehams, awaited them at the altar.

Then, it had been only herself and Edward crowded into a small parish office, with a pair of housemaids called in to witness the transaction. The initial exhilaration she had felt upon taking her destiny into her own hands had faded by that time, and after a very long, jolting carriage ride, Emma had been worn out, and yet still alert and fearful of pursuit. Edward had simmered with ill-tempered eagerness to get the thing done. At the time, Emma had been pleased, thinking that he desperately wanted to make her his wife. What he had wanted was to fix his claim to her fortune, she thought wearily now. Her money was the only thing about her that had ever really excited him.

Colin took her hand, ready to slip the ring onto her finger at the bishop's bidding. Was she making another dreadful mistake? Emma wondered suddenly.

The last week had flown past in a whirl of preparations. There had been no time for calm, rational thought. But she had been prey to wild fluctuations of emotion. At one moment, she found Colin warm and beguiling; at other times, he seemed cool and distant, barely interested in what she was saying. He had the capacity to shut out everyone and everything, she had discovered. And at those times, the expression that shadowed his face was chilling.

Emma's gaze swept along the church pews. There was her father beaming in the first row, flanked by Robin, the young brother she scarcely knew. Some cousins of her mother's, total strangers, sat behind them. On the other side of the church were Colin's mother, her expression stiff; his sister Caroline, smiling beside her husband; his great-aunt Celia, benignly autocratic; and an assortment of other relatives. The only touch of gaiety among the onlookers was provided by the bright military uniforms in the back, where grins and friendly jostling were also visible.

It was time for her to say the words—the final moment for changing her mind. She looked up at Colin. He met her questioning gaze steadily. His violet eyes showed nothing of his feelings, and Emma had a sudden intense wish to know what they were. But he simply looked at her, as the pause in the ceremony grew to an awkward length. Emma heard the onlookers begin to stir in the pews behind them. Her father harrumphed softly, like a bull elephant about to give way to panic. Then Colin raised one eyebrow. One corner of his mouth quirked up very slightly as he continued to meet her gaze. Despite his frequent melancholy, he was a man who laughed, Emma thought. That was a hopeful sign. It couldn't be a dreadful mistake to marry a man who laughed. Taking a deep breath, she gave her promises. A collective sigh, conveying a variety of emotions, went through the congregation. Colin's violet eyes showed a subtle twinkle, almost as if he understood what had gone through everyone's mind, including Emma's. She couldn't help but smile up at him in response as the bishop pronounced them wed.

The wedding luncheon provided by George Bellingham for the small group invited to witness the ceremony was lavish. He had wanted to ask many more people to attend, and it had taken the combined efforts of Emma and Colin's aunt Celia to convince him that this was inappropriate. He consoled himself by procuring every delicacy available to serve his guests and by providing cases and cases of champagne.

The military men greeted this bounty with loud enthusiasm, and at once appropriated several cases for their own use. As family members eyed them with disapproval, envy, indulgence, or amusement—depending on their temperaments—the men gathered in one corner of the room and began proposing toast after toast among themselves, downing a full glass of the fine wine with each. After a bit, a few of the young cousins from both sides joined them. Robin Bellingham, also welcomed into their revels, soon found his senses swimming as they emptied one bottle after another with increasing exuberance.

The time came for Robin to give his own toast to the bride and groom and assembled company. As he wavered to his feet, he felt powerful and sophisticated and suave. Gesturing with his glass, he spoke, and was horrified to hear his voice slur over the words he had so carefully prepared. "I wish every happinessh to my shister and her hushband." Flushing bright red, he sank back into his chair, only to miss the waiting seat and tumble to the floor, amid loud laughter from the soldiers around him and cries of, "He's drunk as a wheelbarrow."

"Oh, dear," Emma murmured, watching Robin stumble to his feet, aided by several soldiers who were hardly in better condition. "Oh, dear," she repeated, as the whole group crashed to the floor together and lay there in a heap laughing and cursing.

Colin laughed as well. Emma threw him a look. "Someone should take Robin in hand," she said.

"From the look of your father, he'll be well raked over the coals."

Seeing her father's thunderous scowl, she shook her head. "That's a sure way to make it worse."

"He's a young man finding his feet on the town," Colin added. "Not much harm in it."

"You did the same, I suppose?"

"No doubt I would have, if I hadn't joined the army."

She acknowledged it with a nod. "This doesn't worry me so much." She watched Robin waver into his chair once more, a foolish grin on his face. "But the gambling . . ." She shivered a little. "He never came to see me, as he said he would," she remarked.

Colin merely sipped from his glass, still watching his friends. They looked far older than the boys they had been the first time they all drank together, he thought. And of course, there were many faces missing—far too many.

"I wanted to explain to him the dangers of gaming," Emma went on.

Colin started to speak, but she foresaw his comment before he could make it. "He probably wouldn't listen."

"Youngsters seem to find that difficult," he agreed.

"Perhaps *you* could speak to him," she suggested. "You must know precisely how to influence young men, since you commanded so many of them in the war. I'm sure he would listen to you."

The muscles of Colin's face had stiffened.

"You would have every excuse to speak to him," she added, "having become a member of his family. And your opinion must have greater weight than—"

"I don't see why," interrupted Colin in a rather harsh voice.

Emma turned to him in surprise.

"He wouldn't appreciate my interference," he added abruptly.

"But—"

"In fact, I already mentioned the matter when I returned his notes of hand, and he clearly resented it very much indeed."

"Things are different now. You have become—"

"The boy has a father, friends—a sister, for that matter. This is none of my affair." His tone was forbidding.

"It is everyone's affair when young men are being ruined," snapped Emma angrily. "And a matter of simple kindness to make some effort—"

"I contracted to marry you, not your family," he said sharply. "I'm sure Robin will get a bellyful of advice just from those in this room. I shan't add to it."

His tone was so cutting that Emma was silenced. She sat straighter in her chair, her jaw clenched on further protests. Here were the limits of marriage as a rational bargain, she told herself. There were things she could expect, and others she could not count on. And if she stepped over those boundaries, Colin would make it very clear. It was not an experience she cared for in the least. In fact, she hated it, and she longed to tell him so in the strongest possible terms. But Emma had long ago had her fill of public scenes. Besides, she had agreed to the bargain, she reminded herself, controlling her anger with the skill of long practice. She had known quite clearly that this was no impulsive love match, and been thankful for it. She had wanted stability as much as Colin. But she would see that she remembered his limits in future, she vowed, because just now she felt like spitting.

There were more toasts from the military group, followed by a long, rambling, slightly incomprehensible one from Lord Wrotham, which had Caroline tugging at his coattail to get him to sit down before he finally finished.

Colin sat silent through all of this, his face somber and impassive. Seeing his old friends again, and something about the conversation as well, had roused the grim memories he always strove to keep at bay. Scenes from wartime flooded his mind, and most particularly faces—very young faces, of those who had died under his command. He had had far more than his fill of trying to guide young men past the shoals of life. It had brought him some satisfaction, but mainly pain—pain that did not go away.

A brief grimace escaped Colin's rigid control. He was doing his best to put all that behind him now, but his best wasn't very impressive. At moments like this, he despaired of success. Glancing briefly at Emma, he considered again a question that had been plaguing him ever since the marriage had been set. Was he taking advantage of her? He had been honest about the darkness that the war had left in him, but not about its extent. There was no way to convey that to one who had never experienced war. And even if he could, such revelations could only frighten and repel her.

His jaw set. Things were best left as they were. He was giving her an honored name and a secure home. And he was well able to go on playing the part he had assumed at his homecoming. Marriage would do nothing to change that.

Suddenly, Colin found he could not tolerate another moment of the noise and jollity of the party. "We must be on our way," he said rather abruptly to Emma. "It is nearly four, and it is a long journey to Cornwall."

Silently, without looking at him, she rose and gathered her things.

Colin frowned slightly as he too rose and offered his arm. They did not speak as Emma took it.

There was a flurry among the crowd. A loudly congratulatory group, formed mainly of military officers, escorted them to Colin's comfortable traveling carriage, which was waiting outside with their luggage already tied in back. Comments shouted by some of Colin's old friends made Emma flush.

They climbed in, and Colin struck the carriage roof with his stick to signal the driver. "At last," he said as they started to move away.

Emma waved through the window, and then sank back on the cushions as the wheels rattled over the cobblestones taking them out of London. She had done it, she thought—the mistake she had sworn never to repeat. She had married a man she hardly knew, and here she was alone with him, as she would be for the next few weeks. Now she would find out what he was really like—the quirks and impulses that made up his true nature—and experience told her that she would not find the process pleasant.

Colin, gazing at her profile from the other side of the carriage, found it startlingly forbidding. "It looks as if we shall have good weather for the drive," he said.

Emma made a sound. It could not have been described as actually impolite, but it was far from encouraging.

"Weddings are exhausting," Colin added.

"Are they?" she replied. "I have been to only two." She continued to gaze out the window at the passing street scene. "And the first one scarcely counted as a ceremony," she added under her breath.

Colin didn't hear the addition. "I have found them so," he told her. "So often the gaiety seems forced."

"Forced," repeated Emma rather tartly. "Really."

"Perhaps I mean artificial," he amended. "In most cases, the event simply cements an alliance between two families. Sometimes the two people involved hardly know each other. Why pretend otherwise?"

"Why indeed?"

He saw his mistake. "Of course, I did not mean that today—"

"There is no need to elaborate, my lord. I understand you very well."

"You know that I am most pleased to be married to you, Emma."

"Pleased. Yes, of course."

"I was speaking in general terms. It had nothing to do with us."

"On the contrary, it was very much to the point. We hardly know each other, after all."

"I thought we had come to a comfortable understanding," he objected.

"Comfortable?" The word almost exploded out of her.

"Will you stop repeating everything I say? What is wrong with you?"

Finally, she turned to him. "Wrong? With me? Nothing at all, my lord. You are the one complaining of fatigue."

"I did not complain of fatigue. I merely remarked—"

"Sleep if you like," interrupted Emma. "You needn't be concerned for me. I shall be very happy not to talk."

"I thought you had more sense than to be offended by general remarks," he said.

"I am not the least offended by your opinion of weddings," she replied hotly. "No doubt you are quite correct."

"Then what has overset you?" he demanded. "I have never seen you so prickly."

"Have you not? Well, I suppose we shall both learn a great many things about each other in the next few days," was the sharp reply. Emma gripped the sill of the coach window so tightly her knuckles whitened. She was furious. It went beyond anything he deserved, but she couldn't seem to quell the rage that had erupted in her.

Colin examined her face, half turned away from him again. His slow, inexorable anger hadn't really been kindled, but he did feel impatient. "We won't learn much in this idle sparring. What is the matter?"

"Nothing," cried Emma, defeated by her own emotions. "Just let me be!"

Silence fell in the carriage. The sound of hooves on the cobblestone, the cries of street vendors, seemed suddenly loud. They slowed, and the vehicle swayed on its springs as the driver negotiated a turn in the narrow London street. They had reached the main south road, Emma noted mechanically as the coach picked up speed. Soon, the outskirts of the city appeared, and after a little while longer, they were traveling through countryside.

Emma's anger faded with the turning wheels. She had been a bit hasty, she thought. What man would agree, on his wedding day, to assume responsibility for advising a wild young relative that he had barely met? It was a good deal to ask. And whether or not it was reasonable, she didn't want this kind of marriage. She didn't want it to begin in quarreling and coldness. She remembered the word Colin had used—comradeship. Their bargain had been based on that, and she had welcomed the idea. Was it already lost, in just a few hours?

She was afraid to turn and look at Colin. She was afraid she would see the sort of rage and distaste Edward had directed at her whenever she made any complaint or demand. The thought of facing that sort of hostility again made her feel almost physically sick.

"I think you will like Trevallan," said Colin calmly. There was no hint of rancor in his tone.

Emma took a breath.

"It is built on cliffs above the sea," he continued. "A stone house, for which one is very grateful during storms."

She let herself lean back against the seat, releasing her grip on the window.

"Not that the climate is violent," Colin went on. "In fact, I believe you will be surprised at how warm it is at this time of year. But we do get some weather off the ocean, of course."

Emma faced him. He met her eyes gravely, but one

corner of his mouth was quirked slightly up, and his
dark brows were raised just a bit.

"Truce?" he said.

Something deep inside Emma relaxed. She had not
made a dreadful mistake. She was not a foolish, headstrong child any longer. She had made a sensible, well-
considered bargain. And it would be kept. They were
both quite capable of controlling their emotions. "Is
there a village near the house?" she asked.

Colin hesitated, as if he wanted to say something
else, then nodded.

Much later, Emma woke from a light doze to find the
late summer sunset just fading from the sky. Blinking,
she watched a flight of blackbirds take off from a huge
oak beside the road and dip and wheel in the last glow, a
confetti of black silhouettes against the red stripe at the
horizon. The driver of the coach was turning off the
road into a narrow lane bordered by high hedges. In a
few minutes, he turned the team again, into the drive of
a large house built of gray stone.

"What is this?" asked Emma.

"The home of a friend of mine," said Colin. "We are
staying here tonight."

"A bride visit?" asked Emma, a little dismayed.

"No, Ralph is not here. He merely offered me the
use of the place."

"Instead of an inn?"

"I do not intend to spend my wedding night in a
common inn," Colin declared a touch haughtily.

Emma raised her eyebrows at his tone. "I beg your
pardon, my lord baron," she murmured.

He smiled slightly. "It is not the sort of occasion for
clumsy inn servants knocking to ask if we require things
that we do not require, or crowds of drinkers raising a
din in the taproom at an . . . inopportune moment."

Emma had stiffened. He had no way of knowing
how closely this described elements of her first wedding

night, she told herself. He meant nothing by it. Certainly he was not taunting her. And what lay ahead was nothing like the past. But she could not stop an unwelcome flood of memories that kept her still and silent as the carriage stopped before the front door of the house.

It was opened by a footman as soon as they pulled up. One of their own servants was already at the carriage door, folding down the steps so that they could descend. Colin turned to get out. It took Emma a moment to gather her wits enough to step down onto the gravel drive and enter the fine front hall.

It was obvious that the staff had received advance orders. They were cordially greeted by the housekeeper and shown the suite of rooms prepared for them on the second floor—a spacious parlor with a comfortable bedchamber opening out on either side. Their luggage was brought up and stowed. After that, everyone disappeared, leaving them alone.

Emma's nervousness increased. Telling herself not to be foolish, she went to one of the casement windows, open on the soft evening air, and looked out over the back of the property. There was just enough light left to see that the lawns sloped down to a broad, meandering stream where clumps of willows dangled their yellowing leaves into the water. Several horses grazed in the lush grass on the opposite bank. As she watched, a trio of swans drifted into view, very white against the dark water, floating effortlessly across the surface of the stream, their necks curved in arcs of utter grace. She heard footsteps behind her, and then Colin's voice close to her ear. "It's beautiful, isn't it?"

"Yes."

"I visited here often when I was a boy. There is a summerhouse in the midst of those willows there"—he pointed, his hand brushing her shoulder—"where one is surrounded by whispering leaves."

"It sounds lovely," she said, too aware of his nearness.

"Perhaps there will be time to show it to you tomorrow." His arms slid around her waist from the back.

Emma tried to relax against him, but she couldn't quite manage it. She was trembling slightly, she noticed, and she began to fear that she was going to make an utter fool of herself. She pulled out of his embrace. "I just . . . excuse me a moment," she said, and moved quickly into one of the adjoining bedchambers, closing the door behind her.

Everything was completely different, including herself, Emma insisted silently, as she stood rigid in the luxurious room, fists clenched at her side. But all she could think of was that night eight years ago, when she had been left alone with her new husband in the bedchamber of a run-down inn and suffered the first great disillusionment of her marriage.

After a very long day of travel and tension over whether they were pursued, they had both been tired, Emma supposed. She had been exhausted, and disappointed by the haste and plainness of the wedding itself. She desperately wanted some sort of reassurance—a declaration of love, a promise for the future, even a simple smile to say that despite the difficulties, he was glad to be there with her.

But Edward had just stripped off his coat and begun to struggle with the bootjack, taking off his muddy boots.

Not knowing exactly what to do, Emma had laid aside her cloak and gloves and taken the pins from her bonnet, setting it on the wide window ledge. The only furniture in the room was a large four-poster bed. There wasn't space for anything else.

When she turned around again, Edward had removed his shirt and was standing before her wearing only riding breeches. He was smiling at last, but it was not the sort of smile Emma had looked for. Thinking of it now, Emma realized that it was rather predatory. He had stepped over and turned the key in the door, saying, "We don't want to be disturbed, eh?"

And then he had come and given her one of his crushing kisses that mashed her lips against her teeth. He pulled at her gown, and grew impatient when he couldn't find the fastenings. "We'd best get into bed," he'd said, drawing back. "This room's damn cold." And with that he had turned his back, taken off his breeches, and climbed into the high bed, leaving Emma standing beside it, trembling.

Somehow, she had stumbled out of her clothes. He had enjoyed watching that, she realized now. He had always enjoyed it when she was feeling clumsy and afraid. When she got into the bed, he had jerked her against him and given her another bruising kiss. His body was hot and seemed full of sharp angles. Very soon after that, he rolled on top of her, fumbled for a moment, and then consummated their marriage. When Emma could not restrain a small cry of pain, he had laughed. And though she had tried to tell herself since then that he had mistaken her reaction for enjoyment, she knew it wasn't true.

A knock at the door made her jump. "Emma?" said Colin.

No two men could be more different, she reminded herself. Colin found no enjoyment in tormenting others, and he certainly had not married her for her fortune. But though she called up the memory of his kiss, she still could not move.

"Emma?" he repeated. "Is something wrong?"

She was being ridiculous, Emma told herself. She was not a girl any longer, but a grown woman. She had made a bargain. It was too late to regret it or draw back now, and in any case, she kept the promises she made. Moving a bit jerkily, she went to the door and opened it.

Colin was standing just outside. He examined her face very carefully as she emerged, but said only, "They've brought supper. Are you hungry?"

She had no idea, but the respite was more than welcome.

A small table had been set up before the fireplace,
where a fire burned despite the mildness of the evening.
There were slices of cold chicken and fresh bread, a
round of cheese, and a compote of apples and pears that
gave off a rich, fruity scent. Colin poured a glass of wine
and offered it to her. Emma took it eagerly and drank
nearly half in one quick swallow before seating herself
on one side of the table.

Colin raised one eyebrow and seemed about to
speak. Then he thought better of it and took the other
chair. "Ralph and I were at school together," he offered
as he began to fill their plates. "We became fast friends
at the age of six, when we discovered a mutual passion
for ferrets."

Emma smiled, partly from relief. She was hungry, she
realized, extremely hungry. She began to eat.

"He had actually brought one of his favorites with
him to school," Colin went on. "And he managed to
keep it, secretly, living in his pocket for nearly a week
before the masters found out. My admiration for him
never wavered after that."

"One can see why," replied Emma. She drank deeply
of her wine again.

During their meal, Colin chatted amiably about the
house and his friend Ralph and the adventures they had
shared there. His steady voice soothed Emma as much
as the food and wine. And she was soon calling herself
six kinds of idiot for her earlier behavior. By the time
they rose from the table, a mellow glow had replaced
her tension, and she felt prepared for whatever was to
come. Indeed, she didn't want to put it off any longer,
for fear she would lose her nerve again. Taking a quick
breath, she marched up to Colin and put her arms
around his neck.

He looked a little startled.

"I'm ready," she declared.

"Ready?" he echoed.

"Yes." The word came out loud. She had had more
wine than she was used to, Emma realized. But that was

probably all to the good. Standing on tiptoe, she placed her lips on Colin's and closed her eyes.

He gave her only a light kiss. "Ready for what, precisely?"

"To . . . to do my wifely duty," she asserted. She was not going to think of anything at all, she decided. And she felt much better now in any case.

"Duty?" he repeated, sounding half amused, half outraged.

"Yes." She tugged at his neck, trying to pull his head down to her again.

"Is that how you see it?"

"I do not go back on my bargains," Emma declared, slightly irrelevantly. "I've married you, and I know what that means."

One side of his mouth twitched. "Do you indeed?"

"Of course I do!" The wine was like a muffling blanket over her wits. "I'm not a child."

His violet eyes gazed very directly into hers. "Do you want to tell me what is the matter?" he asked.

"Nothing," Emma insisted. "Are you going to kiss me?" she added a bit querulously.

Colin gazed at her for one more long moment, then said, "Oh yes, I am going to kiss you." He pulled her close and did so—slowly and for a long time. His lips were soft and coaxing, by turns gentle and exploratory and urgent.

Emma was dazzled. It wasn't that she had forgotten his kisses, just that old, bitter memories had diverted her from more recent ones. She let herself melt against him, feeling the strong length of his body supporting her. When she raised her head briefly, she found that colors seemed brighter. She let out her breath in a long sigh.

"Yes?" said Colin. He looked pleased with himself, and yet still perplexed about something as well.

"Perhaps it will be all right, after all," slipped out of her mouth.

"All right?"

"Not so unpleasant," she clarified.

"Unpleasant!"

"You keep repeating everything I say," Emma pointed out dreamily. Her mind was even fuzzier, and she was starting to feel extremely sleepy as well.

Colin drew back.

He had an odd look on his face, Emma mused. "We should get this over with," she suggested. "It's hard to stay awake."

"Hard to . . . !"

"You're doing it again."

His jaw hardened. "It has been a tiring day," he said. "You should get some rest."

She was too surprised to answer.

Colin escorted her into the bedchamber where her luggage had been placed. Her legs were wobbly, Emma noted. And the walls were showing an inexplicable tendency to waver. "Do you require assistance?" he asked crisply. "Shall I ring for one of the maids?"

"But what about the bargain?" she wondered. "You said an heir . . ."

"That is something we can consider at another time," he retorted. He turned and strode out, shutting the door with a snap behind him.

Emma had a vague sense that she had made a mistake. But fatigue was overwhelming her. She fumbled out of her clothes and put on the nightgown that had been laid across the bed. When she crawled between the sheets, there were a few bad moments when it seemed the room was spinning sickeningly around her. Then sleep descended with irresistible force.

Sometime in the night, Emma woke to a great swath of moonlight across the coverlet. The air held the scent of starched linens and river mist and was filled with the sounds of crickets. Her head ached a bit. Moments passed before she remembered where she was.

Stiffening, she sat up in bed. She remembered the events of the evening all too clearly. Wasn't one supposed to forget the idiotic things one did under the influence of alcohol? she asked silently.

With a soft groan, she put a hand to her forehead. "Not so unpleasant," she murmured aloud. "What a charming thing to say." She had been as witless and tactless as any of the budding debutantes Colin had refused to marry, she thought. No doubt the same thing had occurred to him.

What had come over her? She was *not* the sort of person who indulged in groundless fears or made great fusses over small matters. She did not enact dramatic scenes. She was reasonable, practical, clear-headed. She *never* overindulged in wine or spirits.

Emma groaned softly again.

Unable to sit still, she threw back the covers and went to look for her dressing gown. When she had put it on, she quietly opened the door into the sitting room and stepped through.

A few coals still glowed in the fireplace. With moonlight streaming through the windows, she could see that the remains of their supper had been cleared away, though the table and chairs had been left in front of the hearth. The sofa and armchairs on the other side of the room looked gray and ghostly. The ticking of the mantel clock was barely audible, and simply emphasized the silent emptiness.

Emma went over to the door that led into the other bedchamber. It was securely closed, the bland white panels offering her no information. She could open it and walk in, she thought. She was married; she had the right. But the idea was intimidating. Did she propose to wake her new husband from a sound sleep in the middle of the night to . . . what, apologize? To explain that she had been thinking of the disappointments of her first marriage, and that had made her act so irrationally?

Emma shook her head and turned away from the door, only to be stopped by a sound from within Colin's bedchamber.

As she turned back, it came again, sharp and exigent—a cry or a protest. It was his voice, yet so harsh and agitated that she just barely recognized it. Even as she wondered, she heard it once more. It sounded like, "No!"

"Colin?" said Emma tentatively.

There was no response. Probably, she hadn't spoken loudly enough to be heard through the door, Emma thought. After a brief hesitation, she grasped the door-knob. Taking a breath, she readied herself to step inside. She twisted the knob, and found that it wouldn't turn. She tried turning it in the other direction; it rattled a little, but didn't move. The door was locked.

Emma took a step backward. He'd locked the door against her. He had quite consciously shut her out of his bedchamber.

Standing alone in the silent parlor, she wrapped her arms around her waist. Was he so angry over her behavior tonight that he didn't want her in his room? she wondered. But he hadn't seemed so when they parted earlier; she could remember that much. She remembered his kiss as well—vividly. What could have led him, after that, to go into his room and turn the key in the lock?

She heard another sound from within—an agitated muttering that rose and fell for nearly a minute before silence surrounded her again. She drew her arms tighter around her body. What was it that he did not wish her to know or see?

Emma waited for a long time outside that locked door. Though she strained her ears, she heard nothing further as the moon shadows wheeled across the carpet and the crickets continued to rasp outside. When at last she returned to her own room and to bed, she did not sleep. She lay staring at the pale canopy over her bed and wondering what unexpected darkness lay at the heart of this marriage on which she had gambled every-thing.

•   •   •

After six days of hard traveling south and west, they arrived at Trevallan on the coast of Cornwall just at twilight on a still, warm August day. Leaning out of the carriage as they drove up, Emma could see the outlines of a long stone building with many windows—only two of them lit. The air smelled of sea salt and evergreens; spines of gray stone pushed through the earth here and there on the property. There was a good feel to the place, she thought, a kind of energy in the atmosphere that penetrated even her deep fatigue.

Though Emma had not noticed anyone along the road, somehow the staff had been made aware of their approach. When they climbed stiffly down from the carriage and walked through the wide front door, they found a long line of servants waiting to greet them in the cavernous great hall. Candlelight illuminated the white aprons of the housemaids and starched collars of the men against a backdrop of dark wood and tapestries and swaths of thick shadow. Emma was tired from the long jolting journey, but she summoned up reserves of strength to smile and respond to the introductions of the housekeeper and other senior servants. The housemaids and footmen merely curtsyed or bowed as she was led past them.

Everyone was very kind, but fatigue made the offers of assistance, the well-cooked dinner, and the covert appraisals by the older servants something of a blur. Emma was very glad to go to bed early. "Her ladyship always sleeps in this room," the housekeeper told her complacently as she showed her into a large square bed-chamber. "The master's through there, with a dressing room between."

Emma looked at the indicated doorway. It was slightly ajar. She did not go near it, however. She felt as effectively barred as if a great metal padlock secured it.

That was the way the subject of their wedding night was being treated. She had tried to say something the following morning, perhaps make amends for her child-ish behavior, as well as discover some reason for his locked door. But Colin had brushed her attempt aside as if it were a matter of no importance, and indeed not much interest to him. And yet he had shown no resentment. He had chatted with her and maintained a calm concern about the strains of the long journey. And at each inn they patronized along the way, he had engaged a separate bedchamber for her, making no move to join her there. It was as if the night had never happened. It was almost as if their marriage had never happened, and they were simply cordial acquaintances journeying together.

He was so skilled at keeping things on the surface, thought Emma as she got wearily into bed. Perhaps that was what he wanted, what he had meant by comradeship and a comfortable bargain. She, however, was finding it something of a strain. Maybe things would change now that they were settled in his old family home? As Emma fell asleep, she found herself fervently wishing that it might be so.

Though he was also tired from the journey, Colin found that sleep eluded him. He lay quiet in the thick darkness, listening to the distant rhythms of the sea and to the familiar creaking of the old house. He had many memories of this place, going back as far as memory went, but this particular arrival had brought back one of the few painful recollections he associated with Cornwall.

Just before his father died, when he was seventeen, the former baron had called Colin to him in this bedchamber and committed his mother and sister to his care. "The name is yours now, Colin," he had said, "to uphold and to carry on. I know you'll bring honor to it, lad."

The pain of that early death returned to him now. It had been so hard to lose his father. And along with the personal loss and grief, he had felt such a heavy weight of responsibility. Honor and duty—those had been his watchwords ever since, and they had almost never let him rest.

This was why he had brought Emma here first of all, he realized. As if he could present her to his dead father and show that he had done well—that the name would be carried on, that he had not forgotten his obligations despite going off to war. Though he loved Trevallan, he had hardly come here since his father's death. The atmosphere had become oppressive to him, heavy with expectation. But now, that feeling was gone; he felt as if a weight had been lifted off his chest. The place was his in a way it had never been before.

And Emma? inquired a sardonic inner voice. She was not his, Colin acknowledged. Not yet. But now that they were no longer spending their days in a jolting carriage, and their evenings in a public inn, there would no doubt be time to remedy that. He would find the cause of the apprehension and reluctance he had seen in her eyes that first night, and banish it. And then she would give way to the eager response he had felt in her more than once, he thought, and she would find he had much to show her. Much, he repeated silently as he at last fell asleep.

The rambling old stone house settled into silence. Outside, the sea wind fingered its walls, as it had done for hundreds of years. The waves murmured on the rocks below. The kitchen cat prowled through long grass, alert for the scent of field mice on the salt-laden, piney air. It was a soft, warm night, with a thin haze, like a gauzy shawl, over the stars and no moon as yet. Colin moved restlessly under the bedclothes and muttered softly in his sleep. Emma turned over without waking. Everything about the scene suggested peace and tranquillity.

But in Colin's dreams, it was far otherwise. Through his sleep, he staggered across a blood-soaked battlefield, pain sharp in his head and chest, up to his ankles in foul water and mud. As far as he could see across the ravaged terrain, dead bodies were piled in grotesque poses—arms sticking straight up, legs twisted at impossible angles, teeth bared in grimaces of rage. The soldiers' gaudy uniforms—all the colors of the rainbow—were stained in varying shades of black and red with gunpowder and blood. Acrid smoke from the guns drifted over the scene, obscuring, then revealing more corpses. A riderless horse with a gash in its side stumbled away in the distance. The only sound was the raucous call of the ravens, summoning their fellows to feast.

Dreaming, Colin staggered through this scene of carnage looking for something. He did not know what. But as he passed each corpse, he checked it, only to find, in every single case, a friend. There was Teddy Garrett, whom he had known since he was six years old and they were both uneasy newcomers at Eton. There was John Dillon, who had joined the regiment at the same time he did and soon become his closest companion among the officers. There was Jack Morley, whose gaiety and eye for the ladies had been a running joke. There was Colonel Brown, whom he had respected so deeply and made into a sort of substitute father for three entire years. Every face he looked at, he knew. All of them had died during the last few years in one or another of the battles against the French, while time and again Colin himself had gotten off with a few minor wounds, the agonies of grief, and a growing darkness of spirit. There was no escaping that desperation now. It rose like a storm cloud on the horizon and came down over him, choking and foul. Despair engulfed him; hope became a mockery. In his sleep, Colin began to moan.

The sound was deep and grating. It rose above the whisper of the waves and the hiss of the wind. It drifted through the open door of the dressing room, heavy with hopelessness and pain. It woke Emma at once.

She blinked in the darkness, gathering her faculties, searching for the emergency that she had sensed even in deep sleep. When the next moan came, she sat up, searching for the source of this frightening sound.

It did not take her long to find it. It sounded just as it had on their wedding night. Quickly, she slipped out of bed and made her way across to the dressing room. Its wooden floor was cool under her bare feet. The door on the other side was slightly open as well, and she stepped through it, her heart beating a little faster.

The room was very dim. She had to grope her way over to the bed, guided by Colin's continued harsh moans. On the small table beside it she found a candlestick and lit it, revealing Colin rigid among the tumbled bedclothes, his body slick with sweat. His head lashed back and forth on the pillow and he was repeating, through clenched teeth, the word "no."

The light washed his face, showing an expression that scared her. The muscles stood out, hard as iron. His lips were pulled back in a snarl. His brow was furrowed like a much older man's. He looked as if he was being tortured, she thought.

She took hold of his shoulder and began to shake him free of whatever horror had him in its grip. "Colin," she said. "Colin, wake up."

He twisted away from her grasp toward the farther side of the bed.

Emma scrambled up onto the mattress. Rising to her knees, she began to shake harder. "Colin," she insisted. "It's all right. It's just a nightmare. Wake up!"

With an anguished shudder and an inarticulate cry, he heaved upright, striking out with one hand as if to fend off an enemy. Emma just managed to duck under the blow. Losing her balance, she threw an arm around his bare ribs to keep from falling. "It's all right," she repeated. "It was a dream. Only a dream."

Colin went still, but he did not relax. Emma could feel the tension in his muscles and the hard rigidity of his back. "That's the trouble," he answered, in a distant, blurred voice that seemed to come from some other place, as if he wasn't truly awake yet. "It isn't just a dream. It's all true."

"What?" she said softly.

"Death. They're all dead. Shattered by bullets or run through with cold steel. All of them gone. Nothing left but to haunt me." He shuddered again, and his skin felt clammy and cold suddenly. Emma tightened her grip.

"You never knew, when you came back to camp, who it would be. Who would have fallen in that battle. You just knew that some of them wouldn't be there. Some of the friends you'd been riding with, and eating with, and drinking with the night before. After a while, you started wishing for the bullet yourself, because then . . ."

Colin stopped short, as if he'd bitten off the words. He sat straighter and looked around as if he were just taking in his surroundings and realizing where he was. He took a deep gasping breath. He turned to look at Emma, his eyes wide and dark, his mouth a grim slash. For a moment, he seemed to concentrate on identifying her. "I . . . I beg your pardon," he said.

"It's all right."

"I didn't mean to frighten you," he added.

His tone was growing more normal, and more distant, Emma thought. "I'm not frightened," she insisted, even though she was, a bit.

"I'm sorry to have disturbed—"

"No." She could feel him starting to shiver as the sweat dried on his skin. "Get under the covers," she said, urging him down.

He didn't move, but when he spoke again, his voice sounded completely normal, as if they were chatting in the carriage or attending an evening party in London. "Emma. Return to your own room. I'm sorry I exposed you to this."

This was why he locked the door, she realized. "No," she said again. When she pushed him this time, he yielded slowly and lay down, letting her pull the covers around him. "Tell me about the dream," she said.

"No."

"It might help," she argued.

"Nothing can help the dead," he replied sharply.

"Not them," she agreed. "You."

He turned his head away.

"Were you fighting?" Emma prompted.

He remained stonily silent.

"Was it one of the battles you—"

"All of the battles are over," he said harshly. "We will not speak of this."

"It seems they are not all over," she pointed out, referring to the dream.

He said nothing.

"Did you lose so many friends?" she ventured, remembering what he had said to her once.

"Yes." The word was clipped, almost as if he was angry with her.

"I'm sorry," she whispered.

Another shudder went through him. He pulled further away from her. "You must go to your own bed," he repeated.

"No," said Emma.

For the first time in months, Colin was afraid. He was afraid the horrors would spill out of him against his will and touch this woman and this place which should never be sullied by such things. "Then I will go," he said, and started to throw back the covers.

"Please don't leave me," said Emma.

The plea went through him like the sabers he had been dreaming of. "You don't understand," he cried. "I must."

"I don't want to be here alone right now. Please."

His fists clenched involuntarily. He wanted desperately to protect her. And he felt that he could only do so by leaving her. Yet she asked him to stay and give comfort he did not possess. "You don't understand," he burst out again, against his will. "I have lost every close friend. Men I loved like brothers. Toward the end, I stopped having friends. I couldn't stand to see them die."

"Oh, Colin." Her voice choked with tears.

Something about that muffled sound shook him so deeply that the images still burning in his brain tumbled out. Before he could stop himself, he was telling Emma about Teddy and Jack and Colonel Brown, about the officers and men in his company, the bonds that formed in a regiment through the horrors of battle and the lighter intervals in between. He couldn't stop himself. He described the mud and the laughter, the boredom and the fear, the wearisome years of life in camp that drained away everyday emotions and left a man empty.

Emma listened and tried to understand both the words and what might lie behind them. This was the source of his melancholy, she thought. This was the thing that set him apart. She was moved to tears more than once, but she blinked them back, not wanting to distract him and stop the flow of confidences. When at last he fell silent, staring at the ceiling, his muscles limp, she put a hand on his bare shoulder in comfort.

"You're freezing," he exclaimed. "You've been sitting there in nothing but a nightgown." Suddenly, he was aware of the thin cotton of this garment, and of the way it revealed rather than concealed the luscious curves and hollows of her body.

"I'll get under the covers," she said, and did so before he could protest. Their bodies touched at hip and shoulder. Desire seared through Colin like violence, pulsing through his body, making his hands shake with its intensity. He wanted to turn and crush her beneath him, drown every jumbled thought and feeling in a fierce torrent of sensation.

Abruptly, he shifted away from her. He couldn't touch her now. If he had frightened her somehow before, the way he was feeling now, the strength of his need, would terrify her. Silently, he struggled for control.

Predawn light was filtering through the closed curtains. The atmosphere seemed gray and almost tangible. A current of cool, brisk salt air wandered in, brushing their faces with dampness. Outside, the rush of the waves was muted by mist.

"My God," said Colin quietly. "What have I done? I've never spoken to anyone of these things. And now

I've forced them on you, who have never seen the least violence—"

"I've seen men brawling at the gaming tables," Emma interrupted. "And drawing knives on one another in the streets."

"Not the same."

"No. I know that. But it is all to the good."

Colin turned to look at her. Her face was very close. "Emma," he began.

"Don't you see? Because I have never witnessed a battle or lived in a camp, I don't have the memories that haunt you. They don't have the same power over me."

"That doesn't matter," he said. "I had no right to describe such horrors to you."

"Hearing about them is nothing to living through them," she answered evenly. "And it is not a matter of rights."

At a loss for words, he stared at a strand of her hair that had strayed across the pillows. She didn't look frightened or repulsed. He couldn't understand it. She was a woman, with all of a woman's soft graces. She had intelligence, imagination, sensitivity—all the traits that had become a curse to him as the war went on and its dreadful progress was engraved in his soul. Where did she get her strength?

"We made a bargain, remember?" said Emma, as if reading his thoughts. "I am not one of those London chits. I know what it is to endure. You don't have to shield me from hard truths."

As she spoke, a great surge of emotion went through him. He wanted to protect her from any trace of unhappiness, he realized. And yet it was too late. Like his comrades in war, she had already been subjected to far more than she deserved. It was all a muddle, he thought. He didn't know what he was feeling among all the conflicting currents pulling him this way and that. "It is too much of a burden," he murmured, wondering if he had done right to marry her. He would not have shared these dark things with one of those London chits. And what right had he to reveal them to anyone? When he had offered her comradeship, he had not imagined anything like this.

The terrible images he had planted in her consciousness lingered as Emma wondered whether the sadness would ever leave him. How could it after what he had seen and done? She had discovered his inner darkness, she thought; as she'd feared, she had uncovered the hidden depths of his nature. And they had turned out to be so different from Edward's. Instead of contemptible weakness, Colin had strength. The demons that tormented him were lost friendships and the privations of war, not risk and greed and gratification of his own obsession. She had been of no help whatever to Edward, Emma thought. And after a while, she had stopped trying, or caring. The pain of that failure remained, and she didn't know if she dared take such a risk again. And yet, she thought—comradeship, fellow feeling, endurance of hardship. These were the words Colin had used, and these were things she understood. Perhaps she still had something to offer after all, she decided, as they lay side by side, each wrestling alone with the shadows of the past.

When Emma woke at nine, she was in her own bed, and alone. Colin must have carried her here, she thought as she rose and pulled on her dressing gown. She walked quietly to his room, but it was empty. Returning to her own, she moved about the large square bedchamber, examining her new home in the light that crept in through gaps in the worn curtains. The walls were papered in a floral pattern that had long since faded to an indistinguishable wash of pinks and greens. The furniture was old as well, in the fashion of fifty years ago. The carpet was good, but the draperies had faded in the sun and no longer matched it. Emma went to a window and peered out. Her breath caught in a gasp. The ocean stretched before her, a huge blue expanse all the way to the horizon, glittering in the sun. Directly below was a narrow band of garden, and then a cliff dropping vertically to foaming waves and outcroppings of gray stone in the wild water. It was a dramatic and incredibly beautiful landscape.

"I'm amazed every time I see it again," said Colin. She turned to find him standing, already fully dressed, in the outer doorway. When he smiled at her, Emma could see no trace of his nightmare in his face.

"Are you all right?" she asked.

His face showed mild surprise. "Perfectly," he responded, as if nothing unusual had occurred in the night—or ever. He went and pulled the curtains open, first on the window she had been looking out, then on the others. Light flooded the room. "It is beautiful," he said, gazing out over the water.

It was the old Colin back again, Emma saw. And they were to resume their light cordial manner, pretending that the nightmares did not exist, that no difficulties or misunderstandings or troubles of any kind existed. She felt a pang of keen disappointment, an impulse to say something irrevocable and shake him out of his urbane placidity. But when he turned to look at her, she remembered the pain in his voice last night, and she found she couldn't quite risk the words. "It's gorgeous," she replied lightly instead. She opened one of the casements and leaned out, taking in a great gulp of the sea air. "It's so warm," she exclaimed.

"Have a care." Still smiling, he joined her at the window. "If you fall, everyone is sure to say I pushed you, as one of my ancestors is rumored to have done."

"Pushed his wife out the window?" she echoed.

"And married a neighbor's daughter only a few weeks after," added Colin.

"The blackguard," exclaimed Emma. "*I* would have come back as a ghost and driven the new bride shrieking from the house."

"Alas." His eyes twinkling, Colin shook his head.

"She was apparently made of very stern stuff. She did not frighten easily."

"You mean you do have a ghost?" cried Emma. "Of the poor wife?"

"So they claim. I have never seen her."

"I'll find her," Emma declared.

"Before you go looking, I should tell you that she was said to have locked up her daughter when she reached the age of fifteen, out of jealousy for her youth and beauty. The poor girl had nearly pined away before her father took matters in hand and made use of the window."

"Nonsense," said Emma. "I expect her husband just said that to justify himself. I suppose his second wife was quite young and beautiful?"

He cocked a dark eyebrow at her. "Only a year older than his long-suffering daughter."

"There, you see?"

"I see that you are not easily duped," he replied humorously.

"Indeed. You will have to think of a far better story than that if you wish to deceive me."

"I'll keep that in mind should I ever wish to change wives."

"Do, my lord." Emma was laughing by this time. "And also be warned that *I* would choose to haunt *you*."

"How fortunate, then, that I have no such plans," he said.

"Are there any other disreputable family members I should know about?" she asked.

"Oh, any number. Our fortunes rise from a doubtful character they say was an assassin for William, Duke of Normandy, before he came to these shores."

"Did he build this house?" she wondered.

"No, no. That was much later, when the crown needed someone to fight off pirates in the Irish Sea. The king chose the nobleman who most resembled the enemy and granted him an estate just here."

"And was he successful?" asked Emma.

"Thoroughly. The pirates were terrified of him. So were his wife and children, by all accounts."

"There appears to be a sinister trend toward tyranny among the Wareham men. I see that I have taken a great risk in marrying you, my lord."

"Indeed," he agreed. "Who knows when the tendencies of my family will surface and goad me to some desperate act?"

"I'll keep a sharp eye out," Emma assured him. "Will you show me the rest of the house? Where was your room when you were young?"

"At the other end. My mother did not care for our noise."

"Come and show me," she urged again.

He looked around her bedchamber. "The place is sadly out of repair, Emma. Mother never cared to be here, and since I joined up, I have only made a few flying visits." He frowned at the threadbare draperies. "I have not spent much thought or money on the house, and I see that it shows. It is hardly fit for a new bride."

"Well, then, it's time you looked over it and made plans for repairs," declared Emma. "And you may as well know that I have already set my heart on new wallpaper for this room. I hope you are not too attached to this pink."

He examined it more closely. "Mother always said it was the color of a diseased tongue," he told her.

"Why didn't she replace it, then?" said Emma, torn between laughter and indignation.

"She only cared about getting away to London," he replied absently. "We might do some refurbishing, I think."

"Oh, it is decided. And after the new wallpaper, I shall install some sturdy bars on these windows."

He turned to look at her, startled. Then he threw back his head and began to laugh.

The valet Reddings, who was tidying the adjoining dressing room, cocked his head like a hound on a strong scent. It had been so long since he had heard that sound that for a moment, he wasn't sure. Then he relaxed. It really was his master's laughter, which he had feared was gone forever. Deeply gratified, Reddings allowed himself a small smile.

Emma dressed, and then she and Colin made a rapid progress through the closed and muffled rooms of Trevallan. Everywhere, she threw back decaying draperies and let the sun in, suggesting new paint and cloth to brighten the dark corners. "Were you often here as a boy?" she asked when they stood in the third floor bedchamber that had been his.

"Most summers," he replied. "And whenever I could manage it on holidays. It was always a sore spot for my parents. My father would have spent a good deal of the year here, perhaps going to London only for the height of the Season. But my mother found the place deadly dull."

"She would," muttered Emma to herself.

"What?"

"Nothing. It is lovely here in summer."

"It was paradise for a boy." He looked out at the ocean, his eyes faraway.

"I think *we* should come here for summers," said Emma. "And other times as well."

"You're so certain after only one night?" he replied, smiling.

"Yes."

"I appear to have married a woman of decision."

"Didn't you know that?" Emma asked absently. "I saw gardens down below. Let us go look at them."

Colin caught her arm as she started from the room. "We will walk along the terrace on our way to the dining room," he commanded. "I want breakfast."

"Tyrant," accused Emma, matching her steps to his.

"In the blood," he answered, leading her toward the stairs. The young housemaid polishing the paneling on the landing grinned to see her master smiling at the new mistress.

"Would you like to go riding?" said Colin a bit later, over coffee and eggs and fresh baked bread with honey.

"I've probably forgotten how," said Emma. "I haven't ridden in years."

"Why not?"

A cloud passed over Emma's face. There had been little opportunity for carefree rides as she waited in shabby lodging houses wondering whether her last few pounds was being lost at the gaming tables.

Colin looked conscious of a misstep. "I keep a few horses here," he said, "eating their heads off in luxury in the stables. Let us go and see what we can find."

"I don't have a riding habit," she said regretfully.

"There are trunks of clothes in the attic. Mrs. Trelawny can find you something."

"But—"

"We'll ride along the coast," he said. "I'll show you the singing caves."

This sounded too intriguing. Emma abandoned her objections.

An hour later, she found herself mounted on a docile bay mare and dressed in a musty black velvet riding habit from the previous century. "I look ridiculous!" she complained.

"No, you don't," answered Colin. The habit had been made long ago for a young girl—perhaps even his great-aunt Celia, Colin thought—and it was tight on Emma. It clung to every contour of her body, revealing all the subtle curves that her everyday garments only suggested. Watching the rise and fall of her breasts as she breathed, Colin was roused. "Come," he said, turning his horse toward the gate.

Colin's mount was not up to his usual standards, but perhaps that was just as well, he thought, as they reached the cliff path and started along it. He did not know the level of Emma's skill, and a spirited horse might have spooked hers and sent them into danger.

Turning, he checked her position. She had a good seat and held the reins lightly, looking very much at home on the mare. She was, perhaps, paying a bit too much attention to the foam-flecked sea spreading below them and too little to the trail. But the mare knew her way and would not be tripped up by the loose stone. Taking a deep breath of the crisp salt air, he picked up the pace.

Emma followed. Though she was a little bothered by the tightness of the riding habit across her chest and shoulders, it was a small annoyance, and the glorious scenery more than made up for it. The path meandered along the headlands, each turn revealing another breathtaking vista of cliff and sea and veils of tiny flowers falling over the stone. Already, she felt completely at home on horseback, as if she had last ridden a few days ago instead of years.

"Care to try a gallop?" asked Colin when they came to a straight section of the shoreline.

Emma smiled and kicked the mare's flank, darting past him and away. With a startled exclamation, Colin gave chase, and they pounded along the sandy path with the air streaming through their hair.

Leaning over the front of the saddle, Emma felt the armhole seams give way on the riding habit. The pressure on her shoulders eased as the old thread tore and gaps opened in the cloth. Now she really looked a sight, she thought. Probably she ought to turn back, but she didn't want to. With her knees and heels, she urged the horse on.

They galloped in a great loop around a bay, pulling up on the far headland where the waves crashed on both sides of a narrow point and splashed high in the air. "Wonderful," cried Emma. She spread her arms, and more of the sleeves came loose from the bodice of her dress.

"The riding habit is not a complete success," Colin remarked.

"I think it's older than Mrs. Trelawny remembered," said Emma. "The thread is giving way."

"I see that it is. Shall we turn back?" The glimpses of pale skin through the holes in the black velvet were disturbing.

"Must we? There's no one about. You promised me singing caves."

"So I did. But there's some weather brewing. I didn't notice it earlier; I have been away so long I'm losing my weather sense."

Emma followed his pointing finger to a bank of clouds on the far horizon. "Those are miles away," she protested.

"A squall can blow up quickly on the sea."

But Emma was filled with the elation of the ride and the sea air. "Oh, come," she urged, and set her heels to the mare's flank once again, racing farther along the coastal path.

Colin spurred his mount after her, knowing that he should insist, but caught up in her gaiety. They pounded along side by side until the twisting path forced them to slow to a walk. "Where are these caves?" demanded Emma, her cheeks glowing from the exercise, her eyes bright with enjoyment. A strand of pale hair had come loose and curled along her temple.

Her beauty silenced Colin for a moment, and filled him with a sharp longing. "A little further," he said. "In the next bay. But Emma." He indicated the clouds again. They were racing in from the sea and now covered a third of the sky.

She looked. It was obvious he was right; a storm was on the way. But Emma was reveling in the first feelings of freedom she had allowed herself in a long time. "We can shelter in the caves until it passes," she said, and moved away before he could argue.

She kept her horse to the best pace she could manage, but on the winding path, that was not rapid. As the clouds raced across the sky, Emma realized that she had miscalculated. They would never be able to reach the next wide bay before the rain. She was just turning to admit as much to Colin when the first drops began.

There was a flurry of rain, like spray from the sea, and then, suddenly, a heavy drenching downpour that pounded on her head and shoulders. Gasping, Emma bent her head to keep the water out of her eyes and mouth.

Colin rode up beside her. "Give me your reins," he said. He had to repeat it in a near shout before she understood and handed them over. Leading her horse, he began to pick his way along the path, now running with water like a small stream. Slowly, they made their way toward the final headland.

Slumped under the pounding of the rain, uncomfortable in soaking wet velvet, Emma felt an odd loosening, slithering sensation. The storm was too much for the ancient riding habit, she realized then. All its seams were giving way, and the bodice was literally sliding off her in tatters. She grabbed a part of the front and tried to hold it against her breasts, but the waist of the dress was sagging over her hips now, and she had to shift her fingers to that, afraid the whole garment would abandon her for the ground. Sheets of rain sliced over her bare shoulders. Emma started to shiver with cold.

Colin could scarcely see the path, the rain was so heavy. But he knew the way from countless boyhood excursions and soon had them twisting down the cliff on a narrow shelf that slanted toward the shore. Wiping the streaming water from his eyes, he peered at the rocks. Where was the blasted entrance? There. Urging his mount forward, he rode under the tall arch of stone, pulling Emma's horse after him.

The relief was immense. From pounding rain roaring in their ears, they came into dry silence. Four feet behind, the downpour continued, but they were safely out of it, though soaked to the skin. Colin turned back to Emma, who was plucking futilely at the trailing remains of her bodice.

"My poor Emma," he said. The black dress was sliding off her as if it were made of liquid instead of cloth. Not only the seams, but the very fabric itself was giving way. Colin dismounted and went to lift her down from the mare. The riding habit completed its disintegration as he did so, ending in a sodden heap on the stone floor and leaving her standing before him clothed only in her soaked shift. The rain had turned the thin cotton nearly transparent, he noticed. Her breasts were perfectly outlined by the clinging material, their tips erect and pressing against it. The cloth clung to every curve of her waist and hips. "Emma," he said again, in quite a different tone, his eyes wandering over her.

When she met his gaze, she flushed and looked down.

He couldn't take his eyes off her. With her silver-gilt hair falling about her shoulders, she looked like a nymph risen from the sea. The pearl and rose of her skin shone through the soaked shift. He felt himself growing aroused by the glorious, sensuous picture she presented.

Wrapping her arms around her chest, Emma shivered in the damp breeze from outside.

"You're cold," he said, forcing himself to look away from her. "I'll light a fire so that we can dry our clothes."

Emma let out her breath. "How will you make a fire here?" she wondered, looking at the rock and sand. They were in a shallow cave that narrowed some twenty feet back into a crevice. There was nowhere to retreat from the open arch at the front.

"With a flint and steel, and driftwood. There's some in that crevice."

Emma walked over and examined the splinters of smooth gray wood lodged in the back of the cave. "Does it come from the sea?"

"Yes," answered Colin, his voice a bit gruff. Coming up behind her, he had to tear his eyes away from her again in order to pull the wood from cracks in the stone and gather it into a pile in the center of the cave. Keeping his eyes resolutely lowered, he took out his knife and began to make a pile of shavings from the driest piece of wood. When she came and knelt beside him, drawing the shift tight against her hips and thighs, he almost cut himself. And his hands shook a little as he struck the flint and steel together, creating sparks to ignite the tinder. At last he managed the thing, and tongues of flame curled up among the sticks of drift-wood. Colin rose and stepped back. "We won't be able to dry everything," he said. "But we can do enough to get home creditably."

"The riding habit is ruined," Emma protested.

"You can wear my coat," he said. "And we'll fix up something with the skirt."

"Your coat is soaked, too," she pointed out.

"True." He hesitated. "We need to hang everything over the fire if it's to dry at all."

"Everything?" she asked, a bit alarmed.

He hesitated again, then seemed to come to a resolution. "As much as possible," he replied. And he began to strip.

"Colin!" Emma looked away. But after a few moments, she couldn't resist turning back. She found Colin using some of the longest sticks of driftwood to try to prop his garments before the flames. He wore only his wet riding breeches, which the dampness molded to his athletic form.

She found herself fascinated by his bare shoulders and the muscles that played along his arms and flexed in his thighs as he moved. There was something deeply exciting about the strength in his hands and the unconscious grace in all the lines of his body. His entire frame was eloquent of explosive power under strict control—a sort of fierce, careful gentleness that informed his every action. A narrow red scar ran across two of his ribs; from the war, she thought, and was shaken by a sudden rush of feeling.

"There." Taking a last look at his makeshift supports, he turned back to her. "That should do . . ." He broke off as Emma flushed scarlet, the color burning down her neck and bosom as well as her face. What he saw in her expression sent a blaze of heat through him and made him acutely aware of the arousal that had been building since he lifted her from her saddle. If he moved, he thought, he would pull her down onto the rocks and sand and take her right here in this decidedly unprivate place.

They stood stock-still, gazing at one another as if they would never get enough of the sight, and completely unable to tear their eyes away.

Rain pocked the waves outside and hissed into the sand. Soft, damp air flowed languorously over their skin, heavy with the scents of pine and the sea.

"You look like a siren," he whispered finally. "Set to lure men to madness."

"And what about you?" murmured Emma. "What sort of spirit are you?"

Outside, a gull screeched. The sound caused one of the horses to move impatiently, its hooves thumping on the floor of the cave. The other blew out a snorting breath in response. Emma jerked, the spell broken, and turned. "What . . . what do you suppose they think of all this?" she asked a bit disjointedly, looking at the animals who screened the front of the cave for them.

Colin took a deep breath. He ran one hand over his face. "They will worry about us at Trevallan," he said, a little abruptly. "I don't know how long this rain will last. Perhaps we had better just ride back through it."

Emma didn't argue. The calm settled atmosphere of Trevallan seemed extraordinarily appealing just now. She went to the sodden pile of velvet that had once been a riding habit and retrieved the skirt, wishing futilely for a packet of pins.

By the time they were ready to depart, the rain was slackening a little. But even so, the baron St. Mawr and his new baroness arrived back at their stately home in a scandalous state. Emma wore a man's riding coat that was much too large for her and a sodden velvet skirt that continually threatened to slide off her hips to the ground. Her hair was blown to bits. Colin sported a soaked linen shirt and breeches that felt as if they had shrunk significantly. His neckcloth was nowhere to be seen.

"Lord have mercy," said the housekeeper, Mrs. Trelawny, to his lordship's valet. "Will they be angry with me about that habit, do you think? It looked fine when I brought it out."

Reddings surveyed Colin, whom he had known in every variety of circumstances over more than ten years, and the new mistress, whom he had been observing with acute interest at every opportunity offered. "I don't believe they are much concerned with the riding habit," he said dryly.

Mrs. Trelawny frowned at him, then hurried forward to help Emma into the house. "Too bad your maid didn't come with you, my lady," she sympathized.

Emma giggled a bit hysterically. Her only servant, Ferik, had very much wanted to come. But he had not seemed just the person to take on a honeymoon.

"A hot bath is what you need," the housekeeper continued. With a sharp glance, she gathered two of the housemaids and sent them for hot water before bustling Emma up the stairs to change.

When Colin and Emma met for dinner some hours later, each was once again respectably clad. They took their places at the table with suitable dignity and helped themselves from the various savory dishes offered with practiced good manners. They ate—somewhat sparsely, it is true, but not enough to cause concern in the kitchen.

The conversation, however, lagged. When one of them ventured some innocuous remark, and the other looked up to respond, a charged silence tended to fall when their eyes met. They would each look quickly away, and the topic raised would be lost in the confusion.

"They seems sommat tired," concluded one of the footmen as he returned a tray to the kitchen.

"I expect they've caught their death of cold," replied the cook. "Out in that rain for hours. I'd best put together a posset."

When Emma rose from the table a little later and passed through the door the footman was holding open for her, she was at a loss as to where to go. She didn't want to sit alone in the huge drawing room. It seemed silly to maintain town conventions when there were only two of them. And the truth was, she didn't want to sit still. She was deeply restless and unsettled.

Fetching a shawl from upstairs, she let herself out onto the terrace that ran along the back of Trevallan and into the cool night air. The sky had cleared some time before, and the flagstones were dry. It was a perfect place to pace and to grapple with the fact that she could not stop thinking about Colin as she had seen him in the cave today. The picture kept rising in her mind no matter how she tried to banish it, and she found herself imagining what it would be like to run her fingers along the muscles of his arm or through the dark hair sprinkled over his chest. The memory of his kisses illuminated these scenes and intensified them, and she was shocked at her own desire.

Even more, she was deeply distrustful. Such feelings were dangerous; they clouded reason, distorted reality, and led one to make terrible mistakes. Hadn't she learned that, in years of misery? And though it was true the situation was completely different now, it had also been clear that these sorts of feelings weren't part of the bargain that was her marriage. Comradeship, Colin had said. And he had certainly not shown much eagerness to share her bed.

Emma turned and began pacing rapidly the other way. When he looked at her today, it had not seemed to be comradeship in his eyes, she thought. It had been something far wilder, something that sent shivers of alarm and anticipation through every fiber of her body. And yet he said nothing, did nothing, about it.

She turned, and paced even faster. A worried inner voice kept declaring that she was in serious trouble.

Sitting in the dining room with his second glass of port, Colin was equally restless. He was thinking of the rosy hue of Emma's skin as it had shown through her shift, and of the enticing outlines of her breasts under the transparent cloth. He was recalling the enflaming curve of waist into hip and imagining quite vividly how it would feel to run his hands along that beautiful line before he crushed her against him. His mind would not be torn from these images and others, and as a result, he was beginning to feel acute physical discomfort.

The point of marrying Emma had been that the match would not be subject to agitations and upheavals, he thought with annoyance. They were supposed to have a clear understanding, an agreement. They were both adults, with some knowledge of the world. And yet here he was plagued with unfulfilled visions of his own wife.

With a muttered oath, he drank again. The problem was, with the long journey and so on, the thing had simply been put off too long, he concluded. And the delay had blown it all out of proportion. The solution was to carry through the first time, and then everything could return to normal. It wasn't as if there was some mystery, something he had never done before. Aware of a keen pulse of anticipation that somewhat belied his reasoning, Colin drained his glass and rose from the table. "Fine," he said aloud, and went to look for Emma.

She was not in the drawing room, or the study. Her bedchamber was empty. The upstairs room that the lady of Trevallan customarily used as a private sitting room was also empty. Striding down to the library, and finding it similarly untenanted, Colin began to feel irritated. Where the devil was she?

In rapid succession, he checked the morning room,

the blue parlor, and the billiard room. He was simmering with frustration when he startled a footman in the hall and demanded, "Have you seen her ladyship?"

"I . . . I believe she's out on the terrace, my lord," was the stammered reply.

"The terrace," he echoed, as if this were an incomprehensible choice. "I should have known."

Emma started slightly when he walked through the glass doors onto the flagstones, but Colin was beyond noticing such things by this time. "It's late," he declared without preamble. "Time we went to bed."

"What?"

"I said—"

"I heard you." As he came closer, Emma took a pace backward.

With two quick steps, he was beside her, gripping her shoulders and forcing her to look up at him. He saw his own memories of the day mirrored in her eyes. She couldn't suppress them any more than he could. Bending, he took her lips in a breathless kiss, his fingers tightening almost painfully on her upper arms. Though Emma felt awkward at first, his mouth was intoxicating—coaxing, softly enticing her to yield. His kiss went on and on, and she was caught by it, astonished once again. Her mouth softened and opened of its own accord. Aroused and exulting, Colin let his hands slide up over her shoulders and then down, lingeringly, over her breasts to encircle her waist and pull her tight against him. He deepened the kiss until it seemed there was nothing else in the world but that link between the two of them. Emma, her senses swimming, melted in his arms, and felt the insistent hardness of his body along the length of hers.

"Come," he said after a long while, leading her inside the house to the stairs.

In her bedchamber, he captured her mouth again and gently coaxed it open so that he could use his tongue to tease and enflame her. Emma responded, at first tentatively and then with more confidence, giving herself up wholly to the kiss. He let his lips move to her neck, then dropped kisses on her shoulder and the swell of her breast above the neckline of her gown while his finger-tips brushed across it.

"Oh," she breathed.

She was so beautiful, he thought, gazing up at him with wide dark eyes blurred with passion. He was iron-hard with desire. She breathed his name, and his hands jerked a little.

Quickly, he undid the buttons at the back of her dress. His hands followed the blue cloth as it slipped off her shoulders and down her arms, over her hips. When it pooled on the floor around her bare feet, she was once again clothed only in her shift, the candlelight gleaming through it.

Colin flung his coat aside. His neckcloth, boots, and shirt soon followed, so all that remained were his breeches, straining against his arousal. He bent and slid his hands under the hem of her shift and pushed it up, running his palms lightly along her thighs, her hips, her waist, her breasts.

Emma made a sound—part enjoyment, part protest.

He threw the thin garment aside and gazed at her, standing before him naked, her pale skin burnished by the leaping candle flames. "My god," he murmured, gazing at the beauty she offered up to him. Without thought, his hand rose to cup one perfect breast, his thumb teasing the rosy nipple and making her gasp. His desire was almost pain now. He couldn't stop himself from enfolding her and pushing her backward toward the bed.

When he took one of her breasts in his mouth and teased it with his tongue, she cried out with the pleasure of it.

Colin could bear it no longer; he had to unfasten his breeches and free himself. When he turned back, naked, he found Emma staring at him, obviously startled and fascinated by the sight of his manhood revealed. Another mark against the wretched Edward, he thought with fierce satisfaction, then banished the blackguard from his mind as he captured his wife's lips once more, demanding now, his hands and lips urgent as he joined her on the bed. Drunk with the feel of her, Colin savored the lovely curves of her breasts and the soft skin of her belly.

Emma let her hands roam over his muscled arms, into the crisp dark hair on his chest. A sharp urgency that she did not understand was rising in her. As if he knew, Colin's hand moved to the ache between her legs and caressed her. Emma gasped, gripping his muscular shoulders. She thought she might faint with the intensity of the sensation. She felt as if she had stepped out of reality into a dream world. She had never imagined anything like this.

Her reactions were overwhelming the last shreds of Colin's control. He was wild for her. Her soft panting breaths filled his senses. Her eager movements against his fingertip enflamed him beyond all reason. In fact, he realized, he could not wait a moment longer.

As he rose above her on the coverlet, his busy caresses took Emma to a peak of pleasure that she had never even imagined. It rose and rose until all her muscles were rigid with glorious anticipation. She felt as if she would fly apart. She knew that if he stopped touching her now, she would die.

Rising on his elbows, he dropped quick kisses on her neck and shoulder as he readied himself.

"Don't stop," cried Emma, clutching his hard upper arms, then reaching up to kiss him pleadingly.

Her need drove him over the edge. "Only for a moment," replied Colin thickly. With a groan, he plunged inside her, and nearly exploded with the wonderful feel of her so tight around him.

As he began to move urgently, Emma once again experienced a tidal wave of feeling. Only this time, he was with her, filling her, and making the torrent of sensation even more intense. There could not be more, she marveled dazedly, but there was. And then it burst through her body like a shower of fire, a flood that saturated every cell of her body with wave after wave of glorious sensation. Emma cried out at the amazing splendor of it. She didn't want it ever to end. It flooded through her, making her dig her nails into the powerful muscles of his back and cling to him like a drowning woman. The last crescendo was just receding when Colin cried out once, holding her in a grasp of steel, then collapsed in her arms.

For a while, then, they lay in a tangle of limbs, hearts thudding, sweating lightly, cooled by the soft air from the window. Emma heard the call of a thrush, lamenting the darkness. The scent of the sea mingled with pine. "I had no notion," she marveled.

"About what?" Colin's voice was lazy, at once softened and roughened by desire.

"That marriage could be so . . . exhilarating," she told him.

His head turned on the pillow. He gave her a slow tigerish smile. "You haven't been married to *me*," he replied.

There was something magical about this place, Emma thought. She was standing alone in the narrow terrace garden of Trevallan, among the summer flowers. Gazing out across the wild cliffs and over the sea, she could watch the sun setting in a blaze of orange. It was as if a spell had been laid over the estate by the lulling rhythm of the waves and the scents of pine and sea salt and the clean blues and greens and grays of the landscape. This was the best part of the year here. It seemed a shame to return to London, as they were scheduled to do in just three days.

She heard footsteps on the gravel path behind her, and recognized them as Colin's. "Perhaps we should just stay here," she said without turning.

"We would miss the end of the Season," replied Colin, coming up to stand beside her. He put one hand on the stone balustrade that ringed the outer edge of the terrace and joined her in watching the sun's fiery disappearance. "My mother has planned a ball in our honor." Colin had already begun to think of London and of certain plans he had made. He needed to make sure they were still in place. To him, it was too obvious for comment that they must go back. Disappearing into Cornwall immediately after their marriage would rouse even more gossip than their unconventional match. The malicious members of the *ton*, of which there were always far too many, would assume that he was ashamed of his choice or that his bride was not presentable after all and he was hiding her from society. They would spread the most outrageous stories they could fabricate, he thought contemptuously, and the whole of society would enjoy them immensely.

Colin looked down at Emma, lovely in a gown of pale blue muslin trimmed with knots of dark blue ribbon. A fierce protectiveness, so strong that it was almost like rage, flooded him. So much had been taken from her, he thought. But in this case, unlike the losses of so many others in his life, he had the power to restore it—the laughter and gaieties of peacetime life. Emma would have them all. And the polite world would be *made* to acknowledge her and offer some recompense for the years she had spent in exile.

To Emma, his reply had sounded merely polite, and she took it as a gentle reprimand. She had, she felt, received a number of these during their stay. It had seemed to her, at first, that the blazing physical passion Colin had revealed to her on that night after their ride in the rain must change everything. She had never experienced anything like it in her life, and it seemed as if a new epoch had dawned. But the morning after that first night he had been the same as ever—polite, solicitous, amusing—just as he had been on the day after sharing his nightmare. He had not referred to the intimacy they'd shared. He had acted as if nothing worthy of note had happened.

As their time in Cornwall passed, he took her riding, showed her the surrounding countryside, introduced her to neighbors. And each night he came to her chamber and dazzled her with the most amazing caresses. After which he went to his own bed. He still had the nightmares, too; she heard them.

Emma sighed silently. She didn't understand him. But she had taken the point that they were to present a picture of unbroken, amiable compatibility to the world and even to each other. Perhaps this was precisely what she was supposed to comprehend, she thought, what their bargain had really been about—that the level beneath the surface of things was not to be discussed or even acknowledged. Perhaps this was truly why he had not wanted a giddy schoolgirl who would be continually plaguing him and think herself head over heels in love. And if she was discovering a distressing tendency to feel such emotions, she had best keep them hidden.

Colin had no desire to stay here alone with her, she thought. No doubt he had many friends he wished to see and things he preferred doing in town. She would have to develop her own round of activities and circles of companions. "Of course, I must order the new wallpapers and draperies for Trevallan," she said with determined cheerfulness. "And a few carpets as well."

"You have a free hand," said Colin with a smile.

"Take care, my lord. Aren't you afraid I'll indulge in an orgy of spending?"

"Not in the least."

"You think I am too careful and frugal?" asked Emma, wondering whether she liked such a prudent characterization.

"I think your taste is too good for excesses. You will buy exactly what is needed to refurbish the place, and I believe I can easily afford that."

Emma laughed. "I see through you, sir. This flattery is designed to keep my spending within bounds."

"Indeed not," he replied, but amusement glinted in his eyes.

"No, no. You imagine you have put me on my mettle, and that I will not exhaust myself searching out bargains to prove you right."

"I had no such plan."

"Good. For I mean to go to the most expensive merchants in town and order their finest goods."

As she had intended, Colin laughed. But then he remembered some of the things she had told him about her life in the last few years, and some that he had worked out for himself. "Do," he urged. "I'll instruct my bankers to pay any bill you present to them."

Something in his voice stopped Emma's teasing. But she couldn't identify just what it was. Puzzled, she turned back to the sea, dark now that the sun was gone. The sky above it still held a little light, and it was a clear, deep blue with a scattering of stars. How wonderful it would be, she thought, to live amid all this beauty. Then she shook herself a little and returned to reality. "Shall we go in?" she said. "Mrs. Trelawny will be waiting dinner for us."

Chapter Seven

Mud-spattered, behind a tired team, the Wareham traveling carriage clattered over the London cobblestones and pulled up before the front door of St. Mawr's townhouse. Emma stumbled a little when Colin helped her out. Her legs were stiff from days of traveling, and she was exhausted by the endless jolting. The weather had broken during their journey back, with a steady cold rain that turned the roads to morasses and slowed their progress to a crawl. It hadn't done much for tempers, either; there had been intermittent flare-ups between the coachman, Reddings, the footmen, and the outriders. It was obvious from their quick movements and the relief in their faces that everyone was exceedingly grateful to be home. Emma herself was longing for a bath, a cup of hot tea, and her own soft, clean bed.

The front door opened before they could knock, revealing a tall, imposing figure in black whose face might have been carved from granite. Emma groped for the name of St. Mawr's butler and majordomo—Clinton, she remembered from her single introduction. But had he looked quite so forbidding then?

Colin confirmed her memory by greeting the man by name. Emma echoed him. "Everything in order?" Colin added, and walked inside without waiting for an answer. Clearly, he had never received a negative to such an inquiry, Emma thought with slight amusement. She entered the grand front hall, with its black-and-white marble floor and elegant staircase curving into the upper stories.

"Not precisely, my lord," replied Clinton as the carriage clattered around to the back of the house and the great front door was shut behind them.

Colin didn't hear. But Emma was at once on the alert. "What has happened?" she had begun to ask when a bloodcurdling shriek rang out from the lower regions of the house, reverberating through the hall like a regimental bugle.

"What the devil?" exclaimed Colin.

Clinton's face merely grew stonier, Emma noticed. He did not appear at all surprised. She began to get a sinking feeling in the pit of her stomach. "That would be Nancy, my lord," he told Colin glumly.

"Nancy? Who in blazes is Nancy?" Colin was also very tired, and rather irritable.

"The second housemaid, my lord," said Clinton in a sepulchral tone.

"The . . . ?" Colin's violet eyes fixed his butler with a look that had caused more than one line of enemy infantrymen to waver. "What's wrong with her?" he demanded.

Before Clinton could answer, a second, lesser shriek rang through the house. It ended in a gurgle that sounded very much like laughter to Emma. The sinking feeling grew stronger. She began to be very much afraid she knew the explanation for these unorthodox noises.

"Nancy is an excitable girl," said the butler.

"Evidently," responded Colin.

"She cannot seem to restrain her . . . enthusiasm for the stories told by *Mr.* Ferik," the man added.

"Oh dear," said Emma, her fears confirmed.

"I have *suggested* that he refrain from entertaining the younger members of the staff with his, er, reminiscences," Clinton continued. "They do not seem to me at all suitable for a household such as ours. *Quite* the contrary, my lord. But he has not chosen to heed my advice."

"Oh dear," said Emma again.

"And I fear, my lord, that some of the footmen encourage him," Clinton concluded. "They appear to forget all the training they have received here when they are in his presence." His face remained absolutely expressionless, and his voice was glacial, but Emma thought she saw a spark of something like fury at the back of his pale eyes.

"I'll see to this," she said.

"Mr. Ferik did mention, my lady, that he takes orders only from you." Clinton did not look at her as he said this.

"I'm very sorry, Mr. Clinton," she replied. "I did explain the household to him, but Ferik does not always . . ."

The butler continued to stare at the far wall as she trailed off. Colin looked impatient with the entire subject. Pushing aside her weariness, Emma added, "I'll just go down and speak to him."

"Yes, my lady. Thank you, my lady," said Clinton frigidly. He stood stiff as a wax figure, every line of his body expressing indignation.

Emma sighed. Although she had known there were likely to be adjustment problems, she had hoped for domestic peace. Resignedly, she headed for the back staircase and made her way down. As she neared the entrance to the kitchen, she could hear Ferik's deep resonant voice rising and falling in a near-hypnotic cadence. She paused to listen before going in.

"And I saw that he was chasing me through the

streets with a great cleaver in his hand," Ferik was saying.

"Gor," responded a high female voice. "Why would he be doing that?"

"He was very angry," Ferik pointed out.

"I'd say so," agreed a man. One of the footmen, Emma thought.

"And, you see, the punishment for this intrusion was to be made a eunuch."

There was a short silence.

"What's a unik?" inquired the woman then.

After a meditative pause, Ferik replied gravely, "The horse Riley is a eunuch."

There were sniggers. More than one footman was present, Emma thought.

"You mean they cut . . . with a person?" Nancy's voice rose toward a delighted screech once again.

Emma could almost see Ferik's slow nod.

"And so, I ran like the wind."

"Didn't you just!" exclaimed a footman. "That would be the thing to give a man legs, it would! A cleaver! Lord have mercy."

"This lord had none," Ferik pronounced.

"That's blasphemy," accused a hostile male voice.

Emma decided it was past time to intervene. She pushed open the door and stepped into the kitchen. Ferik sat in a wooden armchair, his hands on his knees, looking like a giant idol. Two young housemaids, three footmen, and the scullery maid had been clustered around him, gazing upward with rapt attention. When they saw her, this group scrambled to their feet. The tiny scullery maid ducked her head and scuttled away as the others bowed or dropped curtsies. Ferik climbed ponderously upright, a huge smile lighting his face. "Mistress," he said. "You have returned safely, thanks be to God."

"Yes, Ferik." He had been convinced that she would be murdered on the road without his protection. "I wish to speak to you," she added sternly.

"Of course, mistress." Like a monarch, he waved the other servants away. "Take this chair," he suggested, offering the one he had been using with a broad gesture.

Emma shook her head. "Ferik, I thought I explained to you very clearly that Mr. Clinton is in charge of all the staff here."

"Of course, mistress." The huge man gazed back at her with bland innocence.

"You must accept that that is the way of things in this house, and you must not annoy him," she commanded.

Ferik drew himself up and crossed his heavily muscled arms on his chest. "I have been very polite to Mr. Clinton," he replied, deeply offended. "Even though he is a—"

"Ferik!" She knew very well what he had been doing. He had been pretending to defer while he undermined Clinton's authority in a host of subtle ways, making certain there was nothing specific anyone could accuse him of. In the time they had been together, she had learned from his stories and his behavior that Ferik was addicted to intrigue. "You must not keep the other servants from their work," she admonished.

A look of injured astonishment descended on Ferik's mobile face. "I, mistress?"

"As you were just now, when I came in."

He spread his hands. "A few moments taken from the day. A small rest."

He was hoping to form alliances, Emma knew. He also loved attention and admiration. "No more reminiscing," she said.

"Remin . . . I do not know this word."

"No stories," she clarified.

"But they take such joy in—"

"And you must stop plotting, Ferik."

He spread his hands again and opened his eyes very wide, the picture of a man wrongly indicted.

"That is not the way things are done in England," Emma insisted. Then, recalling details of some of the stories he had told *her* over the last year, she paled slightly. "And you are not to put anything in Mr. Clinton's food," she commanded, looking as stern as she could. "Or anyone else's food. Do you understand me, Ferik?"

He was scowling. "I do not need to use poison," he informed her haughtily.

Emma heaved a sigh of relief. "Good," she said.

"I can rise to the top of this household without any such—"

"Mr. Clinton is in charge," repeated Emma. "And he will remain in charge. He has been with his lordship for years and years."

Ferik grew more alert. His frown gave way to a look of intense concentration. "Your lord husband favors Clinton?" he asked.

"Y-yes," said Emma, not liking the look in his eyes.

"Clinton has been in his service for a long time?"

She agreed warily.

"Perhaps since the lord was quite young?"

"I'm not certain. I think so."

"Ah." Ferik nodded to himself as if he had suddenly unraveled some complex problem.

"So, you understand what I have told you?" Emma said.

Ferik smiled. Emma didn't like the look of it at all. But he said only, "Yes, mistress."

"And the stories will stop?"

"Of course, mistress. I am at your command." He bowed slightly, one hand on his massive chest.

As long as she knew the precise commands to make, thought Emma skeptically. For Ferik, anything that was not expressly forbidden was fair game. "I told you that you must conform to the rules of this household," she added.

"Conform, mistress?"

"Follow the rules, obey them."

"Ah. I have been doing my best. But there is always some new thing that I do not understand."

It was true that he had been taught an entirely different code of conduct, Emma thought with a twinge of guilt. He could not be expected to know English ways. "If anything puzzles you, ask me," she told him.

"Yes, mistress. Thank you. There is one thing."

"What?"

"John the footman says that he is about to 'lob a shot over Nancy's defenses.' Could you tell me the meaning of this expression?"

Emma searched for words. "Well . . ."

"I fear it may involve a dishonorable act," Ferik added.

"Uh . . ."

"I like John. I would regret it very much if I had to kill him," he informed her solemnly.

"Kill him!"

The giant gazed at her. He seemed surprised at her reaction. "To defend the honor of your household, mistress."

"Oh." It had been far simpler when she had no household, Emma thought. She and Ferik had dealt very well together then. He had folded his massive arms and glared at anyone who treated her with disrespect, and such people had promptly melted into the woodwork and disappeared. But Mr. Clinton was not going to disappear. Neither were John and Nancy. "You will not kill anyone," she said firmly. "I forbid it."

"But—"

"Absolutely, Ferik. Put the thought from your mind. Anyway, the, er, honor of the household is my responsibility."

He looked doubtful. "In England, the mistress watches over the honor of her women?"

Emma nodded.

"But you cannot fight. How are you to punish wicked men who try to violate your attendants?"

"There are laws to take care of that," she said, with more conviction than was quite warranted. "But the point is, Ferik, that you need not concern yourself with this. Do you understand that?"

"England is a country of many laws," he replied, shaking his head. "I do not see how you remember them all."

"We are trained in it," Emma lied. "So you must do nothing without consulting me. Promise, Ferik."

The huge man sighed heartrendingly. "It is all very confusing, mistress. Have I not guarded you well as we traveled here?"

He had been vital to her survival, Emma thought. And she was grateful to him. "Very well," she acknowledged.

"But now you do not need me. You have your lord husband and his servants to guard you."

The truth of this roused a guilty protectiveness in Emma. "You will always be my companion and guardian," she declared.

His face lit.

"But you must do as I say," she hastened to add. "No more talk of killing."

"Of course, mistress," said Ferik. "I am at your command." He bowed again.

"And you must listen to Mr. Clinton and do as he asks," said Emma.

Ferik gave her a serene smile. "As you say, mistress."

Emma eyed him. He spoke as if this was a matter of no importance, and she knew that was not how he felt. He was still plotting, she realized. "Mr. Clinton is in charge of the household," she repeated yet again.

"So you have said."

"And so you agree?" she insisted.

"Of course, mistress."

Though she was not at all reassured by the spark in his dark eyes, Emma could think of nothing else to forbid. As she walked back upstairs, she determined to keep a sharp watch on Ferik. Then she sighed because she knew that would be next to impossible.

At least he was safe for now, she thought. He would

not attempt any new schemes so soon after talking with her. She could have her cup of tea and lie in her comfortable bed without fear of upheavals. Emma stretched her stiff shoulders. She could almost feel the pillows supporting her aching head, the cool sheets, the delicious relaxation of her whole body.

Clinton was waiting for her in the front hall. Was he expecting a report on the success of her mission? she wondered.

"You have a caller, my lady," he said.

"Now?" replied Emma, dismayed.

"I told him you had just arrived home and were undoubtedly fatigued," he said. "But the young man was most insistent."

"Young man?"

He held out a visiting card. "Your brother, I believe, my lady?"

Gazing at Robin's card, Emma sighed again.

"He seemed rather agitated," Clinton told her.

Was the butler punishing her for Ferik's transgressions? she wondered. But she could find no trace of this in the man's face, which remained, as always, completely unreadable. "Is he in the drawing room?" she asked.

"Yes, my lady."

"Very well. Thank you, Clinton." Emma took deep breaths as she walked up another flight of stairs. She wanted to grow closer to her brother; she only wished he had chosen another day to begin the process.

Robin was standing before the fireplace when she entered the drawing room, half turned away, kicking at an ember that had fallen from the coals with his highly polished Hessian boot. He was gravitating toward the dandy set, Emma decided, taking in the massively padded shoulders of his coat, the strangling height and complexity of his neckcloth, and a waistcoat in astonishing stripes of yellow and orange. He didn't need to go to such extremes, she thought. He was quite an attractive youth without any embellishments. "Hello,

Robin," she said, smiling and moving into the room. At once, he turned to face her, and she was struck again by his strong resemblance to their dead mother.

"Hullo," he replied. "That toploftly butler said you wouldn't wish to see me, but those fellows are always trying to fob one off."

He spoke with a mixture of bravado and uneasiness that prevented Emma from telling him she was worn out. "Sit down," she suggested, and subsided gratefully onto the sofa.

"I wanted to call at once because I didn't get to see you before you left town," he added. "The thing is, I didn't know where you were staying."

"I must have forgotten to tell you. I'm sorry."

"Oh, well."

How soft the sofa cushions were, Emma thought. Almost as comfortable as her bed.

"And I wanted to apologize." He flushed. "At the wedding, you know. I had a bit too much champagne. Not used to it. Those soldiers. Made a muck of my toast."

"It doesn't matter," Emma assured him.

"Does," he insisted. "I wanted to make a good showing, you know. Only brother. All those Warehams about. Have to hold up our end."

"It was all right," said Emma sleepily.

"They laughed," objected Robin, as if he were accusing her.

One could practically lie down on this sofa, it was so broad, Emma thought. And most importantly, it did not bounce or tilt or throw one suddenly into a hard coach corner. It was heaven. "They didn't mean anything by it," she responded dreamily. "You have to admit it was rather funny."

Robin's flush deepened. "I don't see the joke," he replied, aggrieved. "I might have hurt myself, you know. Falling like that."

"Well, I'm sure you will not drink so much again."

This sofa was like floating, Emma thought. She would just close her eyes for a moment, only a moment.

"Now you sound like Father," complained Robin.

"Do I?" murmured Emma. "How dreadful."

"I thought you were different."

"I am," said Emma, forcing her eyes open again. Sleep was dragging at her like a drug. She couldn't recall when she had been this tired.

"I had hoped that we might become acquainted," Robin continued. "For one thing, it's deuced odd, having a sister one hardly knows. People think you're some sort of fool."

"Yes," said Emma, her voice a bit slurred with fatigue. "We must learn all about each other quite soon. Let us set a day to . . ."

Looking pleased, Robin scooted the chair in which he was sitting closer to the sofa. "Well, you know, right after you, er, went away, they sent me off to school. Awful place up north. Cold as . . . cold as ice. And the masters were horrid. Not one of them less than sixty. They made us wear knee breeches and . . ." He launched into a detailed history of his troubles during his early years at school.

In a distant sort of way, Emma realized that Robin was complaining about the dreariness of his school holidays. She felt as if the sofa were a deliciously comfortable, huge white cloud, and she was sinking slowly into it—down, down.

"But Father just left me there, no matter what I told him. Kept on saying I needed discipline. That discipline was the most important thing in life."

She had to fight her lassitude, Emma thought. Robin was speaking to her. But somehow, his words were merging into a dream of the sound of ocean waves at Trevallan. A soothing rhythm that was utterly impossible to resist.

Robin went on talking, covering each of his years at school and a long succession of disputes with his father. Ten minutes passed, then fifteen.

"So I came up to town for good eight months ago," he went on. "He couldn't keep me away any longer. And I've been on the toddle every since." His pride in using this bit of slang was palpable.

"London suits me down to the ground," he added. "I think I shall be a great success here, if only . . ."

Pausing, Robin cleared his throat.

He had come to the crucial part of his speech—the place where he revealed their father's shocking rigidity about money and recruited his unknown sister as an ally. Since the first proof of her sympathy was to be a rather large loan, he was finding this part of the conversation difficult. Looking at the floor, Robin stumbled through the words he had spent days composing. He had so wanted to appear urbane and sophisticated before Emma.

At last, it was over. He had said it all. As he waited for her reaction, his eyes remained on the carpet. Anything would be all right as long as she didn't mock him, he thought.

The silence lengthened. The soft pop of the dying fire was fully audible.

Had he made her angry? Robin wondered. Or was she just trying to decide how to refuse? Unable to stand the suspense, he sneaked a sidelong look at her, keeping his head bent.

Robin's pale brows came together. He straightened. Unable to accept what he saw, he rose and took a step forward. It was true. His eyes hadn't deceived him. She was fast asleep. "Blast it!" he exclaimed, quite loudly.

"Uhh." Emma jerked awake and blinked up at him, seeming, briefly, to wonder who he was.

"That tears it," said Robin savagely.

"I . . . oh dear. Did I drop off? I am so sorry. It was such a long journey, and the inn last night was dreadful—"

"It is I who must apologize," interrupted Robin through clenched teeth. "I did not realize I was such a *bore.* You may be sure I will not trouble you with my . . . my dull conversation ever again."

"Oh, Robin." His face was red. He was working himself into a tantrum. Things were so hard when you were that young, Emma recalled.

"If you are going to mock me . . .!"

"I wasn't mocking," Emma protested.

He ignored her. "Then it's best that I go," he said, his voice throbbing with emotion. He made a gesture, as if throwing something away, and stormed out. Struggling up from the deep sofa cushions, Emma heard him thundering down the stairs to the front hall. He was calling stridently for his hat as she hurried to the stairs. And by the time she reached the hall, he was gone.

"An impetuous young man," commented Clinton, with what seemed to Emma a hint of smug satisfaction.

"Oh, damn," she said.

Clinton raised his eyebrows.

Emma gave him a look that caused him to lower them again, and to stand up even straighter, which hardly seemed possible. Satisfied, she turned and marched up the curving staircase toward her bedchamber, determined that nothing would prevent her from reaching it this time.

Nothing did. But unfortunately, the abrupt ending of her encounter with Robin had driven off sleep, at least temporarily. She would, however, have her tea at last, thought Emma, ringing the bell and ordering a pot when the maid appeared. By the time she had removed her crumpled gown and slipped into a wrapper, the girl had brought the tray, and Emma settled into an armchair with a steaming cup beside her and her feet on a footstool. So far, it was not particularly pleasant to be back in London, she thought. And it was perfectly obvious that more difficulties with both Ferik and Robin lay ahead. She felt a moment's sharp longing for the peace and beauty of Trevallan, and at once suppressed it. Colin wanted to be here. His friends were here. And she had determined to make a success of life in London, as he wished. There was a pile of mail awaiting her on the small desk in the corner. Many of the envelopes had the heavy, square look of invitations. Tomorrow she would open and accept them all. Tomorrow.

Emma rested her head on the chair back. The tea was just right; her headache was receding. She wondered if Colin had already gone to bed.

As if cued, he opened the door between their adjoining chambers and came in. "I thought you would be fast asleep by this time," he said.

"There were . . . things to take care of," she answered.

"Ah, yes. Domestic harmony restored?"

Clearly, he had dismissed all concern about the scene when they arrived, Emma thought somewhat enviously. She nodded.

Colin came to sit in the other armchair, stretching his long legs out before him on the thick carpet. "You know, I've often wondered how you acquired an attendant such as Ferik. Hardly a usual choice for a lady."

"It wasn't exactly a choice," said Emma.

"Why does that fail to surprise me?" replied her husband with a humorous look.

"Yes, Ferik has his own mind," she acknowledged, smiling in response. "But it wasn't he, so much as the circumstances."

"And what were they?"

Emma looked down. "We were traveling toward Constantinople, and we had stopped for the night at a village . . . I suppose you would have to call it an inn, though I'm reluctant to honor it with the name."

Colin examined her face, though she continued to gaze at the floor.

"They had nothing decent to eat there, so I determined to visit the market that was set up in the village square and purchase some provisions for our dinner. I enlisted two of the . . . employees of the inn to accompany me."

"And where was the unlamented Edward?" Colin inquired tersely.

Emma grimaced. "He had already found a game of some sort and would not be pulled away from it."

Colin sat up straight. "Your husband allowed you to set off alone with two strangers from a mean inn in a Turkish village?"

She shrugged.

He made a sound rather like a snarl.

"We walked to the market and I began to examine the foodstuffs offered. It was very colorful, and there was a wonderful smell of spices." Emma looked distant, remembering. "I did notice that people stared at me," she went on. "Almost all the women there wear veils over their faces, so it was obvious I was a foreigner. At any rate, all seemed well until I took out my purse to pay for the things I had chosen. I didn't have a great deal of money, but most likely it was still a fortune to the men escorting me."

"Very likely," growled Colin.

"One of them grabbed me from behind, and the other pulled out some sort of club, I believe to knock me unconscious."

"My God, Emma!"

"I was quite frightened," she admitted.

"Do you know there is a flourishing slave trade in Turkey?" he demanded.

"It's odd that you should mention it, because of what happened next," she said. "I was struggling as hard as I could, in vain, when I heard a kind of roaring sound. The next thing I knew, the man holding me had let go, so quickly that I fell to my knees on the ground."

Colin muttered something inaudible.

"When I looked around, I saw what looked like a giant attacking the two who had tried to rob me. He was shouting at them in their own language, which of course I did not understand. But his meaning was clear."

"Indeed?"

"Curses," she elaborated. "He hit one of them hard enough to send him flying. Then he threw the club over the heads of people nearby. It clattered when it landed."

She remembered it all so vividly, Emma thought. Fear had engraved it on her memory.

"The men ran away. A crowd started to gather around us. And I saw that some of them were pulling at my rescuer as if to draw him away. And then I saw that he was bound with long heavy chains on his wrists and ankles." Finally, she turned and looked at Colin.

"Ah."

"He was for sale!" she informed him.

"Was he?"

"Yes." Emma clenched her fists just thinking of it. "Can you imagine anything more horrible?"

"A barbaric practice," Colin agreed.

"No one there seemed to think so. They just stood and watched as he was taken away. One of his captors even had a whip!"

He watched her face.

"He looked down at me, not pleading, you understand, not as if he expected anything from me."

"Certainly not."

Emma frowned slightly. "He didn't, Colin."

"Very well."

"Naturally, I had to buy him."

"Naturally."

"Well, I could not just leave him in that condition after he had saved me."

Colin said nothing.

"And he has been completely loyal to me ever since and an indispensable guardian in . . . in any number of situations."

Colin scowled. He hated to think of the situations in which Emma had found herself. Ferik had his gratitude, he thought, and a place in his household no matter how troublesome. But he could not help but wonder. "Did he ever confide the, er, reason for his predicament?" he asked.

"What do you mean?"

"Why was he being sold?" Colin elucidated.

"Oh. He was in debt."

"Ah." That was much better than it might have been, Colin thought.

"He had tried to open a hostelry of his own in the village, a better one than the place we stayed. But he didn't have enough money to back it properly, and a string of bad luck drove him out of business."

"I see."

"And then he *belonged* to his creditors," she added. "Can you imagine such a thing?"

"It is rather harsh."

"It is outrageous."

"But you saved him from his fate."

"And gave him his freedom at once, of course."

"It goes without saying."

Emma looked at him. "Are you laughing at me?"

"On the contrary. I am most admiring. I am trying to think of any other woman of my acquaintance who could have thrown off the effects of such an attack and gone on to purchase a gigantic slave with such aplomb."

Emma considered this. "What else could I have done?" she wondered.

"Fallen into a fit of hysterics?" he suggested. "Fainted from the strain? Burst into tears?"

She cocked her head. "What good would that have done anyone?"

Colin started laughing. "Not a particle of good, my indomitable Emma," he replied.

The new baroness St. Mawr walked slowly across the square toward her London townhouse, preoccupied with the two scraps of wallpaper she held. She looked back and forth between them, unable to decide which she would prefer to have hung in her bedchamber in Cornwall. "What do you think, Ferik?" she asked, holding them up so that her giant servant could see them. "Do you like the rose garlands, or the stripes?"

"Neither of them is as beautiful as the other one, mistress," was the reply.

Emma sighed. Ferik had become inexplicably attached to a different pattern at the shop, his interested participation in the choice thoroughly scandalizing the prim proprietor. "I will not have galloping horses and raging storm clouds on my walls," she repeated for the sixth time. "It must be one of these."

"The other is more exciting," he insisted.

"Too exciting. No, it must be one of these. I will not look at another pattern. After just one morning of it, my head is spinning."

"The things in English houses are in-sipid," said Ferik.

Emma looked up at him in surprise.

"I have learned a new word," he informed her proudly. "From that silly little man in the shop."

When she did not appear to comprehend at once, he added, "He said the yellow paper was in-sipid."

"Yes, I remember."

"He meant dull and without life," Ferik continued. "*He* was in-sipid."

Emma stifled a laugh. "You must not say so, Ferik," she admonished.

He grunted. "Not to say, not to do, not to notice—this is the English," he muttered. Looking petulant, he lapsed into silence.

But Emma was used to his complaints by this time. She merely held up the wallpaper samples again. "It is so difficult to imagine what they will look like on the walls when you have only a small piece," she said.

"The horses would look very fine," insisted Ferik. "Strong and splendid."

Emma imagined lines of snorting blue horses racing along her bedroom walls. She imagined Colin's reaction to them. "I know, I will ask Caroline," she decided. She tucked the samples into her bag. Colin's sister had been

very enthusiastic about Emma's plan to refurbish
Trevallan. Indeed, in the week they had been back in
London, she had made a great effort to further their
acquaintance. Colin's mother, on the other hand, had
done only her duty, procuring the invitations Colin demanded for his new wife and introducing her to the
leaders of the *ton* but showing no great enthusiasm for
the task.

Approaching the house, Emma sighed. They had attended some evening party or event every night since
their return. Obviously, she had been right in thinking
Colin was extremely fond of fashionable society. She
herself found much of it dull and irritating, but she was
determined to do her part. He would not lose the life he
loved because of her.

There was a woman standing before the house,
Emma noticed, gazing up at the windows as if they held
some important secret. She was dressed from head to
foot in expensive black mourning clothes, and in one
hand she held a formal bouquet tied with long pink
ribbons. The odd thing was, the flowers in the bouquet
were dead; they were brown and withered to mere
sticks. Puzzled, Emma stopped to examine the woman.
As if sensing her regard, she turned, and Emma saw that
she was much younger than she'd thought, hardly more
than a girl, and very pretty.

The unrelieved black of her costume set off shining
golden hair, creamy skin, pouting pink lips, and wide
blue eyes. The girl was small and delicately made, her
head just topping the level of Emma's shoulder. She
looked, Emma thought, like one of the very costly dolls
displayed in the most exclusive shops—except for her
expression, which was willful and stormy.

Emma walked toward the house. The girl watched
her unself-consciously, surveying every detail of
Emma's dress and appearance.

"Are you going to visit *her?*" the girl asked in a high
little voice, when it was clear that Emma meant to enter
the Wareham townhouse.

"Her?" repeated Emma, confused. This didn't look like the sort of girl who would accost strangers in the street. Everything about her, from her stylish gown to her aristocratic accent, suggested a sheltered daughter of the upper classes.

"The new baroness St. Mawr," drawled the girl, as if there was something deeply offensive in the phrase.

"Oh, no, I—"

"*I* am," declared the other. "I don't care what *anyone* says. I'm going to tell her to her face how she *ruined* my life." She gestured eloquently with the dead bouquet. A withered blossom broke off and fell to the pavement.

"Ruined?" Emma frowned.

"He was *going* to offer for me," the girl continued. "I know he was, no matter *what* my mama says. I could tell he meant to. There are little signs, you know. But then my grandmama died, and we had to go out of town for *weeks* and this awful creature came along and trapped him."

"Did she?" said Emma, beset by conflicting feelings.

"Yes!" The girl's pretty mouth turned down like a child's. "And she is a widow and *old*, and probably fat and ugly as well, and it is all just so unfair." Once again, she punctuated her point with the bouquet. A few more dry fragments floated to the ground.

"He was going to offer for you?" asked Emma.

"Yes! He danced with me at the Boyntons' ball and again, two different nights, at Almack's. Susan said he was quite taken with me."

One of the girls Colin's mother had urged upon him, Emma thought. "And you with him?" she asked.

"I am *deeply* in love with him," replied the girl passionately. "I will never love anyone else. I shall pine away and *die* of a broken heart." She put her free hand over her black bodice as she said this, her doll-like blue eyes flashing. "And so I shall tell the . . . the *creature* who stole him from me."

Despite a host of dissimilarities, for some reason, she

reminded Emma of another girl who had insisted just as passionately upon marrying Edward Tarrant. "What is your name?" she inquired.

The girl blinked, as if becoming conscious that she had poured out her most private grievances to a total stranger. "Mary," she answered. "Lady Mary Dacre."

Emma sorted through her memories of the people she had met or had had pointed out to her recently. This girl was the daughter of a duke, she thought. She was extremely rich, eminently well born, and totally suitable for a nobleman's wife. In fact, she was precisely the sort of daughter-in-law Colin's mother had wished for. Emma glanced at the girl's obstinate expression. Perhaps, she amended silently. "I am the baroness St. Mawr," she said.

The girl stared. "You?" She looked at Emma as if really seeing her for the first time. She took in the silver-gilt hair, the lovely face, and elegant bearing. "But you are not fat or . . ." She bit her full lower lip and fell silent.

Emma gave a little shrug. There was nothing really to say in this situation.

Recovering remarkably quickly, Lady Mary stared at Emma even more avidly, as if analyzing every element of her appeal. "You're fair, like *me*," she said at last, as if this explained a good deal.

Emma blinked.

"But too tall," the girl added complacently. "And your hair is *not* golden."

She had never encountered anyone quite this self-absorbed, Emma thought. Fascinated, she watched Lady Mary catalog her various features, obviously finding fault with them all.

"*This* is for you," declared the girl dramatically, shoving the dead bouquet into Emma's hands. "It is a . . . a symbol of my blighted hopes." Rather too artistically, she choked on a sob.

Emma looked down at the dead flowers, pressing her

lips together to keep from smiling. "Very appropriate," she couldn't help saying.

The girl drew herself up, throwing her head back. "*He* gave them to me," she informed Emma, and tossed her golden curls.

"For your first ball?" asked Emma. It was the custom for gentlemen to send flowers on such an occasion.

"Yes." The word was defiant. "And I chose to carry *his* flowers, even though I received a dozen bouquets. And I told him so when he danced with me."

Emma wondered what his reply had been.

"Pink roses," added Lady Mary meaningfully. "The card he sent said they were just like me."

Walking in the gardens at Trevallan, Colin had told her he found pink roses pallid and uninteresting. However, no one would use those words about this girl.

"His mother told me I was *meant* to be his baroness," the girl added. "She was *prodigiously* kind to me."

Light began to dawn. "She presented you to him, I suppose."

"She was determined to throw us together," replied Lady Mary. "I was her *ideal* for his wife."

"Were you indeed?" replied Emma dryly. She was torn between annoyance, concern, and laughter. She began to wonder if the baroness had actually sent the bouquet.

"Yes, I was. And now you have ruined everything!"

The girl was glaring at her as if she expected some immediate recompense for her supposed loss. "Do you expect an apology?" Emma wondered.

Lady Mary's pretty eyes narrowed. Her doll-like face set. She looked like an extremely spoiled child. "I'll make you sorry," she replied. "See if I don't!"

It was a child's threat, Emma assured herself as the girl whirled and hurried away, but a thread of uneasiness remained. There had been a truly determined glint in those blue eyes. And Lady Mary could certainly do damage if she fed the gossip that still circulated about St. Mawr's unusual match.

Ferik, who had been hanging back while his mistress talked to the young lady, now came forward. "Not well behaved," he sniffed.

Not for the first time, Emma noted that Ferik had a very rigid sense of propriety for one who had lived in the teeming streets of Constantinople. "She is in love, Ferik."

"Love!" He snorted.

"You do not believe that she is?" Emma wasn't at all sure whether to believe it herself.

"I do not believe in love, mistress," was the giant's reply.

Emma gazed up at him, curious. "Not at all?"

"It makes nice songs," he allowed. "It is a thing for singers and poets."

"But not you?" Was Ferik lonely? she wondered. Did he wish for a wife and family of his own?

He shook his head. "Me, all I ask is a big dowry and a nice firm bottom." He pursed his lips, considering. His huge hands drifted up in front of his chest. "And maybe two—"

"I get your point," said Emma hastily.

"Yes, mistress. Shall I take that to throw away?"

She was still holding the withered bouquet. Emma looked at the brown petals and leaves. "No, I'll keep it for a little longer," she replied, mounting the steps to the front door. Inside, Emma asked the footman in the front hall whether Colin was home.

"In the library, my lady," was the reply.

After leaving her bonnet and wrap in her room and tidying her hair, Emma went down to the library, carrying the bouquet with her. Colin was bent over a sheaf of documents at the desk. He looked up when she came in and smiled in a way that made Emma's heart beat a little faster. "Have you found your wallpaper?" he asked.

"I am trying to decide between two patterns."

"I hope you have not come to show them to me."

"No. I will try Caroline when we dine there tonight."

"Just the thing," he agreed. Noticing the dead flowers in her hand, he raised his eyebrows. "Some new fashion I've not heard of?" he asked.

Emma turned the thing in her fingers. "Do you know a girl named Lady Mary Dacre?" she answered.

Colin considered. "One of Morland's daughters? I may have met her." His expression grew wry. "In fact, I must have. That family would have been high on my mother's list. I don't remember anything particular about her."

"Really? I . . . I met her today, and she seems out of the common run of debs."

"Indeed? Is she the reason you're carrying dried-out roses?" Colin joked.

He really had no memory of her, Emma saw. As she'd suspected, the romance between them had been all in Lady Mary's mind, nutured no doubt by the marked attentions of Colin's mother. She debated whether to tell him about her encounter, and decided against it. "I was just taking these to throw away," she answered.

"Is something wrong?"

"No," she replied quickly. "I should let you get back to your work." She eyed the piles of papers that lay before him.

"I brought these from Trevallan," he said in response to the look. "I'm following your lead in setting the place to rights. The estate has not received the attention that it should have had these last years."

"What are you planning?" she asked, curious.

Leafing through one stack of documents, he pulled out an architectural drawing. "The steward suggests we pull down that row of cottages to the south and rebuild. The foundations are unsound."

Emma bent over the plans. "If you're going to rebuild, you should move them into that hollow close by," she said. "They would be out of the wind and much more comfortable, I imagine. Their gardens would probably grow better, too. It was much more lush there."

Colin gazed at the drawings. "A very good point," he murmured. He made a notation on the drawings. "I see that you will be a great help to me in estate matters," he added. "Remind me to hand along all these documents so that you may read them and give me the benefit of your advice."

He was teasing her a little, but he meant it, Emma saw. He actually respected her views. Her throat tightened with pride and a touch of astonishment. She was not much accustomed to having her opinion heeded. No chit of seventeen could match this, she thought.

"What time are we to be at Caroline's this evening?" Colin asked.

"Seven."

"Will the young terror be in bed by then, do you think?"

"You mustn't speak so of your nephew," admonished Emma.

"Wait until you have known him a little longer," responded Colin. "Wait until he pours milk on one of your gowns or drops honey in your hair."

"Did he . . . ?"

"Strawberry jam rubbed into my best coat," he said. "Reddings was furious."

Emma laughed. "I suppose he will improve as he gets older."

"Do you?"

"Most of us did."

Colin cocked an eyebrow. "Are you saying, my dear Emma, that you were such a demon child?"

"I'm told I dropped my father's pocket watch in the honeypot," she admitted.

He laughed. "I'm shocked."

"Oh? I suppose you were an utter paragon? The sort of child mothers pointed out to others as an example."

Colin grimaced at the picture. "There was an incident with some ferrets," he mused.

"Aha! Ferrets again. I begin to see a theme here. What?"

"I was allowed to keep ferrets down at Trevallan when I was a youngster," he told her. "But I was not permitted to bring them into the house."

"Very sensible," put in Emma.

Colin smiled. "But we had a violent, unseasonable cold snap, you see. And there was a litter just born. And I was afraid they would die of exposure."

"So you brought them in," she concluded.

"In a sturdy box," he assured her. "And they did quite well until . . ."

"Yes?"

He shrugged. "When they got a bit older, one of the more enterprising chewed through the box, and the whole litter found they preferred the walls of the house to such confining quarters. A few mornings later, my mother sat down to breakfast and found herself eye to eye with a young ferret seated in the middle of her plate."

Emma started to laugh.

"I imagine he wanted toast," Colin added meditatively. "I'd been feeding them the scraps left from the morning meals."

"What did the baroness do?" asked Emma through her laughter.

"Oh, well. Screamed. Knocked over her chair and a tea urn. Turned the place upside down searching for the poor creatures."

"I can hardly blame her."

"I had already recaptured three," responded Colin defensively. "I would have gotten them all in a day or two more."

"With toast?" giggled Emma.

"A very effective lure," he agreed. He hadn't smiled, but his violet eyes were glinting with amusement. "Perhaps there is hope for young Nicky," he conceded. "If Caroline will stop spoiling him."

"When his new sister, or brother, arrives next year . . ." Seeing Colin's surprised expression, Emma stumbled. "Hasn't Caroline told you? I didn't realize."

"It's quite all right. I'm pleased to see you becoming friends."

"She's been very kind."

"Caroline's a good sort—always has been."

"Did she like ferrets?" asked Emma mischievously.

"Thought they were charming," he assured her.

The clock on the mantelpiece struck the hour. "Oh, I must go," said Emma. "I have an appointment with the dressmaker."

"Does your protégé still have time for you, then?" he teased.

Emma smiled. Since she had begun going about in society, and other ladies had seen her gowns, Sophie had been besieged with orders. Emma had amused Colin one night by describing the Frenchwoman's complacent delight at this development. "Always," she answered.

"I'll look forward to the results," he said, as she moved toward the door.

She hurried out. Colin sat back in his chair, but did not at once go back to his estate papers. Emma's light, beguiling scent hung in the air. The smile she had brought to his lips lingered there.

He saw much less of her here in town, he thought. Of course, that was only natural. She seemed to be enjoying the distractions of the Season, and she was, of course, demonstrating to the gossips that she was entirely suited to be a nobleman's wife. She had dignity, easy manners, an air of distinction—in short, everything that one could ask for. It was ridiculous to become nostalgic about an earlier Emma, soaked to the skin with her hair falling untidily about her shoulders, clutching at the tatters of an ancient riding habit.

Colin shook his head. He had arranged his life most rationally and satisfactorily. He ought to be—he was—completely contented. And there was an end to the matter. Determinedly, he returned to his work.

As she was about to leave the house on her way to Sophie's, Emma was accosted by Clinton in the front hall. "A . . . person has called, my lady," he said. His disapproval was palpable.

"Who?" said Emma, pulling on her glove. "I can't see anyone now. I'm late for an engagement."

Silently, he extended the small silver salver he held, upon which rested a pasteboard visiting card.

Emma took it and read the overly ornate script. Then she closed her fist around the card and crumpled it into a tiny ball. "Tell Count Orsino that I am out," she said angrily. "And do not admit him to this house again."

Clinton looked gratified. "Yes, my lady," he said.

"The rose garlands," Caroline said without hesitation. "You'll tire of stripes in a month. This pattern is far better." She handed the two pieces of wallpaper back to Emma as if there were no more to be said on the subject, and turned to exclaim, "Nicky, do not climb on the mantel shelf. You'll hurt yourself."

The ladies sat in Caroline's drawing room after the splendid dinner she had offered her guests. The gentlemen still lingered over their port in the dining room. The party included Colin's great-aunt Celia as well as Emma's father, but the rest were not family members.

The sound of porcelain smashing brought all the women's heads around. Nicky, who had continued to try to shinny up the marble column that decorated the side of the fireplace, had gotten his hands on the china figure of a shepherdess and knocked it off. It lay in pieces on the slate hearth. "Oh, Nicky," said Caroline. "I told you to stop."

The nursemaid hurried forward and began pulling the boy away from the broken figurine. Nicky protested strenuously, howling at the top of his lungs and kicking out at her. As most of the women gathered in a loose circle around the struggling pair, Great-aunt Celia's penetrating voice was heard to remark, "Why doesn't someone slap the child? In my day, we were taught to behave."

"Nicky," said Caroline. "Stop this at once or you will have to go upstairs and you will not get a macaroon." She looked over her shoulder at Emma and another guest. "I promised him one from the tea tray."

Nicky continued to howl.

"When we have children," said a soft voice behind Emma, "they shall be shut in the nursery the moment they are born and not let out until they reach the age of reason."

Emma turned to find that the gentlemen had joined them, and that Colin stood close by. Caroline's husband was wading through the crowd toward his son. "Nicky is overexcited and tired out," said Emma. "He should have been put to bed long ago. He seems to me too young to be brought down for an evening party."

"You appear to have a solid grasp on these matters," approved Colin. "I shall leave them completely in your hands."

"Oh, no, you won't," answered Emma. "There are times when a father's influence is vital. See how well Lord Wrotham is dealing with his son."

His lordship had swept the little boy up into the air, stopping his howling with this surprise attack. He set him on his shoulder, where Nicky surveyed the room with blinking, reddened eyes. "Won't be a moment," said his lordship, striding toward the door with the nursemaid at his heels. " 'Ware your head, Nick," he added, ducking through the archway and into the hall.

"You see?" said Emma.

The howling started up again in the distance, fading as a door shut.

"Indeed," replied Colin.

The tea tray arrived, and Caroline took her place behind it to pour. One of the young ladies seated herself at the piano and began to play softly. Colin received a preemptory summons from his great-aunt and went to sit at her side.

"Things are going rather well for you," began the old

woman in her usual no-nonsense manner. "Pleased with yourself, are you?"

"Modestly," he answered, teasing her.

"Humph. She's doing all right," she added.

There was no need to ask who she meant. They both looked at Emma, who was talking amiably with one of the other guests.

"One thing, though."

Colin raised an inquiring brow.

"Can't you persuade her to get rid of that pirate, or whatever he is, who follows her about town?"

"Ferik?"

"No notion of the fellow's name, but he's causing talk. Foreigner. Odd-looking. Not a proper attendant for a baroness." She fixed him with her gimlet eye. "Frightened Julia Winters out of her wits at Gunter's, I hear."

Colin returned her gaze unmoved. "I do not know the lady, but—"

"You wouldn't like her," interrupted his great-aunt. "Bird-witted, prone to hysterics. However . . ." She rapped her cane on the floor when Colin would have broken in, "a first-class gossip. Knows precisely how to tell a story. Damned entertaining."

"I see."

"Can't you get rid of the man? Pension him off? Or at the least, find him some other position, so he's not trailing around town after Emma?"

"He is her servant," said Colin coolly. "It is not my decision."

"What sort of nonsense is that? You're the head of the household. Tell her there's no place for him!"

"But there is. Ferik has been of . . . immeasurable service. He will not be turned off."

"What sort of service?" demanded the old woman.

Colin was silent.

"Eh?" She glared at him. "What sort?"

"I'm not going to tell you," he answered.

Great-aunt Celia fixed him with the look that reduced most of the family to quivering jelly. Colin remained unmoved, and after a few moments, she gave it up. "I warned you," she said petulantly then. "If you don't want my help, there is of course nothing more to be said."

"I am deeply grateful for the help you have given me. However, in this case, I cannot—"

"Oh, go away," she said. "I suppose people will get used to the fellow in time. If you want to make things more difficult, that's your lookout. Fetch Caroline. I wish to talk with someone more biddable."

"Someone you can terrorize?" ventured Colin, as he rose to do as she asked.

"Don't try to cajole me. I am quite displeased with you."

"Then I shall take care to stay out of your way." But he rested his hand briefly on her bent shoulder before going to give Caroline the bad news.

The remainder of the evening took a conventional course, with music and a hand of cards and a great deal of talk. As it neared eleven, most of the guests departed, and Colin and Emma were about to go when there was a sharp ring at the front door, then the sound of urgent voices in the hall. "What can this be?" wondered Caroline.

In the next instant, her mother erupted into the room. "Something dreadful has happened," she cried. "I have just heard, and it will be all over London by morning."

"What?" said Caroline. "Mother, your hair has fallen out of its pins." This in itself was shocking. She had never seen her mother less than perfectly groomed.

Colin led his mother to a sofa against the wall. Lord Wrotham poured brandy into a glass and brought it to her.

"No, no," said the dowager baroness. "I don't want it. We must think what to do."

"About what?" shrilled Caroline.

"I am trying to tell you," was the acerbic reply. She

fixed Emma with a glare that made the others turn and look at her as well. Mystified, Emma looked steadily back at her. "This afternoon, the duke of Morland's eldest daughter dressed herself in a white ball gown, arranged herself carefully on her bed, and took a dose of laudanum which she *may* have thought was enough to kill her," Colin's mother informed the group.

Emma felt cold apprehension spread through her.

"I say *may*, because she carefully arranged matters so that she was discovered almost immediately and revived," she added. "She sent notes well ahead of time to three of her closest friends explaining the reasons for her 'desperate' action."

The others were beginning to look puzzled. "That is terrible," said Caroline. "But . . ."

"What has it to do with us?" her husband finished. "Dreadful thing, of course. Very sorry for the girl and her family . . ."

"The notes *said*," declared the baroness in a loud, ominous voice, "that she wished to die because Colin had jilted her."

"What?" exclaimed Colin.

"She also mentioned that she had encountered the new baroness St. Mawr and that she could not bear to do so ever again." She glared at Emma. "What did you do to her?"

Heads swiveled toward Emma.

"Jilted her?" said Colin. "I cannot even remember her." He, too, was looking at Emma, recalling their conversation earlier in the day.

"Not remember her?" replied his mother in an outraged voice. "Not remember Lady Mary Dacre?"

He made an impatient gesture. "No doubt she was one of the many girls you threw at me."

The dowager baroness walked over to him and stared belligerently up into his eyes. "Lady Mary Dacre," she said, emphasizing her words with a forefinger jabbed into his chest, "is one of the girls you pretended to court in order to spite me. You took her driving, sent her flowers, danced with her. You must remember her!"

Colin backed up a step, looking slightly self-conscious. "I, er, courted a number of them," he answered.

"Just to drive me mad," responded his mother bitterly. "To raise my hopes, and then dash them."

"To persuade you to stop meddling in my life," retorted Colin. "And I think this Lady Mary must be mad. It was obvious I was not serious. None of the other chits thought I was."

Balked of her prey, his mother turned to Emma. "And what about you? What did you do to the girl?"

"Nothing," said Emma quietly. Everyone's eyes were on her. "She was outside the house this morning. She accused me of stealing Colin from her, said he was about to offer for her when she had to go out of town."

"Ridiculous," said Colin.

When Lady Mary had promised to make her sorry, Emma thought, she had not imagined this kind of dramatic, public gesture. Emma realized that she was trembling.

"Obviously, the girl is unbalanced," said Colin. "I am sorry for her, but it has nothing to do with us."

"Nothing?" sputtered the baroness. "Don't be an idiot. Half the people who hear this story will believe you jilted her to marry Emma, and that Emma then drove the chit to suicide. The rest will think it must be even worse than that." Putting her fists to her cheeks, she groaned aloud. "And after the gossip about your marriage. The family will never recover from this."

"We will say it isn't true," put in Caroline, who had moved close to her husband and looked rather white.

"Well, of course we will *say* it," exploded her mother. "But no one will believe us. On the contrary, the more we deny it, the worse it will be."

"We will ignore it," said Colin. "It is not true, and we will not dignify such a story by speaking about it."

His mother groaned again. "The notes went to the

daughters of two earls and a viscount. There is no doubt they will believe it. We must *do* something."

Emma was shivering—not with upset, but with anger. She clenched her fists in her lap. How dare the girl do this to Colin? She had claimed to love him. Could she be so self-involved that she did not realize she was ruining him?

Noticing her distress, Colin pulled her to her feet. "We are going home," he said. "We can speak of this tomorrow when heads are clearer."

"Tomorrow it will be all over London," protested his mother.

"I do not see how we can prevent that," he answered, taking Emma's arm.

The sight of his solicitude was too much for the dowager. "It's all *her* fault," she said, glaring at Emma. "None of this would have happened if it weren't for her."

Colin turned instantly, his violet eyes blazing. "Be silent! I do not want to hear that again, Mother. Do you understand me?"

"If you hadn't insisted on marrying her, we—"

"If I hadn't married Emma, I would probably have throttled you by now," Colin declared. "Leave it, Mother!"

She gaped at him. Before she could think of a suitable reply, he had turned away and was escorting Emma down the stairs and out to their carriage, which had been summoned some minutes ago. "You know there was nothing between this chit and me," he said as they drove away.

"Yes," answered Emma, almost absently. She was wondering if there was anything she could have said to prevent this catastrophe.

"You didn't tell me she had approached you."

"I . . . it didn't seem important. If I had realized what she would do!"

"Clearly, she is a lunatic," he said curtly. "Perhaps we should suggest that she be shut up in Bedlam."

Emma said nothing. But her mind was racing. There had to be something she could do to save this situation.

"I will not let anyone hurt you," Colin added. "You may be sure of that."

Emma's eyes filled with tears at the determination in his voice. Facing the loss of his respected position in society, which was so important to him, he still thought of her and defended her. She would not allow disgrace to fall on him because of their marriage.

The first shock was wearing off. As they reached home, Emma gathered her wits and began to think. Through the long hours of the night, she went over things again and again, examining every angle. Gradually, she started to form a plan.

When she finally did fall asleep, near dawn, Emma slept heavily, and she did not wake until well past her usual hour of rising. The slant of light through the partially open curtains told her it was after nine. For a few minutes, she lay in bed, reviewing her thought processes of last night, searching for flaws. Though she acknowledged a number of risks, she could not improve upon the plan she had outlined. It had to work.

Rising, Emma dressed to go out and left the house on foot with only Ferik to accompany her. Within twenty minutes, they reached the home of Colin's mother. Ferik knocked, and they were admitted. "My lady has not yet come downstairs," the butler informed Emma.

"I will go up," she replied. "Wait for me here, Ferik."

"Yes, mistress."

"But you can't just . . ." began the butler. Ferik stepped into his path like a human wall as Emma hurried up the stairs. She passed the drawing room and started up another flight. There, a startled housemaid directed her to the dowager baroness's bedchamber. Emma stepped up to it and knocked briskly on the door.

"Yes?" came a voice from within.

Taking a deep breath, Emma opened the door.

"Good morning," she said, sounding more confident than she felt.

The baroness was sitting up in her bed, wearing a fetching creation of lace and pink silk. A breakfast tray was before her, bearing the remains of coffee and toast, and she was holding a letter from the pile that lay beside her cup. "You?" she said.

Emma took the stool from the vanity table and placed it close to the bed, then sat down.

"What are you doing here?" Colin's mother demanded, putting the letter aside.

"I have come to talk to you about the situation with Lady Mary Dacre."

The baroness groaned. "Such a complete disaster. I don't want to think about it."

"We must."

"We?" replied the older woman, with a touch of hostility.

"You gave her a great deal of encouragement," Emma pointed out. "She told me of it."

"Well, what if I did?" she blustered. "She was perfect for Colin. Breeding, family connections, fortune. And she had some spirit as well. Colin was always complaining that the girls I presented to him were insipid."

"That is certainly not the case with Lady Mary."

"If you had not—"

"If *you* had not encouraged her so markedly, she would not imagine herself in love with him now," Emma interrupted.

They glared at each other for a long moment.

"I know you don't like me," continued Emma more temperately then. "But we must work together if we are to spare Colin humiliation."

"Oh, it's Colin you're worried about, is it?" responded his mother. She sat up straighter and rang the bell beside her bed. When a maid looked in, she said, "Take this tray. Can't you see that I'm done with it?"

The girl bustled in and removed the breakfast tray.

"Yes, it is Colin I'm worried about," said Emma

when she was gone. "I won't have people believing that he behaved dishonorably."

Meeting her dark blue eyes, the baroness found no guile in them. "And what of yourself?" she asked.

Emma waved the question away as if it were irrelevant. "Here is what I think must be done," she said. "And I cannot do it without you."

As the baroness listened to the plan Emma laid out, her expression slowly shifted from petulance to dawning respect. Her unwanted daughter-in-law had truly thought this out, she realized. She had anticipated the difficult spots and made plans for those as well. For the first time, the baroness really focused her full attention on her son's new wife. She was beautiful, no question about that. But apparently she was intelligent as well. Unlike Caroline, she had grasped the important points at once. And it seemed that she cared far more for Colin than his mother had understood. To herself, the baroness admitted the possibility—only the possibility—that the marriage had not been a dire mistake.

"So?" said Emma. She had finished her explanation, but Colin's mother just continued to stare at her.

"I don't like it," the older woman said slowly.

"But—"

The dowager held up a hand. "However, I cannot think of a better solution."

Emma sat back.

"It could work, if they will cooperate."

"Surely they will wish to stop the gossip about Lady Mary as well?"

"One would imagine so."

"Then you will help me?" asked Emma.

There was a short pensive silence. "Yes."

Emma let go the breath she had been holding. "I shall see that it works," she declared fiercely.

Colin's mother looked at her once again. Her jaw was tight, her back straight. The look in her eyes was almost intimidating. Yes, she thought, there is far more to Colin's wife than I had any notion of.

Emma rose. "This afternoon, then?"

"No reason to wait," agreed the baroness.

"I will come for you in the carriage at two."

The older woman nodded. When Emma did not leave at once, as she clearly wanted to do, she looked inquiring.

"Thank you," said Emma with some difficulty.

Her face softening, the baroness smiled.

A few minutes before two, Emma came downstairs dressed in a pale green muslin dress sprigged with rose and dark green. She had had her hair dressed rather severely, and it was nearly hidden by a straw bonnet trimmed with rose and green ribbons. Pulling on her gloves, she went through the door that Clinton held open for her and climbed into her barouche, directing the coachman to the home of Colin's mother. Once there, the vehicle paused only long enough for that lady to climb in, then continued on to a large stone house in Grosvenor Square. "You sent word?" Emma asked.

"Yes," answered the baroness. "I had no reply, but I know they are at home."

Emma nodded. One of the footmen hopped down from the back of the carriage to knock on the door, while the other handed them down to the pavement. When Colin's mother's announced herself, the butler looked doubtful. "I don't think, my lady, that anyone is—"

"I must see the duchess," the baroness replied firmly. "It is a matter of some urgency. You must tell her."

With an uneasy sidelong glance at Emma, who had not given her name, the butler said, "I will see whether she is at home." He ushered them into a parlor to the left of the front door and left them.

"Will he throw us out?" murmured Emma when the man had gone.

"I have known Frances Dacre for thirty years. Since she was only Miss Fanny Phelps. She would not dare refuse me." But her tone was not as confident as her words.

"Come on," said Emma.

"Where?"

"I think we had better find the duchess and tell her our business ourselves."

"Emma! You cannot . . ." But Emma was already in the hall and starting up the stairs. After a moment's indecision, the baroness went after her.

"Where is the drawing room?" she asked as they ascended.

"There," said Colin's mother, pointing right.

Emma opened the door. "No one there."

"Shouldn't we wait . . .?" But Emma was already on the next flight of steps. "Jane has a sitting room next to her bedchamber," the baroness remembered.

"Good," said Emma. "We'll try that. Which way?"

"Emma, this is not at all the thing. What are we to say to her when we come bursting in?"

"I won't sit quietly with folded hands and then be asked to leave," she replied. "Or wait for Colin to be whispered about and laughed at by all his friends."

"Yes, but—"

"If you do not wish to come with me, just tell me where to go."

Something in her tone made the baroness draw herself up. "This way," she declared, leading.

They reached a closed door farther down the hall just as the butler came out of it. "What are you doing here?" he exclaimed, profoundly shocked. "I put you in the parlor. You cannot—"

"What is it, Ellis?" called a voice from inside the room.

On a deep breath, the baroness pushed past the butler, saying, "It's me, Jane. I simply must speak to you."

Emma slid into the room behind her, quickly taking in the pleasant peach-colored walls and hangings, the comfortable furniture. The Duchess of Morland sat at an exquisite escritoire beside the window in the midst of writing a letter. She was a small, spare woman with blond hair that might once have been as bright as her daughter's and alert blue eyes. Just now, she looked surprised and annoyed. "Catherine," she said. "I cannot, really cannot bear to see you just now."

"I've come to help," insisted the baroness.

"There's nothing to be done," was the reply. "I'm taking Mary into the country until this—"

"You mustn't do that," interrupted Emma.

The duchess turned to stare at her, suddenly haughty.

"My son's wife," murmured the dowager baroness, and the duchess's expression hardened.

"Please listen to me," begged Emma. "You mustn't run away. We can set this right, if we go about it correctly and work together."

The duchess looked at Colin's mother, who nodded. "She has a good idea," she confirmed.

Their hostess drummed her fingers on the top of the desk as she carefully examined Emma. "Very well," she said crisply. "Tell me."

Chapter Eight

"It was in that wretched little village on the mountainside," said Major Laurence Graham. "You know the one. Don't recall whether it was in Portugal or Spain. I'd lost track by that time. But the streets were damned precipices and bumpy as washboards."

"The place where we sat out the winter storms?" inquired Captain Sir Richard Clarke from across the dining table.

"That's it. Remember we had the big snow, and Snodgrass got hold of one of those tin baking sheets from the cook tent and went sliding down the main street sitting on it. Nearly rattled his teeth out of his head, and broke his fool arm, too, when he couldn't stop at the bottom."

"He was going so fast he killed a chicken that ran into his path," recalled Colin.

Graham, who had been drinking deeply from his wineglass, sputtered and nearly choked. "That's right. We ate the bird that very night. Gave him a final salute before we carved. Casualty of war."

"We paid five times what it was worth for that stringy old rooster," complained Sir Richard.

"Aye," agreed Graham. "But it was a bargain for the laugh Snodgrass gave us."

A shadow seemed to pass over the convivial table. All three men lost their smiles for a moment, and looked suddenly older and tireder. The remains of the roast, the crumpled napkins, the half-empty bottle of claret lost their festive air and became scattered detritus ready for the trash heap. The bustle and hum of Colin Wareham's elegant club dining room—the rich draperies, the warmth, the glow of candlelight—faded into the background. And the bone-chilling cold and endless fatigue of the battlefield extended icy tendrils into the group.

"Dead these three years," said Sir Richard quietly.

Major Graham, who had had quite a bit of the hearty red wine, thrust out his glass. "Here's to Jimmy Snodgrass," he declared thickly. "And all the others, too. Every man jack of them, who ought to be here with us now."

In silence, they drank. Colin gazed at his former companions, taking in the changes that time and hardship had made in their faces since he met them six or so years ago. They were far from old, yet compared to the men who surrounded them in this room, they looked hard and grim and weather-beaten.

When Graham had suggested this reunion dinner, Colin had been a little reluctant. As he had noticed at the wedding, seeing old comrades from the army was a sharp reminder of the bad times as well as the good. But he knew these men better than anyone else in his life, and he could not refuse the invitation. It was a strange bond, he thought now. He had never met their families, or learned much of their early years. But the things they had been through together knit them closer than an entire shared childhood could have done. He remembered a battlefield where he and Graham had both lost their mounts in heavy fighting. They had stood back-to-back in the bloody mud and wielded their sabers through an endless carnage, until the lines had at last drawn apart and they had been able to stagger back into camp, supporting one another, and collapse, exhausted, on the cold earth by the fire. Nothing could erase that sort of connection.

Still, it was damned difficult to see his own bleakness mirrored in their faces, to watch their mouths draw into thin lines when certain words were used. It made the melancholy even more palpable. It was like the nightmares, he thought—insistent reminders of a past that would never go away. And yet, in the last few weeks, the power of the dreams seemed to be diminishing a bit. "I heard Jennings's wife had a son," he said, willing the mood to lift.

Sir Richard brightened. "Did she? An heir for the crumbling acres, eh?"

"He called them that, but I understand it's a tidy little estate. And very good prospects from his wife's father," put in Major Graham.

The cloud passed by. Colin refilled their glasses with the last of the claret.

"You'll be setting up your nursery before we know it," Graham said to him. "A real beauty you've got yourself. I said so at the wedding."

"Repeatedly," agreed Sir Richard.

"Well, she is. Do you deny it?"

"Not me, old boy. Colin's a lucky man. It almost tempts one to follow in his footsteps."

"Who'd marry you?" mocked Major Graham.

Sir Richard, whose engaging homeliness had never hindered him with the ladies, merely grinned.

"There he is!" exclaimed a tipsy voice behind them. "Just the man we were speaking of. Hi, Eddie! Here's St. Mawr."

Several diners began to converge on their table from different directions. One of them staggered and slumped onto a seated guest, who pushed him off with a frown. Colin cursed softly under his breath. None of those approaching were men he liked, and all were chiefly known for the extremes of their wardrobes and their propensity to gossip.

"St. Mawr!" A heavy hand dropped on Colin's shoulder.

They had made his presence a focus of attention for everyone in the room, he thought with gritted teeth. "Steyne," he acknowledged tersely.

"Man of the hour, eh?" declared the newcomer. The scent of brandy wafted over the table, carried on his breath. "Never knew you were such a one for the ladies, old man."

"Got to watch the quiet ones," said one of his companions in a slurred voice. "Always up to something on the sly."

"Got them dying of love for you," giggled Steyne. "Or nearly. Morland's daughter is recovered, they say."

"A sad misunderstanding," Colin managed. His fists were clenched under the table.

"That wife of yours must be a saucy little piece, to lure you away from a dowry that big," laughed Steyne. He leaned down to speak confidentially. "A widow, eh? No green girls for you. She knows a thing or two about keeping a man satisfied, I suppose?"

Blood slammed into Colin's temples, and molten rage gripped all his limbs. His vision reddened. Before he could think he was on his feet and had somehow gotten Steyne's throat between his fingers. The sensation as he squeezed and watched the man's face darken and eyes bulge was enormously gratifying.

"Here," babbled one of Steyne's companions ineffectually. "Here, now."

Colin had a vague impression of men rising from tables, of voices raised. But all he could really see was Steyne's purpling features and the fear in the man's close-set little eyes.

"Colin." Someone tugged one of his arms, but he resisted.

"Colin, lad." Someone else had the other arm. The two of them were pulling him off Steyne. He struggled.

"Come along," added Sir Richard. "Let go. There you are."

Regaining his senses, Colin let his hands drop to his sides.

"No need for a public brawl," Major Graham assured him. "We can easily find an excuse for you to call this numbskull out. And you can run a sword through him without breaking a sweat."

Steyne, who had been gasping and sputtering and holding his bruised throat, started to cough at this. "Apologize," he croaked, beginning to back away. "Meant no offense."

"Great fuss over nothing," chimed in one of his friends. He took Steyne's arm and urged him off. "All a mistake," he added.

The pair stumbled, but recovered quickly.

"Heard him incorrectly," jabbered the friend. And then the whole group of intruders turned and fled.

Sir Richard eased Colin back into his chair. He turned a blandly threatening gaze on the crowd in the dining room, who suddenly found their dinners of interest once more.

"Worm," muttered Graham. "Like to set him down before a French cavalry charge and watch him disgrace himself."

"All right now?" asked Sir Richard. He poured wine from his own half-full glass into Colin's empty one and offered it to him.

Colin waved it aside. "I'm fine," he replied rather irritably.

"Are you?" Sir Richard examined his face. "Not like you, to fly off like that."

It wasn't, Colin thought. He had been known throughout his regiment for being slow to anger. They had called on him to settle disputes and intervene in quarrels. His men had relied on him to be even-tempered and coolheaded.

"Fellow deserved it," muttered Graham. He gestured

peremptorily at the waiter and ordered another bottle of the claret.

Something had snapped when that idiot, who really didn't matter in the least, Colin acknowledged, had made slighting remarks about Emma. It had been intolerable.

"We could go after him," suggested Major Graham. The wine arrived, and he filled his glass. "Give him the thrashing he deserves. Saber's too good for him!"

"Do be quiet, Laurence," said Sir Richard.

Colin waved them both off. "I'm fully recovered," he said. "Steyne's not worth thinking about. Everyone knows the man's a fount of malice and half-truths."

"There you are," said Sir Richard, obviously relieved.

"Ought to rid the city of vermin like that," muttered Graham. But he was only fulminating by this time, and all of them knew it.

"Let us have another glass and forget the incident," said Colin. "And then I must be on my way." He had an intense, somewhat irrational, need to get home. He wanted to see Emma, to speak to her and make sure all was well. Senseless, he admitted to himself, but wellnigh irresistible.

"To old friends," said Sir Richard, raising his goblet. They echoed him and drank.

Half an hour later, Colin stood in the doorway separating his bedchamber from his wife's and watched her brush her hair. It was like a veil of silver gossamer falling around her shoulders, he thought. She wore a low-cut nightgown of dark blue silk and cream lace. Her skin glowed. Everything about the room—the delicate objects, the light, sweet scent, the roses on the mantel shelf—was new to his life, filling some of the yawning emptiness that the war had left behind.

Following the mesmerizing movement of her arm, he felt an unfamiliar tightness in his chest. It was not desire, though he was certainly feeling that as well. It was not fear. That he knew only too well from the battlefields. And he was not afraid; he had no doubt he could protect Emma from anything that might come. No, it was more amorphous, a new emotion. He could not define, even to himself, its nature. The uncertainty made him uneasy, and he brushed it aside. "Did you have a pleasant day?" he asked moving into the room.

Emma turned to smile at him. "Hello. You're earlier than I expected. How are your friends?"

"Much the same," he answered. He came forward and put his hands on her shoulders, meeting her eyes in the vanity mirror. Emma put down the hairbrush. "Anyone bothering you with this silly gossip?" he asked.

Emma shook her head, setting the candlelight dancing in her hair. "You?"

He ignored the question, fervently hoping that no one would be crude enough to tell her of the incident at the club tonight. "A lovely gown," he commented.

Emma's smile grew impish. "It arrived today. Rather expensive, I'm afraid."

He smiled back. "Worth every penny." He bent to kiss her neck just where it curved into her shoulder, and there was a knock at the door. "What the devil?" said Colin, straightening.

Emma met his inquiring glance with a shake of her head.

"Yes?" snapped Colin. "What is it?" Emma drew a wrapper around her shoulders.

The door opened to reveal Ferik, in all his giant duskiness, carrying a tray on which rested a decanter and two glasses. "I heard you come in, lord," he said. "I was listening for you. I have brought you brandy."

Colin simply looked at him. Emma closed her eyes and shook her head.

"You drink brandy in the evening," added Ferik with a good deal of satisfaction. "I have noticed this." He carried the tray in and set it on a small table in the corner.

"Yes, sometimes," Colin allowed. "But I did not call for any tonight." He was eyeing the huge man with puzzlement.

"You could not," replied Ferik complacently. "Mr. Clinton is asleep. The others are asleep. But me, I do not sleep."

"Not at all?" wondered Colin skeptically.

"Not as long as my lord and my mistress wake," he said. "And there is any service I may perform for them." Clasping his hands on his chest, he bowed deeply to them.

Colin watched this performance with fascination.

"Thank you, Ferik," said Emma. "We won't need anything else tonight. You may go to bed. Really."

Ferik shook his head. "I shall not sleep for a long time," he told Colin. "You may call me if you wish for anything at all."

"I shan't need you," Colin assured him.

Ferik's massive shoulders rippled in a shrug. "Who knows what may come?" he intoned. "I always await your commands, lord." He bowed again, then backed out of the room, shutting the door as he passed through it.

"What the devil was that about?" exclaimed Colin.

Emma's laughter escaped in a sputter. "He is trying to win your favor," she explained.

"My . . . ?"

"And to discredit Clinton, so that he may have his place."

"As butler!" He imagined Ferik opening his door and greeting visitors, and grimaced.

"Well, as head of the staff," said Emma.

Colin frowned. "Clinton has been with me since I first set up my own establishment. There is no possibility . . ."

"I know. I have told Ferik over and over, but apparently he does not believe me. Intrigue is the rule where he comes from, you know. Every servant is always plot-ting against the others."

"Well, he cannot do so here."

"I have told him," Emma repeated.

"Perhaps I had better tell him as well."

"Yes, why don't you," she agreed. "He might listen to you."

"You don't sound confident." Amusement was be-ginning to tinge Colin's voice now.

"Well, Ferik is very . . . unpredictable."

"Is he?" Colin looked haughty. "If he interrupts us here again, he will discover that I am very predictable indeed, and not very forgiving." He wondered whether to tell her about Great-aunt Celia's opinion of Ferik, and decided against it. "Would you like to go riding in the morning?" he added instead. He was thinking of Cornwall and their rides there.

Emma flushed. "I . . . I have an engagement," she had to reply, thinking of the plan she was setting in motion.

"Too bad."

Emma suffered a sudden attack of uneasiness. "Colin?"

"Yes?"

"If I did something that you didn't quite like, that . . . annoyed you . . ." She stopped. She didn't think he would like her plan at all, so she did not intend to tell him about it until it was well under way. But keeping it from him was a bit uncomfortable.

"Like what?" he asked.

"Oh, I don't know." She wished she hadn't brought it up.

"Then neither do I," he replied. "If you took a lover, I would wring your neck."

"Colin!"

"But if you, oh, quarreled with the cook so that she left us, I would merely beat you a little and send you to the kitchen in her place."

"And I would poison you at your next meal!"

He chuckled softly. "What mischief are you planning?"

"None." It wasn't mischief to save him from the vulgar tongues of gossips, Emma thought. But she couldn't rid herself of that nagging uneasiness.

"Then we needn't worry our minds over the question."

"No," Emma said softly. "I'm sure there is nothing to worry about."

Colin rose early the next morning to ride in the park. He preferred the place soon after dawn, when all the fashionable promenaders who would crowd it later were still safely in bed and out of his way. Then, he could almost imagine himself at Trevallan, with miles of open country around him and the possibility of riding as long as he liked without encountering any simpering gossips or insincere heartiness. Had the war spoiled him for London? he wondered as he urged his mount to a gallop in the silent, empty parkland. Not really, he concluded. He had never been much taken with the city, despite his mother's love of it. How he would have liked to remain in Cornwall, he thought, his heart lifting at the idea. Then he remembered recent events. If they ran from the wagging tongues and malicious stares, the *ton* would consider the worst confirmed, and Emma's chances of taking her proper position in society would be ruined. Scowling, Colin turned his horse back toward home. He would have to call on his mother, he supposed, and find a way to combat the gossip. He would far rather have faced a line of French infantry, bayonets at the ready, than deal with this, he thought.

Striding into his own drawing room a little later, still holding his riding crop, Colin found not Emma but a young girl dressed all in black who sprang to her feet as soon as she saw him. "Good morning," he said politely.

"I am not here by my own will," she exclaimed dramatically. Her large blue eyes bored into him. Her lower lip trembled. She brought one small gloved hand to her breast.

Startled, Colin blinked.

"I would never, *never* have intruded upon your household after what has passed between us, but my mother and your"—she choked artistically—"your wife have fixed it all between them. *I* was not consulted."

"Er . . ." temporized Colin, playing for time.

"I *know*," she declared. "It is excruciating. But others do not possess the same depth of emotion as we do, you see. So they have no *idea* what it is like."

Suddenly, he realized who she was. "Good God," he said.

She nodded as if he had expressed something profound.

Colin looked around, hoping to discover some other member of his household nearby.

"I cannot help my feelings," she was continuing, "but I shall not *embarrass* you by expressing them." Belying her words, she gazed at him longingly and twisted a handkerchief in her hands. "You have made your choice," she added, in a voice that throbbed with the emotion of an opera singer. "We shall not speak of regrets, or mistakes." She moved a step closer. "Although *I* shall never recover," she finished in a piercing whisper.

Colin took a step backward.

She followed. "I think you *might* tell me, however, what you found lacking in *me* that—"

"Excuse me a moment," he muttered, backing out of the room.

"Can you not bear it?" she asked, trailing after him. "I do not know how I am doing so myself. My mother says women are the stronger, but I do not think—"

"Must go," said Colin hurriedly. "Duties."

"Duty." She sighed. "We are all of us terribly constrained by duty, are we not? My mother says it is my duty to be here, but—"

Colin turned and fled.

"It is *terribly* hard, seeing one another again," murmured the girl, as if someone was still there to hear, or as if she was composing an anecdote to entertain a sympathetic audience. "To come face to face, alone, with no one to hinder us from opening our hearts to one another. And yet duty prevented it." She sighed again, heartrendingly.

Encountering the footman in the hall, Colin demanded, "Where is her ladyship?"

"I believe she is upstairs, getting ready to go out, my lord," John replied, a bit startled at his master's savage tone.

"Thank you," Colin replied, and started up the steps two at a time.

John rolled his eyes and went to inform the staff that their master was in a taking about something.

"Emma!" said Colin when he burst into her bedchamber and found her at her dressing table. "The Morland chit is in our drawing room."

Emma turned with a smile despite the sudden acceleration of her pulse. Lady Mary had arrived early, and she had been confident they would be out of the house before Colin returned home. "Yes, I know."

"What in blazes is she doing there?" Remembering the encounter, he shuddered. "It's clear the girl really is suffering from some form of mental disturbance. I suppose we should pity her." He grimaced. "I find it difficult to do so. She spoke to me in the oddest way. And the look she gave me, Emma, was enough to freeze one's blood."

"She is somewhat upset because—"

"She?" He turned back toward the door. "To have the effrontery to come here. It shows what a disturbed state she must be in. I'll get John to escort her home, and I'll send along a note to Morland, by God, telling him—"

"No, wait," said Emma. "You can't. We . . . we are going driving in the park."

"As soon as she is gone, we will do so," he replied.

"No," she said again. "I mean, Lady Mary and I are going."

"What?"

"I arranged for her to go driving with me, because—"

"With you?" he exploded. "After the things she has said? Have you gone mad as well? The chit has spread the most insulting rumors about both of us, and you wish to take her for a drive?"

"But don't you see, that's just it. If she is seen to be friends with me, people will be much less likely to believe the stories they hear."

Colin came back into the center of the room and frowned down at her.

"It is a plan I conceived, to prevent a scandal," she continued. And to save you from the whispers and the doubts, she added to herself.

Colin's frown had eased only a little. "You mean to make a show of being friends with Lady Mary Dacre?" he echoed, as if making certain he understood.

"Yes," replied Emma brightly.

"And you believe this will convince the gossips that the rumors are untrue?"

"What will they be able to say, if we face them down with coolness and determination?" she replied.

"Full frontal assault?" he suggested. "Sabers drawn and don't spare the horses?"

Emma wrinkled her nose. "I suppose that is one way of putting it," she acknowledged.

Colin considered in silence.

"Your mother thought it a good plan," Emma added.

"Did she?" Was his mother playing a double game? Colin wondered. But no, she wouldn't risk it with something as serious as this. He tapped his leg with his riding crop, not pleased but not seeing any real objection he could make. "Are you sure the chit has agreed to this?" he asked, recalling some of her disjointed remarks to him.

"Well, not entirely," said Emma. "But the duchess,

her mother, was taken with the idea. I'm sure Lady Mary will come round."

Colin raised one dark brow. "Are you?"

"She will see that it saves her from being the center of a scandal."

"And if she wishes to be?"

"To be what?" said Emma, confused.

Colin shook his head. It seemed to him that Lady Mary Dacre wanted very much to be the center of something. And a scandal would do if that was the only choice.

"I don't understand." Rising from her dressing table, ready to go out, Emma cocked her head at him.

But he said only, "I don't know if this is a good idea."

"How else can we stop this gossip?" inquired Emma. "Do you have a better plan?" She was quite ready to hear it, she thought. Her contacts with Lady Mary so far had not made her eager for more.

"No," answered Colin slowly. He gazed at Emma, fresh and lovely in a gray morning dress with blue piping. He hated the thought of scandal touching her, and even more of her being rejected by the leaders of fashionable society. Remembering the drunken innuendoes at his club, he clenched his fists at his sides. Something had to be done. "Oh, very well," he conceded. "I hope you do not expect me to accompany you, however."

"No." Emma smiled at him. "I do not think that advisable."

"Wise," he replied. "Are you really set on this, Emma?"

"I see no other way," she answered, determined to save him.

"I can't think of one just now," he admitted, thinking only of her.

Their eyes met and held, full of feeling. Each of them wondered just what the other was thinking to make that gaze so intense.

"I . . . I must go," said Emma.

Silently, he held the door for her to walk through.

In the drawing room, Emma found Lady Mary flipping impatiently through an album of engravings. She looked pale and pretty in her black gown and dark, frilled bonnet, but her expression was extremely petulant. "I am here only because Mama made me come," she said as soon as Emma appeared. "I do not wish to go driving with you, or anywhere with you."

Emma bit back a sharp rebuke. "You wish to plunge Colin into a scandal, then?" she asked mildly. "Perhaps you would like to see him disgraced, as your revenge?"

"I would never do *anything* to hurt him!" exclaimed Lady Mary, her seemingly mild blue eyes suddenly blazing.

Emma refrained from pointing out that accusing him of jilting her, and making a show of ending her life as a result, hardly supported this assertion. "But will you do something to help him?" she asked pointedly.

"I'm here, aren't I?" was the sullen reply. "Even though every *moment* I have to spend with you will grate horribly on my nerves and deeply offend my sensibilities." She glared at Emma. "I shall pretend to be your friend for *his* sake," she finished dramatically, "but I shall not really *be* your friend."

"Thank God for that," muttered Emma under her breath. But aloud she said only, "Agreed."

On the short drive to the park, where it would now be the height of the fashionable hour of promenade, they were silent. Lady Mary scowled out one side of the barouche, while Emma gazed in the opposite direction. This was going to be more difficult than she'd realized when she formed the plan, she thought. She wanted nothing more than to shake her companion thoroughly and return her to her home. However, this was for Colin, she reminded herself. At the gates of the park, she said, "If this is to work, you must try to look happier."

Lady Mary turned her scowl on Emma. She looked rather like Caroline's son Nicky when he was forbidden to climb on the mantel shelf, Emma thought. Another carriage was coming up behind them as they turned in, and for a moment Emma despaired. Then Lady Mary straightened in her seat, put her shoulders well back, and smiled.

Emma blinked. The smile changed the girl's doll-like face, giving it human character and warmth. It made Emma think there might be something worthwhile under the petulance after all.

"Like this?" said Lady Mary through her teeth.

Emma's spark of interest guttered out. "Precisely," she snapped, smiling herself in a way that could scarcely be completely convincing, she thought.

They drove into the crowded avenues of the park and began to pass the carriages, mounts, and walking parties of the *haut ton*. Within minutes, they became a center of attention, and people began to whisper and, very discreetly, point them out.

"Will *he* be here?" asked Lady Mary through her fixed smile.

The way she said "he" made it clear she meant Colin. "No," replied Emma.

"I suppose you will keep him from me through this charade," said the girl. "Perhaps it is just as well. It was *terribly* hard, seeing him this morning." She heaved a great sigh through her steadfast smile. "I could tell he felt it, too." She clasped her black-gloved hands together.

Playacting, thought Emma savagely. She longed to tell the chit that Colin had wanted her thrown out of the house.

"*Why* did he choose you instead of me?" demanded Lady Mary passionately then. "It makes no sense."

Since Emma had no intention of trying to answer such a question, she was grateful to the beady-eyed old countess who hailed them from her carriage just then and pulled up to exchange greetings. She was even more relieved when the girl played the part assigned her as they dismissed the rumors as mistakes and exaggerations. The countess took in all they had to say with avid interest; whether she believed it or not, Emma couldn't tell.

"That stupid stuff will not do for Jane and Alice and Eliza," Lady Mary said when the woman drove off.

After a moment, Emma remembered that these were the friends to whom she had sent her "farewell" notes. "You will have to speak to them personally," she agreed.

"I shall tell them the truth," declared Lady Mary with a toss of her head.

"Good," answered Emma. "Then you will tell them that you were mistaken about Colin's intentions, that you mistook politeness for love, that you somehow did not notice that he paid equal attentions to a dozen other girls and roused hopes in none of them. You will apologize for your behavior and ask that they mention the incident to no one."

"That is not how it was at all!" sputtered Lady Mary.

"No?" Emma held her gaze in a battle of wills that seemed to surprise the younger girl. She was utterly spoiled, Emma thought. She was used to getting whatever she wanted without any opposition. But not this time. She wondered how long it would take for the girl to realize she had met her match. Out of the corner of her eye, Emma saw a party of riders approaching them. "Smile," she murmured sweetly, and they turned to face another barrage of questions.

More than an hour passed in similar encounters. Emma found it wearing, but she thought they did very well. She had the strongest of motives to succeed, and she suspected Lady Mary was beginning to enjoy the role she was playing. She was certain, at least, that she enjoyed the attention. And Emma was confident they had begun to stem the tide of gossip, though the battle was by no means won.

At last, she was able to direct the coachman to head for the Morland house, where she would gratefully drop Lady Mary. As he was turning around, however, a high-pitched voice from the side of the road called, "Emma, my dear."

Emma turned, and was extremely displeased to find herself confronting Arabella Tarrant, who stood on the grass verge arm-in-arm with Count Julio Orsino.

"It's vastly fortunate that we should encounter you this way," said Arabella before she could speak. "I'm feeling quite unwell, and I was hoping to see some friend who could drive me home."

Without waiting for a response, she marched up to the barouche and opened the door. Orsino stepped smoothly forward and lowered the steps for her before either of the footmen could move.

"Dizzy, you know," insisted Arabella as she climbed in. "I am distressingly susceptible to heat."

Orsino quickly followed her into the carriage and joined her in the forward seat, where he sat smiling at Emma with smug effrontery.

She could not have them thrown out of her carriage without causing just the sort of scene that would fuel yet more gossip, Emma thought, fuming. She was neatly trapped. She signaled the coachman to proceed. "It isn't hot," she said sharply then.

"Not to those of us who have lived in the South," replied the count. He smiled at her warmly, intimately, as if they knew each other very well indeed.

"The least degree of warmth oversets me," claimed Arabella, fluttering her hands and causing the ghostly green ribbons that trimmed her piercing yellow gown to shiver and sway. "I declare, it's been an age since I've seen you, Emma. You look as lovely as ever." Malice etched her voice like acid.

She had arranged this with Orsino out of spite, Emma realized, because they had ignored her since returning from Cornwall. Colin had sent her a substantial sum of money, yet Arabella wanted only to take advantage of his position in society. She resented that they would not let her use them. A flash of anger shook Emma. Arabella hoped to cause trouble, and she had already gotten her wish. Emma gritted her teeth. She had to find a way *not* to make introductions. Lady Mary was gazing in fascinated horror at Arabella's garish gown. Orsino should certainly not be made acquainted with a young, unmarried, and very wealthy debutante.

"I am sorry that I cannot take you home," Emma said to Arabella. "We are expected at once in Grosvenor Square."

"No, we aren't," said Lady Mary, sensing a mystery. "Mama is visiting my aunt."

Taking the matter out of her hands, Orsino leaned forward, putting his hand to his breast. "I am Count Julio Orsino," he said. "From Italy."

"Really?" said Lady Mary. "My father went to Italy on a grand tour when he was sixteen. He liked it very much. We have a lot of pictures from Italy in our house."

"Your father must be a man of great good taste," replied the count. "Miss, er . . ."

"I am Lady Mary Dacre," said the girl. She held out her hand.

Emma bit her lip in irritation, longing to shake her. But there was no saving the situation now. "This is Mrs. Arabella Tarrant," she added, and noticed the girl perk up at the last name. Splendid, she had heard that gossip as well.

"Enchanted," murmured the count, offering Lady Mary a broad smile. "But I must offer my condolences?" He made it a question, and indicated the deep mourning dress Lady Mary wore.

"My grandmama died," she confided.

"Ah. I am sorry."

The girl nodded. "I am *very* sorry. I miss her very

much. But, you know, she would *want* me to go out and enjoy myself, and not be draped in black and shut away from the world."

The count's eyes gleamed. "Of course she would," he agreed.

If only she had been shut away, thought Emma bitterly. She should have realized that Orsino would not be content to be turned away from her house and would plan some sort of revenge.

"I am surprised you stand for such treatment," the man added.

She had to get Lady Mary away from him, Emma thought desperately. She looked around. They were nearing the gates of the park.

"I had thought to be riding in the park," Orsino offered, "but I was sadly disappointed in a mount."

"Did you hire a horse?" asked Lady Mary.

Orsino shook his head. "I will not allow you to call it a horse, dear lady. It would be a mortal insult to the breed, to every one of the fine animals we see before us." He gestured to the riders on the bridle path. "The . . . creature has been returned to the stables where I rented it. But only after it had bitten my manservant, the landlady's boy, and the man delivering . . . ah, coal, I believe it was. A very large, florid gentleman who threatened to bring the law down upon us."

Lady Mary giggled.

"I have been advised to patronize another establishment, but I have not yet brought myself to, er, confront another English mount."

"No doubt the horses in Italy are much finer," said Emma tartly.

He made an airy gesture. "Shall we say more . . . refined?"

"Why not go back and ride them, then?" she suggested, her patience at an end.

"Ah, if it were possible," he replied, and let out a deep sigh. "But I fear the late war deprived my family of its estates and fortune in my home country. It is sad, is it not, when a great noble family falls on such hard times?"

Emma's lip curled. She had heard more than one person speculate on the legitimacy of Orsino's title. And she was certain that there had never been any lands or fortune. He was a gamester, a swindler, and who knew what else. "Now that the war is over, perhaps you could go back and recover them," she said sweetly.

The count shook his head, but did not offer any reason why this was impossible.

"It is like a novel," said Lady Mary happily.

Probably because it came out of one, thought Emma sourly. She had to get Lady Mary away from this dangerous man. Desperately, she scanned the area for possible rescue, and noticed a hansom cab discharging a passenger on the road outside the park gates. At once, she turned to the footman perched at the back of the carriage. "John, get that cab," she commanded. "Hurry!"

Looking startled, the man jumped down and ran to secure the vehicle.

"I must apologize," said Emma with false sincerity. "As I said, we have an engagement. But fortunately, here is a hansom that can get you home. I hope you feel better very soon, Arabella. Pull up, please, Tobias."

The coachman obediently stopped the carriage. Emma faced down Arabella's obvious outrage and Count Orsino's amusement in silence, merely waiting for them to get down.

They had no choice but to do so. Arabella was beginning to sputter objections, but Orsino simply gave her a bow that conceded defeat—for now—and put her into the cab.

"That was terribly rude," said Lady Mary when they were on their way to her home once again.

"They are not proper people for you to know," answered Emma curtly.

"Why?"

She ignored the question, absorbed in her own emotions. She seemed to have no luck at all in London. Everything she did threatened more social embarrassment. And Colin wanted a wife who did not enact dramas or make his life more difficult. Sooner or later, wouldn't he decide these continual upheavals weren't worth it?

"That man raised his hat to you," pointed out Lady Mary.

Looking up apprehensively, Emma saw her brother Robin on the other side of the street, mounted on a good-looking chestnut. Relieved, she waved.

"I thought we were going home," complained Lady Mary.

"In a moment," promised Emma. They were closer now. "Robin!" she called.

At first, it seemed that he might not approach, but then he turned and came up beside them. "Morning," he said coolly, tipping his hat. He didn't smile. Indeed, Emma's brother was still feeling extremely aggrieved. After their unfortunate encounter at the St. Mawr house, he had placed Emma in the same category as their father—someone who treated him like a child, to be shunted aside and ignored. His bitter disappointment in her had been compounded by the necessity of raising a rather large sum of money quickly. He had been forced to go to a most unpleasant moneylender and, as his friend Jack put it, "sign away his soul." Unfairly, this had simply increased his resentment toward Emma. He had not answered the note she sent him, and had not called on her again.

"Robin, I have been wanting to see you," said Emma.

Hearing the emotion in her voice, Lady Mary perked up, examining Robin with new interest.

"Been dashed busy," he answered. "Rafts of invitations." His airy gesture and bland expression were meant to convey a sophisticate's weariness with these attentions. But he rather spoiled the effect by adding, "Didn't want to *burden* you with my confidences."

"It is not a burden," declared Emma. Her concern for Robin had been the starting point for everything that had happened to her in the last weeks, she thought. She had had his interests at heart from the moment she saw him again. He did not know that however, she reminded herself.

"No need to concern yourself," he replied airily. "I took care of everything. Shouldn't have brought you into it in the first place."

"Into what?" she asked. All her worry over his gambling came back in a rush. If he had been in trouble, no doubt that had been at the root of it. And she knew only too well the sort of things that could befall a young man when the gaming tables got the better of him. "Robin, won't you tell me . . ."

He waved her question aside. "Going to introduce me?" he asked, implying that she had somehow slighted him once again.

Emma gave an exasperated sigh. "Lady Mary, this is my brother Robin Bellingham. Robin, Lady Mary Dacre."

Lady Mary's face fell as the pleasant fantasy she had spun about Emma's betrayal of her husband with a shallow young lover evaporated.

"How d'you . . ." Robin paused. "Dacre?" he repeated. "Dacre? The one who's spreading insulting stories about St. Mawr? What the deuce is she doing with you?"

"Robin," admonished Emma. She looked around; there was no one near them just now.

"It was certainly not *my* idea," answered Lady Mary.

Robin ignored her. "They're saying at the clubs that she's off her noodle. According to Freddy Blankenship—"

"Freddy is *despicable!*" cried Lady Mary. "And it is excessively rude of *you* to talk about me as if I am not even here."

Robin looked her up and down as if she were a mildly interesting specimen at the zoo. "Freddy says she nearly pulled the same trick on him. Claimed he was paying her attentions when he only danced with her."

Lady Mary gasped. She had turned bright red. The glare she aimed at Robin was murderous. "You . . . you . . ." she sputtered.

"Freddy says she thinks herself irresistible."

"You *beast*," exploded Lady Mary, having found her tongue. "You are worse than Freddy. You are the rudest, most unpleasant man I have ever met."

"Well, at least you won't be imagining that I mean to offer for you, then," responded Robin callously.

"*You?* If you were the *last* man on earth, I would not accept you."

"Rest assured, the question won't come up," said Robin.

Lady Mary burst into tears.

"Robin," protested Emma.

"As if I should *ever* look at *anyone* with a waistcoat like that," Lady Mary blubbered.

"What's the matter with my waistcoat?" exclaimed Robin, looking down at this loudly colorful garment.

"It's hideous," she wailed, then retreated into her handkerchief.

"Lady Mary," objected Emma.

"You hellcat," said her brother. "I'll have you know that this pattern is all the crack. Been excessively admired by any number of people with *taste.*"

"It looks like something a child would scribble if she got into a paintbox," sniveled Lady Mary.

Robin drew in an outraged breath. "*This* creature caused St. Mawr to throttle a fellow in the middle of his club dining room? It's a rotten shame, that's what it is. Shouldn't be allowed."

"Caused *what*?" said Emma.

"Disrupted the entire place. Everyone staring. Must have been devilishly embarrassing." Robin shook his head. "I'd have throttled *her* instead, I can tell you that much."

"Robin, what are you talking about?" demanded Emma.

"Perhaps not throttled," Robin was continuing to himself. "Not the thing to throttle a lady. Bad form. Shaken her soundly, maybe. Yes, that's it."

"What happened at Colin's club?" repeated Emma, in a voice that could not be ignored.

"Um? Oh, it was that thing with Steyne. Came up to St. Mawr's table at the club. Said something or other about this whole rigmarole. I never heard what. And St. Mawr went for his throat." Robin looked torn between admiration and disapproval. "They say two of his friends had to pull him off Steyne or he would have killed him then and there."

"Because of *me*?" wondered Lady Mary rapturously, her tears mysteriously dried.

"Insult to Emma, I heard," contradicted Robin. "No one would get into such a taking over *you*."

"Beast," said Lady Mary.

"She-devil," replied Robin cordially.

Emma made a sound, which caused them both to turn and look at her.

"Say." Robin frowned at the expression on his sister's face. "Probably shouldn't have mentioned the incident." He looked guilty. "Know I shouldn't have, in fact. Not suitable for ladies' ears. Hope you won't let on that I was spreading the tale."

"*I* will," Lady Mary assured him.

Robin ignored her.

Colin had already been exposed to acute embarrassment in front of his town friends, Emma thought. Because of her. And he had not even told her about it.

"You all right?" Robin asked.

"Yes." Emma wanted to ask him more about the incident, but not now, in this public place, with Lady Mary at her side taking it all in. She instructed the coachman to turn for home. "Come and visit me," she told Robin as they left him.

With a wave that committed him to nothing, Robin

rode off. Emma then had the pleasure of riding through the streets in an open carriage with Lady Mary sniffing theatrically into a handkerchief beside her. "Do stop," she urged the girl. "You will ruin all that we accomplished today."

"It was not like that at *all*," wailed her companion from the depths of her square of linen.

"Of course it wasn't," soothed Emma, not caring in the least what "it" might be, only determined to forestall more tears.

"Freddy Blankenship was *hounding* me. He sent flowers. He took me riding. He always asked me to stand up with him more than once at Almack's. When Mama told me that we might expect an offer, I took the next opportunity to inform him that I did not *wish* to marry him."

Emma made calming noises, searching the busy street for anyone who might recognize them.

Lady Mary gulped back a new sob. "He is *fat*, and he thinks he knows everything," she informed Emma.

She shook her head, trying to look sympathetic and fervently wishing that they might reach the Morland house soon.

"He called me a starched-up little prig who thought no one was good enough for her. But that isn't *true*. I just didn't *like* him."

"Of course," said Emma, relieved that the crying seemed to be definitely over.

Lady Mary sniffed. "*And* I think he was paying me attentions only because I am the daughter of a duke."

"He sounds like a dreadful person," responded Emma.

"Well, he *is*. And now he is getting his revenge on me by spreading these stories, making me ridiculous."

"Rather like your story about Colin," Emma could not resist saying.

"It *isn't*," wailed Lady Mary. She threw her wet handkerchief onto the seat of the carriage. "I am going to *make* Mama take me into the country."

Would that be best, after all? Emma wondered. She didn't know how much more of Lady Mary she could tolerate. Certainly she wanted her kept away from Orsino. And with Colin creating scenes at his club, perhaps it was all for nothing anyway. She set her jaw. Their appearance together had helped today. Many of the people they had spoken to had begun to doubt the stories; she knew it. She had to continue, which meant that Lady Mary did as well. "That's the same as admitting the talk is true," she argued. "Do you want to give Freddy that satisfaction?"

"What else am I to do?"

"Ignore him. Drive out with me again and show everyone that you are not affected by the silly things being said."

Lady Mary stared at her from reddened eyes. She was not at all stupid, Emma realized. "You just want to help St. Mawr," she said. "You don't care anything about *me.*"

"You said you wanted to help him, too," Emma pointed out.

"Nobody cares about me," the younger girl wailed, groping for her sodden handkerchief once more.

Fortunately, at this moment, they pulled up in front of the Morland town house. Emma accompanied Lady Mary inside. "Showing the *ton* that you are unaffected by gossip will help you as well," she told her. "If the stories about Colin are untrue, isn't it all the more likely that Freddy's malicious attack is also groundless?"

"I *hate* him," said Lady Mary passionately.

"Of course you do."

"I'll *show* him he cannot spread lies about me!"

"Good," encouraged Emma.

"I'll tell everyone he wears a corset. I heard it creak when he bent down to pick up my fan."

"I don't—" began Emma.

But Lady Mary had undergone a sudden change in mood. "We'll look for him in the park, and I'll *cut him dead,"* she added triumphantly.

Emma hid a grimace.

"How fortunate that you began this." Lady Mary gave her a brilliant smile. She seemed to have forgotten her resentment of Emma. "I am not allowed to go out otherwise, you know, because we are in mourning."

"Don't you think that you should—"

"Freddy will be very, *very* sorry he so much as mentioned my name," declared the younger girl with immense satisfaction. She turned and gave Emma her hand like a grand hostess. "Good-bye," she said happily. Holding up the flounce on her skirt, she went tripping up the stairs.

Emma returned to her carriage with a mixture of apprehension and relief. Events seemed to be moving rather too fast, she thought, and not at all in the direction she had planned.

Emma looked for Colin as soon as she reached the house, but he was out. Her desire to speak to him was so strong that she could not settle to anything else. Instead, she paced the drawing room, growing more impatient and irritated by the minute. Her silent commands did not bring him home, however. She had to go up to dress for dinner without having seen him. She did hear him arrive a little later. But the maid was dressing her hair, and she knew that Reddings would be with him. She would have to contain herself until after the evening meal, she concluded in frustration.

"How was your drive?" Colin asked Emma as they ate.

"Unusual."

"From what I have observed, Lady Mary Dacre seems to be an unusual young woman."

"She certainly is that." In an effort to make conversation, Emma recounted the story of her outing. Colin found the exchanges between Lady Mary and Robin Bellingham amusing. "I am developing a strong desire to meet this Freddy Blankenship," he said.

"I leave him to you," responded Emma. "And I pray that our next drive will bear no resemblance to this one."

Colin raised his eyebrows. "Is there to be another?"

"Yes, I think so."

"You really believe it necessary?"

Emma looked at him. "Don't you?" she asked pointedly.

He did not respond to her signal. "You must do as you think best," was his only reply.

"You have no opinion on the matter?" wondered Emma crisply. "You don't think the scandal is spreading?"

"My credit is strong enough to withstand the chit's illusions," he answered.

"I see."

Colin did not appear to hear the irony of her tone. He smiled. "One good thing has come out of this, at least. You have won over my mother."

"What?"

"I encountered her in Bond Street today, and when I ventured a mild complaint about the presence of Lady Mary in my drawing room, she leapt to your defense."

"You're joking?"

"No, indeed. Your efforts to avert a scandal impressed her deeply. She scolded me for venturing to criticize such a brave and quick-witted young woman. Said I didn't deserve you."

"Why would she say that, I wonder?"

Something in her voice finally penetrated Colin's consciousness. "Because you've taken her by storm," he said. "Is anything wrong?"

"With me? No."

"Has someone insulted you? Is that why you're asking about scandal?"

"I don't know," she snapped. "Have they?"

Colin frowned at her. Before he could speak again, the footman entered with a tray, and the second course was served with due ceremony. When they had taken what they wanted and begun to eat again, John stationed himself in the corner, ready to do their bidding, and effectively limiting their conversation as well.

They finished the meal mainly in silence, then walked together through the dining room door, which John was holding for them. "Will you sit in the library, or do you prefer the drawing room?" asked Colin.

"The library," replied Emma decisively. It was much more private than the upper room, and would give them a chance to talk.

They settled on the library sofa before the fire. Colin stretched out his long legs toward the blaze. "This is pleasant," he said. "It has been a long time since we spent an evening at home."

"Yes." Emma half turned to face him. "There is something I wish to speak to you about."

"I sensed that," he responded dryly.

"Why did you not tell—" Emma's sentence was interrupted by a knock at the door. "What?" she snapped.

Ferik entered with a tray containing decanters and glasses. He gave them a dazzling smile as he placed it on the table before them.

"Where is John?" said Colin.

Ferik straightened, spreading his great hands. "Alas, he fell and hurt his knee," he replied. "But I knew that you wanted your brandy, lord, so I brought it at once."

"Is John all right?" said Emma sharply, having a very good notion of how the footman came to fall.

"Oh, yes. He must only rest a little." Ferik gave her a conspiratorial look, and Emma glared at him.

"Clinton will see to him," said Colin, misinterpreting her reaction.

"It is Mr. Clinton's *night off,*" said Ferik, as if mentioning some filthy habit the butler had recently revealed. "*I* do not require nights off, lord." He put his hand across his chest. "Never would I desire such a—"

"Yes, yes," interrupted Emma. "Thank you, Ferik. We don't require anything else."

"Yes, mistress. But shall I not bring more wood for the fire? The box is nearly empty."

"It will last," said Colin. He looked at Ferik, and the giant bowed low.

"Yes, lord, thank you," he said, and went out.

"He has to stop this," Colin complained when he was gone.

"I'll speak to him again," answered Emma impatiently.

"No." He looked thoughtful. "I think we must try stronger measures. I cannot have my footmen injured."

"What measures?"

Colin raised one brow. "I believe I will order Clinton a . . . a new coat. With, oh, silver buttons."

Emma had to smile. "Ferik will be livid with envy."

"Precisely. And he will see that Clinton continues to have my, er, favor, despite his incursions."

"You have a flair for intrigue, my lord."

"I do, don't I?" He reached for the decanter. "Will you join me?"

Emma shook her head, and he poured out one brandy.

"Now then," he added after he had taken a sip and approved the vintage. "What did you wish to talk about?"

"Why didn't you tell me what happened at your club?" Emma asked without preamble.

"My club?" he echoed.

But Emma could see from the flicker of wariness in his violet eyes that he knew exactly what she meant. "I understand you attacked a man there," she continued impatiently. "Publicly, in the dining room. And I have heard it was because of some insult to me."

"Heard from whom?" replied Colin in a soft, dangerous voice.

"Why didn't you tell me?" Emma asked again.

"There was no reason to do so." Colin turned slightly away from her. He was not proud of his behavior during that unfortunate incident. And he was furious that Emma had been told of it.

"No reason? Was it not related to this stupid scandal we are trying to combat?"

"I don't wish to discuss it."

"I insist upon discussing it!" exclaimed Emma.

"It is none of your affair," he snapped.

"None . . ." She couldn't speak for a moment, she was so angry. Her temples were pounding with it. "I see," she said finally through gritted teeth. "We are not, then, working together on this problem. We are not partners with a common cause who can aid each other. We are to care nothing for what the other does, and indeed not to expect that it is *any of our affair*!"

"Emma!"

"I had not realized. I had foolishly assumed that our *bargain* meant that we had shared interests and goals. I beg pardon for having overstepped my bounds, my lord. I shall take care not to do so again!"

"You are making a great deal out of nothing," Colin replied.

"Oh? Are gentlemen constantly throttling one another at your club? I had formed quite a mistaken impression of it."

"You are being purposely irritating," he accused.

"It is no wonder then that women are not admitted," Emma went on as if he had not spoken. "We are not particularly partial to brawling."

Colin took hold of her shoulders, shaking her a little, and forced her to face him. "Stop it!"

His fingers were digging into her arms. Emma took a deep breath.

"Who told you of this?" he demanded.

She took another breath, trying unsuccessfully to be calm.

"I will know," he said.

"What does it matter?"

"Emma!"

"Perhaps that is none of *your* affair," she retorted. She wriggled, trying to shake off his grip.

Colin shook her very slightly again. "If you do not tell me at once, I shall . . ."

"What? Throttle me?"

He released her as if she had burned his hands. His eyes, fixed on her face, narrowed. "Someone you met in the park, I wager," he said. "But a mere acquaintance would not dare . . ." His jaw tightened. "Your brother," he guessed. "He hasn't the wit to keep his mouth closed."

Emma tried very hard to look blank, but he still managed to read the truth in her face.

"Blast him!" growled Colin. "Why can't he be content with his ridiculous clothes and making a cake of himself at the tables. I shall—"

"Tables?" repeated Emma.

Colin looked at her.

She sat up straighter and clenched her fists. "Is he still playing deep?"

"Oh yes. He has no sense in that area either."

"Why didn't you tell me?"

"I just did," he snapped, wishing young Robin Bellingham to perdition.

"Thank you," she replied bitterly. "I suppose you never would have if we had not begun this . . . discussion."

"I'm not his nursemaid."

"No, you made it very clear from the day we were married that you would not help him. And we have established, of course, that we do not act together in any matter. I shall have to do what I can alone."

"Emma," said Colin. How had they gotten to this point? he wondered. He couldn't quite remember.

"I'll speak to him," declared Emma grimly. "I know about these things. I know where gaming can lead. He must listen to me."

"It's your father who should be spoken to," replied

Colin involuntarily. "If he didn't push so hard . . ." He stopped.

Memories of growing up in her father's household flooded Emma. He had always expected perfection from his children, and no doubt her own behavior had made it even more difficult for Robin. She looked into the embers, glowing red in the fireplace. "I don't want to talk to Father," she admitted quietly.

"Well, don't then," said Colin. "Young men grow out of this extravagant behavior, you know. You are making too much of it."

Emma stared at him. A vision of Edward rose in her mind—ravaged by his passion for gaming. Colin did not understand. She felt the gulf that had suddenly yawned between them widen even further. "Don't be concerned," she said coolly, rising from her place on the sofa. "I shall not try to make this any of your affair."

"Well, it isn't," he muttered. He felt as if he were angry with the whole world. Emma was being utterly unreasonable, he thought.

"I know," she said. "Good night, my lord."

When she was gone, Colin refilled his brandy glass and brooded savagely over the fire. Emma was being unfair, he thought. She did not listen. And she had a damned biting tongue. He knew he'd acted like an idiot that evening at the club. He needed no one to tell him so, or to make sarcastic remarks about brawling. Didn't he wince inwardly every time he thought of it? Didn't he have to endure the jokes of acquaintances with pretended good humor? And wasn't he only too aware that his uncharacteristic behavior had made squelching the scandal much more difficult? Had she needed to twit him with that?

Defiantly, Colin filled his glass again and took a good swallow. She might give him more credit, he thought. She might have some notion of how devilishly embarrassing it was to make a fool of oneself in public. But all she cared about was her damned brother. And was he worth it? No! He was a young idiot who didn't have the sense to keep a story like that to himself, or to leave the gaming tables in good time, or to choose a decent waistcoat. Scowling at the embers of the fire, Colin resisted the urge to smash his glass on the brick hearth. One thing was certain; he wasn't going to be saddled with trying to reform Robin Bellingham. A short stint in debtors' prison would be positively good for the young fool, he thought savagely.

Chapter Nine

The next morning, before she had time to think too much about it, Emma summoned Ferik and set out to walk a short distance through the London streets to one that was hauntingly familiar to her. When they reached the neighborhood, she paused at the corner and looked down it. There were the ample red brick houses trimmed in gray stone, the whole street the product of one admired architect. There were the worn cobblestones and the neat pavements punctuated by posts where horses could be tied. There were the scrubbed doorsteps, carefully maintained by dozens of housemaids. There were even, unbelievably, the autumn roses in the windowbox at number sixteen, old Mrs. Grainger's house. It was astonishingly unchanged.

"Is this where we are going, mistress?" inquired Ferik.

She nodded, momentarily unable to speak.

"Who lives here?" he wanted to know.

"I used to." It came out in a whisper.

Ferik bent toward her. "I didn't hear, mistress."

Emma took a breath and stood straighter, recovering herself. "This is where I lived when I was a child, Ferik. The home of my family."

"Ah." The giant looked around with great interest. "A pleasant place," he concluded.

"Yes." Emma began to move again, walking down the right side of the street toward number eleven.

"We are going to see your father, mistress?"

She nodded again.

"Ah. That is good." He strode along behind her looking pleased.

"You approve, Ferik?" asked Emma, slightly amused.

"It is proper to give respect to one's elders. You have not visited your father since we returned to England."

"We did not part on good terms when I left it," she said dryly.

"But now you will make amends," suggested Ferik.

"Amends? He is the one to do that."

As they approached the front door of the Bellingham house, Ferik shook his head slowly. "No, mistress, it is the child who must submit. It is wrong to humiliate the old."

Emma started to argue with him, then thought better of it. "You know nothing about it," she muttered, and indicated that he should knock on the door.

It was opened by another familiar figure. "Hello, Wiggins," she said.

"Miss Emma!" The old butler looked overjoyed. "How good to see you again. We had all heard . . . I mean, may I offer you felicitations on behalf of all of the staff?"

"Thank you." Emma felt guilty under his benevolent gaze. Perhaps she ought to have visited before now. "I'll come down to the kitchen before I go," she said. "Is my father in?"

"Yes, miss. In his study."

Emma stepped inside. Wiggins seemed to notice Ferik for the first time. He started visibly.

"This is my servant Ferik," Emma told him reassuringly.

Wiggins gazed upward in amazement. "Is it, miss?" he said feebly.

Ferik bowed very low. "I offer my respect to the household of my mistress's father," he rumbled.

"Er." Wiggins gazed at Ferik, who remained bent at the waist, then goggled at Emma.

"Just accept," she whispered.

"Er. Yes. Thanks," said Wiggins. Ferik straightened, smiling broadly.

"Wait for me here," Emma told him.

"Yes, mistress." The large man slid down to sit on the hall floor, resting his back against the paneled wall.

"Miss Emma!" protested the old butler.

"He'll be fine. Don't worry." Leaving them to work it out between themselves, Emma hurried off toward the back of the house.

At the door of the study, she hesitated. To be called to this room had meant a scolding when she was a child. She and Robin were not allowed inside it unaccompanied, and their father had always retreated here when he was out of sorts. It took a bit of courage to raise her hand and knock.

"Yes," said a gruff voice within.

Swallowing, Emma opened the door.

Her father was sitting in an armchair next to the hearth. Light streamed into the window behind him, falling on the pages of a book he held. His mane of white hair was a shining nimbus under this illumination, and his craggy face was in shadow. "What is it?" he demanded, looking up. Surprise replaced irritation at once, and he grasped his cane to struggle to his feet. "Emma, my dear, how splendid to see you."

"Please, don't get up." She walked across the room to stand before him.

"What a fine surprise," he added, sinking back into the chair. "Sit down, sit down. You're looking very well."

"Thank you." She took the chair on the other side of the fireplace.

"Nothing wrong, is there?" he asked sharply. "No problem with St. Mawr?"

"No, Father."

"Ah. Good, good. Just wondered, you know. You haven't come round here since . . ." He left this thought hanging and turned to pull vigorously on the bell rope. "Coffee? Tea?"

"I don't . . . A cup of tea."

The door of the room opened. "Bess, Miss Emma's here," he said. "Bring us some tea."

"Yes, sir." The maid dropped a small curtsy. "Good to see you again, Miss Emma."

"Thank you, Bess."

While they waited, Emma kept the conversation on general matters, but when the tea had been brought and poured and they were alone again, she said, "Actually, I came to speak to you about Robin."

Bellingham's smile faded. "What's he done now?" he demanded.

"He hasn't done anything. Or, what I mean is . . ." She braced herself. "I'm worried about his gambling," she said.

"Damn the boy," exploded her father. "Is he still at it? I've told him and told him. I've threatened to stop his allowance altogether. But he will not listen." The older man pounded his fist on the arm of his chair. "I'll have his hide."

Emma couldn't suppress a quaver of apprehension. How often he had railed at her when she was young. "Please," she said.

"What?"

"This does no good."

He glowered at her. "You have some suggestion, I suppose? Wouldn't be here otherwise."

"I don't know," she said. "I thought we might consult together. I'm afraid, Father. I know so well what can happen to a man addicted to gaming."

He grunted.

"I couldn't bear to see Robin ruined like . . ."

"Like that blackguard Edward Tarrant," he finished.

She nodded.

"I told you from the very beginning that he was a worthless fortune hunter."

"Yes. You did."

"But oh, no, you knew better. Found out I was right, eh?"

"Yes, Father," replied Emma tonelessly.

"And now you come around to tell me how to raise my son, do you?"

"No! That is not what I meant. I only want to—"

"That's rich. It is indeed. If I'm hard on the boy, it's all due to you, you know."

"Me?" Emma stared at him.

"I wasn't going to have him running wild, ruining his life the way you did. I've kept a tight rein on the boy. And what if I did?" His scowl was belligerent.

"I know I made things difficult," began Emma.

"Difficult! There's a word. You have no idea what it was like."

"I don't suppose I do," she admitted.

Her father glowered at her from under his bushy white brows. "I was beside myself when you ran off. I'd tried to be a good parent after your mother died, you know. Did the best I could, which wasn't much, perhaps. And then you threw over all your chances and eloped with that . . ." He clenched his teeth. "Well, I vowed that nothing like that would happen again."

For the first time, Emma felt remorse about her treatment of her father. There had been no room in her mind for other points of view when she was seventeen, she thought. "I'm sorry, Father," she said.

He stared at her, his mouth working as if he was chewing over some tough bit of meat. "Never said that to me before," he pointed out.

"I know."

"Humph." George Bellingham cleared his throat, then swallowed.

"Do you think Robin could be rebelling against your 'tight rein'?" Emma ventured after a pause.

Bellingham blinked, then frowned. "Gambling just because I forbade him to do so?" he replied. He shook his head. "No, that's ridiculous. Robin is an intelligent lad."

"Of course," Emma agreed. "But like most young men, he is not averse to kicking up his heels a bit."

"He's no mincing dandy, despite those ridiculous clothes he wears," growled Bellingham.

"No, indeed. I imagine he even enjoys flouting authority now and then. Rather like riding a horse everyone says is untamable."

Bellingham looked at her from under his bushy white eyebrows.

"Or holding a curricle race on the busiest street in Bath?"

The older man cocked his head.

Emma gazed blandly back at him, willing herself to be unintimidated by his glare.

Finally, Bellingham chuckled. "Told you too many of those stories when you were a little lass, didn't I?"

"I remember them all," said Emma, venturing a smile.

"My father tore a broad strip out of me for that race," he added. "Called me six kinds of fool and threatened to restrict me to the country until I turned thirty."

Emma preserved a prudent silence.

Bellingham sighed again. "When he came down from school, I forbade Robin to play anything, even silver loo. Perhaps I did push him too hard."

Emma simply listened.

"He's a spirited boy, as I was myself."

She nodded.

"Gaming is *not* in our blood," he insisted.

"I hate it," she assured him.

Bellingham brooded for several moments. "I suppose you have some suggestion?" He sounded both hopeful and resentful.

"I wondered . . . what if you stopped mentioning the subject of gambling to Robin?" she offered. "Give him nothing to fight against."

"And when he comes to me with his debts?" demanded Bellingham. But before Emma could answer, he frowned, and said, "Not that he has for a long while. I don't know how he's been managing, because he always loses more than he wins. Boy's a damned poor player."

"You could tell him that it's none of your affair, that he is a man now and you trust him to manage his income."

"But he can't," exclaimed her father.

"Perhaps not. You may have to come to his rescue again. But who knows what he may do, given the opportunity and no criticism?"

"Humph," was the only reply. There was an intent look in the old man's eyes, however, and Emma decided that she had best be satisfied with that. Pushing him would accomplish nothing. "You must decide what is best," she concluded. "But if there is anything I can do, you must tell me at once."

"You could keep him occupied," said her father immediately. "Boy wants to be a pink of the *ton*. He's only too happy to attend any sort of fashionable squeeze. Keeps him from the tables, too."

"I can do that," she agreed eagerly. She was suddenly struck by a thought. "In fact, I think I can do even better." It was brilliant, Emma thought. The perfect thing.

Emma and Colin had a long-standing engagement to attend a play that evening with his mother. As she put the last touches on her elegant ensemble, Emma vowed that she would give Colin exactly what he'd asked for in his marriage bargain. She would show him that she was even better than he at keeping to the terms of their partnership. She would be pleasant, but distant; completely agreeable, but superficial; and all in all, the epitome of a suitable nobleman's wife. Taking a final look at her superbly cut gown of ruby velvet and the cascading curls of her pale hair, she gave a nod and went downstairs to join her husband.

The dazzling smile she gave him in the lower hall made Colin look first relieved, then slightly puzzled. If he had expected some recurrence of their earlier quarrel, Emma thought superciliously, he would find he didn't know her as well as he imagined. Holding her head high, her expression and stance a masterful mixture of grace and hauteur, she moved through the door Clinton was holding open for them and allowed the footman to hand her into the carriage.

When Colin joined her, she was carefully settling her skirt so that the velvet would not be crushed. The footman secured the coach door and swung up behind as the horses started off. The vehicle swayed a bit on its springs, and Emma took hold of the strap so that she could remain sitting quite upright.

"Emma," began Colin.

"Have you heard anything about this play?" she asked brightly. "Your mother didn't seem to know the plot, or the actors, or anything else."

"I believe it started last night. That is the extent of my information."

"Ah. An adventure, then," she replied.

"An adventure," echoed Colin, gazing at her.

"It is much more interesting to go to an unknown play, don't you think?" Emma was gazing out at the passing street scene as she spoke. "It may be a failure, of course. There is that risk. But if it is good, one has the gratification of discovery."

"Gratification?" he repeated, as if the word was alien to him.

"I have always loved the theater," she went on. "And I have been privileged to attend performances all over the Continent, and even once in Constantinople. Do you know that there they—"

"What the deuce? Is this . . . mindless chatter some sort of—"

"Mindless?" Emma struggled to keep her voice even and cordial. "I do beg your pardon, my lord. Have I been boring you? You should have mentioned it earlier."

"Is this about last night? Because I wanted to—"

"Last night?" she interrupted, as if she were trying to recall what he could be referring to. "Oh, here we are. Isn't it fortunate we live within such a convenient distance from the theaters?

"Emma!"

But the footman was already opening the carriage door and letting down the steps. Colin's mother and Sir Oswald Staunton, an older man who had been a friend of his father, were waiting for them on the steps of the building. And the group proceeded immediately to the box the older woman had taken for the evening. The time before the curtain rose was taken up with settling in their chairs and commonplace civilities. There was no opportunity for private talk.

When the play began, Emma leaned forward and prepared to enjoy herself. She really did love the theater. Plays had been a diversion and a solace even at the worst times of her life, and she always found herself able to forget her troubles in the unfolding story.

The actors began. Emma rested her elbow on the rail and put her chin in her hand, mentally ticking off the list of characters—an innocent young heroine, a stalwart hero, a wicked old aunt, an unwanted suitor. All too familiar, she thought, disappointed by the quality of the first speeches. It seemed this would be a very commonplace performance.

Then something odd happened. Emma blinked, wondering if she had really seen it, and decided she couldn't have. Or it was an accident, a mistake. The actors moved around the stage, declaiming their too-

predictable sentiments over the heads of the audience.
There was another oddity, and a third that left Emma
openmouthed with amazement. She turned to see if the
others had noticed anything. Sir Oswald looked sleepy
and extremely bored. Colin's mother appeared impatient, her eyes drifting from the stage to the crowd,
searching for acquaintances. Emma glanced at Colin.
His violet eyes held a glint of deep, sardonic amusement, and a smile was tugging at one corner of his
mouth.

"Did you see . . . ?" she whispered.

"I did indeed," he replied before she even finished
the sentence. "A most unusual performance."

They turned back to the stage, and in the next instant, both of them burst out laughing.

"You two are very gay," said Colin's mother. "I
don't see that this play is so amusing. Indeed, I find it
rather irritating."

"I believe the actors agree with you, Mother," said
Colin, "or perhaps they just dislike each other intensely."

"Did you see the one playing the judge stick out his
foot to trip the old lady?" asked Emma.

"She set the point of her heel on it," agreed Colin.
"Remarkably agile for her age. I thought he cursed her
most creatively."

Emma laughed again. "And then all the actors had to
make it part of the play. That tall one playing the hero is
beginning to look quite desperate."

"Don't see anything funny about it," muttered Sir
Oswald. "Damned disgraceful performance, I say. Actors more interested in scoring one another off than in
entertaining the audience."

Emma and Colin looked at each other, identical wry
humor in their expressions. Had anyone ever shared her
reactions so precisely? Emma wondered. So often in the
past she had been made to feel that she was out of step
with others, or unreasonable. She felt a tremor of emotion, and looked away from him.

When the curtain fell at the first interval, the folds of cloth were received with more enthusiasm than the previous scene. Some people were leaving, Emma noted, but when Sir Oswald suggested that they might do the same, a protest sprang to her lips.

"No, no, we must see this through," Colin objected before she could voice it. "I have an intense curiosity about what they will do next. Do you think they will make it through the entire play?"

"I don't know about the young heroine," said Emma. "She looked about to explode just before the curtain."

"We cannot miss that."

"No, please," she replied, smiling at him.

Sir Oswald grunted. "Let us have some refreshment at least," he grumbled, rising a little stiffly from his chair.

The four of them strolled together down to the crowded anteroom, where those who did not care to stay in their boxes greeted their friends and examined the fashions of the other theatergoers. Colin went to procure wine. His mother and Sir Oswald were hailed by a group of acquaintances and turned to join their chattering circle. Emma stood just behind them watching the animated crowd as if it were another drama.

"I don't understand what is going on in this play," a woman to her left was complaining. "It makes no sense."

"The young girl ain't bad looking," she caught a dandified gentleman murmuring to his crony. "Believe I'll slip backstage afterward and get an introduction."

Did anyone in this audience share her amusement about the way the actors were behaving? Emma wondered. Only Colin, she thought, with an inexplicable wistfulness. She looked around for him, and saw that he was still waiting for the wine.

"Good evening," said a smooth, hateful voice near her ear.

Emma turned to face Count Julio Orsino.

"Seeing you here, I thought I would pay my respects," he added.

She said nothing.

"Are you enjoying the play?" Orsino asked as if they were amiable acquaintances. "Not a very good one, I fear, eh?"

"Go away."

"My dear baroness—"

"And stay away from me," Emma added through clenched teeth.

"But you are left here all alone," he responded with patently false solicitude. "I cannot—"

"I am not alone."

"Indeed? Shall I fetch your friends for you?" He scanned the crowd.

Emma grew uncomfortably aware of Sir Oswald and Colin's mother close behind her, and of the fact that Colin himself must be making his way back to them. She did *not* want them to encounter Orsino. If the count thought he could force her to make introductions, he was sadly mistaken, she thought, her jaw clenched. He had still not understood who he was dealing with. If he insisted on a public demonstration, she would give it to him. Trembling with outrage and tension, Emma stood very straight and silently turned her back on him, giving him the cut direct. Anyone who saw would know that she was refusing to acknowledge the acquaintance. It was the most obvious and humiliating insult she could offer Orsino. And how he deserved it, she thought defiantly. This would show him that he must get out of her life, because Emma was certain that if he did not, something dreadful would come of it in the end.

An endless moment passed when she heard nothing of the crowd around her. Then a subtle movement ruffled the hair curling onto her cheek. "You would be well advised to come and see me," whispered Orsino, his lips almost brushing her ear. "I have been very patient. I have endured your contempt. But that is at an end now. If I do not hear from you by tomorrow, believe me, you will regret it."

He withdrew. Emma felt rather than saw him walk away from her. A few people standing nearby gave him curious glances, followed by more furtive, sidelong looks at her. Her hands were shaking, she noted dispassionately, and acknowledged to herself that she was afraid of Orsino. She had seen too much of what he could, and would, do.

A wineglass moved into her field of vision. "Here you are," said Colin.

Emma started violently.

"Did I startle you? I beg your pardon."

She took the wine.

"Who was that you were talking to?"

She looked up at him, and then quickly away. "I? No one. I wasn't talking to anyone." She drank from the glass, keeping it steady with some effort.

Colin examined Emma's averted face. He had distinctly seen her engaged in conversation with a sallow, foreign-looking fellow in rather flashy clothes. He had seen her turn away from him, and seen the man lean in to whisper something that had made Emma turn a bit pale. The man had had an air that he didn't like in the least—full of intangible warning signs that one learned with experience. Emma should not have any contact at all with that sort of man.

But she had had a great deal of contact with that sort of man in her earlier life, he remembered. Colin frowned. It occurred to him suddenly that Emma might have things to hide from the years she had spent with Edward Tarrant. "The stocky fellow with the yellow waistcoat," he prompted, unwilling to let this drop.

"Oh." Emma drew in a breath. "Oh, him. He was just asking, uh, how to reach the third tier of boxes."

If her manner had not been so agitated, he might have believed her, Colin thought. He watched unknowable emotions pass across her beautiful face. Clearly, she had been upset by the appearance of this fellow. And even more clearly, she was not going to tell him why.

The realization disturbed him profoundly.

"Not familiar with the theater?" he couldn't help adding.

"What? Oh, no. I . . . I believe he was from out of town."

He knew her. She could not be concealing anything dishonorable. But why, then, didn't she tell him what was going on?

He wanted to force her to, Colin realized. He wanted to say that it had been obvious from her expression that the man was no stranger, and that he had said something that upset her. He wanted to demand that she confide in him, and perhaps more important, that she explain why she had hesitated to do so.

But he didn't quite dare. He had known about her past when he married her, Colin thought. She had certainly made no secret of it. He had taken it on as part of their bargain. He had no grounds for complaint. Their sane, sensible arrangement did not give him the right to know what she did not wish to tell him. But some fierce, wounded part of him remained completely unconvinced by this rational argument. He wanted her to turn to him. The intensity of his need shook Colin and made him quickly try to wall it off behind practiced defenses. He simply wanted to protect her, he told himself. There was nothing wrong in that. It was his proper role as her husband. He took a deep breath. He would look into the matter of this unknown man quietly himself, he decided. And then they would see.

The bell rang, calling them back to their seats. They were standing in a crowd overpopulated with eager gossips, all of whom could sniff out a tidbit better than the finest foxhound, Colin told himself. It was no place for any sort of private conversation. Emma would never consider sharing confidences under this sort of malicious scrutiny.

For some reason, he felt considerably relieved. And

all he wanted just now was to see that worried frown disappear from her face. "One of the waiters told me that the man playing the judge has been jilted by the older actress, who is infatuated with the young hero," he said as he offered his arm to escort her back to their box. "And he is wavering between her and the ingenue. The whole cast is in an uproar about it."

"Reality intrudes into art?" Emma managed.

"With a vengeance, apparently. Quite literally in this case."

She smiled, and Colin felt an odd tightening in the region of his heart.

"Perhaps they have sorted things out in the interval," she offered as Colin's mother and Sir Oswald joined them in walking upstairs.

"I must admit that I hope not," he replied. When she met his eyes, he raised one brow.

"Me, too," she admitted, with another, easier, smile.

When the curtain rose again, it was immediately clear that the cast of the play had not resolved its difficulties during the pause. Their faces were set in anger as they pronounced the lines of what had been billed as a light-hearted comedy. When one of the men was required to take a lady's hand and bow over it, it was obvious from her look of pain that he crushed her fingers between his. In turn, when she was pouring him a glass of wine, she deliberately spilled it down the front of his knee breeches, leaving an embarrassing stain. His show of teeth in response was feral. "He looks as if he would dearly like to bite her," Colin commented, and was rewarded by another sputter of laughter from Emma.

After that, things only got worse. Cast members stepped in front of one another, spoke lines from completely different plays, and took every opportunity to interfere with their colleagues' parts. The action became a muddle, shifting at the whim of the last speaker, who forced the rest to scramble for a comprehensible response to whatever he chose to say. Emma and Colin found themselves pulled into a guessing game; with each speech, they vied with one another to whisper the name of the play from which the words had originally come. In ten minutes, they counted six unrelated titles.

"Not *Hamlet* again," protested Emma a few minutes later, wiping tears of laughter from her cheek. "The man playing the judge seems to have memorized every line of it."

"And he appears to find much of it very apt," agreed Colin, laughing out loud yet again as the older actress turned a killing glare on the actor in question.

Half-eaten apples, crumpled playbills, and random bits of refuse began to land on the front apron of the stage, thrown by disgruntled patrons in the pit. The ingenue, irritated beyond bearing by what was happening, deliberately kicked one piece of fruit back out into the audience, rousing an ominous mutter. The play's hero grabbed her arm and jerked her roughly around to face him, speaking his romantic lines to her through gritted teeth.

"This is dreadful," said Colin's mother, though she was smiling by now, too. "Come, let us go."

"Don't you want to see how it comes out, Mother?" asked Colin, his voice shaking with laughter.

"It will end in a riot," she replied positively. "And I do not want to be trying to find my carriage in the middle of it."

On stage, the ingenue lost control. Putting her hands on her hips, she confronted the audience and said "Beast!" to a burly man with a striped handkerchief tied around his neck who had just called out an insult. The man responded with an even grosser evaluation of her character and morals and the performance in general.

"That tears it," said Colin.

The young actress began picking up the things that had been thrown onto the stage and hurling them back into the audience. After a moment of frozen consternation onstage, one of the younger actors joined her, while the rest began to edge their way into the wings, hoping to escape notice. The crowd in the pit surged and roared like the sea, and then twenty arms were raised to throw.

"Perhaps we had better go," said Colin.

"Couldn't we just hide behind the curtains here in the box and watch?" asked Emma, her eyes twinkling.

A stray apple core flew past, barely missing the feather that adorned the dowager baroness's hair.

"A strategic retreat," declared Colin. "Come, Mother, Emma. If you will give the ladies your assistance, Sir Oswald, I will take rear guard."

Many of the other denizens of the boxes had come to the same conclusion, and when they reached the theater entry, it was crowded with fashionable patrons trying to get to the door. As they struggled through the crush, the volume of noise rose steadily behind them. They were outdoors and getting into the carriage when a mob of young men burst from the theater and went racing off down the street yelling and waving bits of cloth that looked remarkably like satin petticoats.

"Damned apprentices," said Sir Oswald. "They're a menace. Something ought to be done."

"Indeed," replied Colin, his voice unsteady. "Perhaps they should let them criticize plays for the newspapers."

Emma laughed.

"It is all very well to laugh," grumbled Sir Oswald. "But I don't know what the world is coming to when a pack of rabble is free to run the streets brandishing, er, undergarments. And probably looting as well."

"Oh, I think they've already got what they wanted," said Colin.

The older man snorted.

Fits of laughter continued to break out between Emma and Colin throughout the drive home. "I had a great deal of sympathy for that young actress," said Emma as they entered the house and walked up the stairs together. "I would have wanted to throw things if I had been in her situation."

"Very understandable," Colin agreed.

"But my aim would have been better," she assured him. "I would have hit that vulgar man who shouted the insults right on his big red nose," she added.

"I haven't the slightest doubt of it." They had come to the door of her bedchamber, and Colin hesitated. After yesterday, he was not, he realized, entirely sure of his welcome. The idea was unsettling and annoying. He just wanted everything to be as it had been. "We laugh at the same things," he pointed out.

"Yes," Emma agreed, the laughter still lingering in her eyes and around her mouth.

"That is not so common in my life," he added.

"Nor mine. What does that say about us? I wonder. Do you think our comic sense is warped?"

Looking down at her, Colin felt a tide of powerful emotion rise, frightening in its intensity. He couldn't put a name to it, though he knew it was all centered on Emma. "I was . . . a bit hasty last night," he tried. "I did not mean to offend you." Looking into her dark blue eyes, taking in her beauty, so familiar but always somehow a surprise as well, he could not stop himself from raising his hand to touch her cheek.

Emma put her own hand on top of his.

With an inarticulate sound, he pulled her into his arms and crushed her against him. To his infinite relief, Emma slid her arms around him.

Reaching behind her, Colin found the doorknob and opened the door, easing them both through it into her bedchamber. When it was safely closed behind them, he bent and kissed her glancingly, like the brush of a butterfly's wing.

Emma let out a sighing breath.

He kissed her again. His hand caressed her neck and shoulder, then ran down the ruby velvet of her gown to her waist.

Emma murmured his name very softly.

He continued these soft, quick kisses for some time, letting his hands float all over her body. When she followed his lead, slipping her hand inside his shirt and caressing his skin with the same light touch he was using, Colin shuddered with a fierce, exultant mixture of triumph and desire.

He loosened the fastenings of her dress, and it pooled scarlet on the carpet. Drawing back a little, he stripped off his coat and shirt and neckcloth. Emma ran her hands very lightly over his muscled arms and chest, making his breath catch. His skin was as hot as Emma's felt. His kisses grew more urgent now, but still quick and glancing over her lips and neck and shoulders.

Suddenly, he bent and caught the hem of her shift, pulling it up and over her head as he straightened again. He held her wrists high for a moment as his lips fastened on hers in a kiss that was not gentle at all. As it went on and on, his hands drifted down her arms, across her back, over her hips. He pulled her hard against him. "Come to bed," he said in a thick voice.

As he shed the rest of his clothes, Emma stood beside the high bed, naked, watching him. The feeling of her eyes on his body was wildly enflaming. When he turned and swept her into bed, his heavy arousal was completely obvious, and she began to subject that part of him to the same featherlight caresses they had been exchanging. Colin groaned and clenched his jaw at the exquisite torture of it.

He knew he could not maintain his control much longer, but he wanted to savor every inch of her before that moment came. Rising on one elbow, he began moving his lips over his wife's beautiful body—her creamy shoulders; the mounds of her breasts, where he paused a while to tantalize and enjoy the breathy sounds of pleasure she made; the soft skin of her stomach and the jut of her hip; the smooth length of her thigh.

She was like warm silk, Colin thought, sliding along the length of his body and driving him mad. Making love to her was a magnificent combination of wanting

something to the edge of desperation, and at the same
time knowing that you could have it, and thus wanting
to sustain the event as long as you possibly could. His
free hand found the hot liquid center of her arousal and
flicked over it. "Oh," cried Emma.

She strained against his hand. He didn't want this to
be over; he wanted it to go on and on. "Colin," she
breathed. "Oh, Colin."

The need in her voice shattered the tenuous hold he
retained on his desire. Rearing up, he pulled her close,
crushing her lips with his. Emma clung to him, curling
one leg around his and arching in his grasp. Saying her
name over and over, he plunged into her, both of them
crying out at the intense pleasure of the sensation. He
could not stop himself now. He moved faster and faster,
feeling her move with him, overwhelmed by sensation
and feelings too deep to fathom. Her wild release, and
the way she clung to him, triggered his own climax,
sweeping him into a realm beyond description, where
nothing existed but the two of them and the world they
created together. Nothing could be allowed to jeopardize this, he thought with his last scraps of rationality.
Nothing.

Some time later, when their breathing had slowed
and the pounding of their hearts had eased, Emma un-
tangled herself and looked down at his face on the pillow. "I never would have known any of this without
you," she whispered.

"Any of what?"

"The way it feels," she murmured, still looking at his
face. "The . . . the incredible sensations." She seemed
to struggle for words. "I did not intend to marry
again," she added. "I would never . . . I would have
lived my whole life without feeling so . . ." She sat up,
stretching her arms above her head.

"So . . . ?" he prompted.

"So wonderful," responded Emma. "So amazingly
splendid. Edward never . . ." She bit down on the
words.

"The despicable Edward Tarrant," said Colin. "He never what?"

Emma was silent.

"Tell me," he demanded. The thought of another man touching her blazed in him.

"I think," replied Emma slowly, "that only gambling truly excited him." She wrapped her arms around herself. "With me he was always impatient . . . even a little rough. As if the . . . the duties of marriage were something to get over as quickly as possible. Perhaps even distasteful." A slight shudder went through her. "That is certainly what *I* thought, very soon after the wedding."

Colin felt pity for her, but also a surge of satisfaction, mixed with contempt for that fool Tarrant.

"If I had not met you . . ."

He had the sense that he too would have missed something vital if he had not found her, but he had even less idea of how to explain what.

Sometime in the deep watches of the night, Emma woke and lay still a moment gazing into the darkness. She was in her own familiar room. The quiet ticking of the mantel clock, the trace of her favorite perfume, were cozy and comforting. But there was something different. What was it?

She became aware of a rhythmic sound and an unaccustomed warmth at her side and turned her head. Colin slept beside her. In the dimness, she could just see his lashes in a dark fringe against his cheeks and a faint suggestion of the fine planes of his face. The coverlet rose and fell with his soft breathing. One of his hands lay on the pillow very close to her lips.

Her heart began to beat faster. He had never stayed in her bed before. Wary of nightmares, keeping a certain distance, he had always gone to his own chamber, usually after she had fallen asleep. She would wake in the morning alone and sometimes wonder wistfully what it

would be like to find him at her side. But when she had
thought of mentioning this fact, she had been stopped
short by the limits of the agreement between them.

And now, here he was. Emma listened to his even
breath, filled her nostrils with the beguiling, masculine
scent of him. He hadn't left her tonight. He had trusted
her enough to stay, to risk exposing his nightmares—
and himself. He had offered her the vulnerability of
sleep.

She felt a sudden longing to wake him and search
those extraordinary eyes for evidence of this change and
what it might mean for them. But she didn't dare. The
moment was too tenuous, the chances of disappointment too great. She wouldn't be able to bear it, she
thought, if he woke and denied that this meant anything
at all.

Rising on her elbow, Emma watched him sleep. He
looked peaceful and indomitably strong. Colin was everything she wanted in a man, she thought, and far more
than she had ever hoped or imagined she would find.
She wanted to be here, beside him, twenty years from
now, thirty. She wanted to build a family with him, a
dream she'd given up only a few months ago.

She had fallen in love, she thought shakily, really in
love this time, not the shallow, childish infatuation
she'd felt for Edward. She hadn't understood anything
about love until now. She'd thought it was a pounding
heart and a dazzle like sun on water. But it was much
more like the sea currents at Trevallan, she realized—
sweeping, inevitable, beyond anyone's ability to resist
or control. And she was in its grip, with no hope, or
wish, for escape. All she wanted was for Colin to find
that he felt the same way about her.

Emma swallowed, blinked quickly, and lay back
down. He had never asked her for love, she reminded
herself. Love had been no part of the bargain they made.
In fact, when he offered for her, he had said he no
longer expected it or thought himself capable of it.
Turning her head, she traced the contours of his face

with her gaze. She had agreed. Then, she had welcomed
the idea of a safe haven, a respite from the turmoil and
pain she had endured for years. But those had not been
the result of *love*, she cried out silently now. She hadn't
understood; it was just the opposite.

Too late, said a merciless inner voice; too late to want
more, to ask for another sort of marriage. Honor required that she keep her word. Colin wanted a comrade.
He had said so. He wanted a wife to be proud of before
society, an heir for his name and title, a comfortable
companion who would not plague him with emotional
scenes and pleading for more than he had to give. This
was what she had promised. With this, she must be satisfied.

And possibly, possibly, begged another part of her, a
grain of hope? Things did sometimes change, insisted
this voice. Here he lay, beside her, as he never had before.

Emma felt that hope flicker like the first hints of
flame in dry tinder. Surely there was a chance? Sometimes, when Colin looked at her, it seemed that he was
trying to communicate something far beyond comradeship.

In that fragile moment, as she almost dared to hope,
she remembered Count Julio Orsino, and how close he
had come tonight to meeting Colin face to face. If Orsino continued to hound her, eventually some explosion
would occur, and her chances of a different sort of marriage would be ruined, she thought. She could not allow
that. Orsino must get what he deserved.

Emma woke much later to a chilly, dreary day, with
rain running down the windows and sodden leaves
choking the pavement. Her resolve, however, was bright
and clear. She dressed and went down to breakfast.
Colin was already gone. She tried to eat, but all her
faculties were focused elsewhere, and she found she
hardly tasted the food. At last, she rose and rang the

bell. "Fetch Ferik," she told the footman crisply when he answered it. "And bring my cloak. I am going out."

"I'll order your carriage, my lady," responded John.

"No."

The footman looked startled at her sharp tone.

"Just the cloak," she told him. "And Ferik."

"Yes, my lady," was the puzzled response.

They traveled in a hackney cab rather than Emma's very identifiable carriage. She gave the driver the address she had seen on Orsino's visiting card. Ferik shivered and mumbled imprecations about the weather in his corner of the dilapidated vehicle, but Emma scarcely heard. She felt as if all her being was concentrated into one point directed at the heart of Count Julio Orsino.

The cab pulled up before a brick lodging house in a neighborhood that Emma had never visited before. Obviously, Orsino was short of money, she thought, examining the ramshackle houses and the bits of garbage dotting the street. All of the rage and fear and hatred that had built up in her in recent years, and which she had thought were gone, gathered around this man who would destroy her life without a pang to get what he wanted. Orsino epitomized all the evils she had had to endure and the powerlessness that had nearly broken her. But he would find himself facing a different Emma today, she thought defiantly. Raising the hood of her cloak against the rain, she handed the driver his fare and then jumped down to the muddy street. Ferik was right behind her, splashing the hem of her cloak when he stepped heavily into a puddle. He muttered some Turkish oath under his breath, then said, "What is this place?"

"Lodgings," Emma replied curtly. "I must see someone who lives here. A man I do not trust. You are to wait outside the room and come at once if you hear me call."

The huge man scowled through the rain that was pelting his face. "Who is this person?"

"Never mind that. Come, let us go in out of the rain."

They rang the bell, and were admitted by a scrawny, ill-tempered woman who directed them up the stairs to the third floor with a wordless jerk of her thumb. Keeping her hood well forward to hide her face, Emma went up. The stairs were narrow, unpainted, and very dirty. She held up her skirt to keep it from touching the wood. When Ferik knocked at the upper door, they were met by a small, dark man dressed like a servant who did not seem to speak English. Emma addressed him in Italian and asked for the count.

"Baroness," said a hated voice from the other end of a short corridor. "You are here. Good."

The servant held out his hands for her cloak, but Emma kept it huddled around her. Moving forward, she examined the count's sitting room from the doorway. It was only a little cleaner than the stair. Grime had collected in the corners and streaked the bay window that overlooked the street. The furniture was sagging and shabby, the rug and draperies faded to brown. Some effort had been made to lighten the atmosphere. A colorful paisley shawl had been flung over the ancient sofa. But the overall effect remained depressing. The count must be desperate, Emma thought, and braced herself to face his worst. "Wait here, Ferik," she said, stationing him just outside the door before walking into the room.

"I'm very pleased that you took my advice," said the count. "I trust you will forgive the, er, simplicity of my quarters. Sit down. Angelo will bring wine."

"I don't want any wine," said Emma, letting her hood fall back. "I won't be staying long." She moved a few steps closer to him, not wanting their conversation overheard, but she stayed between the count and the door. "I came here to tell you to leave me, and everyone associated with me, alone," she said tightly. "No more 'chance' encounters or intrusions in my activities. Do you hear me—none!"

The count gave her a bland look. "Of course," he

said. "I am at your command, as soon as you do as I have asked."

Emma stiffened. Her arms were rigid at her sides, her fists clenched. She felt as if she were made of stone. "Understand this," she said. "I will never introduce you into London society, and I will not permit you to harm my friends. You may as well leave England. There is nothing for you here."

His answering smile was predatory. He looked like a hunter who is pleased and excited by the cleverness of his prey. "I had so hoped we could deal together in a friendly way," he said, moving closer to her. "For Edward's sake, I gave you time to consider my very reasonable request. I have not pressed you, even though you have treated me quite shabbily, eh?"

"Have you not? You have continually invaded in my life," said Emma. "But it will do you no good. I will never help you."

"As a gentleman . . ."

Emma made a rude noise.

Count Orsino gave her an admonishing look. "As a gentleman, I have so far refrained from mentioning the true reasons why you *will* help me."

"I won't—"

"But now you leave me no choice," he interrupted. His face had flushed slightly. His lips were parted and his dark eyes glistening. He looked like a man who was about to indulge in his favorite pleasure, Emma thought. And he was looking at her in a way that was both unsettling and embarrassing. She prepared herself for the real battle between them.

"When Edward drank, he became extremely confiding," Orsino said throatily.

"I'm sure you encouraged him to do so," snapped Emma.

"And of course, he drank a good deal," insinuated the count, as if she had not spoken.

"At your insistence," she replied. "It made him easier to fleece."

"He told me so many things about you," Orsino continued. His voice had gone distant, meditative, as if he was remembering some delightful occasion when he had deeply enjoyed himself. "Edward could paint extremely, er, vivid pictures when he wished to," he added.

"He raved when he was drunk," said Emma curtly. She was beginning to be afraid of what was coming.

"Oh, these weren't ravings. They were remarkably lucid. And, er, detailed. He made a particularly gripping story of your elopement." The count's liquid eyes caressed her lewdly.

Emma flushed.

"It was quite entertaining to hear how you insisted upon fleeing with him when your father forbade the match, how you could scarcely keep your hands off him in the coach as you went." His glance became intimate, lingering on the curves of Emma's body.

Her flush deepened. What a toad Edward was, she thought.

"And your . . . eagerness during the week before you were actually married." His teeth showed in a feral smile. "It made quite a *rousing* tale."

She had been eager, Emma thought miserably. She had thought she was in love, and she had believed that Edward loved her as ardently. She had imagined that they would spend the rest of their lives happily together. Instead, she had gotten seven years of hell, and now it was capped by this—the revelation that Edward had publicly humiliated her with his worthless friends. Shame and rage kept her silent.

"No doubt your new husband and his noble friends would enjoy hearing every intimate detail." The count continued running his eyes over her.

"You are despicable," said Emma.

"And when I add certain . . . realistic touches, such as the mole you have on your . . ."

"You dare?" she exclaimed.

"Oh, yes." He looked like a man anticipating something he longed for. "I dare nearly anything when my livelihood is in jeopardy. As you must know."

She did, thought Emma, with a sinking heart. She remembered an occasion in Vienna when Orsino had been at the end of his resources. He had discovered a wealthy young German who was visiting the city to show his new son to his wife's parents. After administering liberal doses of brandy, he had won the young man's entire fortune in one long night of high stakes gaming. The next day, sober again, his victim had thrown himself under the wheels of a heavy cart rather than face his family. And Orsino had mocked his stupidity that night at the tables. He had been flushed and replete, as he was now, feeding on another's pain.

"And I fear," continued the man in a deceptively gentle tone, "that it will appear I have *personal* knowledge of your charms." The tip of his tongue showed briefly along his full lower lip. "Of course, in a sense, I do. Edward was extremely forthcoming." His voice hardened. "And if you do not help me, I shall do everything possible to convince all London that we have been passionate lovers."

"If I tell my husband you are a liar, he will believe me," Emma responded.

Count Orsino shrugged. "If you say so. But others may not be so trusting."

They certainly would not be, Emma thought. The silly stories that had been circulated about them so far would be like candle flames compared to the wildfire of scandal Orsino would delight in stirring up.

Trembling with disgust, Emma turned and walked away from him, taking up a position near the window and watching the rain streak down the glass. She had known that he would have some threat in reserve, she thought, but she had not anticipated this. The raindrops blurred before her eyes.

For seven years, she had lived with a man whose obsession had defeated any impulses he might have had toward the good. One by one, he had destroyed all her hopes and illusions of love. He had dragged her down to the razor edge of respectability, with the constant threat of a plunge right off it. He had raged and sworn at her, abandoned her even as they continued to live in the same house. But through it all, Emma had held on to the belief that once, in the very beginning, he had felt something for her. Now, that belief cracked and disintegrated. Edward had always held her in contempt. He had wanted only her money, never her. And now, from beyond the grave, through Orsino, he was threatening the one thing she had been able to salvage from those years—her good name. There had been days when the only thing that had sustained her was the knowledge that she, at least, had maintained her principles. Orsino threatened to sweep this away as if it were nothing.

"So you see how it is," said the count, shrugging as if there was nothing he could do.

And not just herself, Emma thought. Colin would suffer along with her—or more. She couldn't bear to think of his humiliation if Orsino's lies began to be whispered through the *ton*. It would be the last straw, Emma thought despairingly. They had weathered the irregularity of their match, and Lady Mary's ridiculous allegations, but this would be too much. Colin could not be expected to allow the ruin of his family name. He would have to reject her. She turned and glared at Orsino, rage and contempt in her gaze.

It had no effect.

"But the solution is so simple," he said, once more spreading his hands. "A few introductions, perhaps an invitation or two, and you are rid of me."

That was another lie, Emma thought. Once he had a hold on her, he would never go away. She would be doing his bidding, slowly destroying her self-respect, for the rest of her life. She clasped her hands tight together. She had to have time to think, to discover a way to stop him. "I . . . I must think it over," she said, pretending to be beaten and near surrender. "In a week . . . or, no, two. Yes, in two weeks, I will—"

"Alas, my dear baroness, I fear I cannot wait so long," was the answer. He smiled, and Emma marveled at his ability to look benevolent. He hid his true self so well. And that just made him more convincing, she thought savagely.

"A week, then," she said.

He hesitated. "Very well," he replied finally. "But in the meantime I shall of course cultivate my acquaintance with the interesting young woman you presented to me."

Emma ground her teeth together. "You will leave Lady Mary alone!" she said.

"As soon as you agree to my terms," he replied.

"You devil," said Emma. "You wretched, cowardly—"

With one rapid step, he was upon her, catching her upper arms in a painful grasp and pushing his face close to hers. His breath smelled of spirits even so early in the day. "Take care what you call me," he said softly. "You are alone in my chambers, after all. And I would not be averse to making my claims about our intimacy quite real." He bent to fasten his lips on hers, but Emma jerked away.

"Ferik!" she called.

"Yes, mistress," replied a deep voice from the hall. Heavy footsteps approached.

Count Orsino let his hands drop and moved hastily back. "Blast that overgrown barbarian," he hissed. "I heard what he did to Charlie Todd in Constantinople. He is no fit servant for a civilized woman."

"On the contrary," said Emma, with the first satisfaction she had felt during this interview. "He is precisely the servant for a civilized woman. An uncivilized one would not need him, because she would scratch your eyes out herself. Ah, Ferik, we are going."

"Yes, mistress," said Ferik, looming in the doorway.

"This changes nothing," declared the count spitefully. "You have a week."

Emma left the room, very conscious that she had no answer to this taunt.

Outside, it was still raining, though not as hard as before. Emma started off down the street at a rapid pace, paying little attention to the direction.

"Shall I find a cab, mistress?" asked Ferik, lagging behind her.

"I wish to walk a while. I need to think."

"But it is raining, mistress," said Ferik in scandalized tones.

"That doesn't matter."

"But, mistress." All of the giant's dislike of the English climate vibrated in those two words.

"Please be quiet. I must try to decide what to do," was Emma's reply.

Ferik subsided into offended silence. Emma strode along the muddy street, oblivious to the increasing dampness of her cloak, turning over alternatives in her mind. She felt trapped, like a fly struggling in a spider's web. She knew from experience that Orsino could be horribly convincing, and he had such damning details to embellish his story. Emma had seen the count wreck a dozen reputations with a few well-placed anecdotes and his pose of complete sincerity.

She shuddered, but not from the cold and damp, and pulled her sodden cloak closer around her shoulders.

She could try to discover what crimes the count was fleeing on the Continent, she thought. But she didn't have much hope of success. She didn't know whom to ask, and Orsino had been known to use false names and identities. It was most unlikely that she would happen upon anyone who could accuse him and force quick action under English law.

She could leave, Emma thought bleakly. But he would tell his story out of spite in that case, and it would follow her wherever she went. Colin might, too.

Or he might not, she realized with cold dread. He might let her go in disgust.

Emma drew her arms tight around her chest under the cloak. There seemed no way out. But she was fiercely certain of one thing; she would not let Orsino win.

They came out onto a busy street. Sheets of water splashed from beneath the wheels and hooves of a stream of passing equipages. Pedestrians had their heads down against the rain. Emma turned to look at Ferik. He was very obviously wet and miserable.

Emma felt a pang of guilt. She had been so absorbed in her own concerns recently that she had not given much thought to Ferik. He did not belong in England, she admitted now. She should not have brought him. But she had needed him; she could not have survived without his protection. Her guilt increased at this admission of selfishness. She would have to do something for him, she thought. Eventually, he needed to go home, with a munificent reward for his service to her, though no sum of money could ever repay him. She didn't want to ask Colin for money, however, especially just now. She would have to see to this, also, herself.

But there was, at least, something tangible she could do right now. "Why don't you find us a cab, Ferik?" she said gently.

"Yes, mistress!" He leapt into the crowd, and in a few moments, despite active competition, had secured them a hack. Emma climbed aboard in silence for the ride home.

Lady Mary Dacre called an hour early on the morning when they were scheduled to go out, and Emma was in no mood to see her, or indeed, anyone else. Since her visit to Orsino, she could think of only one thing—how to prevent the man from destroying her marriage and ruining her life. The threat colored everything she did. It made her distant and forgetful with acquaintances. It destroyed her interest in routine household tasks. And worst of all, it made her draw away from Colin at the very moment when she most wanted to move closer, to discover what his feelings for her truly were.

And though she told herself that she must go on with her daily round and not let anyone see that something was wrong, Emma found the girl's stream of chatter as irritating as the buzz of gnats around one's face on a country walk.

"Jane and Eliza think I made the whole thing up!" Lady Mary was saying indignantly. "They don't believe St. Mawr ever showed any special interest in me at all." Her pretty face set in petulant lines, she added, "Alice isn't sure. Not *sure*! How can they treat me so? They are supposed to be my *best friends.*"

Emma murmured something noncommittal.

"If they were *truly* my friends, they wouldn't doubt my word," said the other fiercely. "I won't have *anything* to do with them after this."

"I suppose it's a matter of perspective," said Emma. "People have different views—"

"Friends don't *have* perspectives," interrupted Lady Mary. "They are supposed to be on your side no matter what. Did *you* think people were your friends when they told you not to marry your first husband?"

Emma caught her breath, her attention firmly captured at last. The girl's effrontery was amazing.

"Well, did you?"

She was like one of those small dogs that looked fluffy and harmless, and then fastened its teeth into you with mindless fury, Emma thought "No," she admitted.

"There, you *see*!" said the girl.

"And I was very, very sorry," Emma added, half to herself. She had never been sorrier than right now, as the mistakes of the past threatened to wreck her future.

"Why?" Lady Mary stared at her with wide, china-blue eyes that were completely devoid of tact.

"Because they were right," Emma replied curtly.

"He was a hopeless gamester. He cared for nothing but the tables, and himself."

"You mean he didn't love you?"

"No," said Emma, prepared to be rude if this went on much longer.

"So you cared for someone who did not love you, either," was the response. The thought seemed to give Lady Mary a great deal of satisfaction.

Emma simply looked at her.

"Of course, St. Mawr is not a gamester. I suppose he is a rather admirable person." The girl was tentative, as if she had never considered such a question before.

Emma said nothing.

"So *I* chose better than you," said the girl complacently.

There was something almost awe-inspiring about this level of self-absorption, thought Emma.

"And also, I shan't have to endure *years* of unhappiness. I daresay the gossip will die down soon." Lady Mary turned to contemplate her once more with those wide, merciless eyes. "So, you are not some perfect creature who has always had everything her own way."

Startled, she shook her head.

"And you are not trying to make me look clumsy and ridiculous in comparison to you."

"Why would I do that?" said Emma, shocked at the idea.

"Oh, people do," said Lady Mary. She threw Emma a sidelong glance that suggested she knew far too much about this topic, and perhaps not all of it from the side of wounded virtue.

"Vulgar, hateful people," said Emma firmly.

"Well, but—"

The drawing room door opened and the footman announced Robin Bellingham, who strolled in on his heels.

Emma's brother wore an ensemble so fashionable that he could scarcely move in it. His heavily starched collar points framed his face like a white basket, and clearly made turning his head next to impossible. His neckcloth rose in snowy waves that looked to Emma as if they might strangle him at any moment. The excessive padding in his coat made his stance stiff. Only his fawn pantaloons, stretching smoothly over a creditable pair of legs, accommodated themselves to his movements. When he had made his bow to Emma, he had to turn his entire torso to look at the rest of the room. "You here?" he said rudely when he noticed Lady Mary.

"Why shouldn't I be?" answered the girl, bristling.

"Well, I'd think that was obvious," he said.

"Robin! Could I speak to you?" interrupted Emma. "A matter of family business," she told Lady Mary as she drew him into the far corner of the room. Robin threw a smug look over his shoulder. The girl stuck out her tongue.

Emma had meant to confer with Robin and explain everything before Lady Mary arrived, a plan that was thwarted by the girl's early appearance. Now, she hurriedly explained everything to her brother in a low voice, ending with a plea for his help and support. "I would be so grateful," she finished.

Robin preened a little.

"Of course, it means being polite to Lady Mary," Emma warned, "and appearing to be her friend."

When Robin looked mulish, she added, "Or at least an amiable acquaintance."

Robin turned an unenthusiastic eye on the girl. She glared back at him as if he had leered. "But will she be polite to me?" he wondered.

"It is a great deal to ask, I know," soothed Emma. "But I have faith in you."

"You do?" He seemed startled by the idea.

"Yes. I think you are capable of great things in the right cause," she assured him.

Robin stood straighter. Despite the stiffness of his shirtfront, he pushed out his chest. "I'll do it!"

"I knew I could count on you," replied Emma, relieved that her plan for Robin seemed to be working.

She would keep him occupied and far from the gaming tables. At least she could save *him* from ruin, she thought. "You will escort us to the Royal Academy, then?"

"Pictures?" Robin balked.

"All the *ton* is going to see the new exhibition of paintings. It seemed a good place to show ourselves."

He still looked mutinous.

"Everyone I meet is talking about it," she added. "I feel positively gothic, not having been."

"All the crack, is it?" Robin frowned over this, then gave in. "I suppose I can look at a few pictures."

"Splendid." Emma moved back toward Lady Mary. "Are you ready to go?" she asked.

"*He* isn't coming with us?" complained the younger girl.

"He is my brother, and I wish him to come," answered Emma gently.

Robin gave Lady Mary a smug smile. She wrinkled her nose and sneered at him.

Climbing into Emma's elegant barouche, Robin and Lady Mary argued about who would take the forward seat. Lady Mary claimed that any *gentleman* would not hesitate to face backward to accommodate ladies. Robin maintained that a proper, modest deb would offer to take the less comfortable place, not wishing to thrust herself forward.

Lady Mary won that round by the simple expedient of plopping down in the seat and spreading her skirts around her, giving Robin a look that was both triumphant and defiant. However, Robin got his own back when Lady Mary attempted to direct the coachman to the Royal Academy. He subjected her proposed route to severe, and justified, ridicule and substituted a better one with an annoying superior air.

They were the same age, Emma realized, both just barely out of the schoolroom. And they brought out the lingering childishness in each other. With a tiny bit less control, it might have come to hair-pulling and shoving and shrieks for mother to mediate. She sighed quietly.

At the academy, Robin offered Emma his arm with exaggerated politeness. Lady Mary sniffed and walked through the doors ahead of them, her head high. "We are friends on an outing together," Emma reminded them. "We are having a pleasant time."

Lady Mary smiled, and as before, it transformed her conventionally pretty face. Robin blinked in surprise at the change, and then seemed to have difficulty looking away for quite some time.

"Is that the best you can do?" hissed Lady Mary through her teeth. "You don't look happy. You look poleaxed."

Robin smiled at her.

He also had a beautiful smile, Emma thought. In fact, with his pale coloring and silly, dandyish clothes, you didn't notice precisely how handsome a lad he was until he smiled. Oddly, it made him look more masculine and assured, too.

It was Lady Mary's turn to be startled. Her eyes widened and her lips opened a little, as if something completely unexpected had jumped out in her path. She examined Robin with more care, and seemed to find something of interest in the survey.

"I suppose we must make a show of looking at these pictures," Robin said. But this time he offered his arm to Lady Mary.

Emma, in her turn, smiled as they walked into the gallery together.

But the lift in her mood was brief.

"There is that man we met in the park," Lady Mary commented five minutes later. "The one you were so shockingly rude to."

Robin turned to stare, looking startled at this accusation of his extremely well-mannered sister.

Emma turned as well, and her heart sank as she found Count Orsino approaching them with a broad smile. He had to be keeping watch on her house and following her, she thought with a tremor of fear. His constant appearances could not be mere coincidence. He was purposefully tormenting her. "Turn around," she urged, taking Lady Mary's free arm. "I don't wish to meet him."

The girl pulled away. "I do. He's interesting. Good day, Count," she added in a louder voice.

Orsino took off his low-crowned beaver hat and gave the group a bow. "Ladies," he said, coming toward them, "you outshine the work of the artists around you."

Lady Mary giggled.

"Are you enjoying the display?" he continued as he joined their group.

"We just got here," the girl replied.

"Indeed? I am fortunate. Perhaps you will allow me to take you round. I have some knowledge of art." He offered his arm.

To Emma's intense annoyance, Lady Mary took it. "I told my father I had met someone from Italy," she said. "He spent the whole evening recalling his journey there."

Orsino smiled down at her. "Should I offer you my abject apologies for being the cause of this reminiscence?"

She giggled again.

"We already have an escort, Count," said Emma a bit desperately. "So we will not require your services." When he turned and looked inquiring, she cursed herself, for this forced her to introduce Robin to the man.

"Young Bellingham?" was the response. "But I have heard of you, have I not? Someone was telling me that if I wished to know just how to get on in London, I would do well to model myself on Robin Bellingham."

Robin goggled at him, then flushed. "Me?"

"Yes, indeed. And I can certainly see why. Would you consider it an impertinence if I asked who made that waistcoat?"

Robin's answering smile was like a knife through

Emma's heart. Her brother was far too young and inexperienced to see through this kind of blatant flattery. And he so wished to be seen as a pink of the *ton.* The look the count threw over his shoulder as the three of them moved away from her made it clear that he knew exactly what she was thinking and was enjoying her anguish thoroughly.

She had to get them away from him! Emma looked around the gallery. She saw no one she knew well. Short of dragging her two young companions out by force, she didn't see what she could do.

"Where are you staying in London?" Lady Mary was asking when she caught up with them.

"Alas, I find myself in the clutches of one Mrs. Groat, who provides apartments for travelers. Quite a terrifying woman. I fear I've made a poor choice of lodgings. Last night I heard most suspicious sounds in the wall. Unless I am mistaken, there are rats."

"Ooh," replied Lady Mary with a shudder.

Orsino shot Emma a meaningful glance. For one horrified moment, she thought he was going to mention that she had been to his lodgings, then he turned away again with a smug smile. He was vile, Emma thought, as she unclenched her fists—despicable, ruthless, inexorable. What was she going to do?

Colin was spending his morning in quite different pursuits. He had by no means forgotten Count Orsino's intrusion into their theater party, nor his feeling that he should find out something about the fellow. It was not difficult to identify him; a few well-placed questions at his club soon uncovered a name, for the count had been making determined efforts to force himself upon English society. But no one seemed to know anything more—beyond a general impression that there was something unsavory about the man.

However, Colin had a good deal of influence and many contacts around the city of London, and he used all of these powers now to investigate the history and character of Count Julio Orsino. His hunt led him in many directions and into very different locations.

He spent a profitable hour in a tiny, dark office in the warren of streets near Saint Paul's Cathedral, with a sinister man named, implausibly, Smith. Mr. Smith's business was knowing everything, or at the very least being able to find it out within a very short time. He provided Colin with some very shrewd observations about Orsino and his habits, and why he was in London. His predictions of the man's future plans did not make for pleasant hearing.

Colin spoke to acquaintances in the army. He called at the Italian embassy and spent a cordial couple of hours with an official there who agreed to a speedy search of his government's records in return for certain future favors. In an English government office, Colin spoke with an old school friend and, between reminiscences, got a promise that he would make inquiries through official channels. Finally, Colin interviewed the proprietors of a several exclusive gambling establishments, who were known to have a broad web of contacts among their counterparts abroad.

In the end, as information about the count began to accumulate, Colin's uneasiness turned to dread. The man was not a simple gamester. He had been involved in a hundred shady enterprises and unsavory transactions. There was a suspicion, unproven, that he had been a source for the white slave trade during his time in Constantinople. There were dark rumors of murder. Colin was appalled that Emma should even be acquainted with such a man.

But she was. The life she had been forced to lead had put her in contact with a variety of dangerous individuals. He recalled her story of her first encounter with Ferik and shuddered slightly. He found that his fists were clenched. It was fortunate that Tarrant was dead, because otherwise he would have been forced to kill him, he thought somewhat illogically.

He remembered the way Orsino had bent over Emma at the theater, and the look on her face as he did so. It did not require military instincts to conclude that the man meant her some sort of harm. An irresistible desire to get Orsino's stubby neck between his hands began to build in Colin. He longed to choke the whole story out of him and then see to it that the blackguard never approached his wife again. But even more, he wished Emma would come to him and tell him what was wrong.

As they drove home from the Royal Academy, having shaken off Count Orsino only when they actually got into her carriage, Emma found herself biting her bottom lip to keep from screaming.

"I don't see *how* you can say so," declared Lady Mary Dacre with a toss of her golden hair. "That was quite the *ugliest* painting in the whole show."

"It was far better than those sickly lambs and simpering boy that *you* liked," replied Robin.

"He was a *shepherd,*" said Lady Mary. "And he was *not* simpering. He was under the influence of some powerful *feeling,* a state that I'm sure you would not understand."

"Looked like he had a good deal of feeling for one of those sheep," muttered Robin under his breath.

"What?" said Lady Mary sharply.

"I said he looked like he was about to fall asleep," Robin answered, avoiding Emma's eye.

"He did not!"

"Here we are," interjected Emma, trying to keep the relief out of her voice. They had reached the Morland townhouse, and she was more than ready to take leave of Lady Mary.

The girl folded her arms and looked exceedingly mulish. "I can't go in. I, er, I left my handkerchief in your drawing room."

Emma turned to look at her in surprise. "What?"

"My handkerchief. I must go and fetch it."

"I'll have it sent to you."

"No. I must get it. It's, er, my mother embroidered it for me." It was clear that even Lady Mary found this explanation extremely thin, but equally clear that she was determined to return to Emma's house and that nothing short of a full-scale battle would remove her from the carriage.

Perhaps that was just as well, Emma thought. She had to warn the girl about Orsino and convince her not to speak to him again. And though she longed to be alone, this would provide an opportunity. "Very well," she said. "We will leave Robin at—"

"I'll go along with you," her brother interrupted.

"But it is on our way—"

"Like to walk home," declared Robin. "Lovely day for it."

Exasperated, Emma looked from one to the other. It was some sort of silly contest, she decided. Neither of them was willing to be the first to leave. They really were like children. Mentally throwing up her hands, she directed the coachman home.

It was not far. In a very few minutes, they were climbing down from the barouche and walking through the door that Clinton held for them. Robin was coming inside, Emma noticed resignedly. "Shall we look in the drawing room for your handkerchief?" she asked Lady Mary.

"Oh, I can find it," was the hurried reply. Lady Mary stepped in front of her, putting her foot onto the first stair.

"Of course I will help you," said Emma, with a spark of malice. She had endured much this afternoon, and she was not averse to giving some of it gently back. She was very well aware that they would discover no stray handkerchief in her drawing room.

"I'll help, too," said Robin, following Lady Mary up the stairs.

"I do not require help," exclaimed the girl, "particu-

larly *your* help." She hurtled into the drawing room and
crashed head-on into Colin Wareham.

"Oh!" The girl tottered wildly on her feet. Colin was
obliged to reach out and steady her. "Oh," she said
again.

Perfect, thought Emma. The day needed only this.

"You might watch where you're going," said Robin.
"You could injure someone popping into a room like
that."

"Oh, what do you know about anything!" cried
Lady Mary, and promptly burst into tears.

"Eh?" Robin seemed startled by the strength of her
reaction. He blinked. He turned to Emma, who was not
looking at him. He gazed questioningly about the room,
his eyes finally falling on the tall, handsome figure of
Baron St. Mawr. "Ah," he said, enlightened. "Forgot."

One corner of Colin's mouth jerked.

"We have been looking at the pictures at the Royal
Academy," said Emma somewhat desperately. Lady
Mary's sobs continued in the background.

"Have you?" Colin was at his most urbane. "They
say it is a fine collection this year."

This was a sticky situation, Robin told himself. Sort
of thing Emma had recruited him to help her with. She
was relying on him. He racked his brain for something
to say.

"Very fine," agreed Emma feebly.

"Splendid technique, I've heard," Colin added
blandly.

Emma threw him a look.

Lady Mary let out a piercing wail. "How can you
all—"

"The thing is," cried Robin loudly to forestall her.

They all turned to look at him. Even Lady Mary
choked back a sob and blinked at him in surprise.

"The thing is," he repeated, wondering what the
deuce he was going to say.

Everyone waited.

It was dashed hard to think with people staring at

you like statues, Robin realized. But he had said he would help. He groped desperately for an idea—any idea. "A . . . a friend of mine knows of a boat that takes parties up the river toward Greenwich," Robin babbled, surprising even himself. "That's right. He was telling me about it just the other day. Neat little craft. Flat bottomed, like a barge, Jack says, but very clean."

Everyone was still staring at him. Robin flushed and fumbled for words. "It . . . er . . . I was thinking, we should make an expedition," he said, without thinking the matter through any further.

Three pairs of eyes continued to contemplate him, with varying degrees of surprise and disapproval.

"Take a picnic," he added, thinking that was a nice touch, and feeling more and more pleased with himself. "Row upriver like Queen Elizabeth in the engraving." Where the devil had that come from? Robin wondered, seeing the thought mirrored on the others' faces. Then he remembered a book that had been about the house when he was small, a biography of the famous Virgin Queen with lavish illustrations. One of them must have stuck in his mind all this time, he marveled.

"I've never been on the river," said Lady Mary slowly. She appeared to be examining the suggestion for potential pitfalls while growing increasingly enamored of it. "Yes, let's," she said finally. "It sounds like fun."

"I don't think—" began Emma.

"Oh, *don't* say you won't go," interrupted Lady Mary, galvanized by resistance. Her tears, and the supposed reason for them, seemed completely forgotten. "If you won't come, then it is off. And I am *so* tired of being cooped up at home." She gave Emma a limpid look.

Meaning that if she didn't agree, Lady Mary would make certain any outing they took was pure misery, thought Emma bitterly. The girl was a natural blackmailer.

"I think it's a good notion," said Colin, surprising

them all. "What about tomorrow? I have no pressing engagements."

"You . . . you will . . . ?" Lady Mary stammered to a halt.

"I don't know if I can arrange . . ." faltered Robin simultaneously.

"Colin," admonished Emma.

"I believe it is supposed to be a fine day. Just the thing for a picnic." Colin smiled, seemingly without concern.

"I don't think," began Emma again.

"Well, I *want* to go," declared Lady Mary. "I want to see the boat. I don't care who comes." She looked ready to stamp her foot.

Colin met Emma's speaking gaze, and returned it steadily. "Splendid. It's settled, then," he said.

"I, uh, I'll have to speak to the boatman," Robin pointed out.

"Yes, indeed. Offer him a larger fee if there is any objection," said the older man. "And of course you'll want to look in at Gunters and arrange for the food. They do a very creditable basket for this sort of thing."

"Y-yes." Robin gathered his wits. "But I can't be sure the boat will be free, you know, on such short notice. I'll have to—"

"Persuade him," suggested Colin.

"Well, but—"

"Surely you can deal with a *boatman*?" said Lady Mary.

They were all looking at him. Robin's jaw hardened. "Certainly," he rapped out. "I'll make all the arrangements," he added recklessly.

"Do you really think . . .?" began Emma, then trailed off. Colin continued to gaze at her; his face contained some message, but she could not read it.

"It is settled, then," he said. "We rely on you, Bellingham. Send word of the time."

"Very well," said Robin, like a man who had gotten

in well over his head without knowing quite how it had come about.

"You are not to order lobster for our picnic," Lady Mary said. "I *hate* lobster."

"You needn't eat it, then," Robin snapped. "But I shall certainly have some myself."

"But even the smell makes me feel quite ill. How can you—?"

Emma broke. "Robin, you will escort Lady Mary home," she commanded through gritted teeth. "You may use my carriage."

"Why have I got to . . .?"

"No doubt Lady Mary is tired," she continued, ignoring him.

"No, I'm not," said the girl.

"So you had best set off *now.*" Emma's tone did not encourage argument. And the glare she directed at the two young people seemed to impress them even more.

"Oh, all right," agreed Robin pettishly.

Lady Mary pushed out her lower lip and looked mutinous. But she turned with Robin toward the door.

"I'll have the servants find your handkerchief and send it to you," added Emma sweetly.

Lady Mary looked blank.

"The one your mother embroidered *especially* for you."

"Oh." The girl had the grace to look guilty. "That is, thank you."

"I am completely at your service," replied Emma savagely.

With sidelong looks at her expression, the two young people hurried from the room.

Emma turned to Colin. "What are you doing?" she asked.

"I wished to help you," he said.

"Help?"

"Yes." On his way home, Colin had come to certain conclusions. Emma was annoyed with him because he had refused to do anything about her scapegrace brother. He would show her that he stood ready to aid her, that he could be counted on to stand by her, and then she would no doubt confide in him about whatever problem this man Orsino posed. "I thought to lend my efforts to your campaign to show society that there is nothing in the rumors," he added. "Won't it be even more convincing if I join a party of which Lady Mary is a member?"

"Perhaps," allowed Emma.

He spread his hands.

"But it will be very awkward. I don't think . . ."

"I had another motive as well."

Emma raised her eyebrows.

"It is, after all, a significant sacrifice, to spend a whole day with two bickering youngsters, one of whom fancies herself in love with me," he pointed out.

"You cannot know how significant," replied Emma feelingly.

"But I shall find out."

"You certainly will."

"And so, you see, you were wrong."

"About what?" Emma wondered.

"I do believe that we have a partnership, and an obligation to help one another," he said significantly. "I am ready to do my part."

Emma gazed up at him, her eyes threatening to fill with tears. She could not tell him the real reason for her reluctance—that she was pulled violently in two directions at once. She longed to spend the day in his company. But she was also terribly afraid that she might make some slip, give him some clue about the threat hanging over her before she could eradicate it.

"I mean to hold up my end of the bargain," he assured her.

Emma froze. She was deathly tired of that word "bargain," she thought.

Chapter Ten

As he offered his arm to Lady Mary Dacre to escort her onto the boat that was awaiting them at the other end of the short gangplank, Robin tried to make some order of the multitude of details buzzing in his mind. He was feeling extremely harassed. In barely twenty-four hours, he had had to locate the boatman, bribe him to change his schedule and accommodate them, arrange for food and drink, provide extra funds for the odds and ends the boat suddenly, mysteriously required, and then choose suitable garments from his wardrobe for a day on the river.

His problems had begun when his friend Jack had been unable to remember the boatman's name or location, and they had not ended yet, he thought distractedly. Though Lady Mary was chattering brightly about the sights on the docks and the fine clear weather, Robin expected only the worst from her, and he was very much afraid that the day would be a disaster. And of course, everyone would blame him. This helping people was a good deal more complicated than he had imagined, he thought. It would be quite a while before he tried anything of the sort again.

"Oh, look," said Lady Mary. "How pretty!" She trotted over to the cluster of chairs and small table in the center of the vessel, shaded by a striped awning.

It ought to be pretty, thought Robin bitterly. He had been coerced into financing a new awning, and the rug covering the deck boards had come from home, without his father's knowledge. He looked around to make certain everything else was in place. The boat was actually a small barge, flat and square, with a tiny shack-like house in the rear. The awning spread over most of the middle. The coils of rope and other oddments at the front corners had been tidied as he asked. The boatman and his son stood ready at the back to ply the oars. Baskets of provisions sat on the rug near the table. All seemed to be in order. He breathed a sigh of relief.

"There are no flowers," said Lady Mary as she sank into one of the waiting chairs. "We should have had flowers, don't you think so, Emma? The table looks so bare."

Robin gritted his teeth.

"It is very nice as it is," Emma said absently. She wasn't in the mood to think of anything as trivial as flowers. Though the day was crisply lovely and the sights new and varied, she was conscious of very little but Colin at her elbow.

She stole a glance at him, and found he was looking steadily at her. She didn't understand what was going through his mind lately. His offer to come on this expedition and prove that he was a true partner in their relationship had filled her with hope. Surely it showed he was coming to care for her? It was cruelly unfair that fears of Orsino and the threat of ruin should dominate her thoughts just now, when she desperately wanted to be open with him. This was going to be an extremely difficult day in more ways than one, she thought. She bent her head again and went to take one of the chairs under the awning, behind Lady Mary.

The boatman drew in the small gangplank and cast off from the dock. As the gap of dark water between them and the shore widened, Robin and Colin sat down as well. The two younger people pulled their chairs closer to the front of the awning, so that they could see better, leaving Emma and Colin side by side at the rear.

The boatman and his son worked the oars, and the small barge moved out into the busy river traffic of the London basin. They passed a large merchanter, whose masts towered far above them, and drew some lively comments from a sailor on deck. A waterman's little vessel passed across their bow, taking two passengers across the river. The water swarmed with these floating hacks, which allowed those in a hurry to avoid the congestion of the bridges. Great barges also passed, hauling cargo up and down the Thames. In the distance, they could see another oceangoing ship just coming in, some of its sails still unfurled like clouds against the sky. Their oarsmen moved expertly through this crowd, weaving their way upriver and giving the passengers an excellent view of the London shoreline.

"There's the Tower," said Lady Mary. "That is Traitor's Gate, where they brought prisoners in from the river to be beheaded." She gave a happy shiver.

"Not there," said Robin. "Farther down. See, those steps."

"How would you know? I looked through an illustrated guidebook to the sights of London from my father's library last night, and I am sure that is—"

" 'Tisn't," said Robin, like a much younger lad. "There, see." Another gate had come into view, arched and barred.

There was a silence at the front of the awning. The boat narrowly avoided collision with a waterman who was racing across the river as if his life depended on it, and their boatman exchanged some good-natured abuse with the man.

"Look there," said Lady Mary, as if the dispute with

Robin had never occurred. "That barge is full of chickens."

They were indeed passing a large vessel piled with wicker cages from which a chorus of squawking arose.

"They'll be at the market tomorrow," said Robin.

"Ugh, they stink," said the girl, wrinkling her nose as the breeze brought the smell of the fowl to them. The oarsmen exerted themselves, and they shot forward out of range.

"You know," said Colin, near Emma's ear. "I believe that chit has completely forgotten me."

Emma started, and turned to find that he had shifted his chair closer to hers.

"A very short time ago, she was claiming I had broken her heart and her life was not worth living," he commented. "And now I scarcely seem to exist for her." He smiled wryly at Emma. "It is certainly a cure for excess vanity. Now I know how highly to rate my attractions."

"She's a child," answered Emma. "She doesn't know what love means as yet."

"You were married at her age," Colin reminded her.

"Exactly," said Emma, her voice vibrating with emotion. "What better evidence could you want?"

Colin watched her. Her face was half turned away from him. She sat very straight, as if containing a high degree of energy by sheer will. Her slender figure was lovely in a gown of dark blue. "If you had not run away to be married, and I had not run off to war," he began, then paused, thinking. "Do you think we would have met in some ballroom?" he went on at last. "Danced a set together and parted again, as heedless as those two?" He glanced at Robin and Lady Mary.

Emma clasped her hands in her lap. She was squeezing them very tightly together, Colin noted.

"Or might we have fallen madly in love," he added, "as only the very young can do?"

"Only?" echoed Emma in an odd voice.

Colin examined her face again. It looked strained.

Why would she not confide in him? he wondered. Why would she not trust him? "I think so," he answered. "That kind of madness seems a thing of early youth."

"Nothing that could happen to you," she gibed.

"No more than you would elope," he responded, surprising himself a little with the sharpness of his tone.

Emma caught her breath. She looked a trifle wild, he thought, like a horse shying at a sudden gunshot. "And do you think that is love?" she breathed.

"What?"

"That self-absorption, that insistence on getting one's own way, that . . . that lunacy?"

He was somehow losing the thread of the conversation, he thought.

"You think that is what 'love' means?"

"I suppose there are many kinds of love," he answered, playing for time.

"You suppose? But it is not a subject you know from direct experience?" The threat of tears hovered in her voice.

"Emma, what is the matter?"

She turned to him, and searched his face.

"You can rely on me," he urged. "I am not some hotheaded youth who thinks of nothing but his own gratification. I can stand fast."

"Stand fast?" she repeated in a questioning tone.

"I can be trusted," he replied, feeling resentful at having to say it aloud. "I know the value of duty and honor and keeping one's word."

"Or one's bargains?" asked Emma.

"That is another way of putting it."

She turned her head away.

"So?" he said impatiently after a moment. Surely he had given her every opportunity to tell him what was wrong, every assurance that she could require?

"What?"

"Have you nothing you wish to say?" he added.

"I?"

"There is no one else taking part in this conversation!"

Emma glanced at him, then quickly away. "Were we not having a philosophical discussion, my lord? I fear I have exhausted my small store of knowledge."

Her face had gone smooth and closed. She had drawn away from him. Colin was overtaken by intense frustration.

"Emma," said Lady Mary, turning around in her chair. "Look at the ducks!"

As his wife leaned forward to follow their guest's pointing finger, it was all Colin could do not to curse out loud.

Weaving back and forth through the stream of vessels, their boat passed the congested docks of the city and the more scattered moorings along the outskirts. At last, they left London behind and passed between grassy banks where willows trailed their leaves in the water. Emma doggedly participated in the conversation between Robin and Lady Mary, all the while feeling Colin silent beside her. She felt as if pressure were building deep inside her, and that she would not be able to contain it for very much longer.

They drifted past grand houses with swaths of lawn and private boathouses and past small huts surrounded by vegetable patches with one leaky dinghy pulled up on the muddy shore. The sunlight sparkled on the moving water, which lapped the sides of their boat with a hypnotic sound.

After a time, before they could grow bored with the passing scenery, the boatman began to steer in toward shore. Deftly maneuvering, he brought them up beside a small wooden dock, and his son jumped off to tie up the ropes. "We'll picnic here," said Robin, very pleased with his arrangements so far. "Hawkins says there's a fine spot just over the rise."

The boatman threw down the gangplank, and then he and his son gathered up the baskets of provisions and prepared to escort them to shore. "Not that one," said

Robin, taking one from him. "That one's for you." He set it on deck again.

"Thank'ee, sir," said Hawkins, with a gap-toothed grin.

They walked up the slope of the bank and into a meadow scattered with flowers. "Here we are," said Robin.

"I want to go over there," demanded Lady Mary, pointing to a small cluster of trees on the other side of the meadow, just past a fence.

"This is much better," protested Robin. "It's sunnier, and closer to the boat."

"*You're* not carrying anything," the girl pointed out.

"I know, but—"

"I *want* to go over there," she repeated, looking thunderous.

"Oh, very well!" Scowling, Robin started to trudge through the long grass.

They all followed him. Colin loosened a rail so that the ladies could step over the fence, and the Hawkinses spread a large red blanket out under a tree and placed the food baskets on it before turning back to the river.

"Perfect," said Lady Mary, sinking down in a pool of skirts. "Listen to the wind in the leaves! It is like the ocean."

Robin showed no signs of listening. He was still frowning as he unpacked the provisions he had bought and began to spread them out on the blanket.

"How lovely it all looks," said Emma.

Robin brightened. "We've cold chicken and rolls," he said. "*And* lobster." He threw Lady Mary a look. "There's wine, and these peaches. The woman particularly recommended those. And some pastries as well."

"A feast," responded Emma, winning a smile.

Robin found the corkscrew and began to open the wine. Emma got out the plates and cutlery and spread them out. Colin carved the chickens, and Lady Mary oversaw them all with benevolent approval.

They began to eat. Robin and Lady Mary were arguing over whether it was more enjoyable to picnic outdoors or to stop at a rustic inn. The breeze rustled the leaves and carried birdsong across the meadow. It was an idyllic scene, thought Emma. She could almost feel carefree and forget that anything oppressed her.

Suddenly, Colin stiffened. Emma saw his eyes widen slightly and his jaw harden. She started to turn to see what he could be staring at with such wary intensity. "Everyone sit absolutely still," he said, in a tone that commanded instant obedience.

But only for a moment. "Why?" asked Lady Mary, looking around for an explanation.

"I believe we are sharing this field with a bull," said Colin. "And from the looks of him, he is not a good-tempered animal."

Emma followed his gaze and saw a huge, wickedly horned bull moving slowly toward them. It had a reddish hide with white markings on the face and neck, and it seemed as big as a house. It paused, snorted as if annoyed, and came on.

"Good God!" cried Robin, leaping up. The bull's head tossed in an echo of the movement. "Run for it. I'll distract him." He hurried to the right, but this put him among the trees, where the bull couldn't see him.

"Robin!" cried Emma.

"Get back over the fence," said Colin calmly, pulling both women to their feet and beginning to push them toward that barrier. The bull snorted again, sounding closer.

At the fence he urged them over, and then replaced the rail he had removed earlier. Turning, he saw that Robin had come forward and was waving his handkerchief to attract the bull's attention. "Come *on*," Colin called to him.

But Robin ignored him. "I've heard they do this in Spain," he said gaily, brandishing his handkerchief in wider arcs. "Ha, bull, come and get me!" He capered around a tree, going closer to the giant animal.

"Robin!" cried the two women in unison.

Colin shook his head, briefly closing his eyes in disbelief.

"I need something larger," said Robin. His eyes lit on their picnic, and he went and pulled the red blanket from under the food, knocking most of it helter-skelter into the grass. "Just the thing," he said, turning and waving the cloth in the bull's direction.

"Young fool," muttered Colin. He started toward the boy.

With a bellow, the bull collected himself and lowered his head so that his horns were in line with the center of the blanket. With another resonant snort, he charged.

He came much faster than Robin expected, faster than an animal that size ought to be able to move. Watching a ton of enraged flesh thunder down upon him, Robin suddenly froze, the red blanket hanging limp in his hands. Colin started to run.

"Robin!" screamed Emma. "Get out of the way!"

"Move, you idiot!" cried Lady Mary.

Colin leaped. He caught hold of Robin's waist and propelled the boy forward and onto the ground just as the bull hurtled into the spot where he had been standing. There was a sound of rending cloth, and then the animal was past them, galloping down the field, the red blanket impaled on its horns and waving in the breeze like a victory banner.

Colin sprang up and yanked Robin to his feet as well. As the bull bellowed and shook its head, trying to get clear of the blanket, he dragged the young man to the fence and practically threw him over. "We'd better be on our way," he said, his breath coming hard. "I have no faith in this fence."

"Our lunch," protested Robin.

"A fine time to think of that," accused Lady Mary, "after you dumped it all on the ground playing your stupid tricks."

"You hellcat," gasped Robin. "When I was trying to save your skin!"

"Go!" said Colin, seeing that the bull was free again and rumbling toward them.

"I'll have to pay for the dishes," Robin began to protest, but Colin pushed him along in front of him as the ladies hurried back to the boat.

The boatman looked surprised to see them, and when he had heard their story, he seemed to have a good deal of difficulty hiding a smile. He offered to retrieve the lost luncheon, but when he had gone and returned, he told them that the bull was trampling it into the earth with what seemed to be deep satisfaction. "Pertickly the peaches," he told them with twitching lips. "Seems to like the feel of them under his hooves."

"So we are to have no lunch at all?" complained Lady Mary.

Robin turned on her savagely. "It's *your* fault," he said. "If we had stayed where I wanted, this would not have happened. But no, you always have to have your own way. Everyone must do as you wish. You will never listen to anyone else's opinion."

Eyeing the two youngsters, Colin gave the boatman a discreet signal to cast off and start home. Taking Emma's elbow, he guided her to the chairs they had occupied before and seated her. "Thank you," she said shakily. "You saved his life."

Colin shrugged. "A serious goring, perhaps," he corrected.

Emma was so beset by conflicting feelings that she could not speak.

"He has a good deal of courage," commented Colin, watching Robin shake his finger at Lady Mary as if she were a naughty child and he her governess. He turned to smile at Emma. "Though he could benefit from a bit of military training. He needs to learn to retreat in good order from an enemy with superior armament."

"You risked yourself for . . ." murmured Emma almost inaudibly.

"You know, I think I misjudged the lad," Colin continued, not hearing. "There's more to him than I realized. Most youngsters would have simply taken to their heels and . . ." He smiled again. "And bull take the hindmost."

"What he did was foolhardy and horribly dangerous," protested Emma.

"Oh, yes. He should never have attempted any such thing. But it showed a great deal of pluck, you know."

She would never understand men, Emma thought. "And would pluck matter if he had been killed by that bull?" she asked tartly.

Colin looked surprised. "Of course," he replied, as if it went without saying. "Naturally it is better to be both wise and brave, but a man's honor is always of vital importance."

Emma swallowed, her annoyance dampened. He had been so long a soldier. His own, and his family's, honor mattered so deeply to him. What would he do if Orsino began to sully it? Call him out? Orsino cheated at everything; if they faced one another with pistols, the count might well find a way to kill Colin. And even if he didn't, her husband would never look at her with any sort of affection again.

"They seem to enjoy it, don't they?" Colin commented, nodding toward the younger couple in the front of the barge.

"Hmm?" murmured Emma, trying to recover her equilibrium.

"Continually bickering with one another."

"Oh." She looked at the youngsters. "Yes, I suppose they do."

"I've seen long-married pairs who were the same, but I can't say I understand the attraction of it myself."

Emma shook her head.

"It shows the wisdom of basing a marriage on common interests and shared experiences."

Common interests, Emma thought—a cold phrase. She looked over at him. Though she had moments of hope, at other times, like this, she wondered if he ever felt more than a sedate satisfaction with the arrangement they had made. He saw love as an affliction of youth, and himself as beyond or above it. Would he even *want* love, should it ever descend upon him, as it had, so very definitely, on her?

The following day, Colin Wareham was strolling through the reading room at White's, on the lookout for a friend with whom he was engaged to lunch. He was rather early, so it didn't concern him when he saw no sign of James in any of the comfortable armchairs. He took a newspaper from the table where all the popular periodicals were laid out in crisp rows and went in search of an unoccupied chair where he could settle and read it.

He had spotted one in the corner and was heading toward it when he noticed a gentleman passing by the door of the room. It was not his friend. Indeed, it was not even *a* friend. But Colin knew the man by reputation, and something about him caught and held his attention now.

Colin stood still and considered. Robin Bellingham was a spunky lad, he told himself. There was no question about that. And Emma was worried about him. He didn't want to get publicly embroiled in the lad's affairs. Robin wouldn't thank him for such interference. The impulse to help and protect Emma surged in Colin. It couldn't hurt to gather information, he concluded. Good intelligence was the key to any campaign, and to neglect the opportunity to learn something when it was practically thrust upon him seemed silly.

Colin returned the newspaper to its place and made his way to the gaming rooms at the back of the club. Even at this early hour, there were a few men at the tables, desultorily throwing the dice or looking over a hand of cards. The man he wanted had not yet joined the play. He was standing at the side observing, rather like a gourmand surveying the various delicacies spread at a buffet before filling his plate.

"Hello, Whitman," said Colin when he came up beside him.

The man turned, and looked surprised when he saw who had greeted him. "St. Mawr," he acknowledged.

"I wondered if I might speak to you for a moment?"

Whitman shrugged, as if it were a matter of indifference to him. He was a tall, slender man with dark hair worn rather longer than was the fashion and hooded eyes that were both black and unnervingly cold.

Here was the sort of individual that Emma most hated, Colin thought—the sort she had taken him for at first. Whitman was a notorious gamester, wholly a creature of smoky gaming hells and high-stakes tables. He lived for it. And somehow he also managed to make his living at it, a rare skill, and one that most often left him teetering on the knife edge of survival. Probably because of that, Colin thought, he was not averse to introducing wealthy young men to the pastime that obsessed him and to relieving them of some part of their wealth in exchange for the introduction.

"Have you noticed a young man called Bellingham around town?" Colin asked him. He did not need to specify where. If Whitman had seen Robin, it would have been at the deepest tables. The man went nowhere else.

"Bellingham." Whitman's voice was deep and resonant, but completely lacking in emotion.

"Young," prompted Colin. "Light hair, bit dandyish."

"I've seen him," the other replied, as if he hadn't needed the elaboration. "Rotten player. No sense of strategy, poor concentration. Always looking about to see who's in the room instead of keeping his mind on the game."

"Has he been losing heavily?"

Whitman examined him. "Must be. He never wins." A distant gleam appeared in the man's dark eyes. "Connection of yours, ain't he? You paying off his debts?"

"No," answered Colin forcefully. "He has a small allowance from his father."

"Ah." Whitman's interest waned. These pickings weren't large enough to tempt him. "No wonder he's into the cent-per-cents."

"He's been to moneylenders?"

Whitman gave him a look of great weariness, even perhaps contempt. "Haven't we all?" he asked.

Colin ignored this. The situation was more serious than he'd realized. How could the young idiot have been so stupid as to borrow from moneylenders? His chances of paying off such a loan were meager, since the interest in these transactions practically equaled the entire amount. "I don't suppose you know which?" he asked.

Whitman indicated his ignorance, and massive lack of interest in this topic. "If you'll excuse me," he said, signaling that he was going to join the card players. "Unless you'd care to try a hand?" he added, suddenly more alert.

"I fear not. I have a luncheon engagement," said Colin.

The other turned away at once, all of his attention focusing on the cards that were about to be dealt at the table nearby.

Colin stood alone, frowning. If he gave Emma this news, she would be beside herself with worry. She would insist on taking action. And he was *not* going to allow her to deal with moneylenders. His frown deepened. He could communicate the facts to Robin's father, but that seemed distastefully like talebearing. He could simply forget he had ever heard it, of course. But that would leave catastrophe looming on the horizon, waiting to descend on them at some later time with even greater force.

He would have to find out which moneylender it was, he supposed. That would be simple enough. He could discharge the loan anonymously. There need be no emotional scenes, no painful confessions or furious tirades. Colin's frown lifted completely. He'd found the perfect solution, he thought.

Complacently, he set off to find James and sit down to a good luncheon. Afterward, he would see about tracking down this moneylender.

Colin had no trouble finding the man. Scarcely two hours later, he stood in his place of business handing over a large roll of banknotes. "Thank you, my lord," said the moneylender, not taking his eyes from the bills. "Pleasure doing business with you, my lord. Be assured that you may call on me at any time should you need assistance."

"I hope to avoid that eventuality," replied Colin calmly.

The other man laughed as if he had made a joke. "Well, in your case, I'd say that's likely, my lord St. Mawr. Still, you never know."

"Indeed. May I have Bellingham's note?"

"Of course, of course. I have it right here. Everything in order." He handed over a document over which had been scrawled "paid" and his signature.

"Thank you." Colin folded the page and put it in his pocket. "You understand that you are not to reveal my part in this transaction to anyone?"

"You may rely on my discretion, my lord."

"I do. And if I should hear that you . . ."

The man held up his hand. "Many rely on my silence, my lord. It is a necessity of my business."

Colin turned to go.

"Tell Mr. Bellingham I am at his service in future," said the moneylender. "Always happy to help."

"At twenty per cent a month," added Colin dryly.

"As you say, my lord," was the undaunted reply. "'Tis a valuable service I offer, and worth a good price."

Biting back a sharp reply, Colin left him.

Chapter Eleven

Reddings waited respectfully while the baron arranged the intricate folds of his neckcloth, then held his dark evening coat for him to slip on and smoothed it over his master's broad shoulders. It was a pleasure to serve a gentleman who set off his clothes to such advantage, the valet thought complacently. There wouldn't be another man at the ball tonight who had a finer leg or a better way of carrying himself. As Colin brushed his dark hair, Reddings stole glances at his face in the mirror. The bleakness that had so worried the serving man on their trip back to England was gone, but lately it had been replaced by an intense, concerned expression that rarely seemed to lift. It didn't really worry Reddings, as long as it was not directed at him. But someone was going to catch it, he thought.

It was an odd old world, Reddings told himself. The household wasn't at all what he had expected coming home from the war. They had an unusual sort of mistress, and of course her own servant—the Turk or whatever he was—was so far from usual that Reddings couldn't even think of a word for it. But her ladyship was a real gem, he thought, using an expression in the privacy of his thoughts that would never pass his lips. It was his personal opinion that she'd saved the master from falling into despair.

"Reddings," said Colin. "Where have you gone, man?"

The valet came to himself with a start. "Yes, my lord? Sorry, my lord."

"What were you thinking of?" wondered Colin with a smile. "It seemed to please you."

"Woolgathering, my lord," replied the valet. "I beg your pardon."

Colin waved the apology aside. "What have you done with my cloak?"

Reddings fetched it from the wardrobe and held it up.

"No, I'll carry it. I'm going to see if her ladyship is ready."

Draping the garment over his arm, Reddings cleared his throat.

"What?"

"Nothing, my lord. It is just that I have noticed that ladies sometimes prefer to, er, make an entrance on such occasions. And I did happen to notice . . ."

"Yes. Out with it, man. I can see you mean to tell me."

"A new gown arrived today from Madame Sophie," Reddings confided.

"Did it?" Colin considered. The unspoken tension between him and Emma, and the secrets that lurked beneath it, ate away at him as he kept waiting for her to turn to him for help. Her failure to do so weighed heavily. "You think she wants to dazzle me with the effect?" Colin asked.

"Yes, my lord," was the poker-faced reply.

"Oh, very well. I will await her ladyship in the drawing room," he said.

"Very good, my lord," replied Reddings, looking pleased with himself.

It was not a long wait. Colin had been downstairs only a few minutes when he heard footsteps in the hall. He turned and drew in an admiring breath when his wife appeared in the doorway.

Emma's gown was made of layers of tissue in varying shades of seagreen. Below its snug bodice and tiny puffed sleeves, the skirt moved and rippled like water down to the tips of her matching slippers. Her gleaming hair had been drawn up on her head and then loosed in a cascade of curls in the back. She wore the St. Mawr emeralds in her ears and around her neck.

"Breathtaking," said Colin.

"Isn't it a beautiful dress?" Emma turned, making the tiers of color flow around her. "Sophie is a genius."

"From what you say, she is also well on her way to becoming a wealthy woman."

"Oh, yes." Emma smiled. "She is not in the least surprised about it, however."

"You will outshine every other woman at the ball."

Emma caught a glimpse of the two of them in the mirror above the mantel. Colin was terribly handsome in his dark evening clothes. His chiseled face rose from the snowy neckcloth like a head on a coin, and his mysterious violet eyes glowed with the power of his personality.

"In fact, Tom's wife will be sorry she invited you," he added. "She insists upon being the most sought-after woman at any event."

"Colin! That isn't true."

"No?"

"Not at all. Diana has been very kind to me."

"Yes, I have seen her," he replied, his eyes gleaming with humor. "She is always sending you off into another room, where she is sure you will find something 'vastly amusing' to do or some 'terribly charming' people to talk to. People who are not members of her group of admirers, of course."

"That's silly," said Emma. But as she thought about it, she realized that he was right. She began to laugh.

"Diana keeps her former beaux dangling as if she'd never married. Thank God you don't have a pack of admirers lingering from the past," he teased.

Emma froze in the act of putting on her evening cloak. It was only for a moment, but Colin noticed the flash of fear that crossed her face. It was unbearable, this wall that she had erected between them. What was it that she could not tell him?

"We should go," said Emma. "I promised Caroline we would be early for dinner, to help her manage Aunt Celia. She is afraid of her."

"What nonsense." But Colin could see no option but to offer her his arm.

Caroline met them in a flutter at her front door. "Aunt Celia is in one of her moods," she exclaimed distractedly. "She has already made me send Nicky upstairs, and he was only trying the piano for a few minutes. Emma, come and help." She thrust Emma's cloak at a footman and urged her up the stairs to the drawing room.

Silently thanking Aunt Celia for freeing them from Nicky's boisterous presence, Emma followed her sister-in-law's rapid steps. She didn't understand why everyone in the family was so wary of Aunt Celia. She liked the old woman very much, and felt she understood things better than almost anyone else.

Colin strolled up more slowly. Emma was already seated at Aunt Celia's side by the time he reached the drawing room, and he stood for a moment in the doorway surveying the crowd of family and friends that Caroline had gathered this evening. There was nothing surprising in the collection. Most of them he had met a thousand times before, and he had said everything he had to say to them years ago. Thank God he had not been saddled with a wife as conventional as his sister,

Colin thought. He loved Caroline, but he could not have borne to spend his life in a series of parties like this.

"Beg pardon," said a voice at his elbow.

Colin turned to find Robin Bellingham standing there, resplendent in evening dress of the most extreme fashion and a waistcoat that glittered with gold thread and brocade.

Robin noticed him looking at the bright garment. "Latest thing," he said a bit defensively.

"I'm sure you're right," replied Colin solemnly.

Robin eyed him, as if trying to make out whether he was being mocked. Then he shrugged and abandoned the question. "Wanted to speak to you," he confided.

"You are doing so," the older man pointed out.

"Er, yes. About something particular, I mean."

Colin inclined his head to indicate his willingness to hear.

Robin moved uncomfortably from foot to foot. "Oddest thing has happened," he went on finally. Having said this, he fell silent again, looking around the room to be certain no one else was near enough to hear.

"Yes," prompted Colin after a moment.

"Don't like to mention it to you," blurted Robin. "Thing is, don't want to say anything to Emma. But I can't figure out what the devil's going on."

Growing suddenly wary, Colin said, "You may trust me."

"Umm," responded Robin, looking uneasy at the prospect.

"Shall I give my word that anything you say to me will be kept confidential?" the baron asked.

"No, no. I know you don't blab." Robin flushed. "That is . . ."

"Why don't you just tell me?"

The young man gathered himself visibly. "Thing of it is, I had a pretty large loss at the tables a month or so back." He eyed Colin to see if this admission was going to provoke a lecture; Colin merely gazed at him. "And I hadn't the ready to pay it off," Robin added, and paused again. Once more, Colin offered him no reaction whatever. Robin took a deep breath; the rest of his confession came out in a rush. "Well, I was in the suds, you see. I had to raise the wind somehow. So I went to a moneylender and borrowed it." He swallowed convulsively.

Colin waited for the rest of it. It was quite a time coming.

"Now the man tells me that the debt is paid off," Robin said at last. "Every penny—interest and principal. And the thing is, I didn't pay it! The fellow won't tell me who did, either."

Colin maintained his look of polite interest.

"Says the person 'wishes to remain anonymous,' " continued Robin. "Have you ever heard anything like it?"

Colin indicated that he hadn't.

"Know my father had nothing to do with it," said Robin. "Though I must say, he's been mum on the subject of gaming lately." He frowned. "That's odd, as well. Wonder if he's ill, or some such thing?" He brushed this digression aside. "What I wanted to ask . . ." He seemed to find speech difficult once more. "You didn't have anything to do with it, did you?" he managed finally.

"I?" Colin met his nervous gaze with bland inquiry.

"You gave me those notes back," stammered Robin. "And I know how Emma feels about gambling. Well, and she has reason, I suppose. But I just wondered whether you might have . . ."

If he said nothing, Colin thought, he would not have to lie.

Robin examined his face. The silence grew awkward.

There was a change in Robin's expression. It grew less anxious, harder and more resolute. "Well, if you did happen to know anything about it, I just wanted to tell the person responsible that I'm grateful, of course. And

I should very much prefer to pay the money back, over time."

The lad was by no means stupid, Colin thought.

"And if you . . . if you should happen to . . . to discover the person, I'd like him to know that I've concluded the gaming tables are not . . . not . . ." He trailed off helplessly.

"The best way for you to make your mark in society?" suggested Colin.

"That's it," he responded, greatly relieved. "I don't play all that well," he confided.

"You surprise me."

"I don't," added Robin airily, his spirits rising now that he had gotten through the difficult part of the conversation. "I find most of the games damned dull," he said, as if revealing a guilty secret, "and I'm in a constant worry over the money I'm losing."

Colin waited in sympathetic silence.

"So I just wanted to . . . to pass along that I mean to stay away from the tables from now on. Except for an occasional low-stakes game, among friends," he added hurriedly, as if afraid he would be forbidden even that.

"I think you're wise," said the baron.

Robin nodded sagely. "Because, you know, I believe my talents lie in quite another direction," he said. "A number of people have remarked favorably on my style of dress."

"Have they?"

"Even Farrell," he said, naming one of the leading pinks of the *ton*.

"My congratulations," answered Colin, sternly repressing a smile.

Robin took them benignly. "Not many men could carry off this waistcoat, you know," he informed his brother-in-law. He was now fully restored to his usual manner. "But I have a flair."

"I believe that you do," was the almost wholly sincere reply.

"So you . . . that is, anyone interested in the matter can rest easy," the younger man concluded, a trace of anxiety reappearing in his face.

Colin conveyed his understanding with a silent nod, and Robin offered a small bow before making his way to a circle of young people across the room. It had been a curiously satisfying conversation, Colin thought. The only thing that might improve on the experience was repeating the whole exchange to Emma. But, of course, he didn't intend to do that.

"So, you've taken the Morland chit under your wing?" Aunt Celia was barking to Emma at that precise moment. "Are you regretting it yet? Her grandmother says the child is full of romantic notions and disgraceful self-indulgence."

"She is . . . an original," replied Emma in a quieter voice that did not fill the whole room. "In fact, I should present her to you. You might like her." The idea made Emma smile.

"Hunh," the old woman snorted. She shook her head. "Can't abide mischief-makers." She examined Emma with blue eyes that were exceedingly sharp within the network of wrinkles that creased her face. "Sorry for her, are you?"

"I know how easy it is to make mistakes when you are young and inexperienced," replied Emma, returning her gaze steadily.

Aunt Celia continued to stare for a long moment, then she smiled slightly. "I knew you were just the woman for Colin from the first," she said.

Emma couldn't resist. "From the *very* first?" she wondered.

"Don't try your impertinences on me, young woman," replied Aunt Celia, but her eyes twinkled. "Did you know that Catherine agrees with me now? You've won her over. Indeed, you haven't put a foot wrong. You're well on the way to becoming a darling of the *ton.*"

If she knew about the scandal that waited to break

over all their heads, Emma thought, she would have an apoplexy.

"Colin's prodigiously proud of you," continued Aunt Celia, eyes turned to her great-nephew. "And well he should be. The proper wife is a great asset to one's position in society, you know."

"Yes," said Emma quietly. How could she not know it? Everyone in London continually reminded her of the importance of society's opinion—Colin, his family and friends, the people they met.

"Just as the wrong wife can be ruinous," Aunt Celia added.

Was she making some particular point? Emma wondered. Aunt Celia knew everything. Had she found out something? But when she searched the old woman's face, she could see no sign of that.

"Particularly for Colin," continued the other. "Most men, if they're unhappy in their homes, just amuse themselves elsewhere. Set up a mistress, hang about their club, hunt and shoot and make general nuisances of themselves among the wildlife. But Colin's different— has been since he was a lad. He thinks. He gets himself involved in causes. That's why he joined up, you know, against everyone's wishes and without another direct heir." She snorted again. "There was no talking to him. He takes things too hard. You know?"

She put a particular emphasis on the last words, and Emma was forced to examine her again. The old woman seemed to look right through her. "I know," she answered, more determined than ever that nothing she did would harm Colin or his position.

"Good," declared Aunt Celia, seeming satisfied. She tightened her grasp on the cane she held in both hands before her and pounded it on the floor. "Where the devil is dinner?" she demanded. "I'm perishing with hunger."

•   •   •

Most of the party at Caroline's went on to the ball together, and they found the room already crowded when they arrived. "Diana has outdone herself," commented Colin, referring both to the crush of guests and the unusual decoration. Instead of the conventional flowers, their hostess had hung the walls with pine boughs and clusters of pinecones that had been gilded and tied together with gold and white ribbons. The effect was striking, and the branches released a wonderful fresh smell through the whole ballroom.

Their first task was to get Aunt Celia settled at a whist table in the card room with some of her cronies. She had brought her own two footmen to help her and to run whatever errands occurred to her during the course of the evening. Once she was satisfied with her position and partner, Emma and Caroline returned to the ballroom and their husbands. Colin held out his hand as soon as Emma appeared. "It is a waltz," he said.

She moved into his arms, and he swept her onto the floor full of whirling couples. Emma had loved dancing since she was a child in the schoolroom and first began learning the steps. And it was even more enthralling to follow the music with Colin, who moved with crisp masculine grace and held her with such gentle authority. Emma's spirits rose a little.

"That's better," said Colin.

"What?"

"I could almost see the cloud lift. Won't you tell me what it was?" His eyes bored into hers as if he was trying to force the answer out of her.

She wanted to tell him the truth, Emma thought, shrinking a little under the power of that gaze. She desperately wanted to lean on his ever-present strength. But the risk was too great. "I . . . I was worrying about my brother," she improvised. "I've never found the proper moment to mention his gaming, you know. And I feel I am failing him. What was he saying to you at Caroline's? Did he tell you what this 'important engagement' was that prevented him from coming with us to the ball?"

Colin shook his head. "I believe you will soon see a change there," he could not resist saying.

"A change?"

"In his habits."

"You mean the gambling?" She eyed him. "You seem certain."

"I am a very good judge of character," he replied, swinging her in a turn that made her breath catch slightly.

Emma kept her eyes on his face. "What opportunity have you had to judge Robin's character?" she persisted.

"Well, there was the bull," he suggested.

"Have you done something?" she asked quickly. "Did you speak to him? I knew he would listen to you."

"I did not," replied Colin with conviction. "But I think perhaps he is growing up, as I assured you he would do. And I don't believe you will hear about his gaming losses again."

Emma examined his face, then gave him a tremulous smile. "You did do something!"

"I promise you, my dear Emma—"

"No, don't pretend you didn't. I can tell." Her chest tightened, and she had to blink away a few tears. Despite his reluctance, and the pain that lingered from his past, he had made the effort to help Robin somehow. Emma was overwhelmed by a surge of love for this man, who was so much more than she had ever dreamed of finding.

Colin cleared his throat. He was slightly embarrassed, and yet also curiously pleased that she had guessed his secret.

"I don't know how to thank—" began Emma.

"There is absolutely no need," he interrupted quickly. Here, in the midst of all these people, he didn't know how to deal with the soft light he saw in her eyes.

Music floated through the room. The dancers made a great revolving circle under the glittering chandeliers. The scent of pine intensified as the heat in the room grew. And Emma and Colin danced silently together, neither knowing quite what to say.

When the dance ended and they returned to the sidelines, they were immediately surrounded by a group of chattering friends. In the short time since they had returned to London from Cornwall, they had become part of a circle of lively socialites. A few of them were friends of Colin's, but his long absence from England in the army had broken the ties he had had in his early youth, so many of them were as new to him as to Emma. The baron and baroness St. Mawr were welcomed for their own qualities—beauty, intelligence, wit, and good nature—as well as for their position and wealth and style.

"Is your horse ready for the Derby, Andrew?" Emma asked one of the men.

This launched a heated discussion about horseflesh and the colt's chances in the race, along with those of all the other likely entries. One of the women gave Emma a reproachful glance. "A quadrille," said the woman then, as the music began. "Come, let's make up a set for it." She tugged at her husband's arm.

He yielded, but continued to argue over his shoulder. "Short of bone, I tell you. Hasn't got a prayer."

They danced the quadrille, and a country dance, and another waltz. A cotillion was called just before supper, and then wide doors were opened on another room where tables were piled with lobster patties, ices, tiny sandwiches, and other delicacies. One of the men in their party stuck a champagne bottle under each arm and planted himself at a table in the corner, saving the chairs for them while they piled their plates high at the buffet. Their table soon became a center of laughter and noise, and attracted more than one envious glance. Watching Colin exchange mock insults with Tom,

Emma thought how happy he looked. This really was important to him, she thought.

The first dance after dinner was another waltz, and Emma danced it with Caroline's husband, who had a distressing tendency to step on her feet when they turned. When the music ended and they returned to the sidelines, they found Caroline holding the end of a ruffle that had been torn from the hem of her gown. "Teddy Dunster stepped on it," she said. "I shall have to pin it up."

"I'll do it," said Emma. "Come upstairs."

Going up the steps, Caroline lagged behind. "Are you all right?" Emma asked her.

"Rather tired," was the reply.

Emma took her arm, noting that she looked a bit pale. "Perhaps you should go," she suggested. "You are in a delicate condition, you know, even if it is not yet showing."

"Yes, I shall tell Frederick. It was the same when I was increasing with Nicky. I got fatigued so easily."

They reached the ladies' withdrawing room, and Emma found pins and knelt to repair Caroline's flounce.

"I must tell you, Emma," she said. "It is splendid to see Colin happy once again. When he came home from France, we feared he might never recover his spirits. Mama even imagined he would go into a decline." She laughed a little. "I never thought that, but he was"—she groped for a word—"joyless. But he is much better now. Thank you for that."

Emma stood, the ruffle reattached. It was like a conspiracy, she thought. Everyone seemed determined to remind her of the precarious state of Colin's happiness. Did they imagine that she would ever jeopardize it?

"We are all lucky to have you in our family," Caroline added, giving her a one-armed hug.

Emma felt a wave of affection for the other woman, who had been kind to her from the first.

Caroline and her husband departed, taking Aunt

Celia along with them. After bidding them farewell, Emma danced with Tom, and then with another of their friends. She was standing at the side, making use of her fan, when Colin joined her again. "Hot," he said.

"Horribly," she agreed.

"Would you like to take a stroll in the garden?"

Emma opened her mouth, looked startled, then laughed.

"What?" asked Colin.

"I was about to refuse because it is not at all the thing to leave a ball on a gentleman's arm and go off alone," she said, inviting him to join in her laughter. "That is what I was taught, you see, and I have attended only a few balls since my come-out years ago."

"Quite unacceptable behavior in a young lady," he agreed solemnly. "Very fast. Unless, of course, the gentleman in question is her husband."

"Yes." Emma's smile faded. A walk in the cool air sounded wonderful. But she wasn't sure she could bear to be alone with Colin just now.

"Come." He pulled aside a curtain that covered a glass door.

"I don't know if . . ." began Emma, but he drew her out onto a narrow stone terrace with a broad balustrade on the opposite side. Steps led down into the garden. "Oh, this is wonderful," said Emma, as the outdoor air cooled her heated skin. She couldn't resist. They walked arm in arm along the brick pathway.

"Look," said Colin.

Following his pointing finger, she saw a shooting star glitter across the night sky and disappear. Her breath caught at the beauty of it.

"You get a wish," he said.

"I thought that was on the first star you see," objected Emma.

"Both," he assured her.

"But you saw it first," she said. "It should be your wish."

"I yield it to you," Colin replied.

Gazing upward, Emma wished with all her might that Count Julio Orsino would disappear from her life and never return.

"That must come true," said Colin. "You looked utterly determined."

"I was."

"And what did you wish for?" he wondered.

Emma shook her head. "I cannot tell, or it will not come true."

Silence fell. Emma cast about for something to say.

"Shall we explore that walk?" Colin asked, pointing to a path that led between heavy lines of greenery. He began to lead her in that direction. "I probably should warn you that this is the one where young sprigs try to lure the girls to steal a kiss," he added.

"And how would you know that?"

"It's obvious," he replied. "It's the darkest, the most secluded, can't be seen from the house."

"You sound as if you have a great deal of experience with such places," commented Emma.

"Almost none," he responded. "But it's a well-known bit of male lore, you know. There's horses, sport, tying a decent neckcloth, and . . ."

"Luring young ladies into dark places," finished Emma, smiling. He could always make her smile, she thought tremulously.

"Precisely."

They passed into the shadow of the shrubbery, and the lights from the house were cut off as if they didn't exist. Colin's arms slid around her, and he captured her lips and held them in a kiss that made Emma melt against him. The hard length of him through her feathery dress set her afire. Colin let his hands roam over it, sternly resisting the urge to tear the floating silk from her curves and take her here and now under the pines. They had this, at least, he thought fiercely. Nothing could alter his desire for her, or the breathtaking response he could rouse in her. He allowed himself to push one tiny puffed sleeve down over her shoulder and reveal the perfect globe of her breast with its rosy tip.

"Colin," protested Emma. "Someone may come!"

"Let them!" He took that irresistible tip in his mouth, waiting for her reliable, tiny gasp of pleasure.

The conflict in Emma rose to an agonizing pitch. She loved him and she desperately wanted him to love her in return, and just as desperately she feared losing him when Orsino spilled his poison into public ears. She couldn't stand it! Jerking free, she restored her dress with shaking fingers. "We should go in," she stammered, and fled toward the lights and music of the ballroom.

Colin stood alone in the darkness, outrage and disbelief coursing through him like hot metal. She had pushed him away. She had completed the barrier between them; there was not even a crevice left. The shock and pain of it crashed through him, leaving him incapable of movement for long seconds. She had cringed from his touch. Raw desolation, the sort he knew only too well, threatened to engulf him. He fought it off with anger. He had to get Emma home, he thought, where she would have no excuse to run from him, and have this thing out once and for all.

His jaw set, he strode across the garden and reentered the ballroom. The festivities were now at their height, and many of the guests had indulged too freely in Tom's fine champagne. Colin ran his eyes over them contemptuously, searching for Emma. He finally spotted her talking to their host and went quickly to join their group.

"I have a treat for you," Tom was telling Emma. "You've been keen to attend a masquerade. Well, there's a special one coming up at the Pantheon, and I've gotten a party together to go. We'll take a box. You'll be able to see everything."

"I thought the Pantheon masquerades were vulgar and unfashionable," said Emma.

"They're jolly rackety," Tom agreed. "But if we go

in a large party and leave fairly early, there's no harm. We shan't remove our masks, of course."

"I have always wanted to see all those people in costume," Emma allowed.

"What shall we wear?" exclaimed one of their female friends who was part of the circle. "It must be something splendid."

"I will not wear any costume that does not include trousers," Tom declared. "No Elizabethan doublets and hose or anything similar."

"Of course," said the friend sweetly.

"You've landed us in the soup now, Tom," said the woman's husband. "Be sure they'll choose something that will make us look ridiculous."

"I've always had a fondness for the days of King Charles," the friend mused. "They wore those marvelous wigs."

Tom groaned.

"We have to be going," said Colin abruptly. Everyone looked surprised, but he didn't care. He grasped Emma's arm in an unbreakable grip and began to urge her toward the door. And he did not let go until they sat side by side in their closed town carriage clattering through the dark streets of London toward home.

Silence stretched between them like a spring wound to the breaking point. This was no good, thought Colin. They had to be capable of a rational conversation. He could not go on enduring alternate impulses to crush her against him and to shake her until her teeth rattled. He gazed out the coach window, looking for guidance. "There's Barbara Rampling's place," he observed.

Emma looked, then shivered. If she could not find a way out of the current tangle, she might well find herself inside walls like those again, alone, trying to win enough money to survive for the next few weeks—and terribly unhappy for the rest of her life. She shivered again.

They drove past the front door, where a bright lantern hung to illuminate the step and encourage visitors.

Two men were about to enter. Emma watched the smaller one knock as the other waited a little behind. The door opened, throwing a shaft of golden light in their faces, and, with horror, Emma recognized them both. Faster than thought, she started up in her seat, and then struck a sharp blow on the roof of the carriage. "Stop!" she cried to the coachman above them. "Stop at once."

The vehicle lurched as the man began to pull up the horses. "What the devil?" said Colin.

Though the coach was still moving, Emma pushed open the door on her side and started to leap out. Colin caught her arm and held her until the vehicle came to a full stop. "Have you gone mad?" he exclaimed. "Do you want to hurt yourself?"

"I must go in," replied Emma, struggling in his grasp.

"Why?"

"Because I must!" she cried. She broke Colin's grip and jumped down to the cobbled street. Robin had just entered the gaming house in the company of Count Orsino. It was as if Emma's worst nightmares had come to life before her eyes. In an instant, she saw Robin degenerating in just a few years from a bright youth to desperate, grasping insanity, into a creature who thought of nothing but the next wager. The vision—the memory—clouded her reason, and she could think of nothing but dragging Robin away from this place.

"Emma!" Colin was right behind her as she crossed the pavement and mounted the step to Barbara Rampling's door. "Wait a moment," he said as she knocked.

The door opened and she strode through, heading immediately for the stairs.

"Emma." Colin caught her arm again and forced her to stop near the top of the stairs. Catching hold of her shoulders, he brought her around to face him. "*What* is the matter?"

"It was Robin. I saw him," replied Emma a bit

wildly. "He will be ruined. And it is all my fault. I must tell him. I must stop him." She twisted between his hands.

"How can it be your fault?" he said, cursing young Robin silently. He had thought the boy's word good.

Orsino was here because of her, Emma thought. It was as if she had loosed a terrible plague on people she cared about and must now watch them be destroyed by it. Once again, it would not be her, but someone she loved who was ruined and disgraced. The idea drove her beyond rational thought. "You let me believe you had helped him," she accused Colin. "You lied to me!" She tore free of his hands. "You care nothing about Robin," she cried. "He is just an annoyance to you. It would be different if *Caroline* was in trouble. Then you would stop it."

Her words rang in the air for a moment. They faced each other like adversaries.

"It is true I care more for my sister than for Robin," he acknowledged evenly. "That seems to me only natural. But it does not mean that—"

"Go home!" cried Emma. "Leave me alone. I will take care of my brother myself." Her stomach had knotted and she was on the verge of tears.

But he caught hold of her again. "There is more involved here than your brother," he accused. "Why won't you tell me what?"

"I thought he was occupied," said Emma to herself. "I thought he was not gambling as much as before."

"He is not," replied Colin, hoping it was true.

"Things are worse than ever!" exclaimed Emma. "Tonight he is gambling with . . ." She bit off the last of this sentence and struggled to pull away from him again.

"With whom?" demanded Colin.

"Let go. Leave me alone," she said, overcome with guilt.

"He was with someone. That is what has upset you so. Who?"

"You're hurting my arm," she protested. "Let me go."

"Not until you tell me what has frightened you so."

"I am not frightened!" With a violent jerk that bruised her arm, Emma broke free. At once, she leapt up the remaining stairs. "Go home," she insisted, her voice uneven. "I will see to this."

Colin let her go, watching her disappear into the main card room in a flurry of silk. Naturally, he was not going to leave her alone in this place, but he was too angry to follow just now. She was acting as she had when they first met, treating him as someone who could not be trusted. He had shown her that this wasn't true. She had no right to doubt it.

Looking grim, Colin slowly followed Emma into the large card room. Surveying the occupants, he spotted Robin first, sitting at a table in the corner facing a dark gentleman in dandyish dress. After a moment, Colin recognized him. It was Orsino. Somewhat enlightened, he searched for Emma. It took a few moments, but he finally found her sitting in a window seat, half concealed by the curtains. Her eyes were fixed on her brother, and her body was rigid with tension.

Colin paused, then walked farther into the room. He made sure Barbara Rampling saw him, and one or two of the habitués of her house, so that no one would imagine Emma was here alone. Then he retreated into one of the side rooms, where a game of whist was in progress, and settled himself as if interested in observing. Actually, he chose a place from which he could see much of the outer room.

Emma realized that her hands hurt. She had been clenching her fists for a long time, watching Robin lose money to Orsino. With a great effort, she eased them open. Her shoulders were cramping with tension, and her head was pounding. She saw nothing in the crowded room but Robin and the count, and she followed every move of their fingers, every expression that passed across their faces. Several times, she had to restrain herself from running across the room and dragging Robin away from the table. Only the certainty that he would never forgive her for such a public scene stopped her. And so she waited, painfully alert to any opening that would allow her to get her brother away from that devil.

After what seemed like days, Robin finally rose from his chair and walked toward the back of the room, where he went through a curtain that led to the retiring rooms. At once, Emma was on her feet and hurrying through the crowd. No doubt Orsino would see her, she thought, if he had not already. He didn't miss such things. But she didn't care. It wouldn't matter what he thought if she could just get Robin away from him.

Emma positioned herself just inside the curtain that hung across the corridor leading to the back premises. A gentleman who had clearly drunk far too much reeled by just as she arrived. She thought he might accost her, but he seemed lost in his own world and merely stumbled by, tangling himself briefly in the folds of the curtain before erupting into the room beyond. Emma heard male voices greet him in laughing mockery as she turned to watch for Robin again.

He soon came, walking purposefully along the hall, a frown on his handsome young face. It deepened when she spoke his name and he realized that the shadowy figure silhouetted by the light streaming between the curtains was his sister.

"Emma, what the deuce are you doing here?" he said.

"I must speak to you!"

"Now? Is something wrong?" He looked alarmed. "Is it Father?"

"No! It is you, you . . . idiot." In that instant, Emma's welter of emotion focused into a beam of anger directed at her young brother. "How can you be such a fool?" she demanded.

Robin stiffened and looked haughty.

"Can't you see that Orsino is a sharper?" cried Emma. "How can you let him lead you into—"

"Of course I can," interrupted Robin curtly.

"Then *why* are you here with him?" said Emma, feeling ready to shriek.

Robin gave her a look. "I should think that might be obvious to you," he answered. "You are the one who introduced that court card to Lady Mary."

Surprised, Emma just looked at him.

"He's been hanging about her, you know, filling her head with ridiculous notions and encouraging her to believe she is persecuted because she is in mourning."

Emma blinked.

"She has no experience of the world," Robin continued. "She does not see that he is a danger to her."

"But . . ." Emma faltered. This conversation was not going as she had planned.

"So someone has to keep this Orsino away from her," Robin concluded.

"Yes, I know, but . . ."

"Can't be you," Robin added, "because the man's not proper company for any female, in my opinion. So . . ." He shrugged.

Emma gazed at him in bemused wonderment. This was not what she had expected from him at all.

"I said I'd help you with her," he said in response to her expression. "And I am. Trying to help her as well. Orsino really prefers the tables, you know, to just about anything else. If I keep him busy gaming, he can't be making mischief for anyone else."

"He will take every penny you have," wailed Emma.

Robin made a wry face. "Seems likely," he admitted. "The man's got the devil's own luck."

"He cheats!"

Comprehension dawned on Robin's handsome face. "Does he? That explains it, then."

"You mustn't play with him," Emma insisted.

Her brother shrugged. "Have to keep him busy, Emma. He doesn't have a broad acquaintance in London, you see, and if he is not with me, he'll likely be after Lady Mary."

Emma heard echoes of Orsino in that. It was just the sort of subtle threat he made in order to get what he wanted. Her relief at the knowledge that Robin was not addicted to gaming was lost in the fear of Orsino's association with him. Orsino would find a way to subvert him. Her jaw hardened. "You must not have any contact with Orsino," she urged Robin. "I will see that he does not harm Lady Mary."

Her brother looked skeptical. "How?" he asked. When Emma hesitated, he nodded as if she had confirmed some thought of his. "The man's a rum customer, Emma. You'd best stay away from him."

Emma gazed at him with a mixture of affection and despair. It was unbelievable that he should be saying this to her, trying to protect her. He had been a child in England while she faced scoundrels of every sort. "I can deal with Orsino," she told him. "All of Edward's friends were like him. I am used to the type."

Robin looked shocked. "All of them?" he said. "I thought perhaps . . . I mean, I assumed you didn't realize what a blackguard the fellow is."

"I am all too aware," replied Emma. "Please, Robin, stay away from him. It is not just gambling. He is the worst sort of man."

Her young brother straightened and looked stubborn. "I promised to help you, and I shall," he declared. "I don't slope off as soon as things get difficult, you know. You can count on me."

"But it won't help if I am worrying about you all the time," Emma said.

"Don't need to. I can handle myself."

Emma's eyes filled with tears. She really could count on him, she realized. He was rapidly growing up into an admirable man. The trouble was, she didn't want to count on him in this. He didn't really understand what Count Orsino was capable of, and she wanted him as far from the man as possible. "Robin—" she began.

"You won't get rid of me," he interrupted. "So you may as well not try."

If she had not asked him to help with Lady Mary, he would not even know Orsino, Emma thought despairingly. "It is not a matter of—"

The curtain twitched back, and Colin stood there, a frown on his face. He had seen Emma slip behind this drape some minutes ago, and had become concerned when she did not reappear. Now, he faced two startled pairs of eyes and received the distinct feeling that he was intruding on a private conversation.

"St. Mawr," said Robin heartily. "Glad you're here. I thought Emma was alone."

"No," said Colin.

"Good." Robin gave him a comradely nod. "Have to get back to the table. Orsino will be wondering what became of me."

"Robin," protested Emma.

"Not until you tell me what is going on," commanded Colin.

Robin glanced at Emma for direction.

Anger drew Colin's face tight. Emma bit her lower lip, uncertain.

"Don't worry," Robin said, in an attempt at conciliation. "I have things well in hand." And before anyone could argue with that statement, he slipped out into the card room.

The corridor was quiet and empty. Emma looked at the polished floor.

"*He* has things in hand?" said Colin in a tightly controlled voice. "Something has occurred to upset you, and you have turned to that . . . boy to help you?"

It was too complicated to explain, Emma thought.

"What has passed between you and Orsino?" he asked crisply.

"Between us?" Emma cast about for some innocuous fiction, and did not find it. "He's . . . someone Edward knew," she said finally. "I was afraid . . . when I saw Robin with him . . . But it was all a mistake," she added hurriedly, before he could inquire.

Rage and hurt burned in Colin at the thought that she had told her brother things he was not to know.

"I'm tired," said Emma, not meeting his eyes. "Let us go."

"Not until you tell me what is going on," he insisted.

"I have told you. Nothing is going on."

"You expect me to believe that?" asked Colin.

"Are you suggesting I'm lying?" she snapped.

"You are evading the issue!"

"Nothing that concerns you has—"

"Everything about you concerns me!" he shouted. "And I will have the truth of this matter, Emma. Now."

She raised her chin. "You will get nothing by shouting my name in gaming houses."

Realizing that he had lost control in an unforgivable way, Colin struggled to regain his equilibrium.

"I wish to go home now," repeated Emma. She pulled back the drape and walked across the large room to the door opposite. Colin had no choice but to follow. As he did so, he was conscious of interested eyes watching them, particularly a dark, shrewd pair from a table in the corner.

Chapter Twelve

The footman opened the door of Emma's fashionable barouche and offered a hand to help her climb down. She descended gracefully to the pavement and prepared to enter her townhouse. She was coming from a call on Colin's mother, who had been filled with the greatest cordiality and even approval of all Emma's plans for refurbishing Trevallan, even though the dowager baroness had said, "I always found the place draughty and prodigiously depressing to the spirits."

How much longer could she go through the motions of her fashionable life in London? Emma wondered. She thought only of her dilemma. Her small efforts to discover why Orsino had left the Continent for England had failed. All the schemes she formulated had fatal flaws. And time was rapidly running out.

Emma's nights had filled with troubled dreams in which Colin was looking at her, smiling warmly. Then, gradually, his expression would change to chagrin, as if he couldn't believe what he was hearing, and then to distaste, and finally to cold contempt. In the end, he would be staring directly at her with ice in his violet eyes and revulsion in the line of his mouth, and she would know for certain that they would never be close again. She would wake sitting bolt upright and sheened with sweat, and be grateful at first to find herself alone in her bed. The tears came later.

A sound made her raise her head. Clinton was standing in the open doorway of the house, like a stern sentinel in black, waiting for her to enter. He had cleared his throat to let her know this, and to attract her attention to the fact that she was daydreaming in the public street. "Good afternoon, my lady," he said now. "Lady Mary Dacre has called. She insisted on waiting."

Swiftly, Emma mounted the two steps to the threshold and went in, stripping off her gloves as she walked. She was very tired of Lady Mary's chatter about how much longer she was required to be in mourning and the new ball gown her mother had promised her for the first dance she would be allowed to attend. But she had a duty to attend to, Emma thought. And it could not be put off any longer.

When Lady Mary greeted her, Emma responded by shutting the door of the drawing room with a snap. "I must speak to you about Count Orsino," she said without preamble.

Lady Mary looked surprised. "Count Orsino?"

"You must not allow yourself to be charmed by him," Emma replied.

"Why not?"

"He is not a proper person for you to know."

"But he seems quite pleasant," the girl objected. "I think he's amusing. He makes me laugh."

"He is a scoundrel—a cheating gamester, a liar, a libertine. He is completely unprincipled."

"I thought he was a friend of yours," said Lady Mary.

"I became acquainted with him in Europe, because he hung about my husband in order to win money from him. But I have never been his friend," replied Emma vehemently.

Lady Mary looked more intrigued than shocked. "I have always wondered," she said. "What exactly is a libertine?"

"Someone you should not know," repeated Emma curtly.

"Yes, but why? What does it mean?"

Emma hesitated. She did not believe in the approach that left young girls completely ignorant of the coarser side of life. She thought it often put them at the mercy of those who wished them ill. But she was not in charge of Lady Mary's education. She had no right to make such decisions for her.

"Does it mean he will try to persuade me to run away and marry him, so that he can have my fortune?" Lady Mary appeared to contemplate this possibility with an alarming lack of concern.

This was the least dangerous scheme he might plan, Emma thought. She frowned. She had, after all, been the reluctant means of introducing this man to Lady Mary. She had some responsibility to stop him. "A libertine is a man who will not hesitate to seduce and ruin you if he is given the chance," said Emma bluntly. "Marriage may not be involved."

Lady Mary's mouth fell open.

"Orsino is a fortune hunter," Emma continued. "He wants money, a lot of it, and he will do almost anything to get it. Except, I think, to tie himself for life. He would be much more likely to put you in a compromising position, and then force money from your parents. He enjoys deceiving people and robbing them through some stratagem." Her face twisted. "It makes him feel superior."

Lady Mary looked impressed.

"He will do anything," Emma emphasized again. "And he cares for no one on earth but himself. I have seen the way he treated . . ." She met Lady Mary's wide blue eyes. "Other women with whom he became acquainted," she finished.

"How?" inquired the girl.

"Badly," said Emma.

"Umm." Lady Mary thought this over.

"So you see why you must have nothing to do with him."

"I see that I must take care," was the reply. "You may be sure I shan't let him make a fool of *me*."

"You will not be able to stop him," Emma insisted, feeling a strong desire to shake her.

"I don't see why not, now that you have warned me."

"How can you like him?" Emma exclaimed. "He is so false, so insinuating."

"I didn't realize it was all false," Lady Mary admitted. "I will be on my guard."

Emma made an exasperated noise.

"And I'm not certain I *like* him exactly," continued the girl. "He is very interesting, though. I have never met anyone at all like him."

"Because your parents have seen that you don't." Emma's frustration made her clench her fists.

"Well, that's just it, you see. They have made certain I only met *suitable* young men, and I have come to the conclusion that suitable young men are dead bores."

"Lady Mary—"

"And now, of course, I do not even see *them*, because I cannot go out. They do not offer to walk with me in the park or call to see how I am getting on. *They* just say horrid things, like Freddy Blankenship, and laugh at me."

Emma tried to control her temper.

"So I do not see why I should not enjoy myself with Count Orsino, as long as I am *very* careful."

"Because he will eat you alive!" exploded Emma.

Lady Mary smiled, and Emma noticed a most disconcerting spark in her eyes. "That is what he will think," she confided. "Most people expect me to be quite stupid, you know. I find it very useful at times."

"You do not understand what you are proposing," said Emma.

"But I do. Now. And I thank you very much for your kind advice."

Emma groaned.

"There was something I wished to speak to *you* about," Lady Mary confided, as if the previous subject had been satisfactorily disposed of. "That is why I came. I heard you have made up a party to attend the Pantheon masquerade, and I had the most wonderful idea."

"What?" replied Emma warily.

Lady Mary clasped her hands before her chest as if in prayer. "You could take me with you! No one would know who I was. And so they would not know that I am in mourning and not allowed to attend large parties." She heaved a sigh. "You have no idea what a *penance* it is to be missing all the balls and musical evenings and other entertainments that my friends attend." She frowned. "Eliza takes a positive delight in describing every single detail, and exclaiming over and over what a fine time she had."

It must be hard for her, Emma acknowledged, but she had to shake her head. "I cannot take you to a masquerade," she said. "It is no place for a young girl."

"You are going," accused Lady Mary.

"With my husband, and a number of friends. And we only intend to watch for a while and leave early," responded Emma, trying to make the evening sound unappealing.

The scheme backfired. "Well, you see, there's nothing wrong in that," said Lady Mary. "I would stay in the box with you. Everyone will be masked. And no one would know who I was," she repeated. "I don't see the harm."

"Your parents would never allow it," declared Emma.

Lady Mary waved this boring thought aside. "We needn't tell them. My mother is quite used to my going out with you."

"I could not do anything against your parents' wishes," Emma told her.

"You don't know their wishes," insisted the girl. "And if we do not *ask* them, then they cannot forbid—"

"No," said Emma, in what she hoped was a tone of finality.

"How can you be so cruel?" the girl accused. "I did as you wanted, and told everyone that I had been mistaken about St. Mawr's intentions. I have taken great pains to be pleasant and do as I was told. And now you will not do one tiny thing for me!"

An interesting, and characteristic, interpretation of their situation, Emma thought. She wondered what Lady Mary was like when she was not taking pains to be pleasant.

"You don't care anything about me, really, do you? Now that you have got what you wanted, I daresay you will sever the acquaintance."

Emma gave her a sidelong glance. This was uncomfortably close to something she had thought herself. "Nonsense," she replied bracingly.

"No one cares about *me*," Lady Mary burst out. "It is all family or society or duty. I'm heartily sick of it all!"

Emma wondered if she was going to cry, and wondered what she could say to forestall a tantrum. "I do care about you," she said with partial truth. "But that does not mean I will deceive your parents."

"I do not want to *deceive* them," the girl protested. "If they do not—"

She was interrupted by a knock at the drawing room door, followed at once by the appearance of Robin Bellingham on the heels of Clinton the butler.

"I wanted to tell you . . ." Robin began, but

stopped short when he saw Lady Mary. "Oh, er, hullo," he added.

Clinton offered Emma a note on a silver tray. "This was just delivered for you, my lady," he said. Emma took the folded paper and opened it.

Two more days. I believe I will call on your husband first, before offering the tale to the vulgar crowd.

                                                    Orsino

She stared at the words and felt sick. The room receded from her consciousness for a time, and her thoughts raced in the same futile circles that had occupied them for days. What was she going to do? How could she stop this creature from wrecking her marriage and exposing Colin to the ridicule and pity of all fashionable London? What lever could she use, what weapon? There had to be a way.

When she finally became aware of her surroundings again, Lady Mary was saying, "Well, this is the *silliest* thing I have ever heard. Why should anyone wish to spend *five hundred pounds* on a pair of horses, when you can get *perfectly* good ones for half that."

"These are matched grays," replied Robin, scandalized by her attitude. "Bradshaw says they're sweet goers, too, smooth as silk."

"I have not noticed—" the girl began to object.

"Be quiet!" Emma put a hand to her aching head.

"You have been very bad-tempered lately," observed Lady Mary.

"I have not!"

Both of them looked at her. Emma heard sounds of arrival in the hall below and knew that Colin was home, and that another strained, silent evening loomed before them.

"Was it that note?" Lady Mary asked.

Looking down, Emma realized that she was still holding the bit of paper. She crushed the sheet in her fist just as Colin strolled into the room and wished them all good day. A flash of panic caused her to fumble the note into her pocket, and then to flush bright red at the needless attention she had drawn to it.

Colin's expression hardened.

"My lord," said Lady Mary. "How fortunate. You can settle a dispute for us. Would *you* spend five hundred pounds on a team of horses?"

He didn't seem to hear her. He was looking at Emma, watching her try to recover her composure and pretend that the moment of acute awkwardness had not occurred.

"Anyone would," said Robin quickly, trying to catch Lady Mary's eye and signal her to drop the subject. The tension in the room was almost painful.

"Anyone?" she mocked, oblivious to his winks and grimaces. "What nonsense! *I* would not. And of course, most of the people in London could never *afford* to—"

"Shall we go?" said Robin. "I believe you said you had an appointment." He stared meaningfully into her eyes and made an unobtrusive gesture toward the door.

"Me? I have no appointments." She frowned at him as if he had said something exceedingly stupid. "What is the matter with you?"

Emma wasn't looking at Colin at all, Robin noticed, while he was staring at her with an intensity that was almost frightening. And there had been some odd business with that note when St. Mawr came in. Robin had thought at first that they wanted to be rid of their visitors, but now he concluded that it was something else, some trouble between them.

"You're getting as bad as Emma," said Lady Mary. "Lately, she's completely distracted, or else snapping at us like a schoolmistress."

Robin watched Emma flush and Colin frown. Definitely something wrong, he thought. And he was struck by a sudden impulse to do something, to help the sister who had been the first to put faith in him. He had thought, in a vague way, that her marriage was happy.

That seemed to be the general opinion around the *ton*. If they'd hit a snag, perhaps an outsider could help cut them loose. "Er . . ." he said.

The others turned to look at him.

What was the drill here? he wondered. His mind was a blank. Lady Mary was beginning to glare impatiently. What did you do when things threatened to blow up in your face? Robin thought frantically. "Ah!" he said.

"What is it?" snapped Colin.

"You know, Emma, that servant of yours," was the somewhat wild response. "The huge one. What's his name?"

"Ferik?" replied Emma, surprised.

They all looked a bit flummoxed, thought Robin. But a laugh was just the thing to break the tension. "That's it, Ferik," he continued. "Rather an odd duck, eh? Strange notions."

"He comes from a very different sort of society," allowed Emma, looking rather bewildered.

"I should say. The fellow offered to tip *me* yesterday." Robin looked around the group, waiting for them to catch the joke. They were remarkably slow on the uptake. "Instead of me tipping him," he explained helpfully. "Wanted to give me a five-pound note."

"What for?" asked Colin in a harsh voice.

"That's the oddest thing of all," Robin said, smiling to encourage them all to laugh along with him. "Wanted me to put in a good word for him with you. 'Speak well of me to the lord,' was the way he put it. As if you cared what I thought of your servants. Deuced odd, eh?"

The other three just gazed at him.

"Of course, I refused the money," added Robin quickly.

Lady Mary looked bored. Emma looked miserable. Colin looked grim.

"It's a joke," Robin informed them irritably. "Funny, you see? A servant tipping. Don't you see that?"

"I think it's stupid," replied Lady Mary.

Colin had had enough. "I think it is time you took your leave," he said.

The girl bridled.

"Haven't you anywhere else to spend your time?" he added, good manners quite defeated by the current situation in his house.

"Oh, how can you speak to me so? After the way you . . ."

"Someone ought to speak to you sharply at least once a day," responded Colin, his patience completely exhausted. "And they should have begun a number of years ago."

Robin stared at him with awed respect.

"You're horrid," declared Lady Mary. Her face puckered, threatening tears. "I don't believe I was ever really in love with you!"

"Neither do I," replied Colin callously. "And now, if you will excuse us?" He threw Robin a meaningful look.

The younger man stood straighter and prepared to do his duty. But he could not suppress a muttered, "I'm always having to take her off someone's hands. And she's deuced likely to cry in the street, you know."

Colin gave him a sardonic smile, but no answer. He simply watched the two young people gather their belongings and leave the room.

When they were gone, he waited, watching Emma, who was half turned away from him. The unhappiness in her face and stance tore at him. Moving closer, he asked, "Won't you tell me what's wrong?" much more gently than he had planned a moment ago. "Can't I help?"

She couldn't bear it, Emma thought. She really couldn't bear it. He was everything she wanted, and yet she was being more and more cut off from him. The pain in her heart was like a knife.

"Won't you trust me?" he added, hurt in his voice.

The pressure expanded within her. Her throat was raw and tight. Her eyes burned. Her ribs ached. And then, in that dreadful moment, as she thought she would crack into a million pieces, the solution to her problem sprang full-blown into Emma's mind. She blinked. It was so simple, so clear, that she couldn't comprehend how she had missed it before. Granted, it was an act of desperation. But Orsino inspired desperation. And this would work. Relief flooded through her. The release of tension was another kind of pain.

"Emma?" said Colin.

She took a deep breath. "Everything will be all right," she said. "Don't worry. Everything will be all right."

"What will?" he demanded.

Emma shook her head.

He gritted his teeth, angry and frustrated. For a moment there, he had thought she would yield and tell him the whole. But then something had changed. She had changed. And he was shut out again. It was insupportable. What had stopped her from confiding in him? Colin's determination to get to the bottom of this matter redoubled. He would find out everything, he thought with clenched jaw, and then someone would pay.

The next morning, after Colin was gone, Emma went to her sitting room and settled herself in the armchair by the window. Summoning all her resolution, she rang the bell and sent for Ferik. When the giant appeared a few minutes later and stood expectantly before her, she began, "You have said you would do anything for me, Ferik."

"Yes, mistress," was the reply. "Of course. Have you not seen how I endure this constant evil rain for you? And I bear the insults of Clinton with—"

"I have a serious problem," Emma cut in.

Ferik fell silent at once. Clasping his hands before him, he became deeply attentive.

Emma took a breath. "That man we visited in his lodgings, he was in Constantinople. Count Orsino."

Ferik nodded heavily. "I remember him. He plays cards with young men and takes their money."

"Yes. He is threatening me."

Ferik scowled and clenched his great fists. "He would dare?"

"He is an evil man," said Emma. "I . . . I am afraid of him."

Ferik growled. "I will crush him like an insect," he said. "I will break him into a thousand pieces and feed him to the rats. I will . . ." He paused as if remembering something, then looked sullenly disappointed. "Must we set the law on him, mistress?" he asked.

"The law?"

"Yes. You see how I remember what you have told me. You said the English law watches over everyone. Surely it will punish that man if he is trying to harm you."

Emma bit her lower lip. Ferik never listened to her. Why must he choose this moment to finally recall one of her strictures? she thought. "There are a few occasions," she said, "a very few, when the law can do nothing."

Ferik's dark eyes went wide. "But mistress, you told me . . ."

"I know." Emma felt a tremor. But then she thought of Colin, and Robin, and Lady Mary, and hardened her will. "This is one of those times," she added. "The law cannot help me, so I am turning to you."

Ferik stood straighter, swelling with pride and gratification. "Shall I kill him for you, mistress?" he asked hopefully.

Emma clasped her hands together so tight they hurt. "Yes," she whispered.

Ferik nodded, a satisfied grin spreading over his features, as Emma shifted in her seat. "I will return to his lodgings in secret tonight and—"

"No. I have a plan, a way for you to get to him without anyone noticing."

"Not noticing me?" Ferik looked skeptical. Even after months in England, he was still stared at in the street.

"Yes," replied Emma, and she began to explain to him the scheme that had come to her in the drawing room yesterday.

When she finished, Ferik nodded again. "Very nice, mistress. It will surely work."

"You see no . . . problems?"

Slowly, he shook his head.

"And afterward? You will . . ."

Ferik waved his huge hand. "I will take care of everything, mistress. No need for you to worry."

"Yes. But . . ."

"All will be well," Ferik assured her. "I can easily do this."

"Yes," repeated Emma, feeling rather numb. "Thank you, Ferik."

The Turkish giant shook his head. "You do not need to thank me, mistress. My life is yours." Putting his hand on his breast, Ferik gave her a deep bow.

And so it was done, Emma thought.

Colin spent the day following a number of the threads he had unraveled in his earlier investigations. He visited the English government office once again, and came out looking very satisfied with the result. He spoke with his new friend at the Italian embassy. He met with two somber, extremely muscular individuals who came highly recommended by the elusive Mr. Smith and reached an agreement with them. After lunch at his club, he was on the way to his last destination of the day when he encountered Robin Bellingham sauntering toward the park. "I'll walk with you partway," he said.

Robin agreed a bit uneasily. His formidable brother-in-law still intimidated him slightly, especially after the recent incident in the drawing room. Wareham was everything that Robin longed to be, and when he was with him, it became all too obvious that he had a long way to go before reaching his ideal. "I was, er, just going to take a toddle along the Row," he said, striving for nonchalance.

Colin merely nodded and fell into step beside him.

They began to walk together. "You told me you were going to stay away from the gaming tables," Colin said after a while. "I took you to be a man of your word." He watched his companion unobtrusively, with quick sidelong glances.

"I am," said Robin stiffly. "You don't understand."

"Explain it to me," was the curt response.

"Oh, well . . ." Robin felt trapped. He didn't know whether he might be betraying Emma's confidence. On the other hand, he could not stand to have St. Mawr think he was not an honorable man. "The thing is, I had to help Emma," he said finally.

"Emma?" Colin echoed, in a soft, possibly dangerous voice.

"I had to distract this fellow Orsino. He's been making up to Lady Mary, you know," he confided. "And she can't seem to realize that he's not the sort of man she should so much as speak to."

"And what else?" demanded Colin in the same tone.

"Else?" Robin looked bewildered.

"What else has Orsino been doing?"

The young man stared at him, a bit unnerved by the implacability in his voice. "He's been gambling with me," he offered, and then quickly amended. "But I was just keeping him away from Lady Mary, you see. As soon as he's out of the picture, I mean to give up gaming."

When Colin made no reply, he added nervously. "Emma says he cheats. That's why I've dropped so much blunt."

"What is he to Emma?" Colin demanded, fixing his companion with an inexorable gaze.

"Emma?" Robin fumbled for words. "Friend of her . . . of Edward Tarrant, she told me. That's how she became acquainted with the blackguard, which is something I cannot like."

"No," agreed Colin quietly. He examined Robin's face for a moment longer, and concluded that the young man knew no more than this about the count. And he was convinced that there was more to know concerning Orsino and Emma. Prey to a mixture of relief and frustration, Colin put his hands behind his back as they walked on along the pavement.

"This Tarrant must have been a dashed loose screw," Robin complained, feeling considerably better now that Colin was no longer looking at him.

The baron said nothing.

"I hate to admit it, but I think Father was right about him."

"He was indeed," said Colin.

"Of course, I didn't realize all this when I met Orsino at the Royal Academy with Emma." Robin's handsome face darkened. "Lady Mary was there, too. Unfortunate, that."

"Yes," replied Colin absently.

"But you may rely on me. I'm keeping an eye out in that direction," Robin assured him. "No need to worry."

There was more to young Robin than he had given him credit for, Colin realized. And while he had little interest in Lady Mary Dacre, it was gratifying to observe the lad's growing maturity. He decided to share a small piece of information with him. "You will not have to worry about Orsino much longer," he promised. "Steps have been taken to, er, remove him from the country."

"Really?" Robin looked impressed, and a little envious. "Can't be too soon for me," he said. "I'm dashed sick of being cheated at cards."

"No doubt."

His tone made Robin look at him. "What are you going to do with the blackguard?"

"Make sure that he cannot harm anyone here," said Colin grimly.

"How?" Robin looked eager. "If you need any help, I'm your man."

"Thank you, but matters are well in hand."

"I *could* help, you know," said the younger man resentfully.

"There is really nothing more to be done," put in Colin. "But should anything come up, I will feel free to call on you."

Robin grunted, unsatisfied. "Well, at least Emma must be relieved," he said after a moment. He brightened. "That's good. She's been jumpy as a cat over the fellow." His expression grew even more pleased. "And I won't have to spend any more time with him. I must say, I don't care for him at all." Robin let out an expansive breath and walked with a bit more spring to his step. "Should have known you'd take care of the matter," he added. "You're her husband, after all." He smiled at Colin.

The baron merely gazed back at him a little blankly.

"You all right?" wondered Robin.

Colin nodded.

"Right." Robin took another deep breath. "Actually, I'm glad to have this thing taken off my hands," he admitted. "Wasn't at all sure how to resolve the matter. And I've nearly used up my quarterly allowance on the blackguard as it is."

"I'll replace it," said Colin somewhat mechanically.

Robin looked delighted briefly, then his face fell. "Can't let you do that."

"It is my responsibility," was the reply.

Robin gave his brother-in-law a sidelong glance. He sounded dashed odd, and he had a queer look on his face, too. "Well, it's good to know that you and Emma have settled everything between you," he said heartily.

Seeing the gates of the park ahead, he walked a bit faster, the strain of this lengthy conversation beginning to tell. "There's Jack," he added gratefully a moment later. "Do you . . . do you care to come along with us?"

Colin shook his head, not even noticing Robin's relief. After cordial introductions, he left the two young men and hailed a cab to take him home. Sitting in it, he leaned back against the cushions and listened to mental echoes of the phrases Emma's brother had used. "You're her husband, after all. Good that you've settled everything between you."

Emma was deeply disturbed by the intrusion of this devil Orsino from her past, he thought. That was clear, though her exact reasons remained cloudy. He had the means to remove that threat; indeed, he was in the process of doing so. And he had not told her. He had not even thought of telling her. Instead, he had brooded over her reluctance to confide in him, and left her to fret and worry.

Colin shifted uneasily on the leather seat. He remained unshakably convinced that Emma hid nothing dishonorable from her past life. He had seen too much evidence of her integrity to imagine otherwise. Why, then, had he not openly offered his help?

What if, instead of silently railing at her, he had gone to her and let her know he was having the man expelled from the country? Could he doubt that she would then have told him everything? If he had given her one clear opening . . . but he had held back. As he always held back.

Stubborn pride, Colin muttered to the passing street scene. He would tell her as soon as he reached home, he thought, and then things would return to normal between them. There would be no more of these silences and distances. They would resume their former easy, comfortable relationship.

A tremor went through him. He was afraid that was no longer possible. And he was even more afraid, because—he clenched his fists—because it was no longer what he wanted.

He thought of Emma as he saw her a dozen times a day—sitting at the dining table, speaking to one of the servants, walking briskly along a corridor on some household errand, bending over one of the estate documents that he shared with her. She had made his house a place he longed to return to. She had made his life something far more than the bleak round of duty he had contemplated on the boat coming home.

He thought of their days at Trevallan. She had listened to the worst he had to tell and never drawn back. He thought of the odd circumstances of their original meeting, and how easily it might never have happened at all. And he remembered other times—how she responded to his touch with such ardor and tenderness that it made his breath catch to think of it.

This was love, Colin realized. This rich, complicated web of feelings that occupied his whole soul was the love that he had given up hope of ever finding less than a year ago. He shook his head dazedly. He hadn't understood. He had thought love came in one great sudden swoop. But it was far otherwise. Parts of it had indeed emerged as soon as he met her—the passion, the laughter. But others had come more gradually, adding one to another until he finally, belatedly, reached this moment of revelation.

This was why he hadn't confronted her, Colin saw. What he wanted was not the details about Orsino. He didn't care a snap of his fingers for the man. He wanted Emma to love him. He wanted her to turn to him and tell him she was in love with him, as he was with her.

Colin drew a shaky breath. She had never claimed to love him, never promised to love him. He, blithering idiot that he was, had specifically excluded love from their agreement. He had no right to expect love.

But he wanted it.

She had drawn away from him recently. What if she wouldn't come back? The possibility was more fright-

ening than any battlefield he could recall. Colin Wareham, who had faced countless cannons and bayonets
and lances in his life, sat rigid in the moving hack. He
couldn't bear any more losses. And the loss of Emma
would be a catastrophe beyond any that he had so far
endured.

Colin bared his teeth. He wouldn't lose her, he
vowed. He would fight his way through any obstacle.
He would take the risk. And the time—as much time as
necessary. He would destroy this Orsino, and anyone
else who dared threaten Emma, and he would show her
what it meant to love.

The driver knocked on the roof of the cab. "Here
you are, guv," he said.

Becoming aware of his surroundings once more,
Colin climbed out and paid the fare. He would say
something to Emma tonight, he thought, make some
beginning. Then he cursed softly. The damned masquerade was tonight. He checked the watch that hung from a
fob on his waistcoat. He was late. She would already be
dressing for the wretched thing. Frowning, he walked
through the front door of the house. Tomorrow, then,
he decided. By then, he would most likely be able to tell
her that Orsino was gone. That would make a good
beginning, he concluded with satisfaction. And his campaign could go on from there.

Chapter Thirteen

"I look silly," complained Colin a little later that evening, as Emma made a final adjustment to his costume for the masquerade and stood back to judge the effect.

"No, you don't. You look very dashing and romantic. Here, let me just . . ." She straightened his shirt collar at the back. "There."

Colin wore loose trousers of pale buff cloth tucked into his own high riding boots. His white shirt was also loose; it had an open neck, showing the bronze column of his throat, and broad, billowing sleeves. Emma had just finished tying a dark blue sash around his waist, letting the ends trail rakishly, and inserting a sheathed dagger in it at a jaunty angle.

"You're the very picture of a noble Turkish gentleman," she added.

"And you are, what?" he replied, running his eye over Emma's unusual garb.

She looked into the long mirror behind him with a satisfied smile. Sophie had outdone herself when offered the challenge of creating her costume. Though it was actually a normal silk gown, it was so carefully cut and hung with scarves that it looked like a collection of multicolored, diaphanous veils fluttering around her body. A piece of actual veiling covered her hair, bound across the forehead with a glittering riband. "Why, I am a member of your harem," Emma laughed. "A mysterious lady of the East."

"You are extremely pleased with yourself," said Colin, sounding puzzled and a bit strained.

"Well, you *have* trousers," countered Emma. The truth was, she was in a state of nervous exaltation, anticipating the dangerous events of the night to come. The day appointed for Orsino's elimination was upon them, and she was finding the whole thing unreal—like a story or a dream. Or rather like the few times when she had drunk too much champagne, she thought. She felt giddy, reckless, and slightly sick. She was doing her best to mask her jangled state with superficial gaiety. "Come," she said. "We promised to fetch the Nettletons in our carriage."

As they walked downstairs together, they encountered many more servants than usual as staff members lurked about pretending to work at important tasks and actually hoping to catch a glimpse of their costumes. In the front hall, a small, murmuring group of footmen and maids had assembled. "What the deuce?" wondered Colin. Then the group shifted, and he added, "Good God!"

Ferik awaited them near the door. He wore baggy pants of bright red gathered in at the ankle over low leather slippers. His upper torso was bare except for a jeweled and brocaded vest, revealing his massive muscles to all observers. On his head he wore a turban, fastened at the front, just above the center of his forehead, with a gold pin in the shape of a coiled snake. The snake's green eye glinted ominously above the heads of the smaller Englishmen.

"You're just like a storybook," Nancy the maid cried

shrilly. "I keep expecting you to say, 'Open, sez me' and pull a genie out of a bottle."

"Be quiet, Nancy," said Clinton.

"I look like a palace eunuch," complained Ferik in response, drawing a piercing giggle from Nancy.

For the first time in the history of their association, Colin gave him a sympathetic glance.

"I would never wear such things as this at home, mistress," Ferik continued.

"Well, no one knows that," replied Emma ruthlessly, "and you look splendid."

"It is not dignified," muttered the giant.

"Do you have a heavy cloak?" asked Emma, as if he hadn't spoken. "You will be cold without a shirt."

"Yes, mistress," Ferik replied resignedly in his deep, resonant voice. "I am always cold in this cursed country," he murmured to himself.

Colin raised an eyebrow.

"And your mask?"

Ferik nodded.

"*That* will make him unrecognizable," commented Colin. "We may as well leave ours at home, Emma. Everyone in London knows Ferik by this time."

Emma went pale.

"Though in the crowd these masquerades attract, who knows?" Colin added. "I have heard the costumes are quite fantastic."

She relaxed a little.

"I will stay in the shadows, mistress," murmured Ferik, bending so that no one else heard him. "I will not be recognized."

Reassured, Emma followed the two men out to the carriage, where Ferik swung himself up beside the driver as they got in.

After picking up their friends, they proceeded along the dark streets to the Pantheon, where the masquerade was already under way. As planned, they met the rest of their party outside and, safely masked, went in together.

Tom guided them directly to the box he had reserved,

which was in the second tier—well above the rowdy floor of the building, but low enough so that they could easily observe the scene. An attendant took their wraps, and they spent a few minutes fulfilling their obligation to admire one another's costumes.

Tom had come as a pirate, in an outfit rather like Colin's. His wife was Marie Antoinette; she wore a brocaded satin gown with huge panniers that she had unearthed in an old trunk and an elaborate wig that added almost a foot to her height. The Nettletons were ancient Romans, though Victoria Nettleton seemed to be highly distrustful of her long, draped toga. Every few minutes she would jerk its folds as if she was afraid they were falling off. The fourth couple—Freddy and Liza Monckton—had dressed as Romeo and Juliet, even down to a doublet and tights for Freddy, which made him the focus of a good deal of raillery from the other men. "You've let down our side, Freddy," Tom insisted. "Don't you remember we drew the line at tights?"

Freddy, who was known to be much under the influence of his beautiful new wife, simply grinned good-naturedly and ambled over to investigate the refreshments laid out on a side table.

Emma saw that Ferik was settled in a dim rear corner of the spacious box, then took her seat and looked out over the huge room. The scene spread before her made her draw in her breath.

Tiers of boxes circled the wide floor, filled with groups like their own, some in costume and others wearing regular evening clothes and masks. They chatted together, leaned out to watch, and drank wine from stemmed glasses, forming an animated frieze around the perimeter of the great room. But the truly amazing sight was the dancers, who filled the floor to bursting. There, milkmaids whirled in the arms of multicolored Pierrots, queens partnered pirates, Egyptian princesses danced with Spanish grandees. Some of the costumes were shockingly skimpy, and as Emma began to notice details, she realized that the standards of behavior were

extremely loose. Gentlemen leered and ogled; given any
encouragement, they fondled breasts and limbs left bare
for the purpose. Revelers continually approached those
in the lowest tier of boxes and tried to lure them out for
a bit of dalliance. Often, they succeeded, though Emma
did not believe they were necessarily acquainted with
the boxholders. It was a wild melee, a twirling pinwheel
of color and animated faces lit by a thousand candles.
The air was heavy with conflicting perfumes and the
musky odor of unwashed bodies. Voices rose to a muted
roar. Emma grew slightly dizzy observing it all.

"Do you want to try a dance in that mob?" Colin
asked.

"I think I would rather stay here and watch," she
said. "It is like a play."

"Indeed. Rather like the one we saw the other night,
though with more harmony amongst the players."

She laughed.

Colin brought her a glass of champagne, and they
drank and ate and talked with their friends, pointing out
to one another particularly interesting costumes or incidents in the crowd. Tom tried to persuade his wife to
dance, and was repulsed. The Nettletons did venture
down, and returned looking disheveled to report that it
was a madhouse. Some unknown person had actually
pinched Victoria.

The hour drew closer to midnight, and Emma felt her
body tightening with tension. She continued to gaze out
over the room, responding more and more mechanically
to the others' sallies. It was almost time to put her plan
into action. Now that it was here, she didn't quite believe that she had concocted this scheme. But though
her hands trembled a little, her resolution did not waver.

She was about to rise when her eye was caught by
something familiar in a box across the room. A woman
sitting there wore a black gown trimmed with bunches
of ribbon and embellished with a unique bell-shaped
sleeve. Emma did not have to see the golden hair and

pouting pink lips beneath the mask to identify Lady
Mary Dacre. A groan escaped her lips.

"What is it?" asked Colin.

"There's . . . I saw someone I know," Emma answered.

"Who?"

"Someone who should *not* be here."

"Who?" Colin tried to follow her gaze, but it was
impossible to pick out any one person in the crowd.

"It's better not to say. Perhaps no one will find out."
A male figure in black was seated next to Lady Mary. It
was difficult to make him out against the dimness of the
box, but she was certain it was Count Orsino. No one
else would bring Lady Mary to such a place. "Damn
him," she murmured under her breath. This complicated her plan considerably. She would have to make
certain Lady Mary was not left alone in this unsuitable
place, and was taken home after Orsino . . . disappeared.

"I beg your pardon?" said Colin, bending toward
her.

"Nothing."

He looked at her, unconvinced.

It was time. She had to move now if she was to be in
position, no matter what the complications. Emma rose
and excused herself, knowing the others would assume
she was going to visit the ladies' convenience. As
planned, Ferik slipped out after her, silently and discreetly, and they made their way down the inner stairs
and along a corridor that bordered the main room. It
too was filled with raucous revelers, but Ferik's hovering presence discouraged any of them from accosting
Emma.

Ferik took the lead. He had been here a day earlier to
examine the building and find a spot he considered suitable for this fateful meeting. He led Emma past two
small rooms that held a few masqueraders and into another, smaller one that was empty.

Emma looked around it, evaluating the place she had

appointed, sight unseen, for her meeting with Orsino. It was not a salon. It appeared to be a kind of storage room for broken chairs and torn draperies. Emma found herself thinking that the Pantheon must have many of both, and realized that she was trying *not* to think of what was to come.

"I will stand here," said Ferik quietly, stepping into a deep shadow cast by the open door. "He will not see me until it is too late."

Emma nodded. She clasped her hands together to hide their trembling and walked into the center of the room. The chamber was lit by only two sconces. Most of the light came from the hall, thrown across the floor like a swath of bright cloth. Emma stood in it and waited.

Too soon, she heard booted footsteps approaching. Then, a dark figure appeared in the doorway, paused, and came in. "Baroness," said Orsino's voice, and he bowed deeply.

He wore a black tunic with a somber glitter of silver thread and black hose. In his hand he carried a flat velvet cap, also black. He looked like a renaissance portrait of a wicked Italian duke, Emma thought. His bland round face and the malicious glitter of his dark eyes fit perfectly with the role.

"You like my costume?" he asked, noticing her scrutiny. "I am Machiavelli. You have heard of him?" When she didn't respond, he added, "No? A pity. You English are so ill educated. Machiavelli was the author of *The Prince*, a masterpiece of courtly strategy. It tells the truth about what is behind the smiles around a ruler. He was Italian, of course."

When Emma expressed no interest in this topic, he shrugged. "You English," he added. "No subtlety, no style. The things that pass for humor among Englishmen! It is appalling!"

Emma made an impatient gesture.

"Ah, yes. So, down to business, eh, baroness?"

"Yes," said Emma, her throat dry.

"An odd place for it," he said. "But your week is up."

"I know."

"So? You have decided to cooperate?" He sounded utterly confident. He didn't seem to imagine that she would dare to oppose him.

Emma hesitated. She was to raise a hand to brush back her veil. This was the signal to Ferik.

"After all this waiting, I think I may ask a little more," Orsino went on. "Perhaps further meetings like this, where we can be *private*. Eh? You might find that we Italians are more . . . more exciting than the clumsy English in many, many ways."

He had been drinking, Emma thought. His eyes were glazed with reckless desire and greed.

He started to move closer. Emma raised her hand.

Ferik stepped out of the shadows like an exotic ghost emerging from the wall. Before Orsino even registered his presence, he encircled the man's neck with one massive arm and tightened his grip upon his throat. The count's eyes widened in astonishment. His face began to turn red.

Emma felt a mixture of relief and nervousness. "I will not do as you ask," she said. "And I will not allow you to hurt my husband or my friends. So . . ."

Orsino gurgled. His face was deepening to magenta. Emma looked anxiously at Ferik.

"Better you go now, mistress," the giant servant said. "I will take care of this evil man."

"What will you . . . ?"

"No need for you to know."

Orsino began to thrash and kick. His face was purple. Ferik clapped his other arm around the man's chest, imprisoning him as effectively as iron shackles.

Emma was assailed by doubt. "Ferik, do you think . . . ?"

"No one will ever find him, mistress," was the calm reply. "You may be sure of it. You can trust me."

"But should we really do this?" she questioned.

Orsino produced a frantic grunt. His face was now a dark purple, and his eyes seemed to bulge a little.

"An extremely good question, my dear Emma," said Colin, strolling into the room as calmly as if he were entering a rather dull evening party. "Do ease your grip a bit, Ferik, while we ponder this matter."

Startled, the giant complied. Orsino still could not speak, but the color of his face lightened slightly.

Emma found her tongue. "Colin! You . . . I . . ."

"*What* is going on?" complained Lady Mary Dacre, entering on Colin's heels and pushing her way impatiently around him. "I have been left alone in that box for an *age,* and I think it is excessively *rude* of you to . . ." Taking in the scene, she fell silent, staring from one to another with wide blue eyes behind her mask. "Good heavens," she added feebly.

The little storeroom was beginning to feel remarkably crowded, Emma thought.

"Really, Emma," said Colin. He examined Orsino, Ferik, and the details of the chamber in which they stood. "This is not the way to discourage such scoundrels. Threats have no effect."

"I am going to kill him," declared Ferik.

Orsino began to thrash ineffectually again.

"Ah," said Colin, looking startled. "That would do it."

"But I *wasn't* going to run away with him!" exclaimed Lady Mary. "A hired carriage is fetching me in half an hour to take me home."

Orsino goggled at her. Colin raised his eyebrows. "You know about him?" Emma asked her husband.

"All about him," answered Colin in an almost meditative voice.

"I let him *think* I would go with him because I wanted to see the masquerade," continued Lady Mary. She frowned. "And no one else would take me. Everyone is so gothic and prudish." She caught Emma's glare. "But I remembered what you said," she assured her. "I was very careful, and I didn't believe *anything* he told me."

Orsino gurgled urgently. Ferik shook him a bit, and he fell silent.

" 'Count' Orsino is of great interest to several foreign governments," said Colin, as if Lady Mary had not spoken. "He is not welcome in his own country—or in this one."

Orsino stopped struggling and went very still.

"He is, in fact, slated to be escorted to the coast by the authorities tomorrow morning and put on a boat leaving England."

Lady Mary's mouth had dropped open below her mask. "But I *told* you," she said, "I *wasn't* going to—"

"Aha!" shouted a new voice from just outside the room. "I've found you!" A slender figure in a black domino erupted into the room. Above his mask, he wore a large-brimmed hat enlivened by an ostrich feather, and he was brandishing a long unsheathed rapier with alarming freedom. "I've uncovered your despicable plan," the newcomer added. "And I won't allow it, do you hear? I'll kill you first."

"Robin?" said Emma faintly.

Her brother turned in a half circle, taking in the crowd in the small room through the limited viewpoint of his mask. His sword drooped a little. "Did you know about it already?" he asked, clearly very disappointed.

"Know about what?" demanded Colin.

Robin gestured with the sword, causing Lady Mary to screech in protest and back away. "That . . . that blackguard's plan to carry off Lady Mary and ruin her," he answered. "I only discovered tonight from her maid that he meant to bring her here. I came at once. He has a traveling carriage waiting outside, you know. And two dashed havey-cavey characters waiting with it."

"You came to rescue me?" asked Lady Mary, clearly pleased.

"To save you from your own folly," Robin retorted. "You would have been ruined without me." He paused.

"And, er, the others, of course." He looked around the room again, observing Ferik with great interest. "What are you going to do with him?" he asked.

"Kill him," replied Ferik.

"Really?" Robin looked pleased and impressed. "Going to throttle him, are you? Good man!"

"But there's no *need*," began Lady Mary again.

"Silence!" thundered Colin. Everyone started and turned to look at him. "Our friends are in box number twenty-three," he told Robin, enunciating each word very clearly. "You may take Lady Mary and join them there, or you may take her home."

"But I—"

"Or you may both go to perdition," added Colin, in a tone that made Robin take a step back, "so long as you leave us *now*."

Robin grasped Lady Mary's arm, almost hauling her from the room. "But what's going on?" she wondered. It had finally penetrated her consciousness that the scene in the storeroom was not centered around her fate.

"None of our affair," Robin told her.

"I want to stay and—"

"Naturally you do. Why must you always want the most unsuitable things in creation?"

"I don't!"

"You do."

As their bickering faded into the general noise of the masquerade, Colin turned back and surveyed the other three. "I really think you can let him go, Ferik," he said.

"I am going to kill him," Ferik repeated, in the same calm voice he had been using all evening.

"That won't be necessary. As I mentioned, I have made arrangements for his departure. And unless he wishes to find himself in prison, he will not show his face in England again."

"How did you know?" asked Emma quietly.

He looked down at her. "From your manner."

Emma bent her head.

"How did he threaten you?" asked Colin gently.

She flushed, continuing to stare at the dirty floor of the storeroom. "Edward talked when he drank," she murmured, so softly that he had to bend closer to hear. "He told Orsino . . . things, intimate things, about me. He was going to spread them about, make a scandal, let you think that he and I had . . ." She choked on the rest.

"I see." Colin looked at the count, and the emotion in his eyes made the other man cringe. "Perhaps Ferik should kill him."

Ferik grinned.

With a massive convulsion of his whole body, Orsino broke Ferik's grip, jumping free of the huge man and backing away. Bending, he pulled a large knife from his boot top.

Ferik roared and started toward him. Colin said, "You cannot get through both of us, Orsino."

The count grabbed Emma, throwing one arm around her throat and pressing the knife to her breast with the other hand. "Get back," he said, his voice hoarse from Ferik's manhandling. "If you come near me, I'll kill her."

Colin put out a hand to stop Ferik. "Wait," he said.

"I'm leaving," said Orsino. "And if anyone tries to stop me . . ." He moved the blade slightly. "Get away from the door."

They obeyed, Ferik's face in a murderous grimace.

Orsino half pushed, half dragged Emma into the hallway and along it toward the only exit, which led through the ballroom. Did he imagine that he could take her through the crowd without being stopped? she found herself wondering, even though her heart was pounding with fear.

The roar of the ballroom came nearer. A pair of dancers reeled together out into the hall, then stopped short and gaped when they saw Emma and Orsino. The razor-sharp blade nicked Emma's collarbone, and a trickle of blood ran down her breast and stained the bodice of her gown. The unexpected pain made her falter and trip over one of its trailing veils. Thinking quickly, she let herself fall, trying to take the count down with her. But he pulled free and viciously jerked her arm to get her up again.

With a roar, Ferik surged forward. Emma huddled into a ball away from the knife. Casting one frantic look behind him, Orsino plunged through the doorway and into the crush of dancers.

Ferik and Colin raced after him. Pushing people aside, the three cleaved the sea of masqueraders, leaving a line of angry revelers like the frothing wake of a ship. One irate man struck out and knocked off Colin's mask, so that he was revealed to all the onlookers in the boxes. Emma groaned. A shrieking woman whose headdress was knocked askew took hold of Ferik's vest with both hands, and he dragged her nearly twenty feet through the crowd before the embroidered material gave way and she fell with the rags of the garment in her fingers.

His great chest now bare, Ferik forged through the crowd, his dark eyes blazing, his exotic figure nearly a head taller than anyone else. He reached for, missed, then caught the tail of Orsino's black tunic, jerking the man backward as if he were a doll. Twisting his other hand in the count's collar, he lifted him up over his head, a squirming exhibit for everyone to see. Emma glanced up and saw Tom leaning over the rail of their box, his mouth hanging open. The rest of their friends were similarly riveted, not to mention hundreds of others.

"Ferik, put him down," shouted Colin, tugging on the giant's arm to get him to release his prisoner. "Put . . . him . . . down."

Emma leaned against the corridor wall and closed her eyes behind her mask. Their exposure was complete. Ferik's name was known to many in the *ton* after the fever of curiosity his appearance had excited. There would be no hiding Colin's identity. And no stopping the gossips from ferreting out every detail.

She ventured another look. Orsino was on the ground again, and they had taken his knife. No doubt he would be sent away, as Colin had promised, now that it was too late, now that a scandal far juicier than any so far had been set in motion. All her efforts to keep Colin from being an object of gossip and malice had gone up in smoke.

Sick at heart, Emma made her way around the edge of the crowd and outside. She couldn't bear any more. Trudging up the street, she found a hackney cab to take her home. In her bedchamber, she shed her fantastic costume and left it lying in a heap on the floor. Putting on her wrapper, she huddled in an armchair by the fire, crushed by her failure.

After a while, her maid came in. "My lady, I didn't know you were here. His lordship just sent someone to make certain you were home, and I said you would have rung if you were, but he insisted I check. So I—"

"As you see, I am here," interrupted Emma.

"Yes, your ladyship. I'll send word. Can I get you . . . ?"

"Nothing."

"Yes, ma'am. But shouldn't I . . . ?"

"I need nothing. I'm very tired. You may go to bed."

The girl hesitated, then dropped a curtsy and went out. Emma let her head drop back and stared blankly at the ceiling. The mantel clock ticked out the minutes; the fire fell into itself with a shower of sparks. After an endless time, and a constantly repeating litany of might-have-beens, Emma fell asleep.

It was very late when Colin gently opened the door that connected their rooms and came in, carrying a single candle. He looked first to the bed and, finding it empty, scanned the rest of the room with a frown. Discovering Emma still curled in the chair, he went and stood beside it, setting the candlestick on a small table. He gazed down at her bright hair, which strayed over her shoulders like a shower of gilt, at the beautiful line of her cheek and throat. His heart seemed to turn over in his chest, and he was overwhelmed by love and longing. He knelt beside her. "Emma," he said quietly, putting a hand on her shoulder. "Emma, you must get to bed."

She started awake, bolting straight up and gazing disorientedly about the room. Finally, her eyes fixed on his face. "Colin," she cried. "I'm so sorry. I made a hash of everything."

"Nonsense," he replied. "Everything has been settled quite satisfactorily. Orsino is on his way out of England, and he will not be allowed back. He is also very, very clear on what will happen to him if he attempts to threaten you again." His expression was grim. "Utterly clear," he repeated.

"That is all very well, but—"

"Also . . ." He paused.

"What?" cried Emma, acutely sensitive to the change in his tone.

"Well, there is something else. I have done something you may not like."

"What?" repeated Emma, bewildered.

He met her eyes. "I sent Ferik with the count."

"Sent Ferik." Emma blinked, confused.

"He will make absolutely certain Orsino is gone, and then . . . he will continue on to Constantinople."

"Ferik is gone?" Momentarily, she felt bereft.

Colin nodded. "He was somewhat reluctant, but I, er, painted a vivid picture of the advantages of setting up as an innkeeper in his own country. And I gave him a sum of money that should allow him to do so in grand style." When Emma didn't respond, he added quickly, "The idea seemed to please him. And he sent you his profoundest respect and effusive farewells and thanks."

"He will be able to have his wife with the big dowry and nice firm bottom," murmured Emma.

"I beg your pardon?"

"He will love having his own establishment," she added. "I will miss him, but it is perfect. He wasn't happy here in England. I've been worried about him and trying to think what to do."

Colin let out a breath. "Good. Then all's well."

Emma sat up straighter. "How can you say so? By tomorrow, everyone will be talking about the fight at the masquerade, making up wild tales, whispering and laughing behind your back. It will be a scandal worse than any—"

With a brusque gesture, as if this was a matter of no importance, he silenced her. "Why didn't you tell me when you were in trouble?" he asked. "Did you imagine I wouldn't help you?"

Emma turned her head away, staring at the dying fire. "No," she said finally. "I knew you would help. That was the trouble."

"The trouble?" He frowned at her.

She twisted her hands together. "You wanted a quiet life, after the war. You told me that. You didn't want a wife who would plague you and cause uproars. But these . . . things kept happening. Gossip about me, and then Lady Mary's silly dramatics."

"Those don't—"

"We were getting through those all right," Emma acknowledged. "But then Orsino threatened to lie about me, and I thought it would be too much."

"Emma."

"People listen to him! I have seen them. He can be very convincing. He ruined a number of people with his stories about them. I was so afraid . . ." She caught a gasping breath. "I was so afraid he would cause a scandal greater than you could tolerate. And that I would lose you forever."

Gently, he pulled her to face him again.

"And I couldn't bear that idea," finished Emma forlornly, her eyes on the carpet.

"Couldn't you?" asked Colin in an odd voice. "Why not?"

"Because," she choked. "Because . . ." She bit her bottom lip. Colin wasn't angry about the fresh scandal, she thought. He seemed ready to return to their secure, comfortable arrangement. She had everything she needed. It was ridiculous—childish—to wish for more, for passionate declarations of love from her husband. Remember what your circumstances were just a year ago, she admonished herself sternly. But it didn't help. "Because I love you," she burst out. "I've fallen in love with you, and I don't think I could go on without you."

A dizzying heat swept through Colin, expanding in his chest with something akin to pain, and yet joyous. Her words seemed to ring in his ears. He should tell her, he thought. He knew how much it meant to hear those words. But even now, it was damnably difficult. He cleared his throat. "Emma?"

She seemed to sense something. She gazed at him, her eyes midnight blue pools. Candlelight gleamed on the rose and ivory of her skin, glinted in her tumbled hair.

"I . . . I didn't want to love you," Colin managed at last. "I wanted a safe bargain. I thought that would guarantee that everything could not be swept away again, that it would prevent the kind of pain I felt throughout the war. If I did not love, I could not be hurt, you see. I could not lose what I loved, yet again."

Silent, Emma watched him.

"But I couldn't hold that wall," he added. "Day by day, you breached every defense I had. And even though I fought, and tried not to reveal things to you, I fell in love with you all the same." A muscle twitched beside his mouth.

"You love me?" said Emma wonderingly.

He braced himself. "I love you," he said clearly.

She caught her breath on a sob. "You will never lose me," she promised.

"How can you know?" he answered, his voice like a cry.

"I know!" she responded fiercely.

He caught her to him and held her, feeling her heart beat against his chest, her arms lace around his neck. Time seem to hang suspended as he pulled her yet closer, as if he could merge them into one inseparable being.

"Haven't I said I would come back to haunt you if you tried to get rid of me?" Emma whispered in his ear.

Colin couldn't tell if he was groaning or laughing when he lowered his head to kiss her.

"You aren't to worry about any fresh scandal," he assured her a long while later. "I will see to it that your position in society is not affected."

"I care nothing about that," replied Emma. "I wish we could live in Cornwall and forget London entirely. But I know you would miss your friends, so you must not worry that—"

"I only left Cornwall because I wanted to be sure you were accorded *your* proper position as my wife," he protested. "I thought that after the years you spent abroad, you would want that more than anything."

Emma stared at him. "You wanted to stay in Cornwall?"

"I wished it had been possible," he agreed.

"You left because of me?"

Colin nodded.

"But I left because of you!"

He raised his dark eyebrows.

"I thought you wanted to be here, among society. You had not been down to Cornwall for so long. I thought you didn't want to live there. I thought you wanted to be Baron St. Mawr, admired and respected. I—"

"I don't care a snap of my fingers for that," he interrupted.

"But why didn't you say so?" she wailed.

He began to laugh. "And why didn't you?"

"All this time here, and these silly parties, when we might have been with the sea and the cliffs."

"A situation easily mended," he pointed out.

"You mean . . . ?"

He shrugged. "We will close the house and leave as soon as possible."

Emma hesitated. "But everyone will say we are fleeing the scandal about Orsino."

"Let them," he responded.

"Oh, Colin," Emma threw herself into his arms.

It took three weeks to make all the arrangements for the move to Cornwall. They had to placate Colin's mother, say their good-byes to friends, and purchase all the things that Emma wanted for their country home. It was ample time for the scandal to hit, and each day, Emma waited to hear that they had become the target of gossip and mockery. When she marveled about the delay to Colin, he raised one eyebrow and smiled. "I told one or two of the chief gossips that Orsino and Ferik had been in pursuit of the same young lady, and that I was trying to prevent them from killing each other," he said.

When she gaped at him, he added, "I said she was a milliner's apprentice, who has now left the country for America. Nice touch, don't you think? I believe I am getting rather good at this sort of thing."

"Colin!" exclaimed Emma.

"Leaving no one to ask but me," he pointed out. "And alas, I know no more about the matter."

"How could you?" she asked, holding back laughter.

He shrugged. "It seemed the best solution. The story cannot harm Ferik, and I care nothing for Orsino's reputation, though this could hardly stain it after the things he has done. I had the help of some powerful people interested in silencing the story."

"Your mother?" said Emma.

He smiled. "Yes. And even more, the Morlands."

"Lady Mary!"

"Her family does *not* want it known that she attended a masquerade, and with a man who has since been deported as an undesirable."

"So it will be all right?" marveled Emma.

"It appears likely." He smiled down at her. "We are free to stay in London if we like."

Emma was stricken. "But you said you wanted to . . ." Seeing his expression, she hit him lightly on the shoulder. "Colin, don't tease me that way!"

"I can never resist the temptation," he laughed.

On the night before they were to leave, Emma lay nestled in her husband's arms, feeling completely happy and at peace. "I have some news for you," she said.

"You have spent the last remnants of my fortune on sofas and drapery material," he guessed.

"No."

"Then it must be carpets and china."

"Colin!"

"Yes, my love?"

"I am serious."

"I beg your pardon. What is this portentous news?"

Emma took a breath. "I wanted to tell you that one important part of our bargain is fulfilled," she said.

"Our bargain?"

"Our *marriage* bargain," added Emma.

"As far as I am concerned, it is much more than fulfilled. I got more than I ever hoped for."

"But there was one thing you particularly wanted," she reminded him.

"You," he said, drawing her closer and kissing her creamy shoulder.

"No."

"There is nothing else I . . ." He stopped, then rose on one elbow to gaze at her face.

"I am with child," said Emma happily.

He blinked, speechless.

"I wasn't sure until the last few days. But now it is certain. The baby will be born in the spring."

Very gently, Colin moved his hand to rest on her body.

"Well, aren't you going to say anything?" teased Emma. "You do remember you wanted an heir?"

He blinked again, and Emma saw that he was fighting back tears. Finally he spoke. "What a good bargain I made all those weeks ago."

"*You* made a bargain," she teased. "*I* risked everything on a wager."

"And . . . ?"

"And won," Emma said, smiling at him with love in her eyes.

Jane Ashford grew up in a small town in southwestern Ohio, where she discovered the romance of history at an early age in the public library. After extensive travel in Europe, she settled in Cambridge, Massachusetts. She has written novels of romantic suspense as well as numerous Regency romances. She has also taught literature and writing, and written speeches, book reviews, and newsletters.

For current information on Bantam's
women's fiction, visit our new Web site
Isn't It Romantic
at the following address:

http://www.bdd.com/romance

DON'T MISS THESE FABULOUS
BANTAM WOMEN'S FICTION TITLES

Bestselling Historical Women's Fiction

❧ AMANDA QUICK ❧

____28354-5 SEDUCTION . . .$6.50/$8.99 Canada

____28932-2 SCANDAL . . . .$6.50/$8.99

____28594-7 SURRENDER . . . .$6.50/$8.99

____29325-7 RENDEZVOUS . . . .$6.50/$8.99

____29315-X RECKLESS . . . .$6.50/$8.99

____29316-8 RAVISHED . . . .$6.50/$8.99

____29317-6 DANGEROUS . . . .$6.50/$8.99

____56506-0 DECEPTION . . . .$6.50/$8.99

____56153-7 DESIRE . . . .$6.50/$8.99

____56940-6 MISTRESS . . . .$6.50/$8.99

____57159-1 MYSTIQUE . . . .$6.50/$7.99

____09355-X MISCHIEF . . . .$22.95/$25.95

❧ IRIS JOHANSEN ❧

____29871-2 LAST BRIDGE HOME . . .$4.50/$5.50

____29604-3 THE GOLDEN

                BARBARIAN . . . .$4.99/$5.99

____29244-7 REAP THE WIND . . . . . .$5.99/$7.50

____29032-0 STORM WINDS . . . .$4.99/$5.99

Ask for these books at your local bookstore or use this page to order.

Please send me the books I have checked above. I am enclosing $____ (add $2.50 to cover postage and handling). Send check or money order, no cash or C.O.D.'s, please.

Name _____

Address _____

City/State/Zip _____

Send order to: Bantam Books, Dept. FN 16, 2451 S. Wolf Rd., Des Plaines, IL 60018
Allow four to six weeks for delivery.
Prices and availability subject to change without notice.   FN 16 11/96

Bestselling Historical Women's Fiction

❧ IRIS JOHANSEN ❧

___28855-5 THE WIND DANCER . . .$5.99/$6.99

___29968-9 THE TIGER PRINCE . . .$5.99/$6.99

___29944-1 THE MAGNIFICENT

            ROGUE . . . .$5.99/$6.99

___29945-X BELOVED SCOUNDREL .$5.99/$6.99

___29946-8 MIDNIGHT WARRIOR . .$5.99/$6.99

___29947-6 DARK RIDER . . . .$5.99/$7.99

___56990-2 LION'S BRIDE . . . .$5.99/$7.99

___09714-8 THE UGLY

            DUCKLING . . . . . .$19.95/$24.95

❧ TERESA MEDEIROS ❧

___29407-5 HEATHER AND VELVET .$5.99/$7.50

___29409-1 ONCE AN ANGEL . . . . . .$5.99/$6.50

___29408-3 A WHISPER OF ROSES .$5.50/$6.50

___56332-7 THIEF OF HEARTS . . . . .$5.50/$6.99

___56333-5 FAIREST OF THEM ALL .$5.99/$7.50

___56334-3 BREATH OF MAGIC . . . .$5.99/$7.99

___57623-2 SHADOWS AND LACE . . .$5.99/$7.99

Ask for these books at your local bookstore or use this page to order.

Please send me the books I have checked above. I am enclosing $_____ (add $2.50 to cover postage and handling). Send check or money order, no cash or C.O.D.'s, please

Name _____

Address _____

City/State/Zip _____

Send order to: Bantam Books, Dept. FN 16, 2451 S. Wolf Rd., Des Plaines, IL 60018
Allow four to six weeks for delivery.
Prices and availability subject to change without notice.   FN 16 11/9